Shadows *from the* Past

Shadows
from
the Past

a
novel
by

Richard Neely

⊕ Delacorte Press

Published by
Delacorte Press
1 Dag Hammarskjold Plaza
New York, N.Y. 10017

The lines quoted on page 94 are from "I Have a Rendezvous with Death," by Alan Seeger, from *Poems*. Copyright 1916 by Charles Scribner's Sons; copyright renewed 1944 Elsie Adams Seeger. Reprinted with the permission of Charles Scribner's Sons.

Lyrics from "Just One More Chance" by Sam Coslow and Arthur Johnson. Copyright © 1931 by Famous Music Corporation. Copyright renewed 1958 by Famous Music Corporation.

Designed by Elizabeth Fox

Manufactured in the United States of America
First printing

LIBRARY OF CONGRESS CATALOGING IN PUBLICATION DATA
Neely, Richard.
    Shadows from the past.
    I. Title.
PS3564.E25S5   1983   813'.54   82–14935
ISBN 0–440–08008–8

To Vera,
who was always there

Chapter · 1

It was a hot afternoon in May 1942. I sat in my big, square office staring out at the East River and the huge old bridge that arched across it and disappeared into the Borough of Brooklyn. I was waiting for the phone to ring, for someone to tell me whether the publisher of the *Evening Express*, Charles Dain, lying unconscious in Lenox Hill Hospital with a .25 caliber bullet pressing against his brain, would live or die.

I had just talked to Dave Hewlett, our reporter on the scene, who said he'd been tipped by a resident doctor that Dain was barely hanging on and to expect the worst. Which was about what I'd surmised when I'd stopped by that morning and looked into the face, rigid with suppressed panic, of his wife, Harriet, who had taken a suite at the hospital. She had been told that no attempt could be made to extract the bullet until Dain's vital signs offered more positive assurance that he could survive the operation. No one was willing to predict how long that might be.

The shooting occurred at approximately nine o'clock last night. Charles Dain had left the *Express* building at six thirty P.M. and was driven in his Lincoln limousine to the Stork Club, where he dismissed his chauffeur for the night. At the bar he talked briefly with Sherman Billingsley, the Stork's proprietor, and exchanged pleasantries with Max Gordon, the theatrical producer. Midway through his second Scotch, he went to an unoccupied table and used a plug-in phone to make a call. Returning to the bar apparently in good spirits, he finished his drink, went outside, and took a taxi to a brownstone town house on East Sixty-third Street owned by his wife.

Harriet Dain owned half a dozen buildings on the Upper East Side, all willed to her by her father. Reached by police at her Mount Kisco estate, she said that her husband often stayed in the city overnight but invariably at the Waterford Hotel, also owned by her. She said she had no idea why he chose to go to the town house, a residence kept vacant to accommodate occasional visitors to New York, generally her business associates from abroad. She herself never stayed there, preferring the penthouse suite maintained for the Dains at the Waterford Hotel.

The taxi driver, who recognized Charles Dain, dropped him off a few minutes before eight. An hour later the police got a call from a woman who said that while passing the town house she had heard a series of shots coming from within. She gave the address but hung up before the desk sergeant could ask her name. Minutes later two officers in a squad car arrived, entered—oddly, the front door was unlocked—and found Charles Dain, clad only in a dark-blue dressing gown, sprawled on the living room floor, drenched with blood.

Three bullets had been fired—one lodging in the ceiling molding, another in a red-leather armchair, and the third in the anterior region of Charles Dain's brain. This near-fatal bullet had creased his upper arm and deflected to his cheekbone, slowing its flight as it crashed through his skull. If the slug had entered unimpeded, he probably would have died instantly. The trajectory indicated that the pistol had been aimed from a kneeling or sitting position.

Detectives found no weapon, no sign of struggle, no suspicious fingerprints, no clue whatsoever to the presence of anyone other than Charles Dain.

For most of my life I've considered myself an atheist. Nevertheless, sitting there, feeling the dread rise and grab my throat, I prayed to Almighty God that the phone would ring and some happy voice would proclaim that Charles Dain had beat the bullet. The phone remained silent. Maybe, I thought, God had me on hold.

I waited.

My name is Max Wills. I'm sixty years old, long and skinny, and most of my hair is eyebrows, which still look black because I keep plucking out the gray. The silver streaks on top I let stand because I need all the cover I can get. The lines in my face make a photo of it look like a hatch-work drawing. My nose is thin and bony, my mouth wide but not too bad if I don't smile, which I rarely do unless I'm drunk. These days I try not to get drunk in deference to my oversize liver, which is slowly turning to stone, and because two years ago I got hit with a myocardial infarction, which seems to me a dirty way to say heart attack.

A man so unblessed by nature needs compensations. I

get mine by wearing elegant dark suits and white silk shirts custom made at Tripler's, who also provide my polka-dot bow ties. My black shoes are Florsheim's finest, and my midnight-blue fedoras are Borsalinos. Charles Dain once told me that I looked like a diplomat from some Balkan country who'd gone to too many parties and always stayed too late. I wasn't offended.

My title on the masthead says Editor in Chief, but I'm a lot less than that—and yet a lot more. Less because these days I have little to do with the news side; instead I preside over editorial policy meetings, check out the syndicated stuff, and occasionally write a think piece. More because I'm Charles Dain's alter ego, father confessor, and sometimes his conscience. I've played that role for a quarter of a century, starting when Charles was barely eighteen and when I was thirty-four. He's now forty-three.

I first met Charles in the summer of 1916 at the home of George Fletcher, a man some years older than I who was assistant circulation manager of Hearst's New York *American,* where I was a reporter. It was a Saturday, and George and I had gone to a saloon on Park Row for lunch. We started drinking at twelve thirty, were joined by three other bibulous newsmen, and in a half hour it was past four o'clock. George, a big, brick-faced Irishman with red-blond hair and a voice that rattled glasses, then proposed that the five of us proceed by foot, subway, trolley car, ferry, and railroad to his home in South Orange, New Jersey, where his wife would cater to our appetites and thirsts while we enjoyed a friendly game of poker. The suggestion struck us as being eminently reasonable.

We arrived at George's house shortly before six, after a journey marked by ribald wit and a stop to buy several bottles of rye whiskey. The house was a brown-shingled structure with gables and dormers and a creaking front porch furnished with padded rockers and a wooden swing that hung suspended by chains from the ceiling. George's wife, Edna, met us at the door, smiling wanly and edging away, as one might when confronting a pack of tail-wagging dogs suspected of being rabid. Otherwise she was conscientiously polite and soft-spoken, a small, shapely, blond woman who I thought might once have been a high school cheerleader and then one day woke up to find she hadn't a damned thing to cheer about.

George told her we were taking over the dining room. George told her to get ice and glasses. George told her to whip up some food. And she did what George told her to do, quietly, meekly, as though to protest might fetch her a crack across the mouth.

We were cutting for deal when their daughter came in, accompanied by a young man. I gave him a glance, then forgot he was there: my eyes fell on Sharon Fletcher as she stood in the living room taking off her large, feathered hat. She was blonder than her mother, hair curving across pink cheeks and coiled into a bun at the nape of her smooth white neck. Her eyes were big and deep blue, more the color of amethyst, her nose delicate, her mouth full and rich. She was the loveliest creature I'd ever seen, more beautiful than the Gibson girl.

All the men had lurched to their feet, a couple of them buttoning their vests and fussing with their high starched collars. "Well!" said one, which translated into

"Wow!" Attracted by our attention, Edna led her daughter through the portieres into the haze of cigar smoke and introduced her. I was conscious then of Sharon Fletcher's remarkable figure—breasts taut against her ruffled yellow blouse, waist tiny and curving into rounded hips accentuated by a tapered skirt that ended just above the buckskin tops of her shoes, giving a glimpse of trim ankles. She acknowledged us in a soft, pleasant voice, appearing undismayed by the fatuous smiles and hot stares. She was only seventeen—half my age—yet she had such poise that I felt I was the younger.

Her father was the only one not smiling. His big mick face was set in sullen lines, and his eyes, glimmering with suspicion, peered beyond her to the tall figure hanging back in the living room. Edna signaled the young man, and he came and stood beside Sharon, towering over her.

"This is Charles Dain," Edna said in a tremulous voice.

From beside me, unheard by the others, Fletcher muttered, "Danowski."

That made me look intently at Dain. He was dark, with thick black hair curling over his ears. His cheeks were hollow, the skin stretched tight across a strong jaw and prominent cheekbones. His eyes were deep-set and slightly canted, giving his face an exotic look. The name Danowski would fit, I thought, but only if preceded by Prince. I guessed that his father had dropped the "owski" as a defense against bigotry, an excision that would only aggravate the intolerance of Hearstian flag-wavers like George Fletcher.

Once they had left, George seemed strangely distracted. He'd forget to ante, fumbled with his cards, and at intervals would glare out toward the living room as though to discern an unseen enemy. Finally he got up, strode to the front door, and flipped a wall switch that lit up the porch. The reason for his concern thus became obvious: His daughter and Charles Dain were out on the porch, probably in the swing, engaged in God knows what form of mortal sin.

Back at the table George kept looking at his watch, drank constantly, swore at his cards. An hour passed, and he could stand it no longer. Again he got up, went to the front door, and this time flung it wide open. He spoke from inside the living room.

"Getting late, Sharon."

"Late? Why, it's only eight thirty, Daddy."

"Yeah. Well, anyway, it's too late for you to be outside."

I heard footsteps coming down the stairs. His wife, I thought, hoping to avert a scene.

"I'm sorry, sir," Charles Dain said. Apparently he had left the swing and was facing George, whose hulking body now filled the doorway.

"Sorry?" said George, his tone nasty. "Now s'pose you tell me just what it is you're sorry about."

"Sorry if I've upset you." The young man spoke politely, but I thought I detected a note of disdain.

"No, that's not why you're sorry. Hell, no. Why you're sorry is I broke up whatever the hell's been going on out here."

"We were talking, Mr. Fletcher. Nothing else." He didn't sound at all defensive. He was coolly, quietly, stating a fact. Which was enough to detonate drunken George's temper.

"Look, kid, I don't like your attitude. You act, for chrissakes, like this is your house. Well, it's not your house. It's my house. And that's my daughter! So when I say break it up, that's what you'll do! And I want none of your lip!"

"Daddy, please," Sharon said. "Charles was only—"

"Keep out of this, girl."

"It's all right, Sharon," Dain said. "I'll leave."

"No," Sharon said. "It's early. Daddy didn't mean—"

"The hell Daddy didn't," George said.

"Good night, Sharon."

"Good riddance," George said.

I heard the creak of the porch steps as Dain left. Then George swung away from the door and Sharon marched past, head high, face frozen into a cameo look. She swept past her mother, who stood gazing at George in despair. Not until Sharon reached the top of the stairs did she indicate any emotion—a mewing sound, a whimper, reminding me of the forlorn cries of an expiring cat I'd once owned.

At the dining room table we were all uneasily aware that we'd seen a side of George Fletcher never revealed at the paper. There he was always bluff and hearty, always quick with a grin and a joke, and a fiver if you were hard up. Even when boozing he was good old George, friendly, unflappable, able to take a ribbing as well as give it. The delivery truck drivers—many with ethnic names that were tongue twisters—loved him.

On the surface it wasn't hard to understand his outburst. He was second-generation Irish Catholic, descended from a long line of moody men whose wives accepted without complaint the lifetime role of indentured servant and whose children were instilled with a repressive morality and blind obedience to patriarchal authority. That would be especially true in a case where the child, like Sharon, was both solitary and female. No doubt George viewed Charles Dain—dark, handsome, unflinching—as an emissary of Satan, come to rob his precious daughter of the sacred gift that must remain inviolate until bestowed on a husband, preferably one whose family name did not end in a vowel or a z.

But I couldn't help wondering if there was a less superficial explanation. Was it possible that George, having in effect emasculated his wife, now unconsciously coveted his ravishing daughter? The question might never have occurred to me had I not been dipping into the writings of Sigmund Freud, whose theories about sex were just beginning to shock the country. I immediately dismissed the notion, but not because it struck me as nonsense; only because in 1916 the whispered word incest was applied almost exclusively to Southern white trash and people presumed insane.

Anyway, that ugly incident just about finished the poker game. During the next deal, as though in vindication, George muttered, "Hunky whelp," and, a bit later, "Father's a sewer rat"—which turned out to be not quite true, Dain senior being employed by the county as an all-around laborer.

We played a few more desultory hands, then called it quits, we guests weaving our way back across the Hudson River to fall senseless into our separate beds, mine occupying a single room at the Murray Hill Hotel.

Unbelievable as it may seem, after that night I became a frequent visitor to the Fletcher home. The reasons were simple. George was apologetic, declared his friendship, and thereafter sought me out to share his convivial pleasures. He was the old George Fletcher, outgoing, humorous, generous, which quickly erased the image of the irrational drunk standing in a doorway insulting an innocent young man. Also, I was a bachelor living alone, far from my roots in Illinois, and the prospect of enjoying a home-cooked meal while surrounded by a family seemingly devoted to my well-being was irresistible.

I went out there almost every Sunday, and often George persuaded me to leave the office with him at quitting time on Saturday and spend the weekend. My presence had a remarkable effect on him. He drank little and only before dinner, which seemed to surprise as well as please Edna and Sharon. He was considerate and caring, once even helping with the dishes, and always assisting Edna into her chair at the dining table— acts apparently so extraordinary, they brought a flush to her cheeks and caused Sharon's mouth to drop open. I assumed he was simply redeeming himself, exorcising his guilt at being such a horse's ass on my first visit. I was wrong.

I began to sense I was wrong one Saturday night after Charles Dain had brought Sharon home from an early movie. (George had yielded to an uneasy truce with Dain, treating him with cool politeness but always demanding to know where he was taking his daughter and precisely what time he'd return her.) Edna, George, and I were playing Parcheesi at a collapsible card table set up in the living room. As the young couple came through the door George elaborately consulted his big vest-pocket watch—the time was eight fifteen—and gave a nod of approval. Edna invited Dain to stay, and he sat beside Sharon on the sofa. They talked for a few minutes about the movie—*Madame Butterfly*, with Mary Pickford, as I recall—and lapsed into silence while we finished our game. Then Edna brought out pound cake and coffee, chattering nervously but getting little response. The cake eaten, the coffee drunk, Dain rose and bid us good night. Sharon accompanied him to the porch, lingered there for a few minutes, and came back with the radiant look of a girl who has just been thoroughly kissed.

George pretended not to notice her. He was up and stretching, stifling a yawn to say, "Max, you got to excuse me but I'm going to retire." He shot a glance at Edna.

"Well, you can retire," she said archly, "but I'm going to bed."

They laughed. Apparently their little joke had gotten a lot of mileage over the years. Said now, in the context of a pleasant family gathering, with the menacing presence of Charles Dain removed, it seemed to bring them closer together, in fact to suggest a more exciting intimacy once they were in bed. I looked at Sharon. She was smiling at her parents in a way that betrayed a familiarity with carnal knowledge and an enthusiastic acceptance of it.

I wondered, uncomfortably, how far she'd gone with Dain, quickly dismissing the thought. She was a proper young Catholic lady, strictly disciplined to permit no liberties with her person, except perhaps the holding of her hand, an arm cautiously circling her waist, and, the ultimate, a few romantic good night kisses. But that didn't square with the Sharon I'd seen coming in from the porch. That had not been a demure, seventeen-year-old girl. That had been a sophisticated woman, sensually aroused, aware of it, glorying in it.

From the stairs George said, "Don't mind us old folks, Max. You kids stay up as long as you like."

Old folks! George Fletcher—and by the look of her, his wife—was still on the sunny side of forty. Kids! Hell, I was thirty-four years old. Why would he want to make me a contemporary of his daughter? Unless . . .

Preposterous! George pushing me at his daughter as a replacement for the dreaded Charles Dain, a "hunky whelp," son of a "sewer rat"? Logical, yes, but not realistic. Sure, I had a bushel of hair then and dressed like a dandy—homburg, silk tie with pearl stickpin, chesterfield coat, spats over my polished shoes—but still I was too old and too physically ordinary to be considered eligible for anyone so young and so fantastically beautiful as Sharon Fletcher.

But of course George wouldn't see it that way. It was customary in the Ireland of his forebears for a man to be well into his thirties before taking a wife, usually a young one, and the major requirement of the groom was that he be "a good provider." Although George himself was an exception—he'd married at twenty-two—he was nevertheless heir to such thinking and therefore might consider me a catch. What's more, he liked me, thus in his sentimental mind giving credence to the questionable saying: "I haven't lost a daughter, I've gained a son."

All of this floated vaguely through my mind, evaporating when Sharon began to entertain me. She brought out a stereopticon and we squinted at in-depth pictures of places they had visited—Lake Hopatcong, Bear Mountain, Delaware Water Gap, Atlantic City.

Then the family album, which rewarded me with a profile view of Sharon stark naked—on a scale, at the age of three months. (She was charmingly unabashed.)

After that we just sat and talked, and I discovered that for one so young and sheltered she had an astonishing range of knowledge. Not only could she discuss movie stars like Mary Pickford and Mabel Normand, directors like Griffith and De Mille, but also authors such as Theodore Dreiser and Sherwood Anderson, radicals like John Reed, Floyd Dell, and Emma Goldman, the anarchist who advocated free love.

"You sound like the New Woman," I said, teasing her. "I'm surprised you don't use rouge and lipstick and smoke cigarettes."

She laughed. "Not in this house. Daddy would explode."

"You must have very liberal teachers."

She gave me a calculating look, as though wondering how much to trust me. "Only one. And he's not on the faculty."

I felt my eyebrows go up. "You mean—"

"Yes, I mean Charles." She frowned. "But please don't mention that to Daddy."

"My lips are sealed."

Proudly she explained that Charles Dain was determined to "be somebody." One of eight children living in a ramshackle house in the poorest section of town, he was precluded by local snobbery from mingling socially with the well-born. Though his prowess on the football field won him considerable admiration, it was of the kind accorded a handsome stallion at a horse show; the performance ended, he was returned to his stable. His only salvation, he believed, was through mind rather than muscle, and it was his good fortune to have been endowed with intelligence, perception, imagination. He read, he thought, he observed, and what he discovered he shared with this young lady who, I was learning, ran much deeper than the pink-and-white Dresden figurine of my first impression.

"Sounds like that's what he wants to be—a teacher," I said.

She gave me a sidelong look. "No, a newspaperman. Like you."

I smiled, pleased that a young man so gifted should aspire to a business that was the most fascinating I could imagine. My dream was to be like Richard Harding Davis, the striking, grim-faced gentleman-journalist whose dispatches from abroad were models of elegant prose. He had just returned from a tour of Allied capitals, infuriated by President Wilson's declaration that America was "too proud to fight" and urging our entry into the war.

"It's funny," she said. "At first I think Charles just said he wanted to be a newspaperman because he thought it would impress Daddy."

"Did it?"

"I'm afraid not. Daddy wasn't very nice. He laughed and said that perhaps if Charles tried very hard he might get a job on some street corner selling *The Masses*. You know—that socialist paper."

I nodded. "He'd do better selling it than writing for it. They don't pay for contributions." *The Masses*, started five years earlier in Greenwich Village, was a rabble-rousing publication that attacked the status quo with the devastating talents of men who later became internationally famous: writers like Max Eastman, Walter Lippmann, Carl Sandburg; artists like Art Young, John Sloan, George Bellows. Poverty provided their material, wealth and privilege their targets.

"Charles isn't interested in money," she said.

I thought her naïve, but said, "In that case, he's chosen the right occupation." I added dryly, "The other attraction is that there's no job security."

To illustrate, I ticked off the employment practices of a number of press bosses: Charles Dana, late editor of the New York *Sun,* who was still remembered for firing reporters for a single grammatical error; Frank Munsey, a reckless buyer and killer of publications, who refused to hire fat men and would discharge anyone caught smoking on the premises; James Gordon Bennett, Jr., the rich-born drunken madman who usually ran his *Herald* from Paris, and was known to hire and fire whole staffs via transatlantic cable.

Worst of all, I said, was Charles E. Chapin, city editor of the *Evening World,* owned by the family of the late Joseph Pulitzer, the blind, eccentric autocrat who had directed his enterprises from his three-hundred-foot yacht or from one of his half dozen estates here and abroad. Chapin was without doubt the most terrifying figure on Park Row, as I knew from personal experience. His granite face was decorated with a bristling, military mustache and a tortoiseshell pince-nez strung to his lapel by a black ribbon. He had the voice of a banshee and delighted in running up and down the city room shouting headlines, meanwhile peering over the shoulders of rewrite men, bullying reporters, snarling at copyboys. Exhausted, he would return to his desk, which sat on a dais, and there proceed to gobble up sweets—candy, jam, ice-cream cones, canned peaches—which he believed fermented in his stomach and thus allayed the craving for alcohol that had forced him to take the pledge and the Keeley cure.

"I worked for him for six months," I said. "Then one day as I entered the city room he ran up to me, poked me in the chest, and yelled, 'You're fired!' "

"Heavens! Had you done something terrible?"

"I had. Chapin was a high-style dresser—wasp-waisted suits, pearl tiepin, ascot, spats." I paused, aware that she was looking me up and down and smiling. "Exactly," I said. "Sartorially, we were two of a kind."

"Is that what he said?"

"He said, 'I don't like the way you dress,' and walked away."

She laughed, and for the first time I realized she was enjoying my company. I wasn't accustomed to that. For about a dozen years I'd been a knockabout newsman, working mostly at various papers in the Midwest—Chicago, Detroit, Cleveland—making only transient connections with women, the kind who didn't give a damn about what you did or thought as long as you had the wherewithal for a lively show and a fancy supper, for which they would later reward you at some cheap rooming house or hotel.

I had looked for nothing more. After all, the future Richard Harding Davis, whose beat would someday be the whole wide world, couldn't very well concern himself with a wife and kids, could he?

Sharon Fletcher caused me some doubts about that. Here was a girl who was not only beautiful, articulate, and well informed, but one who actually listened. I can still see her big eyes glimmering with comprehension, her full lips rounding into an O, her delicate hands moving to her bosom as I related story after story of people whose triumphs and tragedies had made headlines.

I was just elaborating on the case of Harry K. Thaw, who publicly fired three shots into architect Stanford White, the seducer of Thaw's wife, Evelyn Nesbitt, when I happened to glance at my watch. My God, it was past two A.M.! George Fletcher would kill me!

But when I lay in bed, I forgot about George's imminent wrath. My mind was too occupied with visions of Sharon, with fantasies such as dining together at Lüchow's as violins played, of riding the Staten Island Ferry on a balmy evening, of meeting her under the Biltmore clock and seeing her eyes sparkle with promise. As I drifted off to sleep I seemed to move backward in time until I was no older than Charles Dain.

The next morning George entered the guest room before I was out of bed. The family had just returned from an early Mass and he was still clad in his Sunday best.

"Max," he said, "I want you out of this house in a half hour."

I sat up, blinking, memory flooding back. "Look, George, let me explain."

"Explain what?"

"Why I kept Sharon up so late."

"Oh, that. Why shouldn't you stay up late on a Saturday night? Hell, you're a young man." He paused, raised his eyebrows, and pursed his lips, as though about to render a solemn judgment. "You're *both* young," he said.

I looked at him. He smiled back benignly. I knew then for a fact that he was an aspiring matchmaker. But

I didn't protest—I was too relieved. And even in the light of a brilliant morning, I could not completely disavow the romantic thoughts that had accompanied me to sleep.

"Well," I said, "if you're not sore, why do I have to vamoose?"

He eyed me ingenuously. "Because Edna's got to work on her roses, and I've got to mow the lawn and paint the back-porch stairs."

"I'll help," I said.

"That you'll do." He shot me a sly glance. "And you'll do it by taking Sharon for a spin in the Tin Lizzie."

I laughed. "George, you're a card—the joker. Now why would a lovely young lady like your daughter want to traipse about with an ugly old fogy like me?" I was embarrassingly aware that I was fishing.

"Ugly you are." He looked me straight in the eye. "Still and all, she likes you. She told me so on the way back from church."

Now everything was clear: his abstinence, his attentiveness to his wife, his whole role as model husband and father. He'd as much as been telling me that I could take pride in becoming his son-in-law.

"Fine," I said. "I like her too. So crank up the Tin Lizzie."

"I already did. It's in the driveway rarin' to go. Edna's putting up a picnic basket. Max, my boy, it's a beautiful day!"

Sitting in my office twenty-six years later, I could still remember my feeling of anticipation at the prospect of bumping down a rutted lane in a Model T Ford with Sharon Fletcher close at my side. I could also recall my apprehension over how Charles Dain might react to my poaching. He was a lot huskier than I. And yes, dammit, a lot younger.

I was jarred back to the present by two phone calls. The first was from Hewlett at the hospital. He said that Dain had just lapsed into a deep coma and the medics were not optimistic that he'd ever come out of it.

The second call was from Terry Donovan, our crack investigative reporter, who asked to see me immediately. I told him to come up.

Chapter · 2

Terry Donovan slumped into a chair and gave me his quizzical look, an oblique glance from under heavy lids that gave the impression he was half asleep. He wasn't. In fact, he was the most wide-awake reporter I'd ever known.

"Max," he said, "you got any idea who might have gunned him?"

I shrugged. "Sure. I could give you a list a yard long."

"You mean crooks?"

"Who else? All of his enemies are crooks."

"And some of his friends."

"Not friends—connections, sources. The same goes for you, Terry." I reached in my pocket for a cigarette. The pocket was empty. Donovan shook a crumpled pack of Camels at me and I took one, lit up, and cut a few minutes off my life span.

"That's what the cops think," Donovan said. "That he got it from someone blasted by the *Express*. So right now they're sweating gamblers, pushers, flesh peddlers, stoolies."

"As I said, a long list."

"But maybe the wrong one. Look, Max, anyone who'd

put a bullet into a man like Dain would have to be crazy." He paused to pile his clodhoppers on my desk. "If he was sane, he'd know he couldn't make it through the heat. Everybody from the commissioner to the rookie cop is after his hide."

I shrugged. "Okay, so he's crazy."

He gazed past me, out the window. "Maybe only temporarily," he said slowly.

"Same thing."

"Not if it was a woman."

I stared at him. "What the hell—"

"If it was a woman, she could have been perfectly sane but suddenly lost all control." He softly snapped his fingers. "Like that."

"That's ridiculous."

"Why?"

I leaned across the desk, hands gripping my lapels. "Because I know Charles Dain better than anyone else on this earth. Do you agree?"

He grinned. "Sure, that's why I'm here."

"Then you ought to believe it when I tell you there's only one woman in his life—his wife, Harriet."

He raised an eyebrow. "Yeah, lately."

"What the hell do you mean, *lately?*" I was annoyed enough to stub out my cigarette.

He flapped a hand. "Take it easy, Max. It's no secret that Charles used to—"

"That was years ago. He was young, susceptible, and women wouldn't leave him alone."

"He's still fairly young—forty-three. And still damned attractive."

"But no longer susceptible. He got all that out of his system. I know."

"Okay, Max, I won't argue it. There's too much on your side. Charles Dain, crusading publisher, civic leader, champion of the oppressed, buddy of Archbishop Spellman, Bernie Baruch, Harry Hopkins."

I smiled. "Add faithful, loving husband and you've got it."

"That's the *public* Charles Dain."

"Now, look—"

"Max, forgive me, but you look. We've got a shooting here, maybe a murder. Chances are it's the work of someone the paper crucified. That's what the cops think, and apparently that's what you think. To suggest anything else might smear Charles's reputation, and I can understand your not wanting to risk that. Well, I say we've got to risk it. At least I do. I'm a reporter, not a press agent."

He had stood up, a big man without an ounce of lard on his six-foot frame. He had the powerful, alert muscles of a fullback, which I'd verified once in the shower room of the New York Athletic Club. Usually he appeared no more threatening than an ungroomed Saint Bernard, with his shaggy hair, wrinkled sport coat, and loosely knotted tie that fell short of his unbuttoned collar. Now he looked like he was about to eat me.

I picked up the bent stub of my cigarette, straightened it, lit it, and took a corrosive drag. "All right, Terry," I said, "now that you've had your say—"

"I'm not finished."

"The hell you're not. Now sit down and shut up for a minute."

He sat down, his eyelids flickering in surprise. It was not my style to talk that way to reporters—or to anyone else. I had never been the Simon Legree editor stereotyped in the public mind by the Hecht and MacArthur play *The Front Page.* I was no Walter Burns, and the only one I knew who fit that role was the prototype for it, Walter Howey, the fire-eating eccentric who had made a circus of journalism in Chicago and now ran Hearst's New York *Mirror.* And Terry Donovan was no glib, flamboyant Hildy Johnson; he usually operated quietly, insidiously, often extracting incriminating statements from people who thought they'd been models of discretion.

I lowered my voice. "I'm not saying you shouldn't have questions. That's your job—you're a reporter. I understand that. As the saying goes, I used to be a newspaperman myself."

He didn't smile, just looked at me.

I kept my tone sweetly reasonable. "I think I know what those questions are because I had them myself, as soon as I got word of the shooting. Let me tell you how I see it."

Obviously, I said, the first question was why Charles Dain would go to a town house owned by his wife, a house he supposedly never used. Answer: He'd probably chosen it as a blind because he expected to meet some man who couldn't afford to be seen with him publicly—a shady politician with information, a big advertiser who wanted help to keep his kid out of jail, a rich investor with an offer to buy the *Express,* which happened all the time.

Donovan started to speak, but anticipating him, I cut him off. No, I didn't think someone like that had shot him. The arrangement to meet at the town house, I said, had to have been a hoax, a setup to murder him.

"Which brings us back to the logical suspects," I said.

"Some no-good who'd been nailed by the paper and wanted revenge."

Donovan didn't appear to be listening. His eyes seemed to be turned inward, as though examining his brain.

"You've probably got a few other questions," I said. "Probably the same ones I had. Why was Charles dressed in a robe, nothing else? That's been explained. He'd taken a shower—the tub and curtain were wet and a towel was damp. Why a shower before meeting a *man*? Because he'd had a long, hot day in a dirty city, that's why."

Donovan stirred. "You don't think it's odd that he happened to have a robe?"

"Not particularly. But the fact is, it was left behind by an associate of Harriet's who'd stayed there some time ago. There were a few other pieces of forgotten clothing, none belonging to Charles."

"Women's clothing?"

"Not so much as a garter." I pinched the quarter inch that was left of the cigarette and scorched my lips with a final drag. "It may also interest you to know that the beds weren't touched."

His mouth hooked in a small smile of disdain. I could guess the scenario that had formed in his mind.

"You're conjecturing he was all set for sex but somehow gave her the fits," I added, "Then suddenly her mind snapped and she started shooting. Is that it?"

He answered with a slow nod.

"Horsefeathers," I said. "You've been writing too much pulp fiction. In the real world a woman doesn't try to murder a man just because she doesn't like his attitude."

"The gun was fired from a kneeling or sitting position. He might have knocked her down."

"Come off it, Terry. Charles never hit a woman in his life."

"He might have had to if she was after his gun."

"For your information Charles doesn't own a gun. We know that because every time his life had been threatened, always anonymously, we—and that includes the police—urged him to get one. He always refused, saying that if anyone really wanted him rubbed out, his packing a gun wouldn't stop it."

"All right, then, *her* gun. In that case, it could have been premeditated. She might have gone there mad as hell and—"

"Now you're hallucinating. Try to get it through your thick skull that there's no woman who'd want Charles dead."

His droopy eyes turned stubborn. "There are still some things—"

"Like what?" I barked it at him.

"Like his wife apparently not knowing about his having a key to the place. Like the door being left unlocked after the shots were fired. Like the police being called by a nameless woman."

I held on to what was left of my patience. As calmly as I could I explained that Harriet was unaware of the key because Charles probably got it from the management company just prior to the near-fatal meeting. As for the unlocked door, I said, it was logical to assume that the gunman, overwrought, perhaps hopped-up, had accidently pressed the latch as he dashed out. That left the woman. Why not go along with the police on that one—she was like most New Yorkers, happy to report a crime but never to get involved in it.

"Satisfied?" I said.

"No," he said. "You're giving me guesses. And you're saying that this so-called professional job was done by a bungler who panicked. It doesn't wash."

So much for patience. "That's enough. Now get your big feet off my desk and listen to me."

He unloaded his feet, sat up straight, and eyed me as though I were Tojo. His expression reminded me of the faces of those grim marines in the photos coming in from the South Pacific. Thirty-four years old, I thought, separated from his wife and without dependents; any day now his draft board would grab him and he'd be taking orders from some snotty kid who didn't know a noun from a verb. A preview might do him some good.

"I don't like the direction you're taking on this," I said. "I don't like it at all. And neither would your publisher, if he were half alive. And you damn well know the reason. Once it gets out that you're poking around into Dain's private life, trying to turn up some woman—who, I'll tell you again, doesn't exist—every scandalmonger in this town will start working overtime. Winchell would pick it up. So would Sullivan, Lyons, Kilgallen. You'd be hearing about it at Lindy's, Toots Shor's, El Morocco; and every time some gossip passed it on, another spicy tidbit would be added, until Charles Dain came out looking like the worst lecher, the sneakiest adulterer, in the long annals of fornication."

Donovan looked about to spit. "Some of that will come out anyway. Just the circumstances will be enough to—"

"It won't happen if the investigation stays focused on where it belongs—on the lawbreakers. And that's where it's going to stay. You'll work with the cops. You'll develop leads. You'll try to beat the competition. What you won't do is look for anything that could smear the character of your boss. Am I getting through?"

"Like a Sherman tank. But you'd better tell that to Paul Zack. He might not agree." Zack was the city editor.

"I'll do that. And I'll also tell it to Lou Volkman." Volkman was managing editor, the job I'd once held. "And they'll either agree or turn in their uniforms."

I stood up, not so much to end the meeting as to loosen the knots in my stomach.

Donovan got to his feet, threw me a mock salute, and headed for the door. "Okay," he said, going out. "You're the boss."

For the first time I realized that, at the moment, I was exactly that.

I lay on the couch, head propped on the cool leather arm, and massaged my stomach, aware that what had once been muscle and sinew now felt like thin dough. To distract myself I thought of when I had first met Terry, then a fresh-faced, laughing kid, and of the father he had idolized—the famous Peter Donovan, whom I'd known when he was one of the most widely-read and respected newspapermen in New York.

All so long ago. . . .

Terry Donovan grew up in a hilly section of northern Manhattan called Coogan's Bluff. The location was important because it meant that his mother could walk him up to the tar roof of the apartment building, where he could gaze out at the great oval structure in which his father often worked—the Polo Grounds. The grandeur of this sight was supposed to impress upon Terry the prestigious nature of his father's vocation: sportswriter for the New York *Herald.* To Peter Donovan, who had suffered the triple disappointment of siring three females, it was essential to his pride that his only son not share the opinion, then held by publishers and managing editors, that the sports page was a distasteful necessity, read principally in barrooms and barber shops along with the *Police Gazette* and *Captain Billy's Whizbang.*

Even if he had been aware of this attitude, Terry would not have been deflected from his belief that the only space of consequence in a newspaper was that alloted to baseball, football, boxing, and possibly lesser sports like horse racing, tennis, golf. This belief was often dramatically supported when he dazzled the neighborhood kids with brand-new Spalding baseballs autographed by such awesome pitchers as Christy Mathewson, Grover Alexander, Cy Young.

During the summer of his eighth year his father took him along on a number of assignments—not only to the Polo Grounds but also to Brooklyn's Ebbets Field, Chicago's Comiskey Park, Philadelphia's Shibe Park—often traveling with the players and sometimes meeting godlike managers like John McGraw (astonishingly addressed by Peter Donovan as "Muggsie"), Miller Huggins, Connie Mack (whose real name, much to Terry's delight, was Cornelius McGillicuddy).

In the off-season Peter Donovan covered other sports, notably boxing, which Terry found even more exciting, if less cerebral, than baseball. He met Jack Kearns, Dempsey's manager, and Tex Rickard, the famous promoter; he witnessed the bloody battle at Boyle's Thirty Acres in Jersey City in which Jack Dempsey broke the nose of the handsome Frenchman Georges Carpentier, who responded by breaking his right hand on Dempsey's jaw. On his fifteenth birthday Terry's father presented him with a small radio that he kept beside his bed, where he could stretch out, clamp on the earphones, and hear a sports event hysterically described by Graham McNamee, while his mother and sisters sat in the living room listening to Billy Jones and Ernie Hare (the Happiness Boys) or the Cliquot Club Eskimos, interrupted at times by the velvety tones of announcer Norman Brokenshire.

In that same year, 1923, Terry decided that he would follow in the footsteps of his admired father. By then the reporting of games played by grown-ups was no longer disdained by publishers; sports had entered a golden era, and newspapers devoted whole sections to the exploits of Jack Dempsey, Babe Ruth, Helen Wills, Bobby Jones, Red Grange, not to mention such novel attractions as C. C. Pyle's Bunion Derby and the Six-Day Bike Race.

Many of the chroniclers of these events became almost as well known as the participants, and whenever sports fans gathered for furious debate, they were sure to advance their arguments with quotes from such authorities as Peter Donovan, Grantland Rice, Damon Runyon, Ring Lardner. The writings of these "sports scribes" were generally studded with historical allusions, lyrical phrases, wild inventions. A goal-line stand by the Fighting Irish might be compared to the Spartans at Thermopylae or the defenders of the Alamo. Jack Dempsey's right fist struck like the thunderbolts of Zeus or the hammer of Thor. A baseball bat was the "ash" or the "bludgeon"; a football the "pigskin" or, insanely, the "oblate spheroid"; a pitcher's throwing arm his "salary wing"; a manager a "mentor," "miracle man," or "generalissimo."

All this was heady stuff to adolescents of all ages. and particularly to the son of a man whose by-line appeared above such effusions. Entranced by these bards of brawn, and also hoping to please his father, Terry embarked on a program to add muscular flesh to his lean frame. Soon the house was flooded with literature from mail-order body-builders, most of it packed with glossy portraits of men in loincloths or fancy jockstraps wearing openwork, calf-high black shoes, the better to display muscles that would be the envy of any self-respecting gorilla. Terry never took the courses, but by studying the poses and analyzing the sales pitch, he was able to approximate the "dynamic tension," the proper lifting of weights, the arcane exercises that had transformed ninety-seven pound weaklings—victims of bullies who kicked sand in their faces—into super-Adonises. The fact was he did become big and strong, which might have occurred anyway, owing to the rigors of being a high school halfback, wrestler, and shot-putter.

But above all his pride in himself was the pride felt for his father when Peter Donovan achieved the pinnacle of his profession by becoming a columnist. There it was, every day, on the front page of the sports section —"Pete Donovan's *Sportslight*"—a temple of enlightenment on the players and performances that, second only to Wall Street, were the source of America's character and strength. What a thrill it was to overhear a subway straphanger exclaim, "Boy, Donovan sure gave it to dem bums today!" . . . or to see a promotion ad headed, "If You Don't Read Donovan, You Don't Know the Score!" . . . or to have a male teacher sidle up and ask,

"Who's your dad picking in the fight tomorrow night?" Of all the stars in the firmament of sports, the brightest to Terry was the flabby, rumpled, convivial Irishman he felt honored to call Father.

Peter Donovan was generous with his success. He moved his family to a luxurious apartment in the St. Moritz Hotel, overlooking Central Park. He gave his wife a Packard, jewels, charge accounts at fashionable stores; he sent his three daughters to private schools and expensive summer camps, showered them with gifts and, after their cathedral weddings, honored them with lavish receptions. For his son, the light of his life, who seemed indifferent to material possessions, he reserved a special benefaction—a trust fund sufficient to carry him in style through four years of college. Terry was delighted; now he was assured that he could go to Columbia and work to become the best student their famed school of journalism had ever produced.

He was facing that joyous prospect, having, at seventeen, graduated from high school, when his whole world suddenly collapsed. His father, his loving, gentle, high-principled father, was exposed as a cheat, a bribe-taker, an extortionist.

There was no question about it. The district attorney had recorded conversations with boxing promoters who confessed making payoffs to Peter Donovan for publicizing their matches. Fight managers, press agents, professional gamblers testified, under threat of prosecution, to the payment of substantial gratuities in order to advance their interests through plugs in "Pete Donovan's *Sportslight*."

Terry's father offered no defense. He expressed no self-pity. He didn't hire a lawyer. Instead, he checked into a room at the Great Northern Hotel, drank half a quart of whiskey, then pressed the barrel of a .38 caliber revolver to the roof of his mouth and blew out his brains.

The tragedy did not diminish Terry's love for his father. The man had been weak, he had broken the law, he had compromised the integrity of a great newspaper; but everything he had done had been motivated by a profound devotion to his family. That did not absolve him, but it did shift the blame to the slimy corrupters who had begun to infest every legitimate enterprise in the city. It seemed only poetic justice to use the trust fund bequeathed by Peter Donovan as a war chest for a future attack on the sort of men who had ruined him.

Terry plowed through Columbia in two years instead of four, graduating at the head of his class with a degree in journalism. No longer was he interested in writing about sports. Nor did he aspire to become another Floyd Gibbons or Vincent Sheean, or a city editor or managing editor, or to hold any position that would require him to tell other people what to do.

He wanted only to be a reporter assigned to the investigation of crooks.

That was in 1927, fifteen years ago. During that time he had changed radically from the eager-to-please son of Peter Donovan. Now he was somewhat remote, introspective, often abrasively independent. As a rebel and a loner (not too unlike myself), he was scornful of conventional wisdom, believing that anything the majority thought right was probably wrong. He specialized in digging, in getting to the absolute bottom of a story and turning it inside out, often demonstrating that what was visible on the surface was no more than illusion. It pleased him to come up with invidious and unprintable material, such as the fact that the now-saintly General MacArthur, when Chief of Staff, had installed a former Shanghai chorus girl, a Eurasian, in a Washington hotel suite as his concubine (he lavished black lace underwear on her, and she called him Daddy), or that New York's pompous governor, Thomas Dewey, wore elevator shoes; or that Joseph P. Kennedy, our recent ambassador to the Court of St. James's, had once been the illicit lover of Gloria Swanson. To editors Terry Donovan was a constant trial, suffered only because his instincts, diligence, and connections so often produced the kind of headlines that sold papers. Charles Dain considered him the best crime reporter since Irvin S. Cobb.

Like Cobb, Donovan was ambitious to write better things. As a start he spent most of his off hours in the newspaper morgue, poring over clips of past crimes and catastrophes, making copious notes, and from them contriving pulp thrillers that he sold, at a cent or two a word, to lowbrow magazines like *Argosy, True Detective, Black Mask*. He hoped someday to become a serious author, reside in Dublin, where writers were accorded reverence but left alone, and thereafter live as he damned well pleased. He once told me that he'd like to be the biographer of Charles Dain, a remark I resented because I'd assigned myself that task a long time ago and had a big stack of notes and correspondence to prove it. I doubted now that I'd ever write that book: my essential collaborators—my heart and my liver— were withdrawing their services. Eventually, perhaps, I'd make Terry Donovan the beneficiary of everything I'd accumulated.

But sure as hell not now. Not when all his perceptions were telling him that this shooting was no calculated act of a vengeful criminal but instead had resulted from the collision of two impassioned individuals, perhaps victims of inescapable circumstances.

The words "victims of inescapable circumstances"— attributed to Donovan but inadvertently my own— stayed with me as I sped uptown in a taxi, on my way to the hospital. They were of course a cliché, but, like so many clichés, had become one because they expressed an eternal truth: We are all victims of circumstances— and not necessarily those of the immediate present.

The bullet now threatening the life of Charles Dain may, I thought, have been awaiting him since the day he was born into poverty. There was no way I could determine that.

But what I could and felt I must determine was the degree to which the shooting was motivated by the circumstances of Charles Dain's life since I had known him.

Which took me back twenty-six years—to the summer of 1916, when I drove high and proud in a black Model T Ford with Sharon Fletcher at my side.

Chapter · 3

George and Edna Fletcher—he now tieless and in shirt-sleeves, she in a printed housedress—stood under a maple tree beside the gravel driveway smiling and waving as I backed out the roaring flivver. Turning, I caught a glimpse of their joyful faces and was swept by the feeling that they were bidding farewell to a bride and groom headed for a honeymoon at Niagara Falls. The feeling was not unpleasant. Rising to the occasion, I grinned, doffed my fedora, flung up an arm and brought it swiftly down in the classic gesture of a cavalry officer ordering a charge.

And charge we did, the spindly vehicle taking off as though blown from a cannon. I gripped the wheel hard, recalling George saying that he had tossed camphor balls into the gas tank to pep up the performance. That was the last thing I needed. I'd driven a Ford only a few times, and then merely to crisscross the stubbled fields of a farm I'd visited, where the car was used not only for transportation but also to generate electricity and pump water. Realizing I was in high gear, I contemplated uneasily the three pedals confronting me from the floor. Experimenting, I managed to get into low gear, then back into high, cutting the throttle on the steering wheel, and thus through elimination discovered that the third pedal was reverse, also functioning as a brake. I was now in full and arrogant command.

For a few minutes we drove without speaking, enjoying the sensation of the narrow wheels gliding over hard-packed dirt, inhaling the sweetness of the summer air whipping in through the open sides, dazzled by the morning sun glinting from the flat-nosed hood. Most poignant of all was my sensuous awareness of the small figure beside me—the scent of her lavender soap, the sidelong glimpse of her blue straw hat secured by a silk ribbon tied under her chin, the gentle touch of her shoulder against mine as the car swayed and rocked.

"Well," I said, turning my head to smile at her, "where should we have our banquet?"

The blue eyes that gazed into mine were warm and the look somehow conspiratorial. There was a coaxing quality to her voice as she said, "I wonder if you'd mind—" Hesitating, she glanced ahead and her lovely features contorted in horror. "Max! Look out!"

I lurched against the wheel as the car plunged downward. We had crested a slight rise and were now careening down a twisting hill. I felt the wheel jerk in my hands, felt the fishtail fling of the chassis, heard a barrage of dirt and stones strike the underside of the fenders as the wheels spun out of control. Frantically I banged my foot down on the reverse pedal. The car shuddered but refused to slow. Using both feet, I hit all three pedals. The car bucked, then veered sideways off the road. I jerked the wheel to straighten out, but went too far. For an instant we were airborne. Then there was a crunching thud, followed by the crackle of twigs, and finally, blessedly, immobility.

We were in a field overgrown with weeds and thickets. The engine was still running; indeed, in the surrounding silence, it thundered as though about to explode. We looked at each other. Her cheeks were not, as I would have expected, white with fear but were a glowing pink, and her eyes shimmered with excitement. Her lips were parted and curved into a small smile.

"Are you okay?" I asked.

"Oh, yes!" She looked like a child who had just got off a roller coaster and was eager to go again.

I got out, went around and, there being no door on the passenger side, lifted her out and set her on the ground. I sat on the runningboard and reached out a hand to draw her down, but she danced away. She was, by God, laughing.

"I must be in shock," I said. "I don't understand what's so funny."

"Not funny. Thrilling. So delightfully thrilling."

I decided then that she was deranged. Any normal girl would be suffering the vapors.

"We might have been killed," I said in a doomsday voice.

"Not us. We're indestructible."

"You, maybe. Me, I died back there on the road."

She came and stood in front of me. Compassion softened her face. "You are all right, aren't you, Max?"

I looked at her closely. Not a blond hair out of place. Blue hat, that almost matched her eyes, still perched firmly on her head. Long, pearl-gray dress unruffled. It seemed unmanly that I should be so agitated.

I stood up, squared my shoulders, and said heroically, "I have only begun to fight."

She bowed and with her thumb pretended to pin a medal on my chest. "You are a man of valor, *mon capitaine.*"

"French?" I said. "This is the French army? In that case, I believe there is a custom that must be observed."

Quickly she rose on her toes and lightly kissed each of my cheeks. I was instantly rejuvenated.

"Honestly," she said, her manner becoming serious, "you were wonderful—a regular Barney Oldfield."

I decided she was not at all deranged. "It was nothing," I said. "In fact, it taught me that I can master the beast."

"Then we can still have our picnic?"

"Certainly."

She looked away, saying, "I wonder if we could . . ." She stopped, apparently disconcerted.

"If we could what? Anything you wish."

Her glance swung back and fixed me with a trusting look. ". . . if we could first stop at Charles's house."

Something inside me crumbled. Suddenly I felt like an aging actor miscast as a juvenile in a romantic play. How long, I wondered, before she would start calling me Uncle Max?

"Fine," I said, and trouper that I was, added, "Onward, fair maiden."

To reach the Dain place required a jolting ride down a narrow lane, past a garbage dump, a warehouse, and a scattering of tarpaper shacks. The house, isolated from its neighbors, sat on a large lot devoid of a single blade of grass but dotted here and there with fruit trees. The structure was an ancient two-story affair with an open wraparound porch and a multitude of windows, indicating many rooms—a necessity, I saw, as our noisy approach alerted a drove of occupants to come pouring out the front door.

I counted nine of them—mother, father, three girls, four boys—then added a tenth as a head popped out of an upstairs window. This last was Charles. He waved and ducked back inside. Then from somewhere, everywhere, the yard was invaded by a pack of mongrel dogs, yapping and racing about and adding to the billowing dust raised by the flivver.

While the children remained on the porch, the parents, wearing broad smiles, rushed up to the car.

"Ah," said Mr. Dain, taking Sharon's hands, "a surprise. How nice. How very nice." He spoke precisely, with the trace of an accent, and I had the instant impression that, despite his obvious indigence, he was no ordinary man. He was of medium height, broad-shouldered, big-chested; and he had the strong, sculpted face and curly silver hair that would have looked exactly right on a bronze plaque.

Sharon performed the introductions. Mrs. Dain, a thin woman with bright, dark eyes and jet-black hair pulled back tightly from her forehead, seemed to bend her knees in a small curtsy. Her husband showed no such humility. He stepped up to me, grinned, thrust out his hand, and gave me a firm grip with a palm that felt like pumice.

"Charles has told us about you," he said. "All very good. A journalist. We are honored to have a distinguished journalist visit our home."

I liked him.

As we walked to the house, Mr. Dain quietly ordered

the dogs to silence, then said to me, "Always you can tell the poor. They have lots of dogs." He spoke in a caring tone.

"And children," I said, smiling at the solemn-faced congregation on the porch.

"Oh, yes." He chuckled. "How else could we support the dogs?"

He introduced the children individually, each stepping forward to shake my hand, the girls accompanying the gesture with a slight curtsy. They ranged in age from ten to nineteen, Charles—who had not yet appeared—being next to the eldest. All were dressed neatly, the girls in muslin dresses, the boys in denim pants and cotton shirts, and all looked well scrubbed. You'd have to look hard to discover personal signs of poverty—the darned heel of a sock, an almost invisible patch, an expertly turned collar.

Amenities observed, they marched in a group to the rear of the house. I must have looked surprised, for Mr. Dain said, "They have work to do. Would you like to see?"

I said I would, which was the truth. Having no family of my own—I had left home when I was sixteen—I felt drawn to these courteous people, who seemed to share a deep communion. While Sharon, waiting for Charles, sat on the porch with Mrs. Dain, Mr. Dain led me around the vine-covered side of the house to a produce garden half the size of a football field. With a feeling of wonder, and a twinge of nostalgia, I gazed at row after row of corn, squash, cabbage, lettuce, string beans, zucchini, and tomatoes.

"Amazing," I said.

He nodded in proud agreement.

"You must do nothing but eat."

"We do well. But of course it is too much for us. Some we give to our neighbors." He flicked a hand in the direction of the tarpaper shacks I had passed. "Some, a lot, we sell."

I looked again and saw his children moving up and down the rows, weeding, watering, raking, hoeing.

"You're a fortunate man," I said.

"Yes."

I had an impulse to draw him out. "These days you don't find many young people willing to spend a Sunday digging around a garden."

He nodded. "With us, it is necessary. What is fortunate is that we all enjoy it." He pursed his lips and tapped them with a finger. "Except, I think, Charles."

"He doesn't garden?" It would not have displeased me to hear he was a lazy lout.

"Oh, yes," Dain said. "He will do his part. But later, when he is no longer with Sharon." He stroked his chin reflectively. "It is just that Charles is different from the others. He is, well, special."

I recalled my late-night conversation with Sharon. "You mean because he's a scholar?"

"Scholar?" He gave his soft chuckle, then assumed a grave expression, raised his chin, and contemplated me with mock condescension, like a lofty savant. "Mr. Wills, *I* am the scholar of the family."

He laughed, and I joined in, moderately because I wasn't sure whether or not he was kidding. To find out, I said, "I should have known. You have the look of a Renaissance poet."

"Poet, no. Student, yes. I am a disciple of the classic writers and philosophers—Descartes, Spinoza, Kant,

Voltaire, Goethe, oh, so many." He shrugged to modify the boast, then added, "I am also crazy about the funny papers."

Again we laughed, but now I was staring at him with heightened curiosity.

He caught the look and said, "I suppose it is remarkable that a man who repairs roads, chops down trees, cleans gutters, should also be fascinated by great thoughts and ideas."

"Remarkable and admirable. It's no wonder Charles is so special."

"Really, they are all special, in their own way. But Charles is the great reader. He devours books; in fact, sometimes must be evicted from the library."

"Yet you say he's not a scholar."

"Not, as I am, a pure one. I read only for enrichment, a sense of fulfillment. Charles, however, reads only for a purpose. He wishes to acquire sufficient wisdom to compete successfully with the best brains in the marketplace. He is what you would call a pragmatist."

"Or a realist. Do you approve?"

"I approve of whatever my children want for themselves, so long as it is legal and not harmful to others." He turned away from the garden and grasped my elbow. "But enough of this. I am becoming sanctimonious."

Returning to the front porch, we found that Mrs. Dain had gone inside. In her place, sitting on the top step talking to Sharon, was Charles. The reason for his delay seemed evident: he had changed into clothes of better quality than those of his brothers, and his hair looked freshly combed. I was struck by his resemblance to his father—the curly hair, the deep-set eyes, the strong facial structure. The chief difference was in his long-legged tallness, and something else—an intensity as he spoke to Sharon, a suggestion of restrained sensuality, an aura of possessiveness that seemed to engulf them both. The word for it of course was love. Charles Dain adored Sharon Fletcher, and she—it was so obvious in the warmth of her glance, in the unabashed forward thrust of her breasts—adored him.

Absurd as it might seem, I felt offended, a reaction exacerbated when Charles Dain, rising, wished me a good morning and added the word "sir," as though I were a contemporary of his father. But it was Sharon, so ingenuous for all her intelligence, who finished me off:

"Max, what fun! Charles is going with us on the picnic!"

The smile I worked up was one of the most hypocritical of my life. "How nice," I said.

Charles looked inquiringly at his father. Mr. Dain looked dubious.

I was overwhelmed by masochistic glee. "Why not, Mr. Dain. As you said, Charles can do his work later."

He smiled ironically. "I shall contribute a bottle of my famous dandelion wine," he said.

Driving away with Charles now at the wheel, Sharon beside him, and me jackknifed in the back seat, I began to regain my perspective. My indignation against these two was really unwarranted. Neither had reason even to suspect they had affronted me. They were the young lovers, their affection declared, while I was no more than a friend of her father's, too old to be considered a suitor, a guest enlisted to distract the daughter while her parents pursued their household chores. The one who deserved my resentment was George, whose fool-

ish machinations had encouraged me to think—oh, I
confessed it now—that this treasure of a girl could possibly become mine.

After driving a couple of miles we reached a wooded
area, where Charles pulled off the road and parked on
the grassy bank of a small stream. We spread a blanket,
uncorked the wine, set out the contents of the picnic
hamper—fried chicken, potato salad, cole slaw, biscuits,
apple pie—and drank and ate to the background melody of rushing water splashing over stones. I spoke only
when spoken to, which was seldom, so entranced were
they with each other, their chatter no more compre-
hensible to me than some impenetrable code, their
flirtatious glances causing the food to lump in my throat.
I wished only to get back to George and in some
gentlemanly way inform him that he was a stupid son of
a bitch.

My dark thoughts were interrupted by Charles saying,
"That's very interesting, Mr. Wills."

"Interesting?" I hadn't said a word.

"Yes, I didn't know you'd covered the Thaw case."

Then I realized that Sharon had mentioned my newspaper reminiscences of the night before. "Uh-huh," I
said. "Murder's always interesting. Especially when the
people are rich and famous."

He nodded. "Yes, but that's not really what I meant.
To me, it's a lot more interesting that you were the
reporter. You knew the people involved, the—"

"Not the dead man, Stanford White. But I interviewed the other two—Evelyn Nesbitt and her husband, Harry Thaw."

"And you covered Thaw's trial."

"Two trials. In the first he got a hung jury. In the
second he was declared insane and committed to an

asylum." I felt an inner easing. "That was in 1906—ten years ago."

"Ten years!" He looked at me admiringly. "Mr. Wills, you couldn't have been any older than I am."

I had been twenty-four, six years older than he was now. But if he wanted to lop six years off my age— making me now twenty-eight—fine with me. "Call me Max," I said.

He smiled, as though I'd bestowed a great honor. Which reminded me that Sharon had said he was eager to become a newspaperman. "I hear you're thinking of a newspaper career."

"More than just thinking. I've made up my mind."

He said it with deep seriousness, like a novitiate vow-ing to become a priest. I thought of myself at his age, sneaking into a city room to observe the commotion, thrilling to the vibration of the giant presses, standing at the loading dock as the bundled papers were heaved into trucks, a driver once handing me one, and my pleas-ure at the smell of wet ink. I felt a sudden kinship for him, negating my jealousy.

"Getting in can be difficult," I said. "You'd be lucky to start as an office boy, let alone copyboy."

"What if he already had experience?" Sharon said.

"What kind of experience?"

"Working for the school paper." She gazed proudly at Charles. "He's one of the editors."

"Well . . ." I said.

"Sharon," Charles said, "that wouldn't get me through the front door. Not in New York, anyway."

"Don't be too sure," I said, warming to him. "I'd say it should at least get you an interview."

"Especially if he had an influential sponsor," Sharon said.

Charles stared at her. "You mean your father? Sharon, he wouldn't recommend me for janitor. Unless of course the job was in some place like Zanzibar."

"Not my father." She gave me an arch glance. "I mean someone very close to you."

Charles flushed. "Mr. Wills—Max? Now, wait a minute—"

"What do you think, Max?" Her voice was soft, intimate.

I wanted to say that getting him on the paper would be a great way to get even with George. Instead I said, "Maybe I can do something. Charles, talk to me when you get out of high school."

"Thank you. Of course all I'd be looking for would be a summer job. I'm planning to go to college."

"He's going to work his way through," Sharon said. Again the look of pride.

"If we don't get dragged into this rotten war," Charles said.

The ice broken, he peppered me with questions about the Fourth Estate. Did my boss, William Randolph Hearst, really think he could become President of the United States? Was it true that Arthur Brisbane, the widely-read columnist and Hearst's editorial chief, made as much as half a million dollars a year? What about this man Scripps, who was constantly buying papers—how could he be such an idealist, always supporting the common people, and still make millions? And Robert McCormick, how could he run such a reputedly awful paper as the *Chicago Tribune*, and also, like Hearst, be pro-German, yet continue as one of the most prosperous publishers in the country?

The answers I gave him were superficial, simply because his questions had little to do with the working press. His interests revolved around money and power, subjects newspapermen often reported upon but rarely enjoyed. Of course that was understandable. At eighteen, poor and socially ignored, yet intelligent and informed, he would naturally fantasize himself as a tycoon living in lordly splendor while casting a great newspaper in his own image.

As we drove away in the late afternoon I was reminded again of the future he envisioned for himself. Passing a long, gray Pierce-Arrow, the most envied of automobiles, he stuck his head out and I caught the covetous gleam in his eyes.

"Nifty car," I said.

He shifted his gaze back to the road. "Mine will be blue," he said.

Although there was a smile in his voice, I knew he was not joking.

Nearing his house, he suggested that I take the wheel, saying with a grin that I might as well practice before driving Sharon home. I knew it was a ploy that would allow them to ride in back, but I readily agreed, having adjusted to the role of indulgent chaperone. We rode the rest of the way without speaking, the only sounds being the jolting of tires, the squeak of springs, and—arousing in me a sense of voyeurism—the rustle of silk and the soft sighs of bliss.

After dropping him off, Sharon said to me, "Max, would you mind not telling Daddy that we saw Charles?"

I had been looking forward to telling him in order to convince him to give up playing cupid. "If that's how you want it," I said. "But why the secrecy? Your parents know you're going together."

"They want it to stop."

"You mean not ever see him again?"

"That's what they'd like—my father anyway. But for now they said I mustn't see him so often, and then only at home, when they're around. Once a week, they said. I know they hope that will end it. But it won't. So the next thing they'll do is forbid me to see him at all."

From what I'd heard coming from the back seat, I could understand their concern for their seventeen-year-old virgin daughter. Nevertheless, it seemed to me that their vigilance was excessively repressive.

"I'm sorry," I said.

"Oh, Max," she said, her voice choking. "I can't give him up. I simply can't. I'd die. I know I would."

I slowed the car and looked at her. Her eyes were glistening and her lovely lips trembled. Everything in me seemed to fall apart.

"Maybe you won't have to," I said.

She gazed full into my eyes and I had the poetic thought that I might drown in her tears. "Do you think so, Max? Do you mean you'd help?"

I hadn't really meant anything. "I'll do whatever I can."

"That's wonderful." She dabbed at her eyes with a lacy handkerchief. She smiled at me. "Then next time you visit we'll pick up Charles again."

That startled me. "Well, now—"

"You're a dear." She touched my shoulder, squeezed it.

"Just leave it to your uncle Max," I said, and hit the accelerator hard.

So I became the reluctant pivot in a lovers' conspiracy. During that fall and the winter of 1916 I spent about a dozen weekends at the Fletchers', and each time, with George's blind encouragement, I drove Sharon into the waiting arms of Charles Dain. Rarely did we meet him at his house lest the deception become apparent to his family, who might then scorn me as a betrayer of my trusting hosts. To the Dains I appeared as no more than a selfless friend—good old Uncle Max —who occasionally found vicarious pleasure in advancing the cause of young love.

Usually we would pick up Charles at a trolley stop or a soda fountain or, most often, on the main road near the cutoff to his place. While the weather was still warm we continued with our picnics, and often I would disappear to tramp through the woods, allowing them to entertain themselves in ways I tried not to think about. When the days grew cold we would go ice skating on some remote frozen pond or find sanctuary in a movie house or simply drive aimlessly about, wrapped in heavy wool blankets provided by my thoughtful sponsor, George.

I was of course disturbed by my treachery but justified it by telling myself that I was simply a shield against an oppressor who, in an earlier time, would have committed his daughter to a nunnery. But in my heart, I suppose, I knew differently. Even though I was no more than a spectator, I felt helpless to resist Sharon's exciting presence, the sound of her voice, the ripple of her laugh, the warmth of her smile.

The emotions she inspired only abetted my duplicity. Arriving back at the Fletchers', George would eye me suggestively, smirk in satisfaction and, after the women had gone upstairs, seek to draw me out.

"Well, Max, did you two have a good time?"

"Fine, George. Just fine."

"I'd say better than fine. Believe me, friend, when she

comes back from an outing with you, she looks like the happiest girl in the world."

I swallowed hard. "You're imagining things, George. She's just got a happy nature."

"Ha. You know what Edna says?" He beamed at me. "Edna says she thinks Sharon's in love with you."

"Come on, quit the kidding."

"No kidding. Edna's got a feeling for these things—women's intuition. But you'd know more about it than anybody." He leaned closer and I caught the smell of sneaked liquor. "Is there anything you want to tell me, Max?"

"Yes."

"What?" His eyes were like bright buttons.

"Shut your big Irish face."

He stared at me, then howled with laughter. "Good old Max, the cautious bachelor. Okay, go ahead, play it close to the vest. But anytime you want to talk about it—"

"George, you'll be the first to know."

He lowered his voice confidentially. "One thing. You can forget about Dain. These days he hardly ever comes around. But I suppose you noticed that."

"Yes, I noticed."

"I guess Sharon showed him she's a decent, moral girl, and that's not what his kind is looking for. Anyway, his staying away isn't bothering her one little bit. Schoolgirl crush, that's all it ever was. Now with you—"

"George!"

"Okay, I'll shut up."

Slowly I came to realize that I was caught in an impossible situation. I became tormented by guilt, by fear of discovery, by anguish at being an intimate participant in a courtship in which I was not the lover. One Saturday afternoon in February, while pacing the windy deck of the ferry taking me to New Jersey, I made my decision: I would tell Sharon that Uncle Max was defecting. After that I would stay away from the Fletcher household until George became convinced that his efforts to acquire me as a son-in-law had failed. Immediately I felt an immense relief—and a terrible emptiness.

When I arrived, George met me at the door. He was drunk.

"Come in, come in," he said. "Have a drink."

Surprised, I stepped into a dark living room. George lurched around switching on lamps, then disappeared into the kitchen and came back with two glasses and a bottle of Old Overholt tucked under his arm. I was still standing, feeling uncomfortable in the dead silence that made the house seem abandoned. We sat on the couch, not speaking, while he fidgeted with the bottle and finally splashed out the drinks. I took a sip, and he took a huge swallow. Then his eyes fixed me with the kind of fiery, outraged look reserved for rapists and murderers.

Oh, God, I thought.

"Edna's in her room," he said, wiping his wet mouth. "She's not feeling well."

"I'm sorry," I said. "Nothing serious, I hope."

He snorted. "Nothin' we need a doctor for."

I set my jaw. "And Sharon? Is she—"

"She's not well, either. Lyin' up there on her bed." He stared into his glass, finished off his drink, and poured another. His face was ugly with liquor and hate.

"That's a shame," I said. "I've heard there's a lot of flu going around."

He sprang to his feet and bellowed. "This isn't, goddammit, the flu! This is—" His lips moved, but no words came out. He shook his fist at the ceiling, breathed noisily through gritted teeth, groaned, and collapsed on the couch.

Startled, I forgot my fear. "George, what's wrong? Can I help?"

He contemplated me blearily. "Help? No, you can't help. No one can help. It's my problem, mine and Edna's."

There was a silence before I said, "I guess I shouldn't have come." I looked at my watch. "If I leave now, I can just catch the four o'clock train."

He shook his head. "No, no, you just sit right where you are. There's something I've got to say to you, and I might as well get it off my chest right now."

I gazed at the floor, my mind frantically preparing a defense.

"Max," he said, "I want you to forget you ever met my daughter." He jabbed a finger at my chest. "Do you get me? *Forget her!*"

My head came up, and I looked him straight in the eye. "George, if you'll just calm down and let me explain—"

"Explain! How d'you explain a daughter who's a bald-faced liar! And a boyfriend even worse! Dirty, lying cheats, both of 'em!"

"Now, George, let's talk about this reasonably."

"What's to be reasonable about? Lies are lies." He gulped his drink and glared at me. "Okay, I'll put it all on the table. By God, I sure as hell owe it to you."

Something warned me not to interrupt.

"All right. Yesterday she tells her mother that, later, after supper, she's going to a movie with two girl friends. She's meeting them there, she says. Her mother says she'd better get my permission, which, when I got home, I gave her. Why not? I trusted her, I always trusted her. Jesus Christ!" He gaped in disbelief. "Then what do you think happens? Well, I'll tell you what happens. She's not gone from this house ten minutes when the phone rings and the call is for her." He squinted an eye at me. "Can you guess who was on that phone?"

"I have no idea." My voice was a whisper.

"It was one of the girls she was to meet at the movies. She'd been away, and she'd just got back half an hour before she called. Which means Sharon hadn't even *talked* to her about a movie!"

"Maybe you got the name wrong."

"That's what Edna said. So just to be sure, I had Edna call the other girl Sharon was supposed to meet. And you know what? That girl wasn't home, and she wasn't at any movie. Her mother said she was out shopping for a birthday present with her father! How do you like that!"

"Still, there could have been a misunderstanding."

"Yeah. So I decided to find out. I walked over to the movie house, bought a ticket, and went in. I stood off on the side, against the wall, and for a while, in the dark, I couldn't make out anybody." He paused to swig his drink. "And then I saw her."

"With two other girls?"

His eyes riveted me. "No. With that son of a bitch, Charles Dain!"

I'd anticipated him, but I affected a look of shock.

"They were in the last row, in the seats nearest the far wall. And—Jesus, don't ask me to describe it—but they sure as hell weren't looking at any movie!"

"Ah, George," I said, all sympathy.

"Max, I can't tell you how that hit me. My daughter, my sweet little Sharon, actin' like a brazen hussy with a dirty hunky not fit to shine her shoes!"

"You've got him wrong, George. He's—"

"The hell I have."

"Let's not argue it now." I was suddenly annoyed. "What did you do—rush across and jump all over them?"

"Believe me, that's what I wanted to do. But I figured, why not give 'em a little more rope, see what they'd do after the movie. So I waited there in the dark, so goddamn mad I just about threw up. But they didn't wait for the end of the movie. They left maybe halfway through." His breath was coming fast, and his eyes seemed to pop from their sockets.

"You followed them?"

"Damned tootin' I followed them. And I thank God I did. You want to know where they went? Well, listen to this. There's a grammar school between the movie house and here, dark as a coal mine and not a livin' soul within shoutin' distance. And that's where they went. They just sort of disappeared." He paused to growl.

"Then you lost them?"

"Like hell. I found 'em all curled up in a doorway that's set back from the outside."

My heart gave a pump. "They weren't—"

"No, no, no, not that, thank God Almighty, not that! But it was bad enough, things nice girls just don't do. And, boy, did she know it! She jumped up like I'd fired off a shotgun, which I might've done if I'd had one. Right then, though, I wasn't after her. I went after Dain."

"Don't tell me you had a fight."

"Damned near. I started to take a swing at him—him just standin' there like a cigar store Indian, not sayin' a word, not even to apologize. My fist was cocked, ready to sock him, but Sharon, she flung up against me, and I couldn't get off a punch. Then she started bawlin' and tellin' Dain he'd better leave and that she'd handle it. At first he said no, he'd stay and have it out with me. But then, she was cryin' so, he saw it was no use, and he left."

Apparently exhausted, George fell back on the couch. I looked at him but felt no compassion—the image of Sharon in her agony was too vivid in my mind.

I said coldly, "So now you've got her under house arrest."

He sat up, swelled his chest, and looked self-righteous. "You sound like you think that's cruel. Well, let me tell you the rest, then see what you think. Once I got her home, I—Edna, too—we started to question her. She wouldn't answer anything, just that she had rights and it was high time we understood that. Rights! Seventeen years old, and a *girl* at that, and she talks about rights! That goddamned Dain has practically turned her into a suffragette!"

"And that's all you know—what you saw last night?" I was anxious to know if she'd involved me.

"No, more. A lot more."

I held my breath.

"Oh, she didn't break down again, not that one. All she did was get mad, defiant. It was like she'd made up her mind to hurt us as bad as she could. She stood up there in front of me, eyes burnin' up, and she let it all go. She told how she'd meet Dain at some girl's house when the folks were away. How when we thought she was playing field hockey, or was kept after school, or was at the library, she was really with that hunky rat. She said, See what we'd done to her, we'd made her into a liar, having to sneak around to do things other parents wouldn't bat an eye at. And she called me a bigot! Me, a shanty Irishman who's had to fight bigots all his life!"

I almost laughed, wishing I could have been an invisible witness.

"Max, no girl talks to her father like that and gets away with it. You agree?"

"I guess so. So you sent her to her room."

"Not before I cracked her across the mouth."

"You what?"

"Just what I said. And then I laid down a few rules. She's never to see Dain again. For a month she's not to set foot out of this house except for school, and then she'll come right home. There'll be no movies, no parties, no nothing." He paused to give me a sorrowful look. "And that includes, I said, goin' out in the flivver with you."

I, Judas, had apparently been spared.

"So, what I owe you, Max, is an apology. There I was doing what I could to get you two together, tellin' you she's got these serious feelings for you, and all the time she's cheatin' on you with this hunky stud."

"I don't see it that way," I said. I couldn't tell him how I did see it—that no matter what she did, I could never find it in my heart to condemn her.

I caught the next train to the ferry. And I never went back to that house in South Orange, New Jersey. That interlude in my life was finished. Just as it was with Charles Dain.

* * *

At the hospital I visited for a few minutes with Charles's wife, Harriet, in the VIP suite she had taken— a bedroom and sitting room furnished in Swedish modern, quite the thing in 1942. Harriet was fairly tall, with a full-blown, imperious figure generally described as handsome rather than stunning. She wore her dark hair somewhat in the style of Kay Francis, the movie actress, combed straight back in sleek waves. Her most arresting feature was her eyes—not large but a pene- trating, icy blue, unnerving in what seemed their ability to illuminate your darkest thoughts. Her mouth was wide and thin, embellished but not enlarged with coral lipstick. She wore a close-fitting, bright yellow dress, as though to refute any notion that she was in premature mourning. In short, she was a formidable woman who, even without all her money, appeared capable of domi- nating any man. But if you thought that, you didn't know Charles Dain.

She waved me in with a black cigarette holder, longer than F.D.R.'s, which she liked to refer to as "my Ger- man spy prop," but was actually a compromise between her incessant smoking and her chronically raspy throat.

After a quick hug and grazing of cheeks, she said, "I'm not a widow yet, Max. Though, God knows, the medics look at me as though I should be calling Frank Campbell's and making the final arrangements."

"He's still the same?"

"*Apparently* he's still the same. But these medicine men don't know what's going on inside that flickering brain. I do. Charles doesn't believe in dying. In fact, he's violently opposed to it. So of course he'll live."

She sat me in a chair that was all blond-wood angles,

then went to the window and stared down at Park Avenue. I could hear the swish of traffic and the muted roar of underground trains.

"I agree with your diagnosis," I said. "Have you seen him?"

"A few minutes ago." She turned from the window. "It's difficult to see him through all the wires and tubes. He looks sort of like a Christmas tree without the ornaments." Her voice caught, and she took a powerful drag from her prop. Her brilliant eyes flashed me an appealing look, then seemed to dim. "I think you ought to go in, Max."

I knew then that she was preparing to give him up; his best friend should at least get a last look at him alive. I wanted no part of it but said, "In a few minutes. First tell me, have the police been bothering you?"

"Not really." She extracted the cigarette stub from its holder, dropped it in an ashtray, and expertly replaced it with another. I lit it with my pocket lighter, which for a long time had seen little use. "No more than you'd expect," she said, sitting down. "Could I think of any suspects? Who were the last people he'd seen? That sort of thing. I wasn't at all helpful, except to confirm what they already thought—a setup arranged by some gangster he'd attacked in the paper."

I shifted uncomfortably. "There seems to be a question about the key. You told the police that he never went to the town house. Yet—"

"Yet the key was found in his pocket. It was on his key chain with all the others. So it could be he'd had it for some time. Is that what you're saying?"

"Yes."

She blew out a smoke screen. "I was too shocked even to think about that when the police first called. Anyway, a little while ago I amended my story. I said that he had occasionally used the town house, but that had been some time ago, and I'd temporarily forgotten. The key, I said, was a duplicate made from one kept at our home."

I looked at her. She had fine white skin, but now it had turned a light pink. "I see," I said. "Then that must have been what reminded you—you recalled him making the duplicate."

Her ice-blue eyes seemed to scan the interior of my skull. She smiled thinly. "Damn you, Max."

I just kept looking at her, smiling back.

"You know me too well," she said. "Probably better than I know myself. All right, then. I don't recall him ever making a duplicate, and I don't recall him mentioning that he ever used the town house." She flourished her cigarette holder. "But it was a good lie, a necessary lie, and you damned well know it."

"Absolutely. The truth, I guess, is that he got the key from your management company." Which is what I'd said to Terry Donovan.

"Perhaps, but I doubt it. If he was using that house for some sort of secret meeting, I don't think he'd want them to know it. Anyway, I'll not embarrass myself by asking. Only one thing is important. The police must believe—as I'm now quite sure they do—that Charles was not trying to deceive me." She lightly smoothed her hair. "If they suspected that, it might turn into a mess. They'd go back years and dredge up all the stupid things I've almost managed to forget. And it would be all over the papers. That I couldn't bear."

"You won't have to. So forget it. You did the right thing."

"I suppose my lie would be called obstruction of justice. But I don't feel any guilt whatever." She leaned forward and spoke intensely. "Max, I simply can't believe there's another woman."

I reached over and patted her shoulder. She was forty-seven—four years older than Charles—but at that moment, contradicting the haughtiness perceived by others, she seemed as vulnerable as an adolescent. "Why should you believe it," I said, smiling. "For about the past ten years Charles has been a paragon of virtue. Take it from me, the man who knows."

"You do know, don't you, Max?" Her look said the answer was of utmost importance.

"You bet I do." I tried to relieve the sudden tension. "Almost as much as I know about you."

She gave a small laugh. "Look at me," she said. "I don't even blush."

I left her to look in on Charles.

He was under intensive care but in a large private room, lying half on his side on a tilted bed, his head wrapped in bandages, tubes and wires sprouting from his body. Two nurses and a doctor, probably a resident, were in attendance, the nurses busy monitoring machines that whirred and hissed and made other disturbing noises. I was reminded of the trauma of my heart attack, which heightened the empathy I already felt for my old and dear friend. I stayed less than a minute, just long enough to stand by his bedside and make certain that no damage had been done to the strong, handsome face that still reminded me so much of his father's.

Returning to Harriet, I smiled and nodded optimistically. "He's a tough bird," I said. "Pretty soon he'll start flapping his wings and fly out of this coop."

"Back to our nest," she said, and pretended to slap her mouth for sounding so sentimental.

As I was about to leave, she said, "Oh, by the way, before you came, I had a visit from your star reporter."

"Dave Hewlett?"

"No. It was that big, beautiful, unkempt creature—Terry Donovan."

I felt an uneasiness. "What did he want?"

"Just expressing his sympathy. We have met, you know. And of course Charles thought—thinks—he's the smartest newsman alive."

"Did you mention the key business?"

"No, only to the police."

"Well, eventually he'll get it from them." We were standing at the open door.

"Oh, he did ask one thing."

"What?"

"Whether the person Charles had phoned from the Stork had come forward."

"Now, why would he ask you that? If you knew, you'd have told the police, and he'd get it from them."

"Perhaps he thought they wouldn't tell him."

"Perhaps. Well, I'll keep in touch. Anything I can do—anything—call me."

She wrapped her arms around my skinny frame and squeezed my bones. "You're a divine man," she said.

"You're very discerning, Harriet."

I took a taxi to the Algonquin Hotel on West Forty-fourth Street, where I'd been living for the past twenty years. Frank Case, the owner and majordomo, who admired any kind of writer, saw to it that I was treated like a sultan and personally provided a lot of laughs and harmless gossip. The hotel was the hangout of former and present newspaper people, all of whom had risen to prominence—Aleck Woollcott, Bob Benchley, Frank Adams, Dorothy Parker, Heywood Broun before he died, and Harold Ross, founder and editor of *The New Yorker*, whom I'd worked with on *Stars and Stripes* in Paris. So I was able to keep loneliness pretty much at bay—vital to a man who had concluded a long time ago that he would never have a wife.

But now I wanted to be alone. Upstairs in my suite— living room, bedroom, bath—I prowled from room to room like a hyena at the zoo. I wasn't thinking so much about Charles Dain and his wife as I was about Terry Donovan. Just that one question he'd asked Harriet— Had the person Charles phoned come forward?—told me he was thumbing his nose at my warning to stick to the police line of investigation. He'd dig and probe, all very quietly of course, and chances were he'd come up with something that, perhaps inadvertently, could explode into a juicy scandal.

I'd been the paper's watchdog over Terry Donovan for many years, ever since as an unlicked cub he'd been fired by the late and lamented *World*. (He was caught impersonating a plainclothesman and trying to sneak a camera into Sing Sing prison to photograph Ruth Snyder burning in the electric chair. A photographer imported from Chicago got the picture with a camera strapped to his ankle and the *Daily News* gave it their whole front page.) I knew how he worked, how he thought; and what I didn't know then, I found out later.

That includes his relationship with Kate Richards, who'd been the café society columnist on the *Express* for about ten months.

So what I'm about to tell you is probably as close to the truth as it would be if it came from Terry Donovan himself.

Chapter · 4

Maybe if he hadn't been such a close disciple of Charles Dain, an admirer of the publisher long before they met in 1928, and after that a trusted associate and sharp-eyed observer both on and off the job—maybe then, thought Terry Donovan, he'd have joined with the police in their dragnet of New York's underworld.

That would have had him conducting undercover talks with mobsters like Lepke Buchalter and Gurrah Shapiro, who ran the city's labor and industrial rackets and sat on the ruling board of Murder Inc.; or with Frank Costello, the former slot-machine king who had ascended to the top hierarchy of the nationwide crime cartel; or with crooked Tammany politicians like Jimmy Hines, fancy front men like Bugsy Siegel, retired killers like Owney Madden. All of them, along with their underlings, many of them psychotic triggermen, had been burned by the crusading wrath of the *Evening Express*. But despite that, any one of them, given the routine treachery of the business, might have named or given a clue to the person who had tried to assassinate Charles Dain.

Assuming, that is, that the would-be assassin was one of their own.

Unlike the police, who revered the publisher as a model of rectitude, Donovan had reason to believe the answer lay elsewhere. Charles Dain, he recalled, had once been a conscientious womanizer, a pursuit apparently in full flower when Donovan had first come to the paper. That was back in early 1929, when Cal Coolidge was sleeping away his final days in the White House; when Franklin D. Roosevelt was governor of New York and Jimmy Walker mayor and toast of the city; when bootleggers and bookmakers were pals of the socialites; when Helen Morgan perched on a piano and sang the sad songs, Texas Guinan welcomed the suckers, and Polly Adler discreetly accommodated the lecheries of the rich and famous.

Charles Dain, even then a renowned publisher though not yet thirty, married to a reclusive heiress, was more circumspect than most of his peers—though frequently a part of the nightlife scene. For one thing, he did not play the field, preferring to concentrate his attentions and gifts on one girl at a time, and between conquests, retire into long periods of abstinence spent with his preoccupied wife, who supervised her various enterprises from their Mount Kisco estate. For another thing, he avoided the big, gaudy nightclubs in favor of intimate, unadorned speakeasies—the Club New Yorker on East Fifty-first Street, the Merry-Go-Round on East Fifty-sixth, the Marlboro Club on East Sixty-first— places whose rakish patrons, upon entering the iron grillwork portals, would not so much as blink at the sight of a prominent man-about-town seducing a cute little blonde from the *Follies*. (After all, wasn't the beloved mayor, the Honorable James J. Walker, conducting a wide-open adulterous affair with Betty Compton, who had caught his eye in the musical *Oh, Kay!*?)

Still, there had been some alarming consequences. Terry Donovan recalled the ingenue from George White's *Scandals* who had slit her wrists with a razor blade after Dain had tired of her; she was rehabilitated by prompt medical attention, the gift of a diamond solitaire, and a trip to Europe aboard the *Berengaria*. Then there was the crazy showgirl who hopped uninvited into his limousine clad in a mink coat and proceeded to strip it off to reveal her stark nakedness while loudly proclaiming her love, much to the consternation of the chauffeur and the delight of Dain's passenger, an important advertiser who owned a large department store. Worst of all was the evening when Terry Donovan and Max Wills were chatting in Wills's office and heard a shot explode from Dain's office next door. Rushing in, they confronted a young actress gaping at a tiny pistol frozen in her hand. From behind his desk, blood blossoming on his upper sleeve, Charles Dain appeared unperturbed. "I thought it was a toy from a Cracker Jack box," he said.

None of this reached the public prints, and what gossip there was remained confined to a circle of sophisticates accustomed to bizarre behavior. Besides, about five years after Donovan had met him, Dain's infidelities suddenly ceased and his image of devoted husband began. Donovan conjectured that this abrupt transformation resulted from a number of influences: Dain had become less impetuous and more mature; his wife, intimidating in her self-assurance, had somehow become a more suppliant partner; and, perhaps most important, as a sometime adviser to the newly-elected president, Franklin Roosevelt, Dain was determined to avoid any embarrassment to his hero.

But now, in the wartime spring of 1942, with Dain, at forty-three, vulnerable to midlife anxieties, and his wife, at forty-seven, perhaps entering menopause, would he not have been tempted to restore his self-esteem, his youthful vigor, his taste for excitement by once again acquiring a beautiful, sensual woman?

He would, thought Terry Donovan.

So forget that lecture from Max Wills. Was it worth protecting Charles Dain's reputation if it meant that his assailant—more likely, murderer—would go free? Would Dain himself have agreed to such an unprofessional, gutless attitude? Christ, no. Assuming he was conscious and could speak, he would, if shot by a woman, have her hunted down and brought to him privately; then, depending on the circumstances, he would either buy her a Cadillac or turn her over to the police, and to hell with what anyone thought, including his wife. The man was no hypocrite. He really gave a damn about justice, despite any risk that its scales might conk him on his handsome head.

Well, that's what Terry Donovan intended to give the only man aside from his father he had ever idolized—justice.

There was an obvious starting point: the key.

The president of Metropolitan Management Company was named Raymond Cogswell. He was a short, oval-shaped man with a pink, rubbery face and combed-back hair that rose on his scalp like a porcupine's. As if to compensate for his lack of stature, he sat on a high leather chair behind a carved desk big enough for Ping-Pong.

"Of course I know of you, Mr. Donovan," he said. His smile, showing large teeth, indicated he was impressed. "In fact, I always look for your by-line on a story. There were a couple of instances, I regret to say, when you covered, uh, certain ugly disturbances that occurred on properties we manage." He chuckled.

"It would be hard not to," Donovan said. "From what I hear, you people handle everything in the city except City Hall."

Cogswell's chuckle crested to a laugh. "Oh, no, just our share, just our share."

"Which includes the Dain properties."

Cogswell's laugh cut off and his loose cheeks sagged in bereavement. "Yes, I assumed that's why you're here. What a shocking, shocking thing! To think that such a fine man as Charles Dain, a great man, really, should be shot down . . ." He shook his head, clucked, then said abruptly, "Don't tell me, Mr. Donovan, that you're going to ask about the key."

Donovan's sleepy eyes sharpened to a stare.

"The key to the town house?" Cogswell said. "Where Mr. Dain was shot?"

"You must be psychic. That's what I had in mind."

Cogswell gave a playful smile. "It was, I understand, on his key ring. You'd like to find out if he recently got that key from us."

"Yes. How did you know?"

Cogswell's smile broadened. "Because yesterday I was asked that very same question." He paused. "By a detective."

Donovan shrugged. "Sometimes the cops get ahead of me. What did you tell this detective?"

"That I would check on it and let him know."

"So now they've got the information?"

"Before I could get back to him, the detective again called me. He said to forget about it because they now had the answer. It seems the key was a duplicate made from one kept in the Dain's home in Mount Kisco. Mrs. Dain knew about it but had not thought to mention it."

Donovan contemplated him, then stood up. "Well, that clears that up. Many thanks, Mr. Cogswell." He turned to leave.

"He apparently lost his other key," Cogswell said.

Donovan swung back. "Other key? You mean he had a key to the town house before he made the duplicate?"

"According to our files, yes. You see, any time a key goes out of this office we require a written record. It's a routine matter, done to safeguard our clients' property. In the case of Mr. Dain, I thought at first that no such record existed. Then, after the detective canceled the search, the woman I'd assigned showed me what she'd dug up."

"When did Mr. Dain get it? Shortly before he was shot?"

"Oh, no. If he had, I'd have thought it strange and phoned back the detective. As it was, I saw nothing suspicious—"

"When did he get it?"

"Nineteen thirty-three. June—I forget the exact date."

Donovan sat down. "Nineteen thirty-three? Nine years ago?"

"Exactly." Cogswell waved a hand. "Plenty of time for it to get lost."

"Who signed it out—Mr. Dain or his wife?"

"It was Mr. Dain." He smiled, thinly this time, and raised an eyebrow. "If it had been Mrs. Dain, we wouldn't have asked for a signature. After all, it is her property."

So Charles Dain had gone there alone, thought Donovan. He said, "I'm told the town house is not for rent, that it's reserved for use by Mrs. Dain's visiting guests. How often would you say it's occupied?"

"Not often. Three, perhaps four times a year. And the guests usually stay no longer than a week."

"And you always supply the keys?"

"Always. Mrs. Dain notifies us prior to their coming and . . ." He stopped to study Donovan's face. "Oh, I see what you're driving at. You're thinking that any of these guests could have had duplicates made."

"It occurred to me."

Indignation flickered in Cogswell's eyes. "Mr. Donovan, you can't possibly be saying that one of these guests—reputable, in fact eminent, people—would have used a duplicate key to enter that door and shoot Charles Dain."

"Just considering everything, Mr. Cogswell."

"Well, I'd say that anyone who's a friend of Mrs. Dain would be the last person to consider. I'm not telling you how to do your job, but it seems to me that the people you should be concerned with are the members of organized crime."

"Mr. Cogswell, you'd have made a good detective. That's who we're after."

Cogswell looked pleased.

Donovan rose. "Thanks for your help."

"The truth is," said Cogswell, "I really haven't helped at all."

The hell he hadn't, thought Donovan, as he joined the throngs on Fifth Avenue. Nine years ago, exactly when he had apparently given up his pursuit of susceptible young women, Charles Dain had appropriated a hideaway that, if discovered, would arouse the suspicions of no one other than his wife. And the risk of her ever knowing was slight, so removed was she from her husband's Manhattan milieu, and so immersed in directing her far-flung companies from the fully equipped office in her Mount Kisco home. (Her belated story that the key had been duplicated from one in her possession was, in Donovan's prejudiced view, simply a cover-up.) So it appeared that Charles had not reformed after all, instead had employed his wife's property as a shield for respectability while continuing to indulge his compulsive sexuality.

Though supported in his theory that a woman was the culprit, Donovan felt only a temporary satisfaction. Considering Dain's fickleness, the possible assailants could number a half dozen or more, all of them, ironically, anonymous due to the secrecy contrived by the victim himself. The prime suspect, of course, was the recipient of Dain's phone call from the Stork Club— who, plausibly, was also the woman who had alerted the police. But there was no way to trace that call; whoever was involved would have to confess it. And that was about as likely as someone walking into a police station demanding to be booked for attempted murder.

He picked up a copy of the *Evening Express* from a corner newsstand, hailed a cab, and sat back to scan the front page. The story was all over it, headlines reading: DAIN STILL IN COMA; POLICE QUIZ CRIME FIGURES; MAYOR

VOWS ALL-OUT PROBE, plus a photo of Dain when he had addressed the Association of National Advertisers at the Waldorf-Astoria Hotel, one of his expressionless wife entering his hospital room, and one of the undistinguished town house on Sixty-third Street. The war had been relegated to a single story at the bottom of the page: MANILA FALLS TO JAPS. The editors of the *Express* knew better than to place a cataclysmic global conflict ahead of an assault on their boss.

Donovan, who was separated though not divorced from his wife, lived alone on the ground floor of a red-brick duplex on Tenth Street in Greenwich Village. It was a furnished rental, featuring high-ceilinged rooms, long, narrow windows, hooked rugs over polished wood floors, and a glut of eclectic antiques that, if he had been at all sensitive to his surroundings, he would have found distasteful. Arriving there, he made himself a dry martini and, from habit, took it to the living room. There he sat at his desk, which stood at right angles to the front windows. He glanced at the yellow sheet of paper in his typewriter and read: "Alfred J. (Jake) Lingle, star police reporter for the *Chicago Tribune*, was rushing to catch a train to the racetrack when the bullets ripped into him. He died almost instantly, an honorable member of an honorable profession, rubbed out by the underworld for disclosing their secrets. At least that was what his employers believed on that day in 1930 when they offered a $25,000 reward for the capture of Lingle's killer. What they did not know until later . . ."

That was as far as Donovan had got, the rest blasted from his mind by the phone call from his city editor announcing that Charles Dain had been shot, perhaps mortally. The story begun in the typewriter, a fact piece, had been assigned to him by an editor at *True Detective* and would bring a payment of two hundred dollars. Now, sipping his martini, Donovan reflected idly on the tragedy of Jake Lingle. His diamond-studded belt, the kind given by Al Capone to his most intimate friends and benefactors. His chauffeur-driven Lincoln. His gambling in the stock market and at the racetrack. His summer home on a Michigan lake and his suite at the plush Stevens Hotel. Yet the man's salary from the *Tribune* was only sixty-five dollars a week. Jake Lingle—a hero who in death was labeled a crook, the mob's go-between with the police and the politicians. His killer, whoever he was, was still at large.

The sell-out imputed to Lingle had reawakened in Donovan painful memories of his father, reinforcing his determination to be free, to be sole owner of himself, to be able to challenge authority, attack hypocrisy, and expose corruption without any concern for consequences. He hoped, as a newspaperman, to become the quintessential professional, and with that achieved, withdraw from the clamor and write novels vibrant with truth. His stubborn independence was the main quality he shared with Charles Dain, and was the basis of their affinity.

Who had Charles telephoned? Who was the woman who had alerted the police?

The questions knifed at his mind, meeting stonewall resistance. In frustration he tore the yellow paper from his typewriter, flung it into the basket, downed his martini, and phoned the hospital. He asked for and got a nurse he knew. She was at the nurses' station and would have to call him back. In a minute, she did.

"Terry, I couldn't talk. Now I can. I'm at a pay phone."

"How is he?"

"The same, I think. Still in a coma."

"Jackie, the minute he regains consciousness, I want to know it."

"If he regains consciousness. Oh, I'm sorry. Sure, Terry, I'll try to get word to you right away. You mean you'll come up?"

"Yes."

"I don't think the police will let you see him. There's a guard at his door."

"I'll need less than five seconds, assuming he can talk."

"You mean just time enough to say who shot him?"

"You're a bright girl."

"You don't know how bright. Why not find out?"

"You wouldn't like me. I sigh a lot. And sometimes I sulk."

"More reason. Anyway, I've got a rumor for you."

"Let's have it."

"There's talk of going in for the bullet regardless of his condition. It may be his only chance."

"Call me if you find out for sure."

"I will, Terry. You know I will."

Hanging up, he sat perfectly still, adjusting to the thought that Charles Dain might die on the operating table. He gave his head a hard shake, got up, and headed toward the kitchen for another martini. The phone rang again. Jackie? Had Dain succumbed while they'd been talking?

But it wasn't Jackie. It was Kate Richards, her voice low and without inflection.

"Terry, I'm home and alone and I don't like it at all."

"I know how you feel."

"Maybe if you came over, things would improve."

He masked his surprise. "They can't get much worse. I called the hospital and—"

"So did I. God, what a lousy world."

"I'll be right there, Kate."

She lived only a few blocks away, on Sheridan Square. But not in the typical Village apartment. Hers was on the twelfth floor of an ultramodern building that looked as if it belonged on the Upper East Side, where, judging by her high-fashion wardrobe, Kate also seemed to belong, and in fact spent most of her working time. But when by herself, she enjoyed strolling the quiet Village streets, idling in Washington Square Park, dining outdoors behind a green hedge at the Brevoort Hotel.

Kate Richards had achieved spectacular success at the *Express*, starting as a part-time summer employee when she was attending Vassar, then hired full time as soon as she graduated. She had pretty much run the gamut, from secretary to cub reporter to women's page features to spot news and, recently, to writer of a column— "Midnight in Manhattan." It had not attained nearly the prestige of Dorothy Kilgallen's "Voice of Broadway" in the *Journal-American*, but it was getting there, thanks to the youthful charm she exerted on influential press agents, as well as on the café society crowd that fawned over such pets as Brenda Frazier and Cobina Wright, Jr. Like Kilgallen, Kate was not merely an observer but an active participant in the foolishness that went on at the silk-and-satin saloons of mid-Manhattan, and though often contemptuous of the company she kept, her ambition drove her to stay on the job until the last morsel of gossip had been extracted from the dawn patrol at Lindy's, Reuben's, or Dave's Blue Room. At twenty-five she was in fact what many of the staff called her—Wonder Woman.

Donovan had seen her around during college breaks, when she was known as "the kid from Poughkeepsie," but had not really known her until after she started the column. Then she would sometimes come into his cubicle and pump him for information on the netherworld of crime, hoping for a link with her assigned world of the prodigal rich. Occasionally he provided a plum—a distinguished theatrical producer who was a pederast, a famous actress who shared her bed with a hoodlum, a popular maître d' who supplied his patrons with dope—which she rendered unlibelous by printing as blind items. Nothing more than that had happened between them until about three months ago, a cold March night when he was working late and she had stopped by before making her rounds of the clubs. Then, as she was leaving, she turned at the door and gazed at him with a wistful look he had never seen before.

"I wish I didn't have to suffer all those emptyheads," she said. "I wish I could stay right here."

He walked over and stood facing her. "Why don't you? You've probably got enough handouts for a dozen columns."

She swayed toward him saying, "Well, maybe . . ." then didn't bother to finish or to dissemble but in an impulsive movement flung back her head, hair the color of honey, and pushed her lovely face up to his for a breathless kiss. He was startled, dismayed, delighted—and, for all his self-assurance, uncertain of how to proceed. There had not been a woman since the day his wife—berating him furiously for his arrogance, his insensitivity, his coldness—had stomped out of the house.

"We've been wasting a lot of time," he said to Kate.

"Let's catch up," she said, and kissed him again.

At her suggestion they went to Chambord, where, among the impeccably dressed diners, he looked dismally out of place in his sloppy sport coat and carelessly knotted tie, not to mention his unbarbered hair. She pretended not to notice, but he sensed she was disconcerted, this young woman in her Saks Fifth Avenue dress and Hattie Carnegie chapeau, without whom he suspected he would not have been admitted. She smiled and chatted, suddenly friendly rather than amorous, and he had not been surprised, only disappointed, when, after coffee and brandy, she said she really must leave him to meet some people she'd forgotten were sailing for France at midnight. It seemed obvious to him that while he might cut a glamorous, romantic figure in the office—folded newspaper sticking from his jacket pocket, battered felt hat shoved back on his head, neither of which he affected that evening but were probably there in her mind—in her social environment he became an embarrassment.

They went out together a number of times after that but always to more plebian places, like Tim Costello's and downstairs pasta parlors in Little Italy, south of the Square. Sometimes he sensed that the spark ignited in his office still glowed, however dimly, but was kept turned low lest it consume the ambitious plans she had for herself. Certainly those plans did not include an undivorced man who dressed like a longshoreman and could not be relied on to say the proper thing, even though she was more than willing to share his company now and then and affirm her pleasure with warm good night kisses.

But that was as far as it had gone—and as far as it would ever go, he had decided. Thus his surprise when, alone in her apartment, she had phoned to ask him over. But once he had hung up, the surprise mellowed to understanding. Charles Dain, at the urging of Max Wills, had encouraged her, promoted her, finally elevating her to a job that was the envy of every celebrity-watcher in New York. Naturally she would suffer this threat to the publisher's life even more acutely than most of his other associates. All she wanted was to be comforted, and for only that purpose had called on a friend whose career had been influenced by Charles Dain at least as much as her own.

What he was about to attend, thought Donovan, was either a vigil or a preliminary wake.

So he was somewhat confounded when Kate Richards met him at the door wrapped loosely in a creamy silk negligee, her hair blonder than he had known it and attractively mussed, her manner subdued, sultry, but changing swiftly to frantic expectancy when her arms went around him and her mouth came up to whisper, "Oh, darl—" the last syllable lost in the lush joining of lips.

And he was speechless when, after one drink and another kiss, she led him across the off-white living room carpet, past the puff-pillowed sofa and chairs, and into a bedroom of shadowed light, where she sat him on a scented bed with satin sheets and, while he undressed, stood back and loosened her sash, parted her negligee, then shrugged from its folds to flaunt her nakedness as it drifted to the floor.

And when she came to him and her slim, polished

legs gripped his thigh, his silence was sustained by a sense of awe and, just as it was with her, the compulsion to explore all the wonders of flesh that until then had seduced only his thoughts. It was not until their bodies had thrashed and bucked and climaxed in a long, dizzying ascending and descending curve and lay in an exhausted embrace that he was able to utter a word.

"Kate. My lovely, beautiful, astonishing Kate."

He could feel her smile against his cheek. "I thought my attitude toward you should be conveyed dramatically," she said.

"Atkinson would give it a rave review."

"And you?"

"Would 'I love you' be adequate?"

"You swiped my line. Oh, darling, I do love you. And I'll be so good for you. You'll see."

"You mean you'll take me to your chichi saloons to meet all your charming playmates?" He hadn't meant to sound sardonic.

"Never. We'll stick to the places where we can smell the disinfectant. Anyway, I'm bored senseless with those oversize children. One more conga line and I'm taking the veil." She kissed him. "Now, if you'll excuse me . . ."

She got up, and he admired her taut, round buttocks as she went through the door to the living room. He felt relaxed yet vital, euphoric in a way he'd never experienced.

She came back with two tall Scotches and then lit two cigarettes. After serving him, then sliding in beside him, she said, "This is the way it starts. I'll spoil you rotten. That way, I've cunningly decided, you'll give me all the nice things I deserve."

"Damned right I will."

"Good. Let's begin by going away together."

"Great. When?"

"Now. Tomorrow, or the next day. But not any later. Otherwise I may be carted off to that place where you're not allowed anything sharp. Oh, Terry, I've got to get away."

"You mean just walk out?"

"I've already talked to Max. He's all for it, says we can use syndicated stuff while I'm gone. But I won't go if you don't come with me."

"Ah, Kate, I can't. Not right now. Maybe in a few—"

"Weeks? You know where you could be in a few weeks? On a drill field, in sweaty fatigues, with some ape hollering at you, 'hup-two-three-four.' Stop laughing. What's your classification?"

"One-A."

"See? That means you're fresh meat. So if you want to sweep me away and ravish me to your heart's content, it's got to be now."

He was silent, recalling his conversation with Max Wills. Sure as hell Max wouldn't object to his taking off.

"Well?" she said, stroking his chest.

He glanced at her curiously. "What about Charles? I'd think you'd want to stay close until we know if he makes it."

"We needn't go far. And we can keep in touch by phone. We'll put it next to your pillow."

He grinned. "After the first day, what makes you think I could lift it?"

"Now you're talking. Okay, will you at least speak to Max about getting away?"

"Sorry, I can't do it."

She looked at him. "Then I've no choice but to confess."

"Confess what?"

"That when I saw Max, I also mentioned you. I said I'd heard you were about to get your Greetings from Uncle Sugar, and I thought it was his patriotic duty to give you a little relaxation before you charged out and won the war. I wasn't sure then that we'd be where we are now, but I figured it was a good bet. Darling, you look funny with your mouth hanging open. Anyway, Max said it was the least he could do for his country."

"You're unbelievable. So now he knows we're—how do you three-dot journalists say it? Oh, yeah, an item, great and good friends, constant companions."

"I'm sure he thought that all along. He knows we've been seeing each other. And he knows that neither of us is the kind who insists on telling it to a preacher."

He was silent, brooding.

"Now will you talk to Max?" she said.

He flashed her a smile. "Sure I'll talk to Max."

That ended the conversation. He stayed all night.

"Max," Donovan said, "I talked to Kate Richards last night. From what she said, I gather you two are involved in a plot to get me out of here."

I looked at him sharply, but smiled when I saw he was half joking. "You sound like a man who hates vacations," I said.

"When I'm drafted I'll take it in pay."

I pulled my eyebrows together and gave him a fierce look. "You'll take it in time off—starting tomorrow."

"You'll have to fire me."

I sat back in my chair. "Scram. Vamoose."

"I'm fired?"

"No, dammit, you're not fired. Get out and start earning your money."

Later I worried a little. I knew he'd learned about Charles's key because I'd phoned Metropolitan Management myself, talked to the president, Raymond Cogswell, and found out that Donovan had been there and what he'd been told. ("Just wanted to be sure he'd got hold of you," I'd said, and agreed that there was nothing suspicious about Dain getting the key way back in 1933.)

Knowing about that key, I thought, wasn't likely to do Terry Donovan any good. The only way to get at the truth behind the shooting of Charles Dain was to take a long look backward in time. Then it might become clear why he had surreptitiously taken over the town house, and whom he'd gone to meet on the night he was shot.

Neither Donovan nor the police were qualified for that job. Only one person on Earth was. Me.

Chapter · 5

After that traumatic afternoon with George Fletcher
in the winter of 1917, I was never invited back. Occasionally I'd run into him in the halls of the *American*
and he'd greet me with a nod and a synthetic smile, then
avert his eyes and hurry on by. I knew he thought he'd
done me an injury—of course, unintentionally he had
—and also was embarrassed that in his drunken rage
he had confessed so much of what to him was his
daughter's depravity. So I took no offense. In fact, once
when we happened to be with the same group at the
bar on Park Row, and by chance were standing next
to each other, I asked him about his family.

"No problems," he said. "Edna's fit as a fiddle."

"And Sharon?" I really wanted to know.

He gave me a slightly startled look, as though just
then recalling that I knew her. "Sharon? Oh, she
couldn't be better. She's a darlin', that one."

"Yes, she is." I said it politely, not wanting him to
know how I lamented not seeing his daughter.

He sipped his straight rye whiskey, then said,
pompously, I thought, "Wouldn't surprise me if we had
a weddin'."

That floored me. Less than two months had passed since Sharon had been deprived of the love of her life and already she had become so enamored of a new suitor that she was preparing for a trip to the altar. Adolescence, I thought, was a disease marked by sudden, inexplicable changes of the heart. But perhaps that was the wrong diagnosis. With Dain now unattainable, she may have rebounded into the arms of another man simply to spite her parents and to gain an exit from their repressive supervision. Whatever the reason, the finality of marriage, banning her even from my fantasies, triggered a small inner convulsion.

"Well, well," I said brightly.

"Fine young fella," George said. Then, more emphatically, "Good family. The best." He smacked his lips and added, "College boy," and turned away to speak to the man on his left.

That was the last conversation I had with George Fletcher.

A few days later I got a call from Charles Dain asking if he could see me. I hesitated, thinking he was hitting me up for a job, feeling relieved when he quickly said, "Max, I've never seen the inside of a real newspaper office. I was hoping you could get someone to show me around." I said I'd do it myself, and invited him in for lunch on my day off.

I didn't feel I was doing him any great favor. I liked him, enjoyed his precocious, well-informed mind and his flattering interest in the work I did. But when the day of our meeting arrived, I was struck by a sense of dread. Oh, God, I thought, I'd have to sit and listen to a long diatribe against George Fletcher and maudlin effusions of love for a girl Charles could never have. I considered canceling the date but feared I'd despise myself for what seemed to me the worst weakness a man could have—cowardice.

We met at a restaurant on lower Broadway not far from City Hall, a place frequented by customers' men from Wall Street and prosperous wool merchants from Worth Street. He was thinner than when I'd last seen him, cheeks gaunt, cheekbones more prominent, eyes haunted and seemingly sunk deeper into their sockets; and his dark suit, slightly frayed at the cuffs and collar, hung loosely on his tall frame. But when we shook hands and he smiled, he seemed no different at all from the young man I'd chauffeured in the flivver and exchanged ideas with on a grassy picnic ground.

We had no sooner settled into a booth than he said, "Have you seen Sharon lately?"

My fears, I thought, were about to be realized. "No," I said, "I haven't been out there for quite a while."

"But you do see her father, in the office?"

"Not very often. He's in the circulation department, on another floor."

"Has he said anything to you about her?"

I decided not to mention my brief talk with George. After all, he had not said positively that his daughter was getting married. "Only that she and her mother are well."

"Nothing else?" His manner had become intense.

"I can't think of—"

"I hear she's getting married." He said it as though she were to be hanged.

"Oh?" I said, raising my eyebrows. "I'm not sure I'm happy to hear that." But I was sure; I loathed hearing it. "Look, Charles, I know about your breakup with Sharon. Believe me, I'm terribly sorry."

He managed a meager smile. "I believe you, Max. No

one could have been more understanding than you." He picked up his menu. "I suppose you think that's the real reason I called you—to question you about Sharon."

"It's a good reason."

"But not the main one. It's what I told you on the phone. I want to learn the newspaper business. So the dickens with any more talk about Sharon. All I care about is becoming another Max Wills."

I grinned. "That would take you from obscurity to mediocrity."

He grinned back. "Okay, then, another William Randolph Hearst."

After we'd been served, we talked mostly about the war. Revolution had just erupted in Russia, the soldiers were deserting in brigades, and the Czar had abdicated. On the Western Front the French and British, immobilized in their foul trenches, were suffering more deaths from disease than from bullets.

"If we don't want the Kaiser to replace Wilson," Charles said, "we have to get into it."

"Oh, no," I said, "Mr. Hearst won't allow it."

He laughed, then eyed me curiously. "Does it bother you, that he's so pro-German?"

"It does," I said. "But not to the point where I want us to join the slaughter."

He spoke of the many young men who had crossed the border to join the Canadian forces, and of the Lafayette Escadrille, the French air squadron made up of American volunteers. His eyes glowed with a faraway look, and I had the impression that his ear had caught the distant strains of a marching band above the noise of the restaurant.

"You sound like you're ready to quit school and take the leap," I said.

He gazed at me with a look of utter frustration. "I've got to do *something*," he said, his tone desperate.

It seemed apparent to me that his concern was not primarily for his country but was concentrated on finding some dramatic way to demonstrate to his lost love that she, in turning to another man—and her father, for forcing that decision—had made a colossal mistake. To do that, I thought, he was prepared to commit a form of suicide, provided it would bring glory to his name. Unknown to him, we were both casualties of the same ardent circumstances, though his wound was deeper and infinitely more painful. At that moment I felt joined to him in brotherhood.

When he arrived in the city room of the *American*, a morning paper, they were preparing the first edition, which would be on the streets late that evening. Standing in an aisle behind a low, slatted railing, we watched while I explained the activities of the shirt-sleeved men scattered about the floor. There at the desk in the center, I said, sat the city editor, who was responsible for the work of reporters and rewrite men who covered news of the five boroughs and adjacent territory. That tall figure bending over the city editor and scrawling on a pad was the makeup man; they were positioning and alloting space for stories on the front page. The man next to them, gripping the upright phone, was the assistant city editor, who, perhaps, was begging the managing editor to yield an extra column or two from the national news. The men wearing headsets and banging away on typewriters, stopping at intervals to tear out yellow sheets of paper and yell "Boy!" were rewrite men making journalistic sense of a welter of facts called in from outside by reporters, also known as "legmen." Over there, behind a table shaped like a horseshoe, were the copyreaders, elderly, scholarly-looking men, some with green eyeshades, who were handed typewritten copy from the man in the "slot" and worked it over with stubby pencils, correcting, trimming, writing the headlines. Down the aisle, behind that steel door that kept opening and closing as copyboys rushed in and out, was the composing room, where the copy was set in type by men working Linotype machines, the result then placed in forms, or "chases," for the separate newspaper pages, which were sent to the stereotyper to be molded on thick sheets of papier mâché into mats, over which molten metal would be poured to make printing plates, which then—

"Am I going too fast?" I asked.

"I'm getting it," he said, and I could see that he was, his eyes luminous and seeming to absorb every word I said.

Leaving the city room, I took him through the photo studio, the art department, and the partitioned sections reserved for sports, business news, women's features—along the way peeking into the empty offices reserved for Mr. Hearst and our two most renowned columnists, Arthur Brisbane and O. O. McIntyre—then to the roaring press room to watch the papers ribbon through the giant rollers.

As we left Charles shook his head in disbelief. "And it all starts when, from somewhere, a reporter picks up a phone and calls the city room."

"It starts before that," I said. "When a wife shoots her husband. Or a politician's fingers get too sticky. Or"—thinking of our publisher's obsessive aversion—"when Mr. Hearst decides to crusade against the vivisection of dogs."

"It—the paper—gives him so much power." His tone implied admiration rather than censure.

"Some people would say too much."

"Not if it's used right."

I resisted an impulse to mention Hearst's past notorious acts of jingo journalism—the outrageous lies that precipitated the Spanish-American War (to artist Frederic Remington, hired to depict scenes of anti-American violence in Cuba, but finding none and asking to return, Hearst had cabled, "Please remain. You furnish the pictures, and I'll furnish the war."); his vicious and relentless attacks on William McKinley, climaxed by an inflammatory editorial ("If bad institutions and bad men can be got rid of only by killing, then the killing must be done.") which was widely blamed for inciting the president's assassination.

These events had occurred just before and just after Charles had been born, and either he had not heard of them or chose to overlook them. Either way, it didn't matter. Given Charles's present mood, the things that impressed him most were great success and even greater power.

A few days later we met again, this time to have dinner at my hotel, then walk the streets around Times Square. He spoke very little, seeming preoccupied with his own thoughts. Only twice did his face sharpen with interest—once as we passed near the Shubert Theatre on West Forty-fourth Street, where he stopped to stare, fascinated, at the elegantly dressed people emerging from gleaming limousines, and then, as we made our way uptown, to gaze wistfully at a display of jewels in Tiffany's Fifth Avenue window.

Sharon Fletcher's name was never mentioned—an indication, I hoped, that perhaps he was adjusting to his loss.

I saw him several times after that, usually to have dinner, then go to my room, where, over beer, we would discuss the carnage in Europe and the failures of Allied leadership. Sharing his views and aware of his loneliness, I began to feel a deep affinity for him, in fact a sense of responsibility for his welfare.

"Would you still like a summer job at the paper?" I asked one evening.

He hesitated before saying, "Do you think they'd take me?"

"I'm not certain. But I think I can work something out."

He gave me an affectionate smile. "You're a good friend, Max."

But I had no chance even to broach the subject. Two days after our meeting—on April 2, 1917—President Woodrow Wilson called on Congress for a declaration of war against Germany.

On the following day, Charles Dain volunteered.

"Mr. Wills? This is Carl Dain, Charles's father."

"Mr. Dain! How are you?"

"Very well, thank you. I hope I haven't disturbed you."

"Not at all." I was in my hotel living room, having just come up from the bar.

"Charles phoned you several times but was unable to reach you. He left no message to call back because we have no phone. He asked me to call."

"Nothing wrong, I hope."

"He enlisted in the army and—"

"Enlisted!" It then occurred to me that I shouldn't have been so surprised.

"Yes, he left yesterday. He wants you to know how much he appreciates all you have done for him."

"But I've done nothing."

"Charles thinks otherwise. You gave him great understanding and treated him as an equal. He says he will write to you from his training camp. I don't know yet where that will be."

"I'll be delighted to hear from him, and you can be sure I'll answer."

"He will appreciate that," Mr. Dain said. "And so will I."

"Was this a sudden decision?"

"It appeared so, but I believe it has been forming in his mind for some time." He paused, and when he spoke there was a touch of melancholy in his voice. "I'm sure you know that Sharon—Sharon Fletcher—is now married."

"No, I hadn't heard."

"I thought perhaps her father had told you. We read about it here in the local paper. About a week ago, I believe."

That was only a day or so before I'd last seen Charles. No wonder he had been so withdrawn. "I'm sorry it had to turn out that way for Charles," I said.

"Yes. Fortunately he has great inner strength. Anyway, it is done and I will talk no more about it. Instead, I will make a happy suggestion. I wish, whenever it is convenient for you, that you will come and visit with us."

"I'll do that, Mr. Dain."

"I will set aside a bottle or two of my famous dandelion wine."

It was some time before I realized how much Charles's sudden enlistment had shaken me. He had become the nearest thing to a brother, almost a son, that I'd ever known, and his disappearance into the great, nebulous mass of the military, evoking images of young men slaughtered by the hundreds of thousands at Verdun and on the Somme, filled me with dread. Often, lines from Alan Seeger's poem drifted into my mind—"But I've a rendezvous with Death/At midnight in some flaming town/When Spring trips north again this year"—and I envisioned Charles crumpled in eternal stillness over some foreign parapet.

Part of the feeling, I knew, arose from my own trepidations, induced by a belated belief that American participation in the war had become crucial if the civilized nations were not to be obliterated under the goose-stepping heels of the hated Huns. Every day my conscience became more urgent in its demand that I follow Charles's lead and join in making the world "safe for democracy." But I resisted, bolstered by constant self-reminders that I was now thirty-five years old, that I was needed at home to help keep the public informed, that I was doing my bit by buying Liberty Bonds, donating blood, observing the heatless, wheatless, and meatless days, collecting fats and metals, even fruit pits, which were burned to make charcoal filters for gas masks.

Still, I was powerless to cope with the patriotic fervor sweeping the country. No longer were people singing "I Didn't Raise My Boy to Be a Soldier;" it had been replaced by George M. Cohan's rousing call to arms, "Over There." Riots against the draft had yielded to giant outdoor rallies at which Hollywood luminaries like Douglas Fairbanks, Mary Pickford, and Charlie Chaplin exhorted cheering crowds to buy Liberty Bonds. Colorful posters supplicating us to help "our boys"— knit a sock, feed a fighter, spot a spy—were everywhere. (Not to mention James Montgomery Flagg's grim Uncle Sam pointing an accusing finger at me—at me alone—and growling, I WANT YOU.) No matter where you turned you were assaulted with reminders that if you were not contributing your utmost to supporting the war, you were a slacker.

And through it all thundered the righteous wrath, the flag-waving chauvinism, of the nation's press.

Until Congress overwhelmingly voted us into the war, Hearst, a dedicated anglophobe, had bitterly opposed it. My own paper, the *American,* had editorialized, "The painful truth is that we are being practically used as a mere reinforcement of England's warfare and of England's future aggrandizement." The Kaiser himself had declared, "Mr. Hearst . . . has helped us very much in your country." Well before those words were reported, Hearst's reputation had hit bottom when a federal judge had found his International News Service guilty of stealing news from the Associated Press. Now, with war fever running high, Hearst became the most detested public figure in the country. The *Tribune,* in a series of blistering articles, likened him to a snake, spelling his name Hears-s-s-s-t. Enraged citizens seized bundles of the *American* and torched them into bonfires. He was hanged in effigy, boycotted by former readers, deserted in droves by advertisers, placed under surveillance by the federal government. And to my own personal discomfiture, his reporters were heaped with abuse.

If I had agreed with his position, or even understood it, I might have been able to shrug off the contempt of people I met on assignment. Instead I found myself inwardly approving of the most vicious attacks on my boss, which began to include rumors of his adulterous affair with Marion Davies, a girl half his age who had caught his eye in Ziegfeld's *Follies* of 1916. Loyalty demanded that I try to justify the man who paid my salary. He was, I argued, a great man, and, almost by definition, great men are bold, independent, often eccentric, always defiant of public opinion when it conflicts with their honest beliefs. But I was too caught up in the tidal wave of patriotism to see the man as anything but a menace to all our country stood for—a judgment that must also apply to the paper that employed me.

And so I moved another long step toward the induction center, drawn by my country's call to arms and pushed by the wish to dissociate myself from a paper widely viewed as treasonable. Still, I wavered. Why should I volunteer when, immediately after Congress had authorized the enlistment of one million men, some nine-and-a-half million had rushed to their draft boards to register? What besides arrogance and vanity made me think that I, a skinny, awkward fellow who enjoyed seclusion and abhorred violence, could add one speck of might to General Pershing's American Expeditionary Force?

Then, in late June, I got my first letter from Charles Dain.

Dear Max:

Please forgive me for taking so long to write. One reason was that I knew you'd been hearing about me from my father, and I about you. (He was very pleased that you stopped in to see him one Sunday afternoon. He likes you as much as I do, and that's saying a lot!)

But the main reason I put off writing was because I was ashamed to tell you what I'd been doing. You probably heard from my father about all my heroic deeds while in training, things I wrote because I knew how proud he'd be. But almost all of that was made up. The truth—which I wish you wouldn't tell him—was a lot different, and I'd rather you knew it.

Max, when I first got to Camp McClellan there was not a single uniform to be had. We marched and drilled in our civilian clothes and used broomsticks for guns! There were so many of us that most of the time the officers just didn't know what to do with us. So they had us digging holes—my God, I've dug a thousand!—and painting barracks and washing windows and fixing fences and doing all kinds of odd jobs, necessary or not. This went on for weeks, until I'd just about decided that our strategy was to overwhelm the Huns with shovels and brooms and brushes and then bury them in millions of holes.

But that's all over with. Now I'm in a uniform with a too-tight collar, too-loose pants, and leggings that hang down from my calves like streamers. My appearance might not win the approval of Black Jack Pershing, but even so, I'm finally becoming a soldier. I've learned how to lay barbed wire, hurl grenades, handle a machine gun and shoot a rifle—and dig bigger and better holes, which I'm told the French consider the only sensible way to survive.

I don't know when I'll be getting out of here. Maybe never, if I believe a story that goes like this. It seems that an evangelist hung up a sign reading, "Where will you spend eternity?" Under it a recruit scrawled, "At Camp McClellan." Well, that's not going to be me. I'll get Over There even if I have to swim.

Max, have you ever thought of becoming a foreign correspondent? If you were, you could cover the war from Paris, and when I got a leave, I could visit you and you could take me to all those places the chaplains warn us against. I'm not just kidding. Give it some thought.

I hear Sharon is married now, to some fellow she knew before I met her. For her sake, I hope he's a tough guy and big enough to bust her father's nose when he pokes it into their business. They live near each other in South Orange. God, that seems so far away!

I often think of the times we spent together, Max. We'll do it again as soon as we make monkeys out of Kaiser Bill and all his Fritzes. Keep the home fires burning, and write when you can.

Always your friend,
Charles

His suggestion that I seek a job as foreign correspondent revived all my romantic aspirations to become another Richard Harding Davis. The more I thought about it, the more convinced I became that Mr. Hearst would be doing himself a favor if he assigned me to cover the battlefields. I wasted no time getting into the office of my managing editor and eloquently asserting my qualifications.

"Max, you don't have a chance," he said.

"Why do you say that?"

"Because we need you here. Most of our younger men have been drafted, or are about to be. At your age you're not eligible, which means we can depend on keeping you around. I wish we had a dozen of you."

"What if I volunteer?" The words popped out, with no thought behind them.

He laughed. "That's a good one. If they took you, I'd figure we'd lost the war."

"I mean it."

He regarded me seriously. "Max, how long since you've had a raise?"

"I don't know. More than a year, I think."

"I'll see what I can do."

I got the raise and it was a whopper, more than enough to offset the skyrocketing cost of living. Along with it came a heady rise in my self-esteem, which I indulged with new clothes and two cases of the finest whiskey, the latter considered a necessity, inasmuch as the government had outlawed the manufacture of liquor. As my managing editor had anticipated, my war fever receded, returning in full force only when I wrote to Charles, carefully omitting news of my good fortune.

In early October Charles wrote that he had been assigned to advanced infantry training. I felt a twinge of alarm but stifled it by reminding myself of the widespread belief that the war would be over before a single American troopship could sail, a view supported by the catastrophic battles in Europe that had already cost millions of lives.

A few weeks later the papers headlined that the first contingent of American troops had landed in France. It was the beginning of the end, shouted the optimists—the boys would be home by Christmas. I didn't believe it; certainly not *this* Christmas.

Then, a telephone call from Charles's father:

"He's there, Max! Charles is in France! He landed at Saint-Nazaire!"

I brooded about my easy life, my fine clothes, my gourmet meals, my supply of excellent liquor.

I thought about my paper, now hypocritically proclaiming its patriotism by adorning the front page with an array of small American flags.

Three days after hearing from Charles's father, I volunteered. Surprisingly, I was accepted. Even more surprisingly, I was selected to be a soldier of rank—my orders were to report for officers candidate training at Plattsburgh, New York.

Before I left, there were two calls I felt compelled to make. The first, of course, was to Mr. Dain. I sent him a telegram, and he telephoned me in the evening at my hotel. He seemed touched by my news—proud, yet regretful. He asked me out for a farewell feast, but I had to decline, saying that there was too much work to clean up at the office. The truth was that I could not bear to be treated as a hero while his son might be shivering in a sodden trench infested with rats and lice. I sensed from his tone that Mr. Dain understood.

Before saying good-bye I got the phone number of

the second person I was determined to speak to—the girl that both Charles and I had lost. I placed the call.

"Max! Max, is it really you?"

"It is. The same guy who drove the flivver."

"Oh, Max, how often I've thought of you! It's been so long! I wanted to call and ask you over, but Father always said you were terribly busy."

"Well, Sharon, I'm going to be busier." I told her about enlisting in the army.

"What a fine thing to do," she said. "I just hope that at your age you won't be sent into battle."

At my age, indeed! "I'll probably command the latrines," I said. "Anyway, I wanted to hear that all's well with you before I left."

"Everything's fine. Look, Max, we're moving in a couple of days—to New York. I'd ask you to dinner, but—"

"Thanks, but I'm all tied up. I'd like to have your new address though. I'll drop you a line."

The address was on 184th Street, in the northernmost section of Manhattan. Writing it down, I thought that she was probably making the move to get away from her overbearing father.

"I'll write," I said. "That is, if your husband doesn't object."

"Don't be silly. I've told Tom so much about you, he practically knows you." Her voice lowered and she said with conviction, "Max, he's a very fine man."

"He'd have to be, to get you. I take it, then, that you're a happy woman."

There was a brief silence before she said, "Yes, Max, I'm very happy."

I wondered if in that silence she had thought of Charles Dain.

Chapter · 6

Terry Donovan paused in the doorway of his office to gaze at Kate Richards, sitting behind his battered desk. She was dressed for her after-dark assignment—pale-green, low-cut satin dress, tiny twist of a hat in matching material, vivid makeup to offset the darkness of the plush saloons.

"Waiting for Elsa Maxwell?" he said.

She pointed accusingly at him with a lit cigarette. "Deceiver. Trickster. Bamboozler."

He slumped into a chair. "Now give me the translation."

"Our vacation. You conned me last night. You said you'd fix it with Max."

"I didn't say I'd fix it. I said I'd talk to him, and I did."

"Sure. And you told him he'd have to fire you before you'd take time off."

"You know why, Kate. I'd feel I was walking out on Charles."

"Uh-huh. But it's all right to walk out on me."

His eyes regarded her sleepily, but something inside

his brain seemed to wake up and stretch. "What's going on with you and Max? Why are you both so hot to get me out of here?"

She stubbed out her cigarette, studying his face. Her voice softened. "I can't speak for Max. But I thought I made my reason pretty obvious last night. I want you to myself for a while, before your draft board gets you."

"I want that too. But once I get the call, they'll give me a little time." He grinned. "To take care of my affairs."

"One affair—me."

"Only you. We'll keep it going till the minute I report."

She was smiling now. "Okay, if that's how it has to be. We'll hire a limousine and make love all the way to Camp Dix." She stood up, plucked a Kleenex from her purse, and wiped lipstick from her mouth. "Now I'd like to be kissed."

He rose and obliged, taking his time.

Drawing back, she said, "We'll save the rest for later. You will be at my place, won't you? About midnight?"

"I'll be there, unless something happens at the hospital. I just came from there. Charles is about the same."

"I know, I called." Her eyes glimmered, and she blinked rapidly. "Have the police got anything?"

"Nothing. I spent half the day with detectives. They're grilling every known criminal they can lay hands on, hoping for a tip. I think they're wasting their time."

"Why?" She was looking into her compact mirror, redoing her lips.

"My hunch is that this has nothing to do with Charles's war against organized crime. It seems like something very private."

She snapped the compact shut. "Sounds like you mean a woman."

"Someone should consider that. From all I can gather, no one's giving it a thought."

"Why should they? Charles's reputation is spotless. If he'd so much as given the eye to another woman, I'd have heard about it from those dirtmongers I hang around with."

She should have known Charles Dain ten years ago, Donovan thought. But then Kate had been only fifteen, and so had most of her current playmates—too young to be interested in the sexual intrigues of older men. Besides, Charles had appeared no more licentious than other privileged contemporaries in their early thirties, married men-about-town who punctuated their respectable pursuits with an occasional fling with a presumably promiscuous chorus girl. He decided not to enlighten her. Why tarnish the image of a man who was her hero and professional benefactor and who was now struggling against death?

"You're probably right," he said. "I've got a suspicious mind—an occupational affliction."

"Well, at least you recognize the cause. My intuition tells me that some gangster put out a contract on him. Whoever did it set him up to make it look like just what you're thinking. But the police aren't fooled."

"The police are prejudiced. Charles is one of the most powerful friends they've got. They'd hate like hell to have him brought down by scandal. But okay, have it your way—blame it on a hired killer."

After she left, he found himself reflecting on his feelings for her. He was ambivalent about her aggressiveness; on the one hand flattered that she had spurned any coy preliminaries before taking him to her bed, on the other made uneasy by a sense of being manipulated. Had there been other lovers with whom she had been equally direct? More likely, as her attitude suggested, she had wearied of the transient seductions endemic to the crowd she ran with, and perhaps, having yielded to a disappointing affair or two, had decided to preempt a man she understood sufficiently to feel emotionally secure with. It was not the most romantic reason for being chosen, but then he had been surfeited with romanticism by a starry-eyed wife who spent her days listening to immortal music, insisted on dining by candlelight, and diminished his lust by reading aloud the ethereal yearnings of Edwardian poets.

That marriage, Donovan eventually concluded, had simply been a case of mistaken identities. Charlotte Latham, recent graduate of Bennington and daughter of a rich vice-president of General Motors, had come to Greenwich Village in 1938 to relive the days of its bohemian pioneers. In place of John Reed's support of the Russian revolution, she championed the Loyalist armies in Spain. Big Bill Haywood, one-eyed leader of the violent Industrial Workers of the World, was transformed into beetle-browed John L. Lewis and his militant CIO. Mabel Dodge's famous evenings were resurrected in the form of weekly bacchanals in Charlotte's spacious apartment on Minetta Street. Henrietta Rodman, fierce advocate of free love, was traded in for Judge Ben B. Lindsey and his crusade for "companionate marriage." As for Charlotte herself, she was transfigured into Edna St. Vincent Millay, burning her candle at both ends while composing melancholy verse for the *New Masses* and ephemeral little magazines.

Terry Donovan had been drawn into this masquerade

late one night when he stopped for a cup of coffee at the Waldorf Cafeteria, successor to Hubert's (which had been replaced by a bank), where uptown tourists once gathered to ogle the Village freaks. Sitting down opposite him, Charlotte struck up a conversation and, learning he was a newspaperman, immediately perceived him as a savant, a mixture of Max Eastman and Floyd Dell, equating his careless attire and shaggy hair with the black flannel shirts and wild locks of her radical associates. Donovan, who had moved to the Village because the rents were cheap and the inhabitants tolerant, was fascinated by this small, dark-eyed, pretty girl who seemed even more dedicated than he to personal freedom.

There ensued a series of dates during which Donovan found himself in such unlikely places as quaint little tearooms with wooden benches, candles, and abstract sketches on the walls; dark cellar clubs where sweating Latins danced the Apache; Victorian mansions on Washington Square where the hostess read poetry aloud while her underprivileged guests devoured her food and decimated her liquor; monster rallies in Union Square where scrawny, dyspeptic men with defiant beards inveighed against "the system." Weeks passed before Charlotte, disarmed by several gin rickeys, allowed him into her bed. He had only half completed his mission when he discovered to his astonishment that she was a virgin. But by then it was too late to abort, and besides, Charlotte had got the hang of it and was delighting him by suddenly turning into a whirling dervish. Later he learned that she had retained at least one bourgeois notion—she proposed that they marry. Temporarily insane, he agreed, even acceding to her request that the nuptials be performed at that citadel of middle-class romance, the Little Church Around the Corner. Once the union was blessed, Charlotte reverted to her bogus bohemianism, while Donovan, aghast at what he had done, immersed himself in writing fiction and probing the activities of sober-minded, clear-thinking criminals. The end had come when he had fallen asleep while she was regaling him with a passage from Emily Dickinson.

In contrast to Charlotte, Kate Richards—the Kate Richards of last night, not the one who flitted about Manhattan's fleshpots—was real, of this world, scornful of pretense, immune to phony fads. For that he was appreciative, rating these qualities even higher than the dizzying pleasures bestowed by her ravishing good looks and extravagant sexuality.

So he was in love with her, infatuated by her—but did he love her? It seemed a puerile question, too precipitant to deserve an answer, yet, for some reason, demanding one. Perhaps, he thought, the reason was that he wanted so much to give of his inner self—that self which his former wife thought, mistakenly, was insensitive—and he was fearful of risking it on a commitment that again might be based on mutual misjudgment. After all, how much did he really know about Kate Richards? Only, in essence, that she was a passionate, independent, intelligent woman whose ambition enabled her to adapt publicly to an absurd society she claimed privately to despise. He wondered if she had ever expressed that attitude to Max Wills, her patron since her first summer job while still a Vassar student, and the one who had pressed Charles Dain to advance her with unheard-of speed. No, he decided; despite her candor, she would not have hinted at her

disaffection lest she alienate the men who might someday elevate her to a position in the paper's hierarchy.
The thought disturbed him. A woman who gained satisfaction from achievement, yes; a woman obsessed with
a lust for power, absolutely not. In the first instance, he
could become a partner. In the second, an adversary.

But he was getting way ahead of himself. This was
now, and now was a very fine time indeed, charged
with excitement and promise. If only it was not haunted
by the specter of the comatose Charles Dain. . . .

The phone rang. It was Lee Radner, the night city
editor, who had just come on.

"Terry, I just read your Dain story. Nicely written,
but it's got nothing more than the police handout."

"That's all there is, Lee."

"Yeah, but usually you work in a few intriguing
touches. You're the only guy here who can make specu-
lation sound like fact."

"On this one I'm not speculating."

"Sure, I understand. I'll shoot it through. We'll try for
a come-on in the head."

The fact was that Donovan had done little else but
speculate, none of it getting him anywhere. Now he
sat back and dredged his mind for some past experience
that might shed light on the shooting. A name surfaced
—Arnold Rothstein. Donovan had known the gambler,
a friendly man, always accessible because his "office"
was a table in Lindy's Restaurant on Sixth Avenue.
Almost fourteen years ago Rothstein had been sum-
moned from that table by a phone call from a fellow
gambler named George McManus, who asked to meet
him in a third-floor room of the Park Central Hotel.
Soon after his arrival Rothstein was shot in the stomach.

Fully conscious, he was taken to Polyclinic Hospital, where he refused to tell police who had shot him. Two days later—on the election day that swept Herbert Hoover into the White House—Arnold Rothstein died, still not naming his killer.

The suspect, of course, was George McManus, and the case against him was overwhelming. The room was registered in his name; his chesterfield overcoat, embroidered with his name, was found in the closet. A maid positively identified him as the man who earlier had occupied the room, where she had observed him drinking heavily. What's more, there was motive: Rothstein owed a quarter of a million dollars to the players in a poker game run by McManus and, despite badgering, had failed to pay up. When the case finally came before a jury, the maid, fearing for her life, decided that McManus was not the man she had seen in the room, and the district attorney staged such an inept prosecution that the judge directed a verdict of not guilty.

Why had Rothstein refused to talk? Some said he was merely observing the criminal code of silence. Others, the insiders, believed it had more to do with his link to corrupt Tammany politicians. A lawyer for Rothstein's family demanded that the district attorney investigate the gambler's business records, declaring, "If those papers are ever made public, there are going to be a lot of suicides in high places."

But the files containing those papers had mysteriously disappeared.

Donovan abruptly sat up in his chair. Surely there must be a file of Charles Dain's private papers. Where? It seemed unlikely that he would transport them to his home in Mount Kisco or to his apartment at the Waterford hotel. That left two possibilities: a safe-deposit box at his bank (doubtful), or the modern steel cabinet, actually a safe, that sat in a corner of his office (probable).

Aside from Charles himself, only one man would know the combination to that safe—Max Wills. And if Terry Donovan really wanted to be fired, all he had to do was mention one word to Wills about its contents.

He started to think of some undetectable way to crack the safe, then interrupted his thoughts with a snorting laugh. Hell, if there was so much as a single item in there that might embarrass Charles Dain, his alter ego, Max, would have spirited it away minutes after the shooting. Knowing Max, he would probably not trust the material to a bank or any place the police might think to investigate through a court order. He would keep it in his possession, not on his person but in some hiding place where he lived—his suite at the Algonquin Hotel. Donovan had visited him there a number of times, always with a small group gathered to drink and hear Max recount tales of the old days. Now he knew that very soon, perhaps tonight, he would visit again, this time alone, uninvited, and with his unsuspecting host safely out of the way.

Considering how he might manage the break-in, Donovan felt no guilt. Why should he? Max Wills's excessive concern for Dain's reputation, while nobly motivated, could in fact be an obstruction of justice. And justice was what Donovan had vowed Charles Dain would get. If that meant rattling some closeted skeletons, then on with the rattling. Time enough, once the assailant was identified, to consider such opposing abstractions as mercy or vengeance.

The immediate question was how to slip surreptitiously into Max Wills's suite. Fortunately Donovan knew certain men who were experts in such matters.

"Hello, Jackie?"

"Hi, Terry. I was just thinking about you. It's a habit I can't seem to break."

"Try chewing gum. How's the patient?"

"About the same, I think. There's been a conference here, and they've decided to hold off on operating."

"Maybe that's a good sign. Jackie, is Mrs. Dain alone?"

"Mr. Wills is with her. I saw him come in a few minutes ago."

"Good. That's who I want to talk to. Can you put him on?"

"I'll ring. Hold on."

He waited, tapping his desk, and in a moment Max said in his ear, "Terry? What's up? You got something?"

"Nothing that's not in the paper. I was checking on Charles and heard you were there. How about meeting for a drink?"

"To talk about your vacation?"

"No, Max, we settled that in your office."

"So we did. You'll be sorry when you're doing push-ups and eating Spam. Anyway, I can't make it. There's a thing going on at the Friars."

"A quick one before you go?"

"You know I only drink soda water. Doctors! I'm due at the Friars now—dinner and a show. At least I can stay up late and pretend I'm raising hell."

"Okay, another time. How's Mrs. Dain?"

"Hanging in. I just wish Charles could see her. Best medicine he could have."

Donovan spotted the man as he swung through the door of the bar on Vanderbilt Avenue. His short, wiry figure was clad in a double-breasted gray suit, and his dark-green porkpie hat, complete with feather, sat squarely above his ruddy face. He had the bland look of a clerk at Abercrombie & Fitch, one who had worked late and was in need of a snort before catching his train to the suburbs from Grand Central Station.

In his right hand he carried a maroon-leather attaché case. Of the dozen or so people in the bar, only he and Donovan knew that it contained an assortment of keys, a small but powerful flashlight, a collection of finely-wrought steel tools, a pair of surgical gloves, and a Colt .45 pistol.

He sidled up beside Donovan, not speaking to him, set down the case, locking it between his feet, and ordered Johnny Walker Black Label on the rocks. He sipped it, nodded judiciously, and murmured, as though in approval, "Tonight?"

"Tonight," Donovan said. "Soon as possible."

"Give me an hour. Eight thirty, say."

"Fine. If there's a slipup—"

"You're offending me. Just turn the knob."

The man drained his glass, placed a quarter on the bar, and left.

The small, old-fashioned lobby of the Algonquin Hotel was crowded when Donovan slipped through and squeezed into an elevator. He got off at the fifth floor and walked in the direction opposite to Max Wills's suite, pausing to study the door numbers but casting glances back down the corridor. No one was in sight, and the only sounds came from radios and cars on Forty-fourth Street pestering each other with horns.

Reversing his course, he strode quietly along the thick carpeting and stopped at Room 519. He knocked lightly, stood back, and waited. Hearing no sound or movement from within, he grasped the knob and slowly gave it a turn. He pushed it gently, half expecting to be frustrated by a dead bolt. But the door opened silently on well-oiled hinges, a mute reminder of Max's fussiness.

Stepping inside, he eased the door shut, snapped the wall switch, and stood perfectly still in the soft lamplight as he surveyed the living room. Everything was exactly as he remembered it—heavy overstuffed chairs and sofa with doilies protecting the arms; embossed brass lamps with thickly fringed silk shades; a solid-walnut drop-leaf table with intricately carved legs; a glass-fronted china cabinet that doubled as a bookcase; pastoral prints by George Innes in rococo gold frames on the walls. It was a scene from a long-ago era—about the time of the first World War, Donovan thought—when men wore starched choker collars and women large hats winged with feathers, and sex was saved for marriage.

He went into the bedroom and snapped on the lights, illuminating a high double bed with a brass-runged headboard flanked by antique cabinets that served as night tables. The cabinets were unlocked, and a quick inspection revealed only books, magazines, an unopened carton of matches, and a few pill bottles. Next, the walk-in closet, where about two dozen suits, racks of silk bow ties, and pairs of wide suspenders hung, and beneath them a low platform supporting a long row of gleaming shoes, all with fixed metal trees. He stretched to examine the upper shelf, seeing only an array of soft felt hats, then stopped to scrutinize the floor, finding nothing, not even a particle of dust. The objects he had in mind were a lockbox, a compact filing cabinet, a small safe, a briefcase, anything that might contain a man's private papers. Perhaps, he thought, they were secured in Max's personal file at the office. If so, the search was over; he could not risk being seen by a maintenance worker while ransacking the office of the second most powerful man on the *Express*.

But he had not finished. Before him now, opposite the foot of the bed, stood a high chest of drawers. He started at the top, his hands gingerly exploring beneath a tray of jeweled cuff links, then under stacks of handkerchiefs, underwear, socks, and in the third drawer, silk shirts. There his fingers touched something cool, pebbled, resistant. Gently, not disturbing the lustrous shirts, he drew it out—a large but shallow cardboard box, the kind that once might have contained a sweater. He backed off with it, placed it on the floor beside the bed and, in the glow of the table lamp, knelt. Slowly he removed the top—and stared at a heap of pictures, mostly snapshots.

He felt a stab of disappointment mixed with a vague sadness. There, he thought, in all its innocence, lay the detached life of a confirmed bachelor, memories of people with whom he had shared an intimacy not much closer than the camera used to freeze them in time.

Donovan was about to replace the lid when his eye was caught by a snapshot of a young girl standing astride a bicycle. She was slim, blond, pretty, and wore a smile that, as he bent closer, seemed to leap into his heart. It couldn't be, he thought. A resemblance, yes, but not the person who had flashed into his mind. Hell, this smiling girl in the picture could be no more than fourteen years old, maybe younger. And that long ago— a dozen years, say—Max Wills would not have known Kate Richards.

Donovan turned the picture over. On the back, written in a precise hand, were the words: Kate, April 1931.

No wonder Max Wills had sponsored the career of Kate Richards. Chances were he'd known her almost all her life, knew her parents, had in effect become a second father. The evidence of that must be strewn throughout this big square box. He set aside the lid, squatted, and picked out pictures at random, tossing on the carpet those that seemed significant. When he had laid out about twenty, he quit to concentrate on them, first reading the inscriptions on the backs.

"Max and Kate, August 1919" (Kate, a toddler, was perched on the knee of a delighted, thick-haired Max); "Kate, Sharon, Tom, July 1921" (obviously her parents, the square-faced father beaming and proudly gripping his lapels, the blond mother—incredibly she was even more beautiful than the daughter Donovan knew— protectively holding Kate by the shoulders); "Max, Tom, Sharon, Kate, September 1927" (a picnic scene with the subjects gathered around a wooden table in a leafy grove).

And on they went: Kate with her father and Max at the zoo; Kate in a white party dress, surrounded by her parents and Max as she blew out candles on a birthday cake; Kate on her graduation from high school and, in black gown and mortarboard, hugging her college diploma—typical family-album shots, with Max often a member, like an honorary uncle.

Only two of the pictures had not been inscribed, both of them faded and cracked with age. One showed Max with Kate's mother—her blond hair in a bun and looking charmingly girlish—standing beside a black Model-T Ford. Max's arm was around her waist and she was smiling up at him as though enjoying his embarrassment. The other was virtually the same pose except that the man—Donovan, startled, jerked his face closer—was Charles Dain!

Even though Dain appeared still in his teens, there was no mistaking the deep-set, slightly slanted eyes, the full-lipped grin, the erect bearing. Now what the hell was he doing there—perhaps twenty-five years ago—half embracing Sharon Richards?

A moment's reflection provided the answer. Max, Donovan knew, had been a friend of Charles's before the first World War. Apparently Charles had been invited along one day when Max was calling on Sharon. Whatever Max's intentions toward Sharon may have been, they had remained good friends despite her marriage to Tom Richards. No doubt Charles had forgotten that romantic episode in Max Wills's life and was unaware of the daughter's existence until Max brought her to his attention at the *Express*. Max may even have remained silent about his devotion to the family lest he be accused of something close to nepotism. Well, the secret, if such it was, would not be revealed by Terry Donovan. No matter how Kate Richards had gained her success, she was now earning it.

Returning the pictures to the box, he spotted more

evidence of Max's long friendship with Kate's mother—
a stack of letters tied with a string. He did not touch
them—he was already conscience-stricken at this invasion of an elderly man's most intimate memorabilia—
but he could not avoid seeing the writing on the top
envelope. It was addressed to Lieutenant Max Wills,
with a return address for Mrs. Thomas Richards on
184th Street, New York City.

Donovan put the box back as he had found it, then
continued with his search, finding nothing. Ironic, he
thought as he left, that in seeking a woman who may
have brought death to Charles Dain, he had instead
found a woman who had brought life to Max Wills.

He wished he could confess it all to Kate Richards
when he joined her at midnight. But that was impossible, unless he was prepared to have himself labeled a
cheap burglar who had assigned himself to the theft of
a great man's reputation.

There was one consolation. He now felt that he knew
and understood Kate Richards a lot better—hadn't he
just met her parents, seen her grow up?—a feeling that
should enhance their pleasure, both in and out of bed.

Chapter · 7

I got two letters from Charles during my training at Plattsburgh, and several more during the late winter and spring of 1918, when I was in Paris. By then he had been overseas for five months and had yet to see battle.

The reason for the delay was apparent in the conflicting viewpoints between the commander of the American troops, the iron-willed General Pershing, and the leaders of France and England, Georges Clemenceau and David Lloyd George, backed by their generals. Pershing was adamant in insisting on an autonomous American force assigned to its own sector of the front, while the French and British were equally adamant in their demand that American troops be employed to fill out the ranks of their depleted armies.

Finally Pershing's view prevailed, but until then Charles's division was confined to incessant training in the wintry fields of Lorraine and on the frigid slopes of the Vosges Mountains. His letters, though bristling with impatience, sought to dismiss his plight with light-hearted comments on the nutritional merits of hardtack, the gourmet delights of limp bacon and weak coffee, and the advantages of engaging in trench warfare without interference from an enemy. And, of course. "I have become the champion hole-digger of the A.E.F., surpassing even the French."

Then, after two months without hearing from him, I got a hand-delivered letter.

June 11, 1918

Dear Max:

I'm sending this to you by way of a sympathetic Red Cross girl because I know that our stupid censors would chop it up into hash. As you can see from my address, I'm in a hospital outside of London, where I was delivered ten days ago to rid my lungs of mustard gas and my legs of splintered shrapnel. The first problem has been taken care of, but I've got about a dozen more splinters to go. I'm hoping to be out of here in a week or so.

Yes, I finally met up with the unfriendly Teutons —at a French town called Cantigny. This, as you probably know by now, was the first Yank offensive of the war (please rise and salute the 28th Infantry of the 1st Division!) The attack was carefully staged, and when it was launched—at 4:45 A.M. on May 28—all hell broke loose. First we hit them with a deafening artillery barrage. Then we moved in with mortars and machine guns, crossing the open fields behind French-made Renault tanks. As we advanced on the town we were preceded by a rolling barrage that kept the enemy pinned down on their bellies. Once we reached the streets, we really went to work, bayoneting them in their trenches, burning them out of cellars, blasting them from shell holes with Mills grenades. In less than three hours it was all over—the remaining Germans had run for their lives, we'd taken the town, and all our goals had been achieved. I'm told I did some things that my father and you would be proud of, but I honestly don't remember them. All I can recall is a tremendous feeling of release, as though a huge hand had suddenly let go of my guts. It didn't last long, no more than a day, but now I know why some men think war is glorious.

Of course what we'd done was considered a mere skirmish by the Frenchies and Brits. And I'm afraid they were right because, soon after, those Huns came storming back in unbelievable force, launching attacks all along the Aisne River, then the Marne, slaughtering the French troops and forcing their retreat at Château-Thierry, Cantigny, and Belleau Wood. (How did you feel when the Huns were only about 40 miles from Paris?!) Three American divisions, including mine, were rushed into a counterattack—and that's when I got it.

A gas attack on the eastern bank of the Marne had put me out of action. Accompanied by another soldier, wounded in the chest, and a helpful medic, I had just crossed a bridge to the other side when the shell—the one you don't hear—struck about twenty yards away.

The medic lost both his legs, the wounded soldier was killed instantly, and I, who for a long time had been prepared to die, only got my butt and thighs punctured with steel fragments. How do I tell *that* to the sweet young girls back home?

Anyway, even without my heroic presence, the

German drive was halted—just a week ago—and from all I hear we're ready to move in for the kill. I doubt that I'll be part of it. I'll probably be stuck in the headquarters of some base camp and spend the rest of the war filling out forms. God, how dismal.

I was sorry to hear that Sharon's mother died. I didn't know her very well, but she seemed like a nice woman (who probably would have been a lot nicer if she hadn't married a monster). That Spanish flu, as they call it, is helping to crowd the hospitals over here—as well as the graveyards. I also heard that Sharon and her husband have a daughter. The best I can say about that is that life is very strange. This news of death and new life came to me from my father, who you might some day want to hire as editor of vital statistics, as well as a writer of inspirational pieces that I find great for my morale.

How I envy you your job on *Stars and Stripes*! I read every word of every issue, starting with your name in the upper corner of the front page, along with those of other newspapermen I've come to admire—Alexander Woollcott (I used to read his drama criticism in *The New York Times*), John Winterich, Franklin P. Adams, Grantland Rice. You say that the editor, Harold Ross, is tough and profane (also a damned good editor). Well, tell him that if he'd like to enlarge his vocabulary, he has only to spend a day with an infantry outfit. (Did you know that the English try to stop their kids from saying fuck by telling them it's the German spy word? I heard a ten-year-old shout at an MP, "You dirty German Spy Word!")

Life here at the hospital is monotonously bland, and I won't bore you by going on about it. However, I do have one routine experience that might give you a smile. At least twice a day this middle-aged nurse pops in and politely asks to inspect my ass. Just checking on my progress, she says, then oohs and ahs in approval. Maybe I'll have a picture taken of it that she can frame and put on her piano.

Anyway, if you really want to do something special for a man who has given his ass for his country, write me a long letter.

Oh, Max, I miss you and do want to hear from you!

> Always your friend,
> Charles

P.S. Please note that I am now a sergeant. I'll thank you for a little respect, Lieutenant!

The letter struck me as an odd mixture of boyishness and sophistication, with more than a hint of recklessness. It seemed to me that Charles, now approaching twenty, was in the midst of the transition from youth to maturity, the process accelerated by the impact of war.

And there was something else about the letter that impressed me—Charles Dain had the makings of a good journalist.

I thought about that for a day before discussing his situation with my fellow editors on *Stars and Stripes*. They authorized me to ignore the chain of command and cut transfer orders addressed directly to the commanding general of the First Division. Arrogant as this might seem, it was within the power of this enlisted man's journal to requisition any soldier anywhere without the formality of prescribed military procedure, a privilege furiously condemned by many a hard-pressed commanding officer. In fact, we had been assigned a special car that bore the insignia of the General Staff, and it was not uncommon for slovenly sergeants to drive around Paris and magnanimously acknowledge the respectful salutes of generals and colonels.

A week passed without any response from the First Division. I put through another order, referring to the original one, and at the same time sent a letter to Charles by courier telling him what I had done. (I had hoped the transfer would come as a surprise.) Still, I heard nothing.

At the end of the second week I was alone in the office pasting up a dummy of the front page when in walked the Red Cross girl who had delivered Charles's letter from the hospital. Her name was Ann Tyson. She looked about nineteen and was pretty in the light-haired, brown-eyed, pink-cheeked way associated with state fairs in the Corn Belt. Ah, I thought, at last a letter from Charles.

"Lieutenant Wills, I have a message for you from your editor, Captain Ross."

"Oh?" The word must have expressed my disappointment, because she smiled in sympathy.

"He wants to see you right away. It has to do with a congressman who just arrived."

I groaned. If there was one thing the doughboys didn't want to read, it was the inspirational drivel of some junketing congressman greedy for space in the papers back home. Had the message not been from Captain Ross, I'd have asked Ann Tyson to report that I could not be found.

Outside in the June twilight Ann led me through narrow back streets to a small hotel. As we passed the desk, the concierge, an elderly woman, gave me an almost beatific smile, presumably induced by the glory reflected upon me by the distinguished representative of the American government I had come to visit. On the landing I heard the sound of music—a scratchy recording of "Dardanella"—growing louder as we went down the corridor and crashing against our eardrums when we stopped before a door. Ann gave me a wry smile and knocked. The music rose in volume until I could feel the floor vibrate. "For God's sake—" I began, and then the door was flung open.

Standing there, hair awry, uniform rumpled, champagne bottle clutched in his hand, was Charles Dain.

I gaped at him.

"Lieutenant," he said, half shouting over the thunderous music, "my orders direct me to report for duty tomorrow morning. Tomorrow, not tonight!"

"Charles!" I found myself embracing him, oblivious of the spilling champagne.

He drew back, grinning. "Right now I'm in transit."

I laughed, feeling as exhilarated as if I'd welcomed home an errant son. "Boy, are you in transit! You're flying high!"

"We'll fly higher!"

Ann went over to a battered Victrola and turned down the music. She remained there, as though sensing that her presence had become an intrusion.

"Champagne for the lieutenant!" said Charles, emptying his glass and half filling it from the remnant in the bottle. "Champagne for the sergeant! Champagne for Florence Nightingale!"

"Florence Nightingale is getting piffled," said Ann, but stepped to a corner and brought back a bottle from a partly empty case. As she handed it to him, she smiled slowly up into his face, her brown eyes melting to warm chocolate, and I knew she was in love with him. He seemed not to notice, fussing with the cork, exploding it, pouring the foaming bubbly into hollow-stemmed glasses with the affected formality of a sommelier, while I hovered about making convivial but inarticulate noises.

Still standing, we raised our glasses in a toast. For a moment Charles's eyes lost their wild intensity and became soft, gentle, almost wistful. "To Max," he said, "my dearest friend."

Solemnly we clicked glasses and drank.

Then he returned to his manic high. "All right, troops! Now let's get this operation cracking! First we'll—"

"First you'll tell me what the dickens is going on," I said.

"You don't get it? I wrote Ann from London and asked her to set this up." His sweeping gesture seemed to include the two lattice-backed chairs, the humpbacked sofa, the untidy bed secluded in an alcove. "I got here about noon and—"

"You've been in Paris since *noon?*" My eyes moved spontaneously to the bed, a glance caught by Ann, who looked away, her mouth hooking in a small, secret smile.

Charles was unabashed. "That's right. Ann and I had some catching up to do. Didn't we, Ann?"

She smiled blissfully.

"I'd planned to look you up earlier, Max. But then, after about the third bottle of champagne, I got this wonderful idea. Why not have a little fun with you? You're not mad, are you?"

"I'd only be mad if I'd found a congressman here. Charles, I'm delighted. But how did you get this place? I thought there wasn't a room to be had in all of Paris."

"When in need, see Ann Tyson."

"I arranged it with the concierge," Ann said.

"The champagne too? A whole case?"

She nodded. "Also the Victrola." She went over and stopped the now-silent spinning platter.

"With only one record," Charles said. "One more 'Dardanella' and I'll be back in the hospital—with the shell-shock cases."

"It must have cost you a fortune to bribe the concierge," I said.

"Not one extra franc, Max. Ann saw to that."

I glanced at her inquiringly, this Midwestern girl who looked so ingenuous.

"It wasn't difficult," she said. "I told the concierge that I had a friend, a soldier, coming from London. I said he'd just got out of the hospital and simply had to have a room."

"Lucky for Charles she was so understanding," I said.

Charles looked at her. "I think you told her one other thing."

"Oh, yes. I also said that Charles was President Wilson's nephew."

We went to the Café Napolitain, where Charles, flashing a bankroll accumulated while in the hospital, stood round after round of drinks. From there we taxied up to Montmartre, going to Nini's, hangout of the *Stars and Stripes* crowd (they were too engrossed in their poker game to do more than wave). Then on to Freddie's, where we drank cognac, sang songs scornful of the Huns, and listened to an emaciated woman half-whisper ballads of loving lament and a long-haired poet recite Baudelaire (after which Freddie passed the hat). Driving back at two A.M., we could hear the distant rumble of a German barrage answered at intervals by the enormous French 145s, which lighted up the sky above the Luxembourg Gardens.

Ann Tyson's head rested on Charles's shoulder, and in the occasional flashes of light I could see her eyes, somnolent and liquid. He was gazing intently at her face—hypnotically was the word that struck me—as though he were a youthful Svengali casting a spell over this Trilby in the uniform of the American Red Cross. He was, of course, quite drunk—we all were—but even so, I wondered later if for him the taxi had momentarily become a Model T Ford, and the girl pressing against him a lovely blonde of seventeen dressed in silk and a feathered hat.

They dropped me at the Y.M.C.A., where I was billeted, and continued on to where he was President Wilson's nephew, a role that would be forgotten when they slipped into bed and merged their identities in mindless pleasure.

From the moment he appeared in the office of *Stars and Stripes*—located in the big, gloomy Hotel Saint Ann, not far from the Palais-Royal and the Louvre—Charles seemed in his natural habitat. In that easygoing atmosphere, where differences in rank were ignored and ability was the sole criterion of worth, he was released from the stigma of poverty and family background that in civilian life had made him unacceptable to the snobbish local establishment. The men on the staff liked him, respected him, and though he was somewhat reserved, often invited him out for drinks and poker at Nini's or to a play at the Odéon. Involved as he was with Ann Tyson, he generally declined in favor of joining her for walks along the boulevards, sipping aperitifs at sidewalk cafés, and, on weekends, spiriting her away to the countryside for marathon lovemaking in some quiet inn.

In the office he took hold immediately, aided by his experience on his school paper and some coaching from me. As he sat at one of our peculiar desks—cast-iron, marble-topped café tables—editing copy, writing, helping with makeup, one would think he was an old hand conscripted from the city room of a big-city daily. Still, he often seemed discontented, restless, a condition signified by frequent after-midnight pacings of the room he now shared with me at the Y.M.C.A.

He first expressed it to me when, accompanied by Ann, we stood on chairs in the Champs-Élysées cheering a parade celebrating the Fourth of July. An American brigade had just passed by, soldiers grinning, sun glinting from their helmets, rose petals showered by the throngs drifting from their erect shoulders. Then came the poilus, sternly proud, every bayonet flaunting a small American flag as they marched to the stirring rhythm of a band playing "Swords and Lances." Overhead, planes circled and looped, dropped cargoes of roses, zoomed down to send breezes whistling through the treetops. All around us people were weeping, and I found myself too choked up to do more than croak my jubilation.

Charles pointed to the disappearing backs of the American contingent. "Max," he shouted in my ear, "I want to go with them!"

At that moment so did I. But I said, "You've been there. You belong where you are."

"No, I belong at the front."

I thought for a minute that he was simply caught up in the frenzy of the crowd. But then, peering at him more closely and recalling his nightly jitters, I realized he had been seriously considering it for some time.

"You're not fit enough for combat," I said. He still favored his right leg and lowered himself gingerly into chairs.

"I'm fit enough to shoot a rifle and hurl a grenade."

Ann, who had been listening apprehensively, said, "So you want me to live in a trench. Very well, but don't expect breakfast in bed."

"I wouldn't be gone long," he said, smiling. "Another month, maybe sooner, and the war will be over." He touched her cheek. "Then we'll have *all* our meals in bed."

She kissed him, almost falling from her chair. "Who cares about eating? But honestly, darling, don't even talk about leaving. It gives me the shudders."

"You could be another Elsie Janis—come up and entertain the troops."

"You're the only troop I want to entertain."

I wondered if he was as much in love with her as she with him. I had to doubt it. Still vivid in my mind was the image of that haggard youth who had informed me miserably over lunch that Sharon Fletcher was getting married. We had never mentioned her name, and I took his silence to mean that the wound was still tender. Thus I never revealed my correspondence with Sharon, her letters aglow with the delights of marriage and motherhood.

There was, I thought, a way to appease Charles's urge to return to action and still keep him stationed in Paris. All of us on the staff were granted passes to the front lines, and in quieter days we would pile into our car with its General Staff insignia and make a festive weekend of touring the trenches. That had stopped when the Germans mounted their great offensive, but now that they were retreating, it seemed reasonably safe to assign a reporter to cover the Allied advance. I discussed it with the editors, pointing out that the logical choice would be a young man who combined newspaper training with battlefield experience. Their answering smiles were indulgent, sardonic—I was known as Charles's godfather—and affirmative.

"Charles, you have just been officially appointed our correspondent at the front."

He looked up quizzically from his marble-topped table. "You mean I can visit the HQs and watch the generals play pinochle?"

"You can go anywhere you like."

"You're not kidding? I can cover the guys who are doing the shooting?"

"You can. But you'll have to get there on your own."

"Max, if I were a Frenchman, I'd kiss both your cheeks."

"Do it to Ann," I said.

Ann failed to share his enthusiasm. She could not believe, as Charles did, that the German armies had been mortally wounded. They would, she feared, regroup as they so often had in the past and lash back with a shattering counteroffensive. Charles, annoyed, dismissed her pessimism as the ravings of a would-be

Cassandra who should stick to dispensing coffee and doughnuts. And he was off to the front.

He had no trouble getting there. Weighted down with knapsack and bedroll, a mess kit, canteen, and shovel dangling from his belt, he would stand at the side of the road and hitch a ride from a staff car, a transport truck, an ambulance, or, in some cases, hike to the railroad yards and join the troops moving north in the filthy boxcars they called "side-door Pullmans." Arriving in a combat area, he would bed down with the doughboys, track them to enemy trenches and machine-gun nests, dive with them into ravines to dodge whistling shells. In his first week he filed enough stories to fill a whole edition, prompting a flood of letters, one infantryman stating "Charles Dain is the voice of the A.E.F.!"

It was an accurate assessment. Charles did not write the polished prose so admired by the press back home. His sentences were short and rough. His words spoke the language of the filthy, cootie-ridden men sweating on the battlefields. His tone was unsophisticated, sometimes sophomoric, an echo of what was in the hearts and minds of frightened youths determined to be brave. Coming back to the office a day or so later with a fistful of copy, he would say, "If an editor cleans this up, he's a traitor to the troops." He would smile, but everyone knew he was serious; and there was very little editing.

He was at the front on July fifteenth when Ann Tyson, like Cassandra, was proved right. The Germans struck back with overwhelming force in the second battle of the Marne.

When several days went by and Charles failed to appear, I requisitioned the staff car and, accompanied by an orderly, drove to where the fighting had been most intense. Never had I imagined such carnage. Men without legs or arms lay dead in shell holes or at the side of the road. Others, the severely wounded, were stacked into trucks and ambulances. Abandoned equipment was everywhere. Huge craters defaced the flattened landscape, with only an occasional stripped and blackened tree to suggest that this had been a land of farms and orchards. Command posts had been vacated, and we could find no central point of information that might have word of Charles's whereabouts. We were reduced to asking passing soldiers, stunned, disoriented youths, who would stare at us with glazed eyes, shake their heads, and continue plodding toward the rear. When darkness fell, we returned to Paris, intending to come back the next day.

Entering my office, I found Ann there alone, sitting at my desk. She rose tensely and peered into my face.

"Not a word, Ann. I'm sorry. But tomorrow we'll drive back and—"

"No, Max, you can't go back." She sank wearily into the chair. "Only essential military traffic will be allowed to the front. Everything else has been stopped. Captain Ross got the order this afternoon."

"I'll speak to him. Maybe we can be made an exception."

"I asked him that. He said absolutely not."

I took her out for a drink at a nearby sidewalk café. It was even more packed than usual, and we had to wait with a garrulous, gesticulating crowd outside the low hedge. Everywhere I looked I saw newspapers, and behind them elderly men and women with avid faces.

When we were finally seated, Ann looked around and shook her head sadly. "They're reading France's obituary," she said.

I said nothing, knowing that in her mind the obituary was for Charles. We ordered cognac, and when it was served, she made no move to pick it up.

"I knew I'd lose him," she said. "But not like this."

"Stop it, Ann. You're not going to lose him."

She smiled wryly. "Oh, yes, I will. Even if he comes back, I'll lose him."

I stirred uncomfortably. "Now, why would you think that?"

"Because"—she clasped her glass, then gave me a direct look—"I doubt if any girl could keep Charles for long."

"Ann, you're upset. Tomorrow you'll feel—"

"No, I've known it all along. But I really can't complain. He's given me all he can—his charm, his humor, a feeling of excitement."

"Well, then—"

She downed her cognac. "Everything but himself," she said.

I avoided a response by sipping my drink. What she had said was true, I thought.

"Max, is there a girl back home?"

Again, I evaded. "Has he ever mentioned anyone?"

"No, but of course he wouldn't. If there was one, you'd know it, wouldn't you?"

"Back home I hardly ever saw Charles," I said. "We didn't even live in the same state."

"But he'd have talked to you about her."

"He's never even referred to another girl since he's been here," I said. "Only you."

"Then I guess there isn't one. But there are times when he acts like a man who's engaged, even married, and I'm the girl he cheats with when he's out of town."

She gave a short laugh. "So much for woman's intuition."

I glanced at the surrounding tables, distracted by the incessant babbling. People were shouting in each other's faces, slapping at their newspapers, raising their glasses in toasts. A man whose chair pressed against mine got up to leave, dropping his paper on the seat. I reached over, fetched it, and studied the headline. Despite my limited French I instantly translated the big black type: ALLIES FORCE GERMAN RETREAT!

Once again the tide had turned. I could only hope that Charles was riding the crest.

This time there seemed no stopping the Allied armies. From Château-Thierry north, French and American troops were devastating the western flank of the German line, forcing the enemy to run for the Aisne to escape capture. Twelve American divisions had stormed into action, and the British were preparing for a drive along the Somme.

And still no word of Charles, despite our constant inquiries to commanders in the field. He had been missing for six days when, sick with worry, I decided to defy orders, commandeer the staff car, and drive alone to the front.

I took off well before dawn and reached the front just after sunrise. The scene had changed dramatically. There were still the mutilated fields and the cadavers of solitary trees, but now the area had been cleared of dead bodies and wasted equipment, and the vehicles bumping along the pitted road were heading *north*. The sharpest contrast was in the men moving up in single file along the embankments. They wore fresh uniforms, stood erect, and marched with purposeful strides, grinning and waving at me as I jolted by. Overpowering the smell of cordite and the lingering stench of decomposed flesh was the sweet scent of victory.

I managed to visit three command posts, but without success. In fact, the officers regarded me almost with astonishment, as though incredulous that I should be so concerned about one missing person, who wasn't even an infantryman, when up ahead hundreds of thousands were drenching the earth with their blood.

Taking a back road toward my fourth stop, I soon found myself isolated from the movement of troops. Suddenly I came upon a rolling hill of green farmland with white-washed fences and a trim little house nestled in a grove of shade trees—an idyllic enclave that somehow had escaped the ravages of war. I pulled over, got out my map, and after careful calculations concluded I was lost. Hoping that the farmer could set me straight, I drove up the narrow lane to the house and parked in the courtyard. A middle-aged woman with a strong peasant face and a sturdy body was drawing water from a well. I walked over and started to explain my predicament.

She smiled and gave a helpless shrug. "No *anglais*," she said.

"No *anglais*?" I said stupidly.

"No *anglais*." Still smiling, she yanked up a huge brimming bucket, set it on the ground, and wiped her hands on her long, billowing skirt.

Defeated by English, I tried my fractured French. Smile intact, she shook her head, then gazed beyond me and fluttered her hand. Turning, I saw another woman, younger perhaps, and certainly prettier than this one, emerging from the house.

"Come," said my companion, and she hefted the bucket and stalked on ahead before I could offer my help. Apparently the woman from the house spoke my native tongue.

She was gazing back at my staff car, visibly impressed, when I came up. She smiled, showing even, white teeth, said, "Hello, Lieutenant," and beckoned me to come inside. The other woman preceded us through the door and excused herself to lug her burden into what I assumed was the kitchen.

We sat in the small living room, furnished with solid, burnished pieces that looked as if they had been in the family for generations. Her name, she said, was Yvonne, and the woman who had toted the water was Danielle. They were sisters, Yvonne a widow who had lost her husband several years ago at Verdun, Danielle a spinster who had lived here all her life with their parents, both now dead.

All this Yvonne conveyed in English that was little better than my French. I got down to business, explaining that I was lost and was looking for an American unit fighting somewhere to the east. She took my map and was puzzling over it when Danielle appeared and whispered something in her ear. Yvonne's eyebrows arched, then joined in thought. She smiled and nodded. Danielle gave me a friendly look and returned to the kitchen. Apparently I was to be treated to food and wine.

Yvonne handed back the map, saying with a sigh and expressions of sorrow that she could be of no help. She rose and invited me into the kitchen, where, she said, her sister had prepared something that should please me. Weary, thirsty, hungry, I was delighted to follow her into a large room redolent of soup, fresh-baked bread, vintage wine. Danielle was not there, but I could hear her moving about outside the back door.

Yvonne led me to the door, smiled mischievously, and drew it open. Curious, I looked first at her, then out to where I half expected to find Danielle ceremoniously presenting me with a few fresh-laid eggs. Instead, to my astonishment, she was standing on a milking stool just beyond the porch. Gripped in her upheld hands was the big oaken bucket, now tilted to flood its contents into a pail suspended from a rafter extending from the roof. The bottom of the pail had been punched with holes, thus creating an improvised shower.

Below the shower, reveling in the downpour and a lather of soap, was a naked man. As the women burst into laughter, he turned and grinned at me.

"Max, would you please get me a towel," Charles said.

The wine flowed like a multitude of rivers, endlessly descending to our glasses from gallon jugs poured by the sisters as we sat in the kitchen at a long, planked table. My initial shock—confusing me with an urge either to kiss him or kill him—had turned to pure relief, progressing rapidly to elation, and now, to hilarity. Charles had spotted me from an upstairs window as I drove up, a sight that inspired his creative mind to contrive our unlikely meeting. He had arrived by chance at the farm the previous morning, face stubbled, body reeking of sweat, uniform and boots crusted with mud. And now he sat beside me freshly shaved, smelling of soap, uniform cleaned and pressed, boots sparkling—services eagerly rendered by his smiling hostesses.

"Don't tell me they think you're Wilson's nephew," I said.

"No, I played it on the level. Well, not quite. I said I was editor-in-chief of *S. and S.*"

"You'll be lucky if Ross doesn't bust you to private and sock you with permanent latrine duty."

"When he sees what I've got, he'll pin a medal on me."

He had been all over the front, dodging bullets and shells as he crawled on his belly to interview riflemen, machine gunners, artillery men, men in tanks and holes and field hospitals. From the pockets of his tunic he pulled out stained and wrinkled batches of copy, slapped them on the table, and said, "Max, there's the *real* war!", then reached across, patted the shoulders of our jubilant allies, and shouted, "*Vive la France!*"

Between all the jokes and laughter and tales of battles, I managed to comprehend the reasons for his prolonged absence. They all boiled down to one thing: his immersion in the conflict was so complete that he had become oblivious of time, unaware that there was any other world than the one inhabited by courageous men who every moment lived with death. He was like an actor playing the greatest role of his life, to whom the sets, the dialogue, the people on stage have become the only reality, while the outside world is dimly perceived as the illusion. He was dumbfounded when I told him that he had been missing for more than six days.

"Oh, no, Max. Two days, maybe three."

"Six. I'll prove it when we get back."

"Back? No, no, I'm not going back. No reason to, now that you're here."

"You know I can't stay."

"Course not. You can deliver my stories and I'll catch up with the troops."

"Charles, Ann is terribly worried. You're not being fair to her."

"Ann?" he said, as though the name were unfamiliar.

"Yes, Ann Tyson. She cares a lot about you. We all do. We need you in Paris." I felt as though I were reasoning with a lunatic.

"Ann," he said again. "I'd like to see her face when you tell her about me."

"You'll see it, because you're the one who'll tell her."

He started to speak, then stopped and appeared to meditate. His dark eyes began to glow, and a smile seemed to tug at his lips. I guessed what was in his mind: Charles Dain, fearless war correspondent, veteran of the fighting that broke the German resistance; Charles Dain, returning to Paris to accept the awed admiration of a surrogate for Sharon.

"It's getting dark," I said. "We ought to get started."

Yvonne sprang up and refilled his glass. He looked up at her and smiled as she gazed at him steadily.

"Let's leave in the morning," he said.

I spent the night alone in a corner bedroom. It was a fitful sleep, interrupted frequently by wild laughter coming from the opposite end of the hall, laughter that dwindled into small cries of ecstasy as Charles reimbursed Yvonne, the widow of Verdun, for her great hospitality.

We arrived back in Paris the next afternoon. Charles's dalliance with Yvonne had apparently been therapeutic —a reminder perhaps that there was as much fascination in earthly delights as in the delirium of war—and he seemed eager to resume his former ways.

We stopped first at the canteen where Ann worked,

and at the sight of him she broke into tears and threw herself bodily into his arms, much to the consternation of nearby soldiers, who considered Red Cross girls the army's equivalent of nuns.

At the office Charles received a hero's welcome, restrained by the arrival of Captain Ross, who demanded to know just who the hell Dain thought he was, and why, goddammit, did he have the gall to think he wouldn't be court-martialed? Charles's answer was that he had been trapped with a beleaguered unit cut off from the main body of troops, and it had been impossible to get transportation to the rear. The fact that this enthralling episode was nowhere mentioned in his dispatches was overlooked by Ross once he had read them. "Jesus," he muttered, and from habit picked up his pencil. Then he threw it down, stood up, and tossed the mutilated sheets to a copy editor. "Give it the whole paper," he said, and stalked out.

The next day Ross posted a notice reminding the staff of the order prohibiting travel to the front. That was his only reprimand for my unauthorized rescue mission, and a warning to Charles that henceforth he was confined to Paris.

During that late summer and fall, as we languished through routine assignments and enjoyed the pleasures of the magnificent city, the Allied armies catapulted ahead. On August eighth the British unleashed its forces in a drive along the Somme, taking tens of thousands of prisoners and forcing the Germans into full retreat. The Americans then cut off the Saint-Mihiel salient, stormed through the Argonne Forest, and battled northward along the Meuse from Verdun to Sedan. And as the staggering blows continued, Germany's allies—Bulgaria, Turkey, Austria-Hungary—surrendered one by one.

Then, with its armies facing total destruction, Germany's home front yielded to strikes, riots, mutinies, and collapsed. The German rulers requested an armistice, which the Allied governments, quarreling among themselves over the harsh terms, took more than a month to agree upon. Finally a German delegation crossed the lines to where Marshal Foch's traveling railroad car stood in a forest near Compiègne. At daybreak on November eleventh the Germans signed. Six hours later, at eleven A.M., the guns were silenced.

At last our dream of home could be turned into reality. Charles, however, had other ideas.

One evening in early December I entered our Y.M.C.A. room and found him lying on his bed staring moodily at the ceiling.

"I just got my orders," I said. "I leave in ten days."

"Congratulations." His tone was anything but congratulatory.

"Don't let it get you down, Charles. Yours should be coming through any time now."

"No, they won't." He gave me a small smile.

"Stop talking nonsense."

He sat up and swung his feet to the floor. "Max, I'm not going back."

"What!"

"I understand the paper will continue to publish. The generals think they'll need it more than ever, for the occupation troops. So I'm staying on."

"Have you told this to Ann?"

"Yes, a little while ago."

"How did she take it?"

"I was surprised. She acted as though she'd known it all along. Anyway, she's leaving the first of the week—back to Michigan." He smiled. "That will give us one more weekend in the country."

After Ann Tyson left Paris, she never again saw Charles Dain.

As for me, seven years would pass before he re-entered—and uprooted—my life.

Chapter · 8

It was nine P.M. when Terry Donovan left the Algonquin Hotel. He thought of going home to catch a nap before meeting Kate Richards at midnight, but tense as he was from the search of Max Wills's rooms, he knew that sleep would be impossible. He decided to return to the *Express*, dig through the files in the morgue, and see if he could turn up anything on Charles Dain that might somehow have a bearing on the shooting.

He knew those files had been consulted innumerable times by editors and reporters assigned to write and update Dain's obituary. As with most famous men, Dain's death notice had been written long before and was kept standing in type, ready, at the mortal moment, for immediate publication in the *Express* and dissemination to other papers and the wire services. Chances were there was nothing that would provide even the slightest clue to the publisher's assailant, but after the surprise of seeing a youthful Charles Dain with a stunning girl among Wills's snapshots, Donovan thought it worth a try.

Joe Altman, head of the morgue—or, more formally,

the library—was at his desk behind the counter when Donovan walked in. Altman was a short, round-shouldered man with stubby legs and a melonlike paunch accommodated by an unbuttoned vest. Beneath sparse gray hair, combed horizontally to veil his scalp, his bespectacled face, once full and ruddy, was gaunt and pale, a transformation induced by a creeping cancer that had required the excision of half his stomach and part of his lower bowel. He was sixty-seven years old and had worked for Charles Dain ever since the *Express* had started, serving as Sunday editor until drained of energy by his illness. Dain had then assigned him to his present job, on a part-time basis but without cutting the salary he had been paid as editor. Even without this benefaction Joe Altman would have doggedly remained a Dain loyalist, ready at any time to do battle for his boss. He and Donovan had become extracurricular students of crime, mutual admirers, and occasional confidants, a relationship encouraged by Donovan's constant forays into the files for material that could be converted into salable magazine stories,

Altman leaned back in his rocker, his face pale-blue under the overhead tubes of fluorescent light, and smiled at his visitor. "What's it this time, Terry? Hatchet murder, strangling, or just a nice, neat, poison job?"

"It seems there's been a shooting, Joe." Donovan looked apologetic as Altman winced. "I thought I'd have a look through the boss's file."

"Why not? Everybody else has."

"You mean the guys handling the obit?"

"And a few others. Max Wills, Kate Richards—"

"Kate? Why would she—"

"Looking for an item, she said. She must've come up

empty, because there's nothing in her column except a tribute." He grimaced. "Thank God it's not his epitaph. I just got word he's still with us."

There was nothing extraordinary about Max Wills and Kate Richards checking the file. Max would want to make sure there was nothing there that could smear Dain's reputation, and Kate's search for column material was simply a matter of doing her job. Sure as hell her competition would have read every last paragraph their papers had clipped on Dain, regretting only that their files were much less complete than the *Express*'s. Still, Donovan felt an uneasiness. During his brief investigation, he had twice been confronted by pressures from Max and Kate—their concerted attempt to enforce a vacation, their ridicule of his theory that a woman might be involved. Could their obstructiveness have anything to do with their familial closeness, revealed by the snapshots taken in Kate's infancy and foreordained by her mother's premarital friendship with Max?

The picture of Max and Kate's beautiful mother posed affectionately beside a black flivver sprang to his mind. Then the almost identical pose, this time with Max replaced by a youth who was darkly handsome and rather debonair, his smile magnetic, a forerunner of—the words demanded repetition—the handsome, debonair, magnetic Charles Dain that Donovan had met in maturity.

Walking to a bank of file cabinets, Donovan recalled that Dain had been among the first troops to land in France in 1917 and had remained in Europe until some time in 1924—an absence of about seven years. Given that long a hiatus, not to mention his sudden ascent to the world of the rich, it was probable that he had not renewed his acquaintance with the woman to whom Max was apparently so devoted. In that case, it could be assumed that Dain had not met Kate until she began her summer work for the paper. That would have been perhaps five, maybe six year ago, when Kate had been nineteen or twenty, a fully-ripened, remarkably attractive young woman—almost a replica of her mother as an adolescent, Donovan thought—who might not have considered herself too young to accept the advances of a vigorous man in his late thirties, which at that time was about the age of Charles Dain.

The thought caused Donovan to recoil from a rolled-out file drawer as though it had delivered an electric charge. From the desk near the counter, he heard Joe Altman's startled voice—"Find something, Terry?"—and with an effort gave his head a negative shake while flapping a hand in dismissal.

Thumbing through the folders, seeing only familiar stories and photos, his mind, acting independently of his will, formed a frightening scenario linking Kate intimately to the famous publisher. Perhaps at their first meeting Charles Dain had seen in the lovely Kate Richards another target for his compulsive philandering and had seduced her. But this time Dain, who had established himself as a faithful, loving husband, had found himself deeply enamored—and with a girl working in his own office—requiring him to meet Kate in some secret hideaway—the town house on East Sixty-third Street. In such a situation it would have been Dain, not Max, who was chiefly responsible for her amazing progress on the *Express*, with Max acting as the doting, unsuspecting front man.

Having tortured himself with that hypothesis, Donovan could not avoid carrying it on to a sickening conclusion. Dain, once a notably fickle lover, had eventually tired of Kate and, as recently as the other night, had decided on a way of letting her down easily. Why not meet her at the town house and, after a physical demonstration of love, tell her that his wife had become suspicious, and they must stop seeing each other for a while? Then, by degrees, he would end the affair, and she, fearful of losing her prestigious job, would quietly withdraw.

So he had telephoned her from the Stork Club, arranged a meeting at the town house, then taken a taxi there to await her arrival. Kate—willful, headstrong, aggressive—had, perhaps intuitively, anticipated his purpose and in desperation had prepared herself to block it, even if it meant . . .

No! Even if all else that his mind had constructed were true, it was inconceivable that Kate Richards could have shot Charles Dain.

Still . . .

Considering the all-night hours required by her job, it was not unlikely that Kate would have carried a gun as protection against assault. If so she might simply have threatened Dain and, during a struggle, accidentally squeezed the trigger, uncontrollably firing three shots. Or she might have pointed the gun at herself, threatening suicide, with the same result. Or she might have been brutalized and shot him in self-defense.

Crazy, Donovan told himself, absolutely crazy—the fantastic inventions of a tunnel-visioned reporter turned paranoid by constantly writing about crime and consorting with criminals. Yet even as he chided himself, another thought rushed in to support his thesis. Last night with Kate!

How suddenly and brazenly she had taken him to her

bed. How wildly uninhibited she had been. And this with a man who, though initially an aspiring lover, had settled into the role of platonic companion.

Why this abrupt and astonishing turnabout? Was it because, having been rejected by Dain in such traumatic circumstances, she desperately needed the comfort and love of a trusted friend? Or was there a sinister reason? Did she think that by claiming him as her lover she could avert suspicion that she had been Dain's mistress? Did she also think that she could then manipulate Donovan's investigation?

And what about Max Wills? If he had learned about her affair with his best friend, he must know or suspect she had shot him. How else explain his rigid position— shared with Kate—that it was the work of gangsters, and his transparent desire—also shared with Kate—to relieve Donovan of the assignment? Torn as Max would be by his divided loyalties, his paternal affection for Kate, seen as a trusting girl exploited unconscionably by Dain, might demand that he protect her in the hope that Dain would recover and mercifully absolve her.

Donovan blew out a long breath. Soap opera, he decided, and no more convincing. The question-and-answer exercise he had just endured was merely his habitual game of "What if . . ."—always a prelude to his creation of crime fiction. Some day he might develop it into a gaudy thriller and sell it to the pulps.

Meanwhile he had flipped through the file and been reminded by the clips that Charles Dain was a man of impeccable virtue.

"Nothing?" Joe Altman said.

"Nothing," Terry said. "Great stuff for a eulogy at Saint Pat's, but nothing for a guy playing detective."

Altman squinted an eye, stretching his pallid skin

tight across sharp cheekbones. "Looking for something in particular?"

"Well, yes and no."

"What's that mean?"

Donovan considered him warily, recalling that Joe Altman regarded Charles Dain as his personal deity. "Joe, if I told you, you'd be offended."

Altman thought about that, removing his glasses with one hand, patting his paunch with the other. "What you're saying is that you're after something that could make Charles look bad."

"That's about it."

Altman returned his glasses to his bony nose and glared at Donovan through the thick lenses. "Terry, I wouldn't give a hoot in hell if it made him look bad— that could be covered—provided it turned up the son of a bitch who shot him."

"Son of a bitch? That says you think it's a man."

"Okay, include just plain bitch, if that'll satisfy you." Altman's eyebrows shot up. "So, that's it. You suspect a woman did it."

"I think it's possible. But I seem to be the only one who's given it a thought."

"No, you're not. I thought of that myself, even mentioned it to Max Wills."

"What did he say?"

"Not much. Looked at me like I'd lost my marbles and said, 'Preposterous!'"

"Anything in particular make you think of a woman?"

"Well, you know as well as I do that years ago Charles was a bit of a rounder. Nothing scandalous, just a young fellow with a few wild oats left in him. So naturally I thought of that."

"And that's what you brought up to Max?"

"Hell, I didn't have a chance to bring up anything. He just walked into his office and shut the door." Altman's emaciated face lengthened in a wounded look. Then he frowned in thought, flexed his jaw, and gazed up determinedly at Donovan. "Okay, Terry, I guess you want to know what I'd've told Max."

Donovan sat down. "I do if it will help break this thing."

"It may not be worth a damn. But here it is." Altman folded his arms across his flimsy chest. "A few days before he was shot Charles asked me to his office to discuss a proposal I'd written up—a new system to increase the efficiency of the library. When I got there he was on the phone, and I waited outside the door. His back was to me and he was talking to a woman and—"

"You heard him say her name?"

"No, he never once mentioned it. But I knew it was a woman because of the conversation. He said a few things I didn't catch—I wasn't *trying* to listen—and then I heard him say he'd meet her at the house."

"He could have meant his house in Mount Kisco. In that case the woman would probably be his wife."

"I guess that's what I assumed. So it didn't bother me at all to listen. But then he told her to take a taxi, and he'd be along as soon as possible. So he obviously wasn't talking to Harriet, but I didn't think about that until later. I was too surprised by what he said next." Altman paused and his magnified eyes narrowed as he thought back. "I can recall his exact words," he said.

"Love stuff?"

"Not like you'd think. He said, 'Darling, I've got a fashion tip for you—the way I'd like you to look when I arrive.'"

"You think he meant naked?"

"That crossed my obscene mind. But then she must have asked what he meant, because he said, half laughing, 'One of those ravishing creations you keep in the closet.'"

Donovan felt his chest tighten, the feeling, he thought, of a hunter closing in on hidden prey. "Something sexy," he said. "Black lace and slits and—"

"Please," Altman said in pretended alarm. "You'll have me fogging up my glasses. But sure—what else? Anyway, that was it. I backed off, waited a minute after he'd hung up, then walked in."

"And you have no idea who the woman might have been?"

"None. Just some passing fancy, I guess. But maybe she didn't like that passing part and—"

"But the clothes in the closet. That doesn't suggest a quickie romance. Wait a minute—there weren't any clothes in the closet, not those kind. All the cops found were some odds and ends left by previous guests."

Altman smiled. "I was afraid for a minute you'd miss that. I figured it out, so don't work your brain over it. What could have happened was that right after Charles was shot, the shooter cleared out all those 'ravishing creations.' Probably had a suitcase there, so it was no big trick."

Nodding, Donovan lit a cigarette. "Then she hit a pay phone and called the cops, pretending she was an innocent bystander who'd heard some shots."

"That's how I figured it. But let's not forget this is just a guessing game."

"Keep playing, Joe."

"Sure. A very thoughtful lady. She even left the door

unlocked so the law wouldn't have to waste time breaking in. Damned good thing she did, because another few minutes and Charles would've—"

"Hold it! Just—hold it—right there—Joe."

"I said something good?"

Donovan's eyes tracked the smoke curling from his cigarette. "I think so. Before, you said that Dain asked her to take a taxi to the house and he'd be along later. I can't see him leaving the door unlocked for her, not in this town. So she must have had her own key."

"Or Charles had the only key but loaned it to her, knowing she'd be the first one there."

"I doubt it. If she kept clothes in the closet, chances are she'd been around for quite a while. My hunch is he had a duplicate made for her."

"Makes sense." Altman grinned. "Now all you've got to do is find a mystery woman who has a key to Charles's town house."

And who had a gun, thought Donovan.

Stopping at his apartment, Donovan phoned Jackie at the hospital and got the usual report—no change. But then she added, "Mrs. Dain's been trying to reach you, Terry. Shall I put her on?"

"Fine."

He waited, his thoughts not on Dain's wife but on Kate Richards. Just how was he supposed to handle himself when he met her at midnight? Sure, he'd dismissed all his speculations about her as unbridled fantasies, but he still could not quite scrub from his mind a residual suspicion.

"Terry?"

"Hello, Mrs. Dain." Though he had seen her fairly

often over the years, he could never bring himself to call this aloof, almost imperious woman Harriet. At first meeting he had suspected why her husband often felt compelled to go elsewhere for his sexual pleasure.

"Terry, I know you're assigned to this awful thing that's happened to Charles. I've been wondering if you've made any progress."

"I'm afraid not—no more than you've read in the *Express*."

"Which is very little. I thought you might have some ideas of your own."

"None that makes any sense, Mrs. Dain."

"Except, of course, the one the police are pursuing— that it was the work of gangsters?"

Donovan hesitated before saying, "They've got a good case for it. I don't have to tell you how Charles— the *Express*—has kept the heat on them. Outside of organized crime, I don't think he has any violent enemies."

"Then you agree with the police?"

He felt cornered. "I agree they're doing the right thing. But I'm trying to keep an open mind. There's always the chance that some nut with an imagined grudge decided to play God."

"Yes, I've read of people like that." She paused and he heard a metallic sound, like the flick of a cigarette lighter. "Terry, I'd appreciate it very much if you'd keep me informed."

"I will, whenever possible."

"You'll please *make* it possible." Her voice had abruptly taken on a sharp edge. "Let there be no misunderstanding. I want nothing published that could in any way discredit my husband."

She rang off before he could express his sympathy. He wondered if Max Wills had said something to her that had fueled her protective instincts. Max would not, of course, have mentioned Donovan's theory that a woman might be involved, but it was reasonable to assume he would suggest prior scrutiny of any significant material. Harriet Dain, her suspicions already aroused by her husband's use of the town house, would interpret such advice as a warning of a possible adulterous relationship.

That suspicion, thought Donovan, must be almost as excruciating as the prospect of Charles's death. It was well known that she worshiped him, thought him infallible, lavished her wealth on him—and at the same time, as the sole owner of the *Express*, held him in her financial grip. True, if she ever left him, Charles's personal savings and investments, made possible by his huge salary and even larger bonuses, would still make him a rich man. But not rich like his wife, who had the resources to buy outright control of great corporations, not rich enough to start another newspaper, the only profession Charles Dain considered worthwhile. Without his wife, he probably could never again be the absolute ruler of any sizable enterprise: instead he would have to take his orders from a board of directors and a multitude of stockholders. But Donovan doubted that his wife would ever let it come to that. Enthralled as she was, she'd probably hang on to him even if it meant degrading herself by having to battle a predatory woman.

"Darling," said Kate Richards as she opened the door, "I just got here a few minutes ago and"—she gave Donovan a sighing kiss—"and the ice is out, and all the fascinating bottles, and I'm about to take a shower."

He smiled at her, feeling his anxieties about her dissolve. Absurd that this lovely blond creature, looking so girlish in her green-satin party dress, could possibly be the calculating adventuress who had deranged his thoughts.

"Have a drink with me first," he said.

"Well, all right, but you may have to carry me to the shower. I permitted my drunken friends to buy me a few too many."

He was mildly disappointed. He had hoped that the intensity of her eyes, her flushed cheeks, her loose, seductive smile were due entirely to his presence. "I'll make yours light," he said.

Sitting beside her on the off-white sofa, tall Scotches in hand, he was aware of a sudden mutual tension. He rationalized it by thinking that they needed time to adjust to a new social relationship after the tempestuous union of last night, an event that perhaps made her reluctant to speak of the merry wastrels she had just left lest he feel excluded and therefore resentful. Finally, after a flurry of minuscule talk, he brought it up himself, simply as an entry to easy conversation.

"How was it with the glitterati tonight?" he said.

She seemed to relax. "Read about it in my column tomorrow. Of course you might have to look for it in the sports pages."

"Okay, you've hooked me. Now give me a preview."

"There was a fight. We'd just piled out of the Club Eighteen when this gang of hoodlums came along and started yelling at us. You know—'Don't you know there's a war on?' 'Back the attack, drink more champagne'—that sort of thing. We ignored them, which was all they needed to get really nasty. The four-letter words started flying and, in no time, so were the fists. It seems that a couple of men in our party decided to prove their manhood. Oh, it was a mess."

"Anyone hurt?"

"Just a few black eyes and fattened lips. The cops came, and pretty soon the paddy wagon, and the hoodlums were carted off. I'd say they're now enrolled in the Tombs."

Donovan looked at her, a thought teasing his mind. "I hope you kept out of it."

"With great aplomb. While the battle raged I went back into the bar and had another drink."

"My fearless Kate."

"Not really. I was scared to death."

"These hours you keep—out on the streets late at night—I'd think you'd be scared half the time."

"Just sometimes—when the mad menagerie goes on to another watering hole, and I'm left alone."

"You should have some protection."

"I do." She jerked up her knee.

"I mean a gun." Noting her startled look, he added lightly, "A nifty little pearl-handled number set with diamonds."

She smiled but was silent.

"I'm serious, Kate. No problem getting one. All you have to do is register it." He swallowed some Scotch. "Which reminds me—that's my boring project for tomorrow. I've got to go through the records and check out every twenty-five caliber handgun registered in New York. It could turn up someone Dain knew who might have a motive."

She stared at him, then gave a sudden, brittle laugh. "Stop when you reach Kate Richards."

His eyebrows shot up. "You mean you do have a gun?"

She placed her glass down carefully, stood up, and stretched. "Not anymore. But I did have one, back when I was the new kid on the beat and was afraid of the dark. I got rid of it. I knew that if I was ever attacked, I'd end up shooting myself in the foot."

He wondered what she had done with it and how long ago, but he was wary of pushing the ploy any further. Besides, why would she tell him anything that she knew might incriminate her?

"Maybe that was the smart thing," he said. "Anyway, try never to be alone."

"Good advice. Then you'll join me in the shower?"

He tilted his glass. "I'll stand guard and await the result."

She left him, saying, "The result will be fantastic."

He sat for a few minutes, gazing into his depleted Scotch, not drinking, then went and stood just outside the bedroom. He heard the rush of the shower behind the mirrored bathroom door, followed by the sound of splashing. Quickly he turned back, going to a glass-topped end table, and picked up her small, sequined evening purse. Opening it and reaching inside, his fingers touched metal, which, when withdrawn and held in his palm, proved to be three keys attached to an ostrich-leather tab. They were of different sizes—the small one apparently for her lobby mailbox, the medium-size one shaped like a conventional door key, the large one looking like it was made for a room in an old hotel.

He stepped to the front door, opened it silently, and

inserted the medium-size key into the lock. He gave it a slow twist and the lock turned. Returning to the table, he paused to hold between thumb and forefinger the large, old-fashioned key—about the same vintage, he thought, as a brownstone town house.

He was standing, bending to make another drink, when she swept in, and at the sight of her all other considerations vanished. She was draped in a diaphanous negligee the color of her blond hair, the netlike fabric revealing glimpses of all he had possessed the night before.

"My exercising outfit," she said, grinning.

He started toward her.

She slunk past and picked up the full glasses. "Let's take them to the gym," she said, and pranced toward the bedroom.

It was not until morning—while she still slept and he was going out the front door—that he thought about the oddly shaped key and the gun she claimed she had discarded.

Chapter · 9

DEAR MAX STOP WELCOME HOME EXCLAMATION
POINT DYING TO SEE YOU EXCLAMATION POINT
CALL SOONEST AND WE'LL CELEBRATE EXCLAMA-
TION POINT LOVE AND HAPPY NEW YEAR EXCLA-
MATION POINT SHARON

The telegram was dated December 30, 1918, and was
handed to me by the desk clerk at the Murray Hill
Hotel four days later, January 3, 1919. I had written to
Sharon before leaving Paris telling her I was on my way
and, with luck, should be home in time to raise a glass
to the New Year. But there had been the usual military
delays, and when the time came to sing "Auld Lang
Syne" I was lying on a canvas bunk aboard a packed
transport vessel gazing up at the depressed rump of an
officer sleeping above me.

I had been discharged that morning and had gone
directly to the hotel. The manager, with whom I used to
have an occasional drink, tactfully moved an elderly
couple from my old room and returned it to me, adding
a bottle of Mumm's Champagne, served by a waiter so

deferential—I was still in uniform—he must have thought I was Sergeant York promoted to captain. I decimated the champagne while soaking up to my collar bones in a hot bath, then exchanged my khakis for one of my nattier suits, kept in storage by the considerate management.

Eager as I was to see Sharon, I did not telephone her for several days. After the delightful shock of landing in New York, I was not quite ready to be enveloped by a family, two-thirds of whom were strangers to me. My most compelling desire—a nightly dream when lying in my bed at the Paris Y.M.C.A.—was simply to wander idly about the city and renew our acquaintance. After a few days of that I would return to the *American* where, I had been told before leaving, my old job would be waiting.

A lot of changes had occurred during the little more than a year I had been away. Most spectacular were the monumental tributes to the victorious doughboys—the huge, elaborately festooned plaster arch on Fifth Avenue at Madison Square; the shrine of pylons and palms, called the Court of the Heroic Dead, before the Public Library; and a few blocks north, the jeweled arch suspended above the Avenue between white pillars, illuminated at night by colored searchlights. Constantly there were parades, fed by the transports from Brest, steaming up New York Harbor, the jam-packed troops (invariably welcomed by Mayor Hylan's mustachioed secretary, Grover Whalen) formed into regiments and briskly marched up the flag-lined avenues while bands blared "The Long, Long Trail" and cheering throngs hurled confetti and ticker tape. Patriotic posters were everywhere, urging Americans to "Finish the Job" by

buying Victory Bonds, a plea many had to ignore because of the skyrocketing cost of living and mounting
unemployment.

Then there were the social changes. Strolling into the
lobby of a hotel in the late afternoon, I would often
hear the sound of a jazz band playing in the ballroom
for a tea dance. Looking in, I would sometimes be
pleasantly surprised by the sight of a couple kissing
rapturously behind a potted palm. Young women were
no longer the shy, demure creatures I remembered.
(Sharon Fletcher had been an exception.) As though
responding with a vengeance to President Wilson's
"New Freedom," all embellished their faces with powder, many with rouge, some even adding lipstick. Their
silk dresses, unencumbered by layers of cotton undergarments, now clung to their bodies and rose six inches
from the floor, revealing, not the expected high-laced
shoes and black stockings, but low pumps and sheer,
light-colored hose, generously exposed when the band
blasted out a hot fox-trot tempo.

It was as though the girls left behind by the fighting
Yanks had conspired to greet their heroes as mademoiselles from Armentières, every bit as seductive as the
fast-steppers that may have been encountered Over
There. Occasionally I would see a young lady who had
gone so far as to bob her hair, a style that nice people
usually associated with Greenwich Village radicals who
carried protest placards, practiced free love, and
smoked cigarettes. And yes, by God, some of them *were*
smoking cigarettes!

Twice I got drunk, a condition induced by a sense
of alienation and spasms of longing for the camaraderie
enjoyed on *Stars and Stripes.* Also I was indignant—as

were most returning soldiers—that the so-called Wartime Prohibition Law, passed by Congress in our absence, would take effect on the first of July. It seemed
only proper that we topers demonstrate against our
lawmakers by imbibing to the fullest before the maligned beverage was banished forever from the land.
However, after my second ferocious hangover, I decided it was time to return to work.

Fortunately the stigma of working for Mr. Hearst had
eased considerably, thanks to his vigorous support of
the war once we were in it and the amnesty granted by
hearts warm with victory. My appearance in the city
room was greeted by slaps on the back, shouts of "oo-la-
la," leering inquiries into the sex practices of my recent
Gallic hosts, and a desk decorated with red-white-and-
blue bunting. For the first time I felt I had truly come
home.

A few of the men I had known were no longer there.
One of them was George Fletcher. After his wife Edna
died, he had continued for a while to live in their old
house. Then, several months ago, he had sought or been
offered the job of assistant circulation manager of the
Philadelphia *Bulletin*. From what I could gather, he
was active in the Knights of Columbus and Democratic
politics, and rarely came to New York.

Hearing that, I overcame my reluctance to meet the
husband and daughter of the girl George was once so
determined I marry. I almost thought I had married her
when I telephoned her, heard her exultant cries of welcome, and was told to be on time that night for dinner.

"She's a beautiful child," I said to Tom Richards.
"Looks exactly like her mother."

"Doesn't she." Tom Richards smiled, and cast a fond look at Sharon and little Kate, hand in hand, disappearing down the hall. "Now if she'll just hold on to that until she's grown, she'll be a heartbreaker."

"She's already won mine," I said.

It was true. From the moment Kate had shaken my hand and chirped "Hi, Max"—unabashed by her father's mild protest at such familiarity—I was captivated. The attraction had appeared mutual, demonstrated when she followed me to my chair, caressed my bow tie, and then curled up in my lap and made a pet of my watch chain, which had been fashioned to resemble a skinny snake.

"She was ready for you," Tom Richards said. "Sharon's talked about you so often—even quoting from your letters—Kate feels you're an old friend." His smile broadened. "Just as I do."

"I feel the same way."

Again, it was true. One look at Tom Richards had been enough to dissolve my resistance to meeting him. He was of medium height, somewhat stocky, his face square and open, unlined cheeks ruddy, light-brown hair straight and parted on the side. I suppose most people would consider his good looks unmemorable, but to me they were vividly impressive, reminiscent of the faces of college athletes whose pictures in the sports pages I had so often envied. But it was his manner that was most affecting—an easy friendliness, an empathy, an uncritical acceptance of me as an individual—inspiring a sense of trust, an assurance that any revelation of my flaws would not risk condemnation.

He was twenty-three—almost four years older than Sharon—but seemed more mature than his years would indicate. The army had rejected him, to his regret, because of a mild heart murmur, which he claimed in no way impaired his ability to function normally.

Sharon had known him before she'd met Charles Dain—since she was a freshman in high school and Tom Richards a senior. He had been attracted to her then but had been discouraged both by her age—a mere fourteen at the time—and the severe restrictions imposed by her family. Later, when she was a junior, he saw her often on his trips home from Amherst, when he would take her to movie matinees, or on daytime drives, or to the local soda fountain. ("I was crazy about her," he said. "I wanted to marry her back then, but I was afraid her father would have me jailed for corrupting a minor.") His erratic courtship ended abruptly when, while he was away at college, she met and fell in love with Charles Dain.

He was aware of that episode and, shortly after I arrived, had not flinched when, during a mental lapse, I mentioned Charles's name while talking about *Stars and Stripes*.

"How is he?" Sharon asked, her expression calm.

"Just fine," I said. "He's staying over there for a while." I could not help glancing uneasily at her husband.

He detected my discomfort. Smiling tolerantly, he said, "I know about Charles Dain, so don't think it bothers me if you talk about him." He picked up a pipe and chewed for a moment on the stem. "Sounds like you and he are close friends. So why shouldn't you talk about him?"

He seemed to be protesting a bit too much. I looked at Sharon. She was regarding him with grateful affection. I quickly changed the subject. While it seemed obvious that the memory of Charles and Sharon as teenage sweethearts posed no threat to this marriage, my own melancholy recollections of their impassioned love made it a subject I preferred to avoid. I resolved never again to volunteer his name, just as I had refrained from speaking of Sharon to Charles.

Now, with Kate tucked into bed, Sharon reappeared to announce that dinner was served. Again I was struck by how little she had changed. Her blond hair, worn more loosely to curve across her cheeks, was still pinned into a bun. Her eyes, like luminous amethysts, still glowed with warmth and humor. Her complexion was still a tribute to good nutrition—we knew about calories but had yet to discover vitamins—and to the advertised wonders of Pears soap. And her figure, in its fashionably shortened skirt and snug aqua blouse, was as slim as when she was childless—and even more provocative. For an instant I had the feeling of being transformed into the credulous Max Wills who, long ago, had so briefly been convinced that Sharon Fletcher could be his.

All through dinner I was conscious of her devotion to her husband. While she was attentive to me—drawing me out about my wartime experiences, recalling the letters and snapshots we had exchanged—it was Tom who enjoyed her ardent interest. His most trivial remark was received by her as though it were the pronouncement of a sage. His slightest need—a glass of water—was anticipated and attended to with quiet dispatch. And when she would rise and pass him on the way to the kitchen, she would touch his shoulder or ruffle the short hair on his neck. Returning to his side, she would catch his glance, and her eyes would glimmer with what seemed a combination of love and loyalty and respect. Charles Dain, I thought, had simply been a girlish crush. This man, Tom Richards, was a lifetime partner. I was more determined than ever to keep this segment of my life entirely separate from anything I might share with Charles.

Tom was a fledgling engineer, working as an apprentice in the blueprint department of a huge firm specializing in plans for factories, pipelines, hydroelectric power plants, and many other industrial facilities. Meanwhile he was attending night school at Columbia, expecting one day to emerge with a master's degree in engineering.

"Once I've got that," he said, "we won't have to live in boxes like these."

It was an apt description. The rooms were small, square, and low-ceilinged, and would have been oppressive had Sharon not made generous use of colorful chintz and an assortment of indoor plants.

"I'm very happy here," she said. "Where else could we find a place with a grocery only a block away and a tailor shop right downstairs? Not to mention a butcher next door who throws in a slice of liver for a cat he knows we don't have."

We laughed, and Tom gave her arm an appreciative squeeze.

After dinner, talking over coffee in the living room, I learned that Tom's parents, apparently quite well off, had wanted him to continue on at Amherst at their expense, even though he had married before getting his diploma.

"Tom politely turned them down," Sharon said, her

voice edged with pride. "He wants us to get ahead on our own. And that's just how I want it."

"With you, it's easy," Tom said. He lit his pipe and added, "But enough about our sterling characters. Let's play the Victrola. Maybe Max will show us how they shake a leg in Gay Paree."

The only leg I'd shaken was to a waltz, but soon Sharon had me trotting around in awkward abandon to scratchy renditions of tunes I'd heard in the hotels— "Hindustan," "I'll Say She Does," "Japanese Sandman." Fearful that my wayward feet might render hers inoperable, I withdrew for a while to watch Sharon and Tom demonstrate how the fox-trot should be performed. Obviously he was an expert—one of the advantages of a college education, I thought—and he twirled her about with such ease that she seemed a part of him. I had been too preoccupied with my own shortcomings to notice, as I did now, how graceful she was, her body sinuously obedient to his as they moved in perfect rhythm. There was no escaping the disconcerting thought that they must find huge enjoyment in the big walnut bed I'd glimpsed when passing their room.

Probably it was this moment of voyeuristic fantasy that encouraged me to inflict myself on her again and again. However, as compensation, I held her at a virtuous distance when we danced, my eyes fixed on my feet as they stumbled joyously over the mock-Oriental rug.

I might have cavorted past midnight had Tom not put on a record that seemed to whisk me from their presence and transport me across an ocean—"Dardanella."

Suddenly I was with Ann Tyson in an old hotel, standing outside a door that reverberated to a record blaring out this same tune. The door swung open and again I gaped at Charles Dain, disheveled, grinning, flaunting an almost empty bottle of champagne—a gift bestowed in gratitude on "President Wilson's nephew." Nostalgia misted my mind and, as I returned Sharon to her husband, I was swept by feelings of loneliness and unimportance, as though I had plunged from some great historical experience into obscurity.

I left soon afterward—the beer and cheese brought out by Sharon antagonizing my stomach, my mind beset by images of raucous nights in Montmartre, of a soldier-correspondent chasing maniacally across battlefields, and by ecstatic cries issuing from a far bedroom in a French farmhouse.

Before going to bed that night I wrote to Charles. It was a letter filled with reminiscence and with only a short paragraph devoted to my homecoming.

Three months passed before I heard from him.

April 8, 1919

Dear Max:

So you think I went over to the communist underground press. Or married a Czarist ballerina and carried her off to Switzerland. Or got lost while acting as a guide for rich—and often obnoxious—American tourists.

None of the above is true. My reasons for not writing sooner are, in this order: covering the interminable peace talks; learning French; drinking absinthe at the Dome; playing poker at Nini's; pursuing mademoiselles; catching mademoiselles; fornicating excessively; recuperating from fornicating excessively.

Seriously, I've practically become a permanent

resident of the Quai D'Orsay, where our high-minded President—"Meester Veelson"—is being battered into submission by three of the toughest guys who ever carved up the planet. Lloyd George seems interested only in getting more pink on the world map. Georges Clemenceau, "The Tiger," wants the northern neighbor restricted to making beer and knockwurst so that they'll never again threaten the borders of France. Italy's Guido Orlando is more modest, as befits the nation that got walloped at Caporetto; he'll settle for Fiume. Anyway, Wilson's Fourteen Points are crumbling fast, and what he doesn't give up here, I suspect he'll lose when he gets home to face those senators who don't want us even to speak to foreigners. Of course I don't report it that way. Hell, we're doing just fine; democracy's been preserved and is now being exported—hallelujah and hats off to Uncle Sam! Meanwhile the crimson carpet that greeted Wilson back in December is now in dead storage.

I moved from the Y.M.C.A. soon after you left and now live on the top floor of a three-story house on the Rue du Chat Qui Peche. In case you're not quite sure of exactly where that is, it's off the Rue de la Huchette and is flanked by the Boulevard St. Michel and the Rue des Deux Ponts. There, that should set you straight. I have one large room, beautifully furnished in authentic Louis XIV Flea Market. Still, it has a sort of disorderly charm and such amenities as a pull-chain toilet and a truly regal bathtub supported by four feet in the shape of badly-manicured claws. The *pièce de résistance*, of course, is the four-poster bed, from which I can look out a window and see the spire of Notre-Dame. Occasionally the bed is used for sleeping, but too much of that can make a man lazy, so I've tried sincerely to put it to more active use. The results have been excellent, sometimes astonishing, and I'm sure you'd be proud of me. Fortunately the *jeunes filles* still think we *Americains* are—what you say?—hot stuff. But this may be changing as the boats arrive loaded with my boisterous countrymen, who seem to think, often rightly, that the dollar is the currency of the gods.

At this point you're probably wondering how I can afford all this luxury. Well, you didn't take my advice and do it, so I did—I'm now a foreign correspondent! Sounds beautiful, doesn't it? But the truth isn't quite so impressive. What I really am is a stringer for a couple of news services, which pay me space rates for anything published. So far I've done pretty well, especially with some sidelights on the peace conference. Add that to what I get from S&S and the favorable exchange rate and you'll understand how I can indulge my gluttonous appetites.

I've got a furlough coming in a week or so. I intend to get out of this frigid city and head for the Riviera, where I'll bask in the sun and try to insinuate myself into the world of the bloated rich. Stop laughing. If I could succeed with a well-known dress designer in Paris—she was a bit thick in the middle—why not with a duchess in Cannes? So don't be surprised if my next letter is dictated while lounging on a marble terrace overlooking the Mediterranean. Whatever happens, I plan to put in for a discharge by summer and take my chances as a footloose newsboy.

I haven't commented on your letter because you told me practically nothing except what I read in the papers. Do you think it's *news* that you're again comfortable at the Murray Hill and back at Hearst's heavenly whorehouse?

Oh, yes, you did say you're well and happy. Now that I think of it, that's the best news you could possibly tell me.

God, Max, I miss you!
Charles

He waited until late summer, after he was discharged, before writing again. It was a short letter, saying he was giving up his apartment and returning to the Riviera as roving house guest of a number of people he had met during his previous trip. He was still freelancing for the news services but felt less of an urgency to be published "now that I can sponge for a while off acquaintances whose greatest physical effort is clipping the coupons of gilt-edged bonds." He could leave no forwarding address, he said, but would keep in touch.

I didn't hear from him again until after Christmas, when I received a belated card, postmarked Constantinople, with a scrawled message: "This is the strangest place—everyone here is a Turk! I quit the Riviera crowd—afraid I'd become like one of those dispossessed White Russians in Paris who live off fat American heiresses. I'm here hoping to interview a general named Mustafa Kemal Pasha, who someday could become dictator." (The general indeed became dictator, changing his name to Kemal Atatürk.) In late March of 1920

Charles wrote from Rome, where he was reporting on a militant group called the Fascio di Combattimento, headed by a firebrand socialist named Benito Mussolini. A month later he was in Rumania talking to Queen Marie, formerly a British princess. Next it was Warsaw to interview Józef Pilsudski, head of the Polish state; then Czechoslovakia for a story on its great president, Tomás Masaryk; then Hungary and Yugoslavia and Greece for a series on the men in power.

By the end of 1921, I was no longer startled to read above a foreign dateline, "by Charles Dain." I could see him: tall, handsome, immaculately dressed in London-cut clothes, striding debonairly about the capitals of Europe, this prodigy who had fought valorously in the Great War, suffered agonizing wounds, but nevertheless carried on as a front-line correspondent. I have to confess that my pride in him was severely strained by envy. All this for a stripling, scarcely twenty-four, who as a cub had been my protégé! It was apparent that if I was ever to sample the glorious satisfactions of a Richard Harding Davis, it would have to be done vicariously.

By contrast, my job seemed not only dull but also, in fact, degrading. I was covering city politics, in which Mr. Hearst continued to be deeply involved, even though denied the mayoralty and, later, the governorship. He was still obsessed with the notion that some day he would be president, a fantasy vocalized in New York by his puppet, Mayor John F. Hylan, a bumbling, vulgar product of Tammany Hall who, by never failing to obey his masters, had gained a reputation for honesty. It was my assignment to report the daily acts and utterances of this pathetic pol, which required me to slant and color every story so that he would be seen by the electorate as a leader worthy of their blessing, therefore to be believed when he stated publicly to Hearst: "The great mass of people know you are their constant and vigilant defender."

In short, while Charles was reveling in the glamor of world events, I was wallowing in hogwash. Some relief came when Hearst was distracted from his political ambitions by plunging into the movies, with the purpose of making Marion Davies the brightest star in the Hollywood heavens. But before that was partially achieved— aided by the orchestrated trumpery of his newspaper chain—he had been bypassed at the 1920 presidential convention and all but destroyed politically by Al Smith four years later.

During this depressing period I began to become dependent on liquor, both for solace and as a tonic for my self-esteem. Even before coming of age I'd always drunk rather heavily, but had never felt a physical need for it and rarely lost control. But now I found myself ducking into speakeasies during working hours or sneaking a drink in the office from a pint bottle kept in my desk or, half in panic, phoning my bootlegger when my supply at home had almost run out. I reassured myself by arguing that I was simply going through a trying time, and once that ended, so would the craving for alcohol. And so I kept on, sustained by self-delusion and encouraged by an occupation that accepted drunkenness as evidence of manliness and an amusing part of its folklore. Somehow I always managed to fulfill my assignments, and I never missed a deadline.

Oddly, abstinence was the choice I preferred whenever I visited with Sharon and Tom Richards. At their apartment I was perfectly content to linger over a beer or two, and when I took them to a fashionable restaurant like Sherry's, one glass of wine was sufficient to maintain my conviviality. Of course when I escorted little Kate on an outing—to Van Cortlandt Park, the Bronx Zoo, the Ringling Brothers Circus—her effervescence was more stimulating than anything I could imbibe.

Otherwise there were no restraints on my drinking other than occasional flashes of fear—generally striking during a wakeful night—that my weakness might eventually make me unemployable. That terrible thought imposed a discipline more severe than if I had committed myself to sobriety—a constant struggle to cover up, to speak, walk, and reason as though in complete command of my faculties. The result was nervous tension and frequent attacks of anxiety, which would then have to be relieved by drink.

During one of my blacker intervals I began to suspect that the help at the Murray Hill Hotel were gossiping about my deterioration and eyeing me with contempt. It was then that, on impulse, I moved north to the Algonquin Hotel and into the sympathetic orbit of its owner, Frank Case. Not until years later did I appreciate the irony of what had occurred: paranoia had driven me to make a happy decision.

I was living at the Algonquin when, in June of 1924, I received a letter from Charles which, unknown to me, was to drastically change my life.

He had taken a staff job on the Paris *Herald* and had settled into an apartment for an indefinite stay. More importantly, he had become fascinated by a woman—"intelligent, well-informed, totally unlike the inane flappers and vamps I've become so bored with." She was thirty—four years older than he—which made not the slightest difference because they shared exactly the same outlook and interests. Her name was Harriet Anthony.

I was delighted that he had at last found someone who appealed to him seriously, who apparently understood the complex emotions hidden beneath his bantering surface. Only one thing in the letter disturbed me— the postscript.

P.S. She is richer than the Aga Khan!

Chapter · 10

It was there in the records—a .25 caliber semiautomatic pistol registered to Kate Richards of the New York *Evening Express*. Donovan was startled—not by finding the registration; she had already divulged that—but by the fact that the pistol fired the same caliber bullet as the one lodged in Charles Dain's head. He had not asked her to describe the weapon once kept in her purse because she would then have instantly deduced his suspicion.

The date of registration coincided with her assertion that she had armed herself soon after becoming a columnist. It was a point, thought Donovan, that should have eased his mind—at least the gun hadn't been bought immediately prior to the shooting—but it didn't. It was erased by a mental image of Kate hurling the pistol, still warm from use, into the East River. However she had disposed of it, he was sure it would remain unavailable for a match-up with the two wild bullets found in the town house.

As for Kate having acquired a gun in the first place, that knowledge wouldn't even raise an official eyebrow.

Didn't Walter Winchell carry one? In fact, Winchell's life was once considered so precarious that on a trip to Chicago he had been guarded by two FBI agents, two Chicago plainclothesmen, and three henchmen of Al Capone's, recruited on instructions from Lucky Luciano, New York's number-one gangster, who feared that the columnist's death by violence would incite a shake-up of the underworld. Granting that Kate was no Winchell, the police would still consider her occupation sufficiently hazardous to justify armed self-protection.

What about Kate's old-fashioned key, that looked like a useless heirloom but might possibly fit the front-door lock of the town house? Donovan, more rational than when he had discovered it last night, now shrugged it off; Kate would hardly be so absentminded as to carry such an incriminating item. Besides, there had to be more convincing evidence than an explainable gun, an antique key, and a fantasized scenario before designating Kate a valid suspect. Lurking somewhere in his mind was an elusive element, unrelated to intuition, that kept hinting at a more plausible link between Kate and Charles Dain. He fretted over it as he walked up lower Broadway, but whatever it was it refused to rise and be recognized.

Back in his office he found a message on his desk to see Paul Zack, the city editor. Now what? Was he about to be told to quit snooping around on his own and spend more time in the press room at police headquarters? If so, he could credit the order to Max Wills.

The first edition had just been put to bed as Donovan strolled into an atmosphere that, except for the muted thunder of the presses, was practically funereal. Most of the rewrite men were slumped in their chairs reading the late editions of the morning papers. At the horseshoe-shaped copy desk, one editor was gobbling a sandwich, another doing a crossword puzzle, a third writing a letter. The idle interval would be brief, ended abruptly by the murder of a housewife in Queens, a shoot-out in Harlem, an embezzlement in Wall Street. Meanwhile the only person who seemed to be working was Paul Zack, who sat bent over his desk in the center of the city room speaking rapidly into the phone. As Donovan reached him Zack hung up, stretched, and clasped his hands behind his head.

"Sit down, Terry," Zack said. "We'll have a meeting, just the two of us." He was a trim, swarthy man in his late thirties, with flashing indigo eyes and thick black hair salted with gray. He had a penchant for candy-striped shirts; the red-and-blue number he wore now looked as if it had been scissored from a nightclub awning.

"Sure," Donovan said, taking a chair beside the desk. "I've got time, plenty of it."

"That's all you've got—time? Nothing on Dain?"

"Zero. Everything I know, you've already printed."

Zack growled in disgust. "That's the hell of it. It's been four days now, and the story's exactly as it was on day one. We're running out of ways to say the same thing and make the customers think it's news." He tweaked his fleshy nose. "I figured the least you'd get would be a quote from some syndicate boss laying it off on his competition. Headline: COLUMBO NAMES MAFIA IN DAIN SHOOTING. Something like that."

Donovan grinned. "Columbo *is* the Mafia. But anyway, forget it. None of these glorified hoods is going to point a finger, not publicly. He'd get it chopped off, along with his head."

"Okay then, so attribute it to 'underworld sources.'"

Donovan lit a cigarette and eyed him drowsily through the smoke. "You sound like you've been talking to Max."

"Sure I've been talking to Max. I talk to Max maybe twice a day. So what?"

"So he's sold you it was a professional job—a triggerman sent by the mob."

"He didn't have to sell me. The cops—"

"Yeah, I know. But you also got some heat from Max. Or am I wrong?"

"Not wrong, just overstating. There wasn't any heat. Max doesn't want us wasting our time. So he suggested —*suggested*, I said—that we concentrate on Dain's obvious enemies, otherwise known as gangsters. It so happens I agree with him."

"And you haven't considered anyone else?"

Zack squeaked forward in his swivel chair and placed his hands flat on the desk. "Look, Terry, I'll level with you. I know you're hipped on the idea there's a woman mixed up in this."

"Max told you that?"

"Why shouldn't he? Right now he's the boss, and he's also Charles's best friend. He's got an obligation to see that a lot of irresponsible stuff doesn't get thrown around."

Donovan blew a smoke ring. "You're saying I'm irresponsible?"

"Christ, you're touchy. No, I'm saying what the policy is on this story—Max's and mine."

"And, of course, Harriet Dain's."

"Damned right Harriet Dain's. And that's the policy you'll follow—unless you want to give up eating."

Donovan gave him a knowing smile, a reminder that

he could walk into any city room in town and be hired on the spot, probably at more money.

Zack sighed, leaned back, and smoothed his striped shirt. "All right, Terry, forget I said that. All I'm asking is that if you get anything at all questionable, you discuss it first with me. I don't want to wake up some morning and find you'd slipped something through on the night side that could be embarrassing."

Donovan regarded him curiously. "Got anything particular in mind?"

"Absolutely not. But I guess if you dug back far enough there'd be something that could be tied in with this thing. Nothing valid. Just a little spicy innuendo here and there that could raise some ugly questions. That shitty rag *Confidential* does it all the time."

"Could you be thinking of Charles's old girl friends?"

"Naturally I've thought of that. But that's ancient history. No sheet in town will touch it, except maybe the *Mirror*, which so far hasn't. Besides, there'd be no connection. Those women are all probably mothers now, with kids to worry about. So who'd ever think . . . Did I say something? You look like I'd given you a red-hot tip."

Donovan snapped his mouth shut and blinked away his stare. Zack's words had tripped something in his mind, releasing the elusive element that earlier had defied recognition. He said, "That was my mildly surprised look, Paul."

"Surprised about what?"

Donovan, his mind working rapidly, slowly ground out his cigarette. "I'm surprised that in all the stories you've run on Dain, there hasn't been a word about his past life. I'd think there'd be a few sidebars on his war record, building the paper from scratch—you know, the great man treatment."

"Uh-huh. We've featured plenty of quotes from the big wheels. But you're right, we held back on the other stuff. Max thought we'd better save that to run if Charles doesn't make it. I've got it all here in a drawer —war hero, crusading journalist, civic leader—the works. Hell, I'd even planned an interview with his father, who'd tell us what a bright, hard-working kid he was."

Donovan tensed and leaned forward. The thought that had sprung into his mind now became clearer with the mention of Charles's father. "How is the old man?"

"Not too well. He's past eighty now and a widower. He's got some vascular problems and a kidney condition. For the past year he's been in a fancy nursing home on Long Island."

"How's his mind?"

"Still functioning. Oh, I hear he has trouble remembering everyday things, but Max tells me his memory's perfect about incidents that happened ages ago. Typical of senility, I guess."

"Does he know about Charles?"

"I doubt it. He doesn't read newspapers or listen to the radio. The family haven't told him because they're afraid of how he'll react. After they see what happens, they'll decide on how to handle it."

"So that's why Max canceled the interview?"

"He doesn't even know I thought of it. When I heard how the old man was, I didn't bring it up."

Donovan spoke quietly. "Paul, do you realize that Charles's father, more than anybody, might have some clue as to who shot his son?"

"Come on, Terry. I said he was senile, or getting there."

"But he remembers the past. Look, Charles and his father were always very close. I know that because Charles often told me so. The old man was his adviser, his confidant, the one he went to with personal problems."

"You've met him?"

"Several times. He used to come into the office now and then. Scholarly type, loved to quote from the classics. He once told me I should stop grinding out pulp yarns and concentrate on writing an important book."

Zack's eyes turned flinty. "Terry, if you think I'd assign you to go out and see him, you're insane."

"Don't assign me—just forget we had this talk. I'd be doing it on my own."

"He'd ask you about Charles. You tell him and your next job will be peddling papers in a home for the blind."

"I won't tell him, and I won't lie to him either. He'll think it's just a social visit. But if he can recall anyone who was a threat to his son, I think he'll tell me."

Zack pulled at his lower lip, swung around, and stared at a far wall, then swung back. "Meeting adjourned," he said. "In fact, it never took place." He picked up a pencil and gazed down at his desk. "Good luck, Terry. Nice to have had you around."

The nursing home, once the estate of an auto magnate, was located near Great Neck, on the North Shore of Long Island. Arriving in the taxi he had taken from the train station, Donovan passed through a wrought-iron gateway set in a high stone wall backed by a screen of tall trees. The driveway ascended to a cluster of white, colonnaded residences that sat on a slight rise ornamented by vivid spring flowers. Obviously it was a refuge affordable only by the very rich—the least he could do, Charles must have thought, for the father he revered.

Donovan entered the reception hall of the main building and introduced himself to the stylishly-dressed woman sitting at an executive desk off to the side. He had telephoned ahead and was now greeted by a bright smile. She suggested that he might prefer to wait on the terrace while she arranged for Mr. Dain to be delivered from his room.

On the flagstone terrace, furnished with umbrella tables and padded chairs and divans, Donovan looked out on a huge expanse of green lawn rolling down to a blue cove that shimmered in the afternoon sun. Several old people, some with canes, sat on benches behind a guardrail at the water's edge gazing out at slanting sailboats and occasionally offering tidbits to swooping gulls.

"Ah, Mr. Donovan."

He turned and faced Mr. Dain, who had raised himself in his wheelchair—a substitute for standing—and was nodding and smiling. His hair was still full but pure white, clinging to his noble head like a cap of lambswool. His face was gaunt, etched with fine lines, and despite the suntan seemed to give off a pallor. He was accompanied by a nurse.

"Mr. Dain. I'm so glad you could see me."

"It is my pleasure," Mr. Dain said as the nurse rolled him to a patch of shade. "A delightful surprise. Let me see, the last time I saw you was perhaps a year ago. I remember because I was visiting Charles in his office, and you had just come from the trial of that German— Hauptmann was his name. Yes, the man who kidnapped the Lindbergh baby."

More like ten years ago, Donovan thought, and he had seen the old man a number of times since then. But he said, "You have a good memory, Mr. Dain." He pulled up a chair as the nurse left. "I remember it too. Anyway, I had some business over in the Hempstead courthouse, and it seemed a good time to stop by and renew our acquaintance. I'm glad you're looking so well."

"Oh, I am well enough." His hand twitched in a disparaging gesture. "It is Charles who thinks I need all this pampering. Still, I am grateful. There are people here with whom I play chess and argue politics."

Politics, thought Donovan. If he argued politics, then he must read the papers, thus know about his son. "It's not very hard to get into an argument about Roosevelt," he said, smiling.

Mr. Dain nodded. "True. Teddy arouses strong emotions."

My God, thought Donovan, the man's mind had regressed some forty years. Probably the only knowledge he'd have of a shooting would be the assassination of McKinley.

". . . but mostly," Mr. Dain was saying, "I read. All the old great books. Thank goodness I still have my eyesight. The library here is fairly well stocked, and what I can't find, Max or Charles will bring." He paused, frowned in thought, then brightened. "How is my son?"

Though prepared with a lie, Donovan hesitated, regretting the necessity. "I haven't heard him complain. I'm sure he'd like to have come along with me."

"Ah, that Charles, always so busy. This morning, no, yesterday, maybe last night, I spoke to his wife on the phone. She said he is surrounded by people, that he can't get away. Of course I understand. It is the penalty of great success. Still, he visits me quite often. But not so often as Max. Now there is a true friend."

"Yes. I understand you've known Max for a good many years. How long has it been?"

"Not so long." Mr. Dain's eyes narrowed as he calculated. "It was in 1916, in the summer. It was a Sunday." He smiled to himself and lapsed into silence.

"That must have been when you lived in New Jersey," Donovan said.

Mr. Dain blinked. "Yes, South Orange." Again he was silent. His gaze seemed to reach far beyond Donovan, reminding him of senescent men on benches in Central Park, faces alight with memories burnished by time.

"And Charles brought Max to the house?"

Mr. Dain's expression remained unchanged. "No, Max came in the black Ford car—a flivver, they called it. It belonged to Mr. Fletcher, Sharon's father."

"Sharon?" Donovan thought of the snapshots, recalling the one with Max and Sharon beside the Model T.

"Sharon Fletcher. She was with Max. Oh, she was such a beautiful, charming girl—only seventeen, but she looked like a woman."

Donovan smiled. "Old bachelor Max. It's hard to think of him ever having a girl."

"No, she was not his girl, though I think he may have wished that. It was Sharon who suggested he drive her to our house. I showed Max my garden, all the children working in it." Mr. Dain's eyes softened in reminiscence.

"All, that is, except Charles. He had far better things to do than cultivate a garden."

"He was away?"

"Only as far as the porch steps. He was sitting there, all dressed up, with Sharon. The way they were looking at each other, I don't think they realized anyone else was there."

Donovan felt a small thrill of triumph. His mind repeated Paul Zack's words when referring to Charles's past affairs: "Those women are all probably mothers now, with kids to worry about"—words that had released the subliminal thought that it may have been Charles, not Max, who had been the teenage beau of Kate's mother, which led inevitably to still another theory joining Kate to Charles Dain.

"Let's see," Donovan said. "Charles must have been about eighteen then. Just the age to imagine himself terribly in love."

Mr. Dain smiled wistfully and shook his head. "Oh, no, Charles did not imagine it, nor did Sharon. Never have I seen two people who cared so deeply for each other. I was certain it would last, and that when Charles was able to support a wife, they would marry."

"But they broke up?"

Mr. Dain's features gathered into a fierce look. "They were *broken* up—by Mr. Fletcher, Sharon's father. George Fletcher was a bigoted man who thought himself superior to anyone born in a foreign country, as my wife and I were. Also, we were poor, and I did manual labor. These were the things he saw in Charles—not his brilliance, not his decency. Oh, yes, there was something else. Charles was handsome, extremely attractive. So I suppose George Fletcher feared that his daughter would be seduced. That I can understand. But it was more the other—his snobbery—that made him forbid Sharon to continue seeing my son."

"That must have been hard to take."

"It was a terrible blow to Charles. But it was not the worst blow. That came when he heard that Sharon had married. I have never seen anyone so crushed. Others may not have known it, except perhaps Max. Charles was always able to hide his true feelings. But I knew, and once or twice I spoke of it—but only to console him with the thought of the greatness he could achieve." Mr. Dain's scowl yielded to a look of pride. "I do not mind boasting that I was right."

"You certainly were. That must have been about the time Charles joined the army."

"Yes. As soon as President Wilson declared that we must fight, Charles volunteered. It was a blessing, but" —he smiled in modesty—"I cannot say I foresaw that. Who could have predicted that after the war he would marry such a splendid woman as Harriet?"

"Or that he'd start a newspaper and turn it into a huge success." Donovan glanced around and saw the nurse approaching from the reception hall. He said quickly, "I don't suppose Charles ever saw Sharon again."

"Oh, no. But Max sometimes sees her—she and her husband, who is an engineer; a consultant, I think. Max says they are very happy, for which I am glad. They have a beautiful little girl, Max tells me. He likes to take her on outings." Mr. Dain paused, then added, "He says she is the image of Sharon."

The nurse interrupted to say that it was time for Mr. Dain's before-dinner nap. Reluctantly he bid Donovan good-bye, expressing how much he had enjoyed talking to someone in whom he could confide.

On the train back to the city, Donovan brooded over the thought evoked by Paul Zack and now confirmed by Mr. Dain. A quarter of a century ago Charles had been in love with Sharon—romantically, intensely, unforgettably.

The sequential thought was as logical as it was inescapable, especially in the light of Charles's earlier, aborted liaisons.

Had he finally discovered in Kate, who so closely resembled her mother as a girl, a virtual reincarnation of his first love? Would he not have grasped this opportunity to fulfill through her the great passion denied him in his youth?

But assuming this was true, it fell far short of being proof that Kate had fired the bullet now threatening the life of Charles Dain. In fact, if Charles had indeed seduced Kate, others might have been motivated to take violent action: either of Kate's parents, to protect their daughter against a man they feared might eventually destroy her, or Harriet Dain—perhaps hiring a killer—in revenge against a husband who, this time, may have declared that he was leaving her for a much younger woman.

Of the three, Harriet seemed the most plausible suspect. An ordinary wife faced with losing an adored husband to a beautiful woman little more than half her age might react merely with tearful pleas. But Harriet Dain was no ordinary wife. She was cold, powerful, ruthless —and rich enough to cover almost any crime under layers of hush money. She and Charles had been married for almost twenty years. Despite her immense wealth it seemed incredible to Donovan that a man so gifted could have tolerated her for so long.

Reaching Grand Central Station, he stopped at a newsstand to pick up an *Evening Express*. He gave the man a dime, then ignored the seven cents change as he stared at the headline: $250,000 REWARD PLEDGED IN DAIN SHOOTING!

The donor, of course, was Harriet Dain.

Chapter · 11

When Harriet Anthony was born in 1895, her parents vowed that with the help of God and contraception, she would be an only child. The birth, in a Palm Beach hospital, had been accomplished after thirty-six hours of agony suffered by a mother who for almost the duration of her pregnancy had been confined to her bed, dosed with potassium bromide, and deprived of her husband's awesome lust while reliving the terror of three previous miscarriages. Following the last of those traumas, she had sworn herself to a childless marriage, a decision reversed by the rapacious man who believed that the delirious carnal pleasure he gave her should be rewarded with at least one heir.

Though he would have preferred a boy, Calder Anthony was grateful that he, who had created a fortune from inanimate objects, had finally created life. His initial disappointment at not acquiring a male heir to carry on his various enterprises was quickly replaced by the resolve to ignore gender, defy convention, and raise this product of his manhood as though she were an extension of his dreams, his ambition, his energy. His wife,

Marion, enthralled by his dominance and unconsciously resentful of the bawling stranger who had inflicted such pain, distorted her figure, striated her loins, attempted no interference.

Calder Anthony was ideally equipped for the job. Throughout his career he had been a molder of men, inciting their avarice, exploiting their opportunism, rationalizing their fears—all for personal gain. As a young man he had helped persuade a rebellious group of independent oil producers to accept the extortionate freight rates imposed by the railroads at the behest of the almighty Standard Oil Company, thus earning the regard of quiet-spoken, ruthless John D. Rockefeller and his allies. In appreciation, these and other industrial buccaneers guided him into ever more lucrative ventures which, in less than a decade, elevated him to an international entrepreneur dominating a consortium that refined oil, produced steel, built pipelines, trafficked in munitions, processed food, operated hotels, owned banks and ships and timberland. When, at thirty-five, he married Marion Cortland, a sheltered innocent from Back Bay Boston, he was a multimillionaire. Five years later, when Harriet struggled into the world, his wealth had become incalculable.

From early childhood Harriet was disciplined in self-reliance and organization. Despite a multitude of servants, she was required to make her own bed, select her clothes and dress herself, and arrange her own appointments. She was taught to ride horses, fence, shoot, play cards—baccarat and poker rather than whist and old maid. She was tutored in French, Spanish, German, and, when older, accounting, international finance, and business law. Her playmates were drawn from the homes of Calder Anthony's business associates, men subordinate to him, who instilled in their children a proper respect for the daughter of their master, the man who lived like a lord in a Connecticut castle and commuted to luxurious residences in London, Paris, Rome, Athens.

Harriet was eight when she first accompanied her parents on a trip abroad. With her father she toured a blast furnace in the German Ruhr, a textile mill in Lyons, an oil refinery beside the North Sea, a distillery in Edinburgh, a glassworks in Milan, a coal mine in Wales, and along the way was schooled in the complexities of hotel management, many of these splendid establishments being controlled by Calder Anthony. Leisure time was spent not at a playground or a zoo or a children's party but at a racetrack, a shooting lodge, or a yacht regatta. Always she was complimented on her intelligence, her poise, her manners—words used by many to conceal their uneasiness at such precocity.

On the voyage home she had her first encounter with sex. She had been placed in the charge of a white-uniformed ship's officer assigned to show her the inner workings of a great transatlantic vessel. He had escorted her through the kitchen, the bakery, the laundry room, the engine room, the wireless room, the wardroom, after which he suggested a look at his cabin. There he offered her a soft drink, surreptitiously spiking his own with hard liquor. They talked. He said nonsensical things to make her laugh. He became playful, swinging her off her feet, then tickling her. It was all such fun—until, sitting beside him on the bunk, she felt his hand creep under her dress, slide over her thighs, and teasingly stroke the aperture that she had thought existed for but a single purpose. She knew nothing of his intentions, only that the privacy for which bathrooms were invented had been invaded. Instinctively she knew what her father would say and, jumping up, she said it.

"You son of a bitch!"

"Miss Anthony! Please! I was just *playing!*"

"Go to hell!"

"Shh, be quiet! Calm down and let me explain."

"Explain it to my father. I'll bet you don't know he owns this ship."

"Oh, my God!"

"Get out of my way!"

"Please, please . . ."

She veered past him and stomped out the door. But she didn't tell her father, fearful that he might throw the officer overboard, which, even with all his power, might send him to die in the electric chair at Sing Sing.

Later, reflecting on that alarming incident, she decided that it had been a salutary part of her education, triggering a curiosity as to just why the ship's officer had been so fascinated by this particular part of her person. She secretly consulted Gray's *Anatomy*, discovering in the area of her interest little more than what she already knew—boys had appendages, girls did not—a fact established long ago when she had seen gardeners relieving themselves behind flowering shrubs and privet hedges. Undaunted, she browsed relentlessly through her father's voluminous library and eventually found, on a high shelf in an unlit corner, a treasure of enlightenment. Having had her literary tastes formed by such classicists as Homer, George Eliot, William Dean Howells, she was astonished and confounded when she first dipped into a French edition of a book titled *Juliette*, written by a Parisian nobleman named the Marquis de Sade. Could such outrageous goings-on really happen between otherwise nice men and women? Apparently they did, else how could the Marquis have described them so explicitly, becoming even more graphic in two subsequent novels found on the shelf—*La Philosophie dans le Boudoir* and *Justine*.

From these Harriet proceeded to other books in her father's sequestered collection, absorbing herself in the titillating adventures of Fanny Hill and Moll Flanders, staring bug-eyed at paintings of strangely coiffed Japanese, kimonos thrown back to flaunt their nakedness, the stoical woman often guiding the man's huge member between her legs. And then there were the small paperbound volumes from France—poetry rhythmically studded with words heard only on the docks or in factories; plotless stories describing men and women, often in groups, engaged in what seemed a carnival of acrobatic matings; and, most startling of all because its contents seemed directed at everyone—including her parents and herself—a book of diagrammatic drawings representing couples in an awesome variety of positions, some requiring the suppleness of a contortionist, and, in aggregate, involving every orifice of the human body.

Having always assumed her mother to be no more than her father's public playmate—a natural role for someone who didn't cook, sew, clean house, or attend to her child—Harriet was now forced to consider that this thin, nervous woman might also be involved in functions of a sensational private nature. The thought was staggering, but more than that, thrilling. Seething with curiosity, Harriet was determined to find out.

The opportunity arose one night when she was awakened by the late arrival of her parents, their footsteps on the long, marble staircase echoing through the great Tudor-style mansion. Their quarters—a segregated apartment really—were at the opposite end of the corridor from her bedroom, and once they'd shut themselves in, no sound penetrated the solid oak door that closed behind them. Harriet waited ten minutes before leaving her bed and creeping silently toward her parent's sanctuary. Outside the door she held her breath, squatted, and squinted an eye to peer through the keyhole.

At first she saw only blackness. Then, as her eye adjusted, she discerned the large canopied bed illuminated by pink and blue night-lights. The figures of her parents, uncovered by sheet or blanket, divested of every stitch, in fact, came into focus. They were together and yet they were separated, her mother up close to the headboard, long dark hair overflowing the white satin pillow, her father crouched near the foot, his face not visible because it was buried in the conjunction of her mother's splayed thighs. Then from her mother came a low, protracted moan, which seemed to rise and grow in her throat until it tore from her lips in a thin, high-pitched wail. Calder Anthony did nothing to comfort her; instead, after the wail subsided to a whimper, he simply grasped her above the waist and, expertly, wordlessly, reversed their positions.

Vaguely disturbed but satisfied that the illicit books had not lied, Harriet started to draw back from the keyhole. Then her eye suddenly caught something that riveted it to the cold metal. Her father had reached down, pulled up her mother, slipped a pillow beneath her stomach, thus elevating her buttocks, and was now thrusting his immense appendage into her rear. This time there was no protracted, ascending moan, only the wail, more piercing than the last and stripped of pleasure.

Harriet did not linger to observe her mother's pain yield to delight. Hand clapped over her gaping mouth, she streaked down the corridor, jumped into bed, and yanked the blankets over her head. My God! Her father —all men—were like wild animals. Never again would she curl up on his lap! Never again would she allow him to so much as touch her!

But that attitude changed when, growing in knowledge, she surmised that her father's anal assault was the surest method he knew of to avoid a pregnancy that might kill her mother. Also, she was comforted by the thought that she would never have to share her privileged status with a sister or a brother.

By the age of sixteen Harriet had developed into a tall, leggy girl, full-breasted but otherwise meagerly endowed, possessing the straight-lined figure that in 1911 was unfashionable but a decade later would be all the rage. She had a tendency to sprawl in chairs, lope instead of glide, shout rather than murmur, and was likely to address her seniors with the unvarnished rhetoric employed by her father. Her mother, finding her an embarrassment and jealous of Calder's preoccupation with her training, finally convinced him that this seemingly androgynous child was in fact female, soon to become a woman, and that if she was not to be considered a freak, she must at least be coated with a veneer of graceful femininity. Harriet's tutors were thereupon dismissed, and she was sent to Miss Porter's School, nearby in Connecticut, there to be "finished" before braving the social hazards of a college campus.

At this point Calder Anthony was in his mid-fifties, his wife eight years younger. Having lost interest in the mere accumulation of wealth, and with his vast holdings in the care of trusted managers, he decided to devote more of his life to leisure. Soon his name all but vanished from the business news only to reappear prominently—along with that of his wife's, "the magnificent Marion"—in the society columns. Welcomed into the orbit of the so-called International Set—fashionable Americans and Europeans, mostly British—they joined in a life of extravagance and frivolity, migrating from London to Paris to the Riviera to Palm Beach in pursuit of ceaseless pleasure.

Informed of all this hedonism while confined to the chaste atmosphere of Miss Porter's, Harriet was stricken with disillusionment. Though her father had always led an active social life, never had he allowed it to conflict with what she had been taught was his duty to expand the benefits of the capitalist system. Instilled in her was a scorn of people whose lives were unredeemed by any purpose larger than self-indulgence—the wastrels, the voluptuaries who had now perverted the energies of the man who had set himself up as her role model.

Was she being too severe? she wondered. Was what she saw as decadence more truly an exploration of the culture and antiquities that had contributed so much to modern civilization? Perhaps the convivial excesses she read about in the newspapers and in magazines like *Vogue* and *Harper's Bazaar* were exaggerations representing merely the fringe on the pattern of her parents' activities. Certainly when she visited them while on school breaks—in Connecticut or Newport or Palm Beach—their social pace seemed no more frantic or bizarre than that of other moneyed people who also managed to attend to the world's work.

In the summer and fall of 1913, eighteen years old and as "finished" as Miss Porter's School could ever make her, she found out the truth. Having refused to be exhibited at a great debutante launching party, she agreed that, as a replacement, she would accompany her parents to Europe—an invitation issued reluctantly, she thought, particularly by her father.

The trip confirmed her worst suspicions. In London, as a courtesy to the distinguished Calder Anthony, she was besieged by the Mayfair set and the clique, many of dubious character, surrounding the young Prince of Wales, most of whom slept all day and caroused all night; and by the titled owners of stately country houses, whose occupants drank brandy for breakfast, paused to mount horses and chase a fox, then returned to lounge in their precise gardens, imbibe champagne, pick and wine their way through interminable dinners, then dance and drink until, come daylight, they staggered to bed, and not always the one assigned.

Paris was even worse. There she was thrust into parties that seemed to begin every other hour—breakfast parties, luncheon parties, afternoon parties, dinner parties, usually preparatory to flamboyant costume balls during which several women would invariably strip to their skins and dance on tables while outside, on an unlighted terrace or amidst the shrubbery, couples only just introduced stretched out on divans and quietly fornicated.

But the Riviera, oh, that would be different. The sun, the sand, the sea. . . . Who could resist lazing on the beach, splashing in a tidal pool, cruising on a long white

yacht? And she was right, except there was no escaping
the rattle of cocktail shakers, the popping of corks, the
blare of bands, the frenzied laughter, the wild phone
calls from villa to villa, hotel to hotel, the promiscuous
couplings, the nightly forays to smoky cafés where the
stranger you danced with might be a gigolo, a cat
burglar, or the king of Rumania.

Sailing home alone on the *Berengaria*—her parents
were "taking the cure" at Marienbad—she reflected bitterly on all she had missed. She had absorbed no more
Old World culture than if she had stayed home, rented
a room at the Plaza, and drunk oceans of champagne
while staring at postcards of London Bridge and the
Eiffel Tower. Never again, she thought, and with that
decision realized with surprise that she had just endured
the most crucial part of her education. From that time
on she would be impervious to the suave sophisticates,
invulnerable to synthetic glamor, unimpressed by titles
or coats of arms or any other unearned emblems of
celebrity. She would judge people by what they could
do, not by what had been done for them. Ironically, by
plunging into childish indulgence she had crossed the
threshold of maturity, achieving the identity her father
had planned from the day of her birth. Now she was
determined to complete his plan, eventually taking for
herself the position so wantonly relinquished by him.
While he and her mother romped and rotted in Europe,
she would . . .

But everything changed on June 28, 1914, when a
Serbian terrorist named Gavrilo Princip traveled to the
Austrian province of Bosnia and, at Sarajevo, assassi-
nated Archduke Francis Ferdinand of Austria-Hungary.

❊   ❊   ❊

The outbreak of the war in Europe at first stunned and then galvanized Calder Anthony. Joined by commerce and social kinship to England and France, he viewed the challenge to their sovereignty by the Central Powers as tantamount to an assault on his native land. Overnight he abandoned his profligate ways, shed his dissolute friends, and reverted to the hard-driving tycoon who had built an industrial empire. The Allies were desperate for oil, coal, steel, textiles, timber; and he, along with magnates like Du Pont, Morgan, Mellon, Rockefeller, controlled the resources to provide them. Suddenly he was again shuttling between his offices in Paris, London, and New York, with hurried side trips to Washington, holding meetings, issuing orders, stimulating production, expanding facilities, expediting deliveries. What social life he allowed himself was spent in the company of cabinet ministers, military commanders, and directors of great corporations. For the first time since surrendering to indolence, he was truly enjoying himself.

Harriet, who had enrolled at Smith College, greeted the news of his dynamic reformation with relief and admiration—which turned to delight when he agreed to her request to leave school and become his confidential secretary. In fact, she became much more than that. She toured mines, mills, factories, quizzed the superintendents, prepared reports on efficiency and the feasibility of new methods. She talked to railroad executives, ship captains, cargo handlers, and formulated ways to increase freight capacity and speed distribution. She dined with politicians and bureaucrats and lobbied them into cutting red tape. At night, eyes glazed with fatigue, she pored over textbooks on accounting, business administration, contract law, international finance. Yet despite all this, she managed to spend most of her time at her father's side while he negotiated, charmed, bullied, dictated—and phoned pacifying messages to her mother, bereft now that he was no longer her sybaritic companion.

In Harriet's eyes London and Paris were transformed into cities populated by doers, by men and women who rose with the dawn, crammed their hours with work and achievement, snatched quick lunches and dinners, and spent their evenings as air raid wardens, watchmen, volunteer firemen, nurses, corpsmen. The parties still raged behind the blackout curtains, but these people, the great mass of the citizenry, were not present, nor were the Anthonys or their associates in the great cause. This was the England, this was the France, that Harriet had hoped to find on her last trip abroad, but which had been obscured by a saturnalia of drunkenness and gambling and lechery. These were the people with whom she now felt comfortable—friendly, dedicated, civilized—far more so than with the show-offs, the climbers, the primitives who were so much a part of America. Someday, she thought, she would reside here permanently and, with her father's counsel, direct the fortunes of his multinational enterprises.

She spoke of it one day as they were eating lunch from trays in his Paris office.

"Father, after the war I think I'd like to stay on in Paris, perhaps take an apartment."

He raised his thick eyebrows and extended his full lower lip, which gave him the look of a Hapsburg. "Not go back to school?"

"I thought of taking a few courses at the Sorbonne."

She smiled, displaying her perfect teeth. "Would you sack me if I didn't get a college diploma?"

His answering smile brought to his face a fleeting moment of youth that belied the pouched eyes, the tiny veins in his florid cheeks, the puffs along his strong jaw, all remnants of his abrogated dissipation. "Certainly not. But later, when you're running things, I wouldn't want you patronized by any Ivy League snobs."

"It would happen only once, Father."

He laughed. "That's what I like to hear. Take no nonsense. Respect is what you want, not love." He flashed her an arch glance. "*That* you'll get from your husband."

She felt herself recoil. Almost primly she said, "I doubt there will be a husband."

"Ah, Harriet, give it time. You're only twenty."

Twenty, she thought, the word sounding like forty. Most girls experienced their first romance at sixteen, but she had yet to enjoy such rapture. The reason, she believed, could not be found entirely in her looks. Though tall, she was slim and well proportioned—her breasts perhaps a bit large—and she now carried herself with grace, in clothes designed by the most elegant couturiers in Paris. Her face, while not conventionally pretty, was attractive, skin white and smooth, eyes an electric blue and wide set, hair dark and worn in a sleek pompadour. If her nose was too high bridged, her lips too thin, it could be said that these deviations from current notions of beauty made her appear more interesting.

What was it about her, then, that caused eligible young men to freeze up, excuse themselves after a few polite words, veer away from her approach at a party?

Was it her father's wealth and power, which could crush them should they in any way offend his precious solitary child? Possibly, but she sensed there was something more forbidding—an aura that signaled she was not quite normal, a remoteness that precluded an accommodation of male pride and ego. In short, she concluded, they had her labeled as an undersexed woman more interested in machines than in men. And she feared they were right—never had she felt a romantic or erotic emotion for any man.

"... and for a while," her father was saying, "you'll be too damned busy to be concerned about suitors. You'll have to be my eyes and ears while I'm gone."

"Gone? Where to?"

"You haven't been listening. Your mother and I are sailing for New York day after tomorrow. I've got business in Washington, and she wants to sell the Connecticut house." He sighed regretfully. "Which I suppose means getting rid of my collection of cars."

"Including the Rolls-Royce?" It had been custom-built and, to Harriet, was a palace on wheels.

"No, I'll keep that, and probably the Bentley. Right now they can't be replaced."

"When will you be back?" she asked.

He consulted his desk calendar. "Let's see, this is the end of March. I'd say definitely by early May. We'll take whatever ship we can get."

He was as good as his word: in early May of 1915 Harriet's parents were aboard a passenger liner outward bound from New York. But they voyaged no farther than the waters off Old Head of Kinsale, Ireland, where on May 7 they were torpedoed and sunk by a German submarine. Among the 1,198 persons drowned were one hundred and twenty-four Americans—including Calder and Marion Anthony. The ship was the *Lusitania.*

Except that Harriet missed her father, the years alone were seldom lonely. There was her compulsion to do all the things that he had done, and try to do them better in order to compensate for being female—a job that suddenly grew and intensified when America entered the war. She took an apartment in Paris and another in London, commuting back and forth to meet with government officials, procurement officers, plant managers—estimating their needs, drawing up contracts, arranging timetables, which were relayed by phone and cable to her associates in New York. She became known as a fierce, tough, driving woman—"a Pershing in petticoats," they called her—as demanding in her impatience to get things done as Britain's commander in chief, Sir Douglas Haig or France's Marshal Henri Pétain.

After the war she continued to live in Paris and London, making frequent trips to the United States to help speed reconversion to peacetime production. In late 1920, frustrated by the political and economic mess in Europe and reminded constantly that the center of corporate power had shifted to America, she moved to New York. Foreseeing a boom in Manhattan real estate, she bought property on the Upper East Side and, as much for her own convenience as for financial gain, acquired the newly-constructed Waterford Hotel, reserving for herself the luxurious penthouse suite. No sooner had she settled in than she began to wonder if she had committed herself to a national madhouse.

The nation, suffering an epidemic of strikes, riots, and

crime, incited by Attorney General A. Mitchell Palmer to lump and label all of these disturbances a product of a Bolshevik conspiracy, stood by in silence as the police, the vigilantes, the Ku Klux Klan, jailed, murdered, and terrorized anyone who so much as expressed a dissident thought—acts that, to America's superpatriots, were vindicated when a bomb exploded opposite the House of Morgan, killing thirty people, injuring hundreds, and wrecking the offices of that revered financial institution. Prohibition had produced the hip flask, the storefront speakeasy, the college-boy bootlegger, who in turn converted the borrowed family car into a combination saloon, boudoir, and lethal weapon. The newspapers were filled with stories of suicides by pregnant teenagers, of youthful joyriders dismembered or destroyed in fiery wrecks, of innocent children run down in the streets. Flaming youth had become a family affair, mothers bobbing and shingling their hair just like their flapper daughters, wearing the same short dresses, suppressing their breasts with flatboy brassieres, dancing the shimmy and the tango (and later the Charleston and Black Bottom); and the fathers joined in, miming their sons in their blazers and white flannel trousers, emulating the dance routines of the now-deceased Vernon Castle, passing out in country-club locker rooms, all the while striving with high-powered cars, showy houses, and liveried servants to keep up with the rich racketeers as well as the Joneses.

The whole scene, thought Harriet, was like an enormously staged burlesque of her revolting experience with the International Set when she was eighteen. She sought to ignore it by investing her leisure time, and occasionally her money, in the theater. While watching a play called *Nice People,* starring Francine Larrimore, she was suddenly struck by the magnetic force of a young supporting actor who seemed to project all of his masculinity right into her heart. Nervous, fascinated, she went backstage, was introduced, was led to Belle Livingston's plush speakeasy, then dancing, then supper, then—and here everything was misted by wine—on to her penthouse, where they listened to the melodies of Victor Herbert and Irving Berlin; and the young actor, knowing exactly who she was, whispered lines that cued them to her bed. There everything changed; perhaps, she thought later, because she was so tense, so apprehensive, so mechanical, but also because all the magic he had projected from a distance vanished with this close encounter. She never saw him again, except on the screen when he became a Hollywood star, but she always remembered him as the man who, though failing to fulfill her, had convinced her that she was quite capable of orgasm.

For almost three years she stayed in New York, enduring endless assaults on her sensibilities. In the spring of 1923, her disillusionment complete, she returned to Europe, again dividing her time between London and Paris. Surprisingly, she suddenly found herself one of the most sought-after women in England and France, courted by distinguished-looking men, young and old, who during the war would not have complimented her with a glance. Her surprise quickly faded when she discovered that these titled Englishmen, these French aristocrats, these Russians named Romanov, were all bankrupt or dispossessed, that they coveted not her but her money. Harshly she renounced them, became reclusive, and immersed herself in business.

Until one evening in mid-September when a member of Parliament persuaded her to attend a diplomatic reception at London's Savoy Hotel.

In the crowded ballroom she was standing alone and reaching to take a glass of champagne from a tray when she noticed a tall, impeccably dressed young man standing but a few feet away. She was amused to see him contemplating the retreating and rolling rump of a woman dressed tightly in black satin. Turning and catching Harriet's eye, he shrugged, smiled, and waved a hand toward the orchestra, which was playing "The Londonderry Air."

"I was admiring her London derriere," he said.

She laughed—her first genuine laugh in years.

He came and took a glass of champagne. "So you like puns," he said.

"*That* one I like."

"Then I guess we should meet." He clicked his glass against hers. "My name is Charles Dain."

Chapter · 12

"Mr. Wills," the nurse said, "I'm sorry, but you can't go in now."

I turned from the open doorway to Charles's room and saw a group of doctors coming up behind the nurse. "An emergency?" I asked. "Or another consultation?"

"Consultation." She stepped aside as the doctors, faces impassive, moved into the room. I got a quick glimpse of Charles's swathed head, his nose and mouth still strung with tubes. The dreadful stillness of his features, in consciousness usually so animated, chilled me with the image of an embalmed body stretched out in a satin-lined casket. I gave myself a shake and went back to Harriet's room, where earlier we'd ingested a meager lunch.

She was just hanging up the phone. I nodded and tried to give her a reassuring smile, the kind I'd seen in the Andy Hardy movies when Lewis Stone would emerge from his wife's sickroom to confront a tearful Mickey Rooney. The mimicry was wasted: Harriet was preoccupied with extracting a cigarette stub from its long black holder.

"That was the police," she said, sitting down and tapping the phone.

"They've got something?"

She smiled wryly. "What they've got is a switchboard jammed with nutty calls." She worked another cigarette into the holder and lit it. "I should have listened to you, Max, and held off on the reward."

My advice, based on past experience, and with which the authorities concurred, had been to wait until the police exhausted their leads. To offer a reward now, I had said, especially one so enormous, would trigger a barrage of irresponsible accusations, most of which would have to be followed up, thus diverting attention from more likely areas of investigation. But Harriet, impatient as always, and fearful that Charles might never regain consciousness to name his assailant, had been adamant. A quarter of a million dollars—certainly that should convert even the most loyal of blood-oath gangsters into instant informers.

"It may work out," I said. "Did any of the callers claim to know Charles?"

"I asked that. The officer said none that he knew of. He seemed to take great pleasure in describing several crank calls, which he said were typical."

"It's not just the extra work that's got them upset," I said. "What they're also afraid of is that they'll lose that quarter million to someone they didn't even think of questioning. Anyway, the reward offer was made only yesterday. In another day or so we may find you did exactly the right thing."

I left her with that thought, though I didn't share it.

Back at the office I got a call from Kate asking to see

me. There was an urgency to her tone, a shrillness reminiscent of the little girl who used to cry out in terrified delight when I took her on scary rides at Luna Park or Coney Island. The thought seemed to ease my foreboding, and I let my mind drift back over the years to when I had been almost a surrogate father to her, when mothers in the park would say to me, "My, what a nice little girl you have" or with envy declare, "Your daughter seems so grown-*up*." If Kate was out of earshot, I would let the error stand, feeling a surge of pride, and for a few moments shamelessly indulge the delusion that I must then be Sharon's husband.

It had been an easy role to slip into. Tom Richards was frequently away from home on engineering assignments, sometimes for a couple of days in another city, sometimes for weeks in a foreign country. Sharon never accompanied him; she was too much the dedicated mother; and besides, Tom would have had little time to spend with her. He seemed not to resent my paternal posture; in fact, smilingly, sometimes teasingly, encouraged it, an attitude which deflated my self-esteem when I considered that it also implied he felt quite safe in leaving me alone with his beautiful wife.

Of course it was apparent that he could have felt secure even if I happened to be Valentino. Sharon was as devoted to him as ever, concerned with his comfort, eager to please him in every way. As for Kate, he need never fear that I could replace him in her affections. She adored her father, just as she did her mother, and looked upon me as an old-shoe family friend and part-time playmate. As she grew up and the bond between us matured, I became her confidant and counselor, a role greatly enhanced after she graduated from

214 · *Richard Neely*

the funny papers to the main news section and saw
above a story of some dramatic event the awesome
words "by Max Wills." Often she would question me
about the workings of a newspaper, and I, flattered that
she should find my profession so fascinating, responded
as I had with Charles Dain so many years before, acting, I'm afraid, like a savant. Soon her conversations
with me became sprinkled with journalese, much to the
wonder of her parents, who had never been exposed to
such terms as "fudge box," "sidebar," "jump page,"
"screamer." She was about twelve, I think, when she
solemnly informed me that someday she would become
a composite Nellie Bly, Adela Rogers St. John, and
Dorothy Thompson. I was inclined to believe her,
knowing that whenever she set herself a goal, she pursued it relentlessly until it was attained.

By then her father had achieved success as a consulting engineer, and they had moved to a handsome apartment on the heights above Riverside Drive, where they
overlooked Grant's Tomb, the Hudson River, and, in the
far distance, the magnificent Palisades of New Jersey.
Despite the Depression Tom Richards was able to send
Kate to private schools and then to Vassar. She had
grown into a fine young lady—beautiful, intelligent, re-
sourceful—the only flaw in her upbringing being that
there had been no flaws. It was as though the forces of
nature had conspired to allow one creature to be born
who would never experience grief or adversity or ugli-
ness—all the traumas that so many writers vaguely describe as constituting "the human condition." She had
been treated with respect and understanding by her
parents and teachers. She had been admired and sought
out for friendship by her peers. She had attracted the
young men who interested her, and when a romance

ended, always at her discretion, managed to retain the young man's good will. She had, I surmised, enjoyed the ultimate intimacy with at least one lover—a moneyed, reckless smoothie who was a tennis star at Princeton— from which she not only emerged unscathed but with greater self-assurance. I would say that she was the quintessential liberated woman, except that there was never anything from which she had to be liberated. Whatever she wanted, she openly pursued, and whatever she pursued, she got.

This was the young lady, age nineteen, that I brought into the office of Charles Dain in the early summer of 1937. I had not told him she was Sharon's child, only that she was the daughter of an old friend and a brilliant student at Vassar who was seeking summer employment. I sensed an affinity between them from the moment they shook hands—a reaction I had anticipated, not only because of her beauty but also because she spoke in the direct, confident manner he admired in his wife. In fact, if he had not then been so obviously faithful to Harriet, having years before abandoned his interest in shapely blond ingenues, I would never have acceded to Kate's constant pleas to be given a chance on the *Express*. Also, I felt certain that Charles's professionalism would preclude any emotional entanglement with an employee—not to mention that he was about twice Kate's age.

A week or so after she was hired, I confessed to Charles that Kate was Sharon's daughter. I recall him rising slowly from his desk and glowering down at me as I struggled not to cringe.

"Max," he said harshly, "of all the people in the world, you're the last one I'd suspect of duplicity."

"Now, Charles, I simply wanted you to know her

before . . ." I was unable to finish without making matters worse.

"Before I decided against any link to Sharon? Is that it?"

"Something like that." I stared down at the carpet. And kept staring throughout a long silence. Finally I glanced up, intending to look him defiantly in the eye.

He was grinning!

"Charles! You knew?"

He burst into laughter. "Sure I knew. When you first told me about her I guessed she might be Sharon's daughter. One look at her and I knew I'd guessed right." He sat down and regarded me fondly. "Max, I know you've been seeing Sharon and her family over the years. You mentioned it a few times."

I fussed with my bow tie. "I don't recall ever—"

"That's one trouble with booze. People often don't recall." He smiled. "Anyway, we'll keep it to ourselves. We don't want the gossips saying that the incorruptible Max Wills is padding the payroll with pals."

I felt relieved. "If it matters, Kate's parents are happy we hired her. That says a lot for her father, because he knows you and Sharon were once . . . close."

"Oh, hell, that was, what, twenty years ago?"

"Twenty-one."

He nodded, his dark eyes suddenly softening in memory. "You know, Max," he said, "I've done some pretty extravagant things for certain people just to get rid of them or to shut them up. Maybe it's time I did something nice just for old times' sake."

"You mean give Sharon's daughter a helping hand?"

"If you want to advance Kate's career, I won't object." His eyes seemed to waver as he added, "I may even coach."

But of course I was the coach, the visible mentor who trained, assigned, exhorted; while Charles, like an owner of a baseball team, remained in the background, pulling the strings, making decisions that propelled Kate to the top of the profession. Fortunately her rapid rise provoked little or no resentment among her associates—she was too able, too well liked. But even if she had been neither, I suspect Charles would have pushed her ahead, for reasons that would occur only to me. Either deliberately or unconsciously, he must have seen in Kate an opportunity, a vehicle, to demonstrate to Sharon what a fine, generous, powerful man he had become.

Putting myself in his position, I could easily imagine how he might rejoice in the thought of Kate relating to her mother some act of kindness he had performed, some brilliant editorial stroke, some courageous thrust against the forces of evil. You see, he would think, I've more than justified all the faith you had in me so long ago, the faith your father must have crushed, else you would have waited and not so quickly turned to another man. It was a very human reaction, particularly for one who had endured discrimination because of poor, foreign-born parents. It took no supernatural insight for me to perceive this—I, too, was at least partially motivated by a desire to impress Sharon. In talking to her of Kate's progress, I did not bother to mention the role played by Charles Dain, nor did either of us speak his name.

Now and then Charles would call Kate into his office, apparently, I thought, to background her on a story, and later, perhaps to discuss an item in her column. Always I wondered if he used those occasions to inquire obliquely about her mother, possibly hoping to learn what Kate had passed on about him. But he never mentioned those sessions to me, and neither, curiously, did Kate, who . . .

. . . who was now coming through the door. She shut it, an ominous sign, impelling me to rise from my desk and, as we greeted each other, lead her to the leather couch, where we could talk more intimately.

"I hope your heart can take this," she said.

"I've got it in neutral. What is it?"

"Terry knows I had a gun."

My heart took it, but under protest. "Now, how would he . . . The police? Did he get that from the police?"

"No, *I* told him."

I stared at her incredulously. "There go the ears," I said. "I'd have sworn you said that you told him."

"Your hearing's fine. So just keep listening."

She explained that two nights ago, in her apartment, Donovan had said he was about to check out the owners of all the .25 caliber pistols registered in New York. Naturally she'd had no choice but to tell him about hers before he found her name on the list.

"I didn't mention the caliber, Max. I guess I felt that the less said the better. But last night he brought it up—oh, so casually—and we damned near had a splituation, as the wise-guy columnists say." She lit a cigarette.

I snatched one from her pack and noticed her hand tremble as she lit it. I took a suicidal drag, holding it, then let the pollution drift out through my nose and mouth. "Tell me exactly how casual," I said.

"He gave me that little smile—the one I usually find so charming—and said something like, 'Kate, when you used to pack a pistol, why couldn't it have been a twenty-two or a thirty-eight, or, better still, one of those laughers that shoots out a red flag?' I gave him my blank look and said I couldn't remember what caliber mine was. I didn't even like looking at it, I said."

"So he enlightened you."

"He did, still smiling, sort of shrugging it off. Mine was a twenty-five caliber, he said, then took his time, watching me, before mentioning that Charles had been shot by a twenty-five caliber bullet."

I inhaled more poison. "And you said . . . ?"

"I tried to be funny. Like, 'Please, no handcuffs. I'll go quietly.' His laugh was less than hysterical. Then he asked me how I'd got rid of the gun. Had I turned it in to the police? I was pretty edgy by then—mad, in fact —and I said, What was this, anyway, the third degree? And shouldn't he show me his badge? Oh, I was great with the snappy comebacks—just like Glenda Farrell in the movies. His eyes got kind of flinty and he said that he had to ask because of the chance that somebody"— her eyes dilated as she stared at me—"might have stolen it."

I heard myself grunt. "Did he say why that thought occurred to him?"

"Sit back, Max. Yes, he said someone could have swiped it to use against Charles. Then, when the police found it and matched it to the bullets, I'd take the rap. A frame-up. Merely conjecture, he said—which, as you know, is what he does best."

"You must have asked him why, if it was a frame-up, the police haven't been able to find the gun."

"Almost my very words. I added that the cops hadn't found it because, as I'd told him before, I'd got rid of it months ago. Of course, I said, if they really thought it was my gun that did the shooting, I'd gladly tell them how to get it. All they'd have to do would be to dress up in diving suits, take the Twenty-third Street Ferry, and somewhere off Hoboken plunge down into the dirty Hudson River and feel around in a few million tons of mud. Because that's where I'd chucked it, I said. One day when I was going to New Jersey to visit a friend."

I filched another cigarette, lit it from the old one, and saw the miserable image of my doctor. "Did that satisfy him?"

"I doubt it. He said I should have told the police, but it was too late now. They'd be suspicious, he said, and they'd bust their guts to turn up something between Charles and me. They'd do anything to get that quarter of a million bucks, he said, even if it meant fooling around with the evidence."

"I imagine Terry'd like to be the one who collected. He could become a country squire and write those big books he dreams about."

She looked at me gravely. "Max, I don't think he'd willingly do anything to hurt me."

"He's in love with you?"

"I think so."

"And you?"

She sighed. "If you'd asked me before last night, I'd have said you bet your boots. I guess that underneath all my put-on sophistication I always wanted a man like Terry Donovan. My other life was enough to prove that. Right now, though, he's got horns."

"I gather your evening wasn't a huge success."

She smiled wanly. "It didn't start any fires. The man actually suggested we go to a nightclub—Café Society

Uptown. That, of course, was so we wouldn't have to talk while we listened to Hazel Scott play the piano. The place was full of uniforms, which seemed to depress him, so we didn't stay long. I went on to the saloon circuit and he went home. He didn't ask to meet me later."

"I could order him off the assignment, but that would only increase his suspicion."

"He'd quit and become a private eye. And the eye would be on me."

We sat in silence for a minute before I said, "Try to act naturally with him. I can't see how he can find out any more than he knows now. After all, who would tell him?"

"One person might," she said.

"Who?"

"Charles," she said. "If he comes to."

Harriet Dain had been required to make tough decisions from the day, twenty-seven years ago, when German torpedoes had blasted her into control of her father's enterprises. But never had she been faced with a decision like this—one which could determine whether the man she had adored for two decades would live or die.

That's what it came down to. The doctors, two of them neurosurgeons, with whom she had just met had been of one mind in stating the dilemma—either go in for the bullet immediately and take an estimated fifty-fifty chance on Charles Dain's survival, or delay the operation until his overall condition improved, meanwhile risking an embolism that could either kill him or reduce him to a vegetable—which, to Harriet, was the equivalent of death. The doctors had shown her X rays and charts, had taken turns in evaluating the alternatives, had finally announced their recommendation—extract the bullet. (In every eye she had detected uncertainty.) But the decision must be hers alone. They must have it by the next afternoon.

In her room, wreathed with cigarette smoke, she sat on the sofa and considered what course Charles would choose. Probably he would smile and say, "I'll take the knife—a sharp one, if you don't mind," confident that his great vitality would carry him through. On the other hand, he might prefer to die while in a coma, thus to avoid exposing the circumstances that had triggered the bullets. The thought sent a shiver through her, prompting her to reach for the decanter of Scotch and pour a stiff drink. She took it straight, then leaned back, closed her eyes, and waited for it to subdue her anxiety. She was startled upright by the staccato ring of the phone.

"Nurse Pritchard, Mrs. Dain. I have a man on the line who says he must talk to you."

"Who is it?"

"A Mr. MacKenzie. Dennis MacKenzie."

"I don't recognize the name. If it concerns my husband, tell him to call the police."

"He says he works for you at the Waterford Hotel. He's the bell captain."

Dennis MacKenzie—Mac! Why hadn't he said so? Instantly his image sprang to mind—the pleasant, wrinkled face, the graying hair, the somewhat bent wiry figure in the green brass-buttoned uniform. For some twenty years she had employed him, trusted him, and affectionately called him Mac.

"Of course," she said. "Put him on."

* * *

Now why would Harriet Dain want to see him? Terry Donovan wondered. And why in her penthouse at the Waterford Hotel instead of at the hospital?

When she had announced herself on the phone he had set himself for a tongue-lashing—either she had heard of his inquiries about the key or of his visit to Mr. Dain or both. But her tone, despite its built-in rasp, had been friendly, almost confidential, as though she were speaking to a person she considered her equal. Perhaps she thought he had stumbled on information that he was not yet ready to reveal either to the police or the paper and hoped to draw it out of him.

Well, all he had was an unwilling suspicion, and there was no way she'd get him to confess that. The scene with Kate last night had produced nothing but mutual tension, which later, alone in bed, he had tried to relieve in himself by constant assertions that the match-up in guns was sheer coincidence. By morning he had failed to convince himself and had spent a good part of the day staring into space, like a mystic awaiting divine revelation.

He had a sense of time running out, not only for Charles Dain but also for himself. The signs of war and his imminent induction into it were everywhere—the young GIs thronging Times Square and self-consciously throwing salutes to newly-commissioned officers; the Helen Hokinson-type clubwomen in Red Cross outfits; the Victory gardens on city lots; the comic strip heroes who had entered the fray—Joe Palooka, Smilin' Jack, Captain Easy—even Daddy Warbucks; the bond rallies, scrap drives, air raid drills, food rationing, blackouts and dimouts; the songs that glorified the military and sentimentalized the girls left behind. It was a Norman Rockwell war—serious, sure, but a lot of fun too—and any day now, Terry Donovan, you're going to prove your patriotism and look and act like everyone else of your generation.

Donovan had no fear, no regrets at going—in fact, it might help to straighten out his feelings for Kate—but it troubled him to think of leaving the Dain case unfinished. Sure as hell, the minute he got his official Greeting, Max Wills would insist he leave and not wait until the day he must report for duty.

Meanwhile here he was at the Waterford Hotel, asking directions to the penthouse elevator from the bell captain—a gray-haired man greeted by a passerby as Mac—and about to confront a glacial woman who had put up a quarter of a million dollars to flush out her husband's assailant while disallowing any inquiry that might tarnish his lily-white character.

He sat in a lounge chair covered in heavy striped silk, facing her on a matching sofa. The large room was a blend of pastel greens, yellows, oranges, the walls covered with oils depicting urban European scenes and a lighted portrait of Charles Dain, looking about thirty. Sliding glass doors opened on a pink-tiled terrace, beyond which he could glimpse the towers of midtown Manhattan, appearing foreshortened, as in a painted backdrop for a musical comedy. Harriet Dain seemed a part of the decor in her elegant beige dress and with her cigarette holder arcing wandlike through the air as she spoke.

"Mr. Donovan, before telling you why I asked you here, I'd like your word that whatever I say will be kept in strictest confidence."

"You have my word."

She gave her dark head a brisk nod. "Thank you.

You'll recall our conversation on the phone, when I said that we must avoid anything that might impair my husband's reputation."

"I recall it very well."

She crossed her long legs and adjusted her skirt. "Now I wish to amend that. You are no longer to avoid it. However, should you discover anything of, uh, that nature, you are to reveal it to me alone. Do I have your agreement?"

"Even if the information proves who shot him?"

"In that case," she said, "I'd appreciate hearing of it first. But of course I would not ask you to withhold it. My only concern is to make sure Charles is not maligned because of any questionable association."

Donovan gave her a direct look. "Are you saying you've learned of a questionable association?"

Her thin mouth tightened into a pink slash and she fluttered a hand to her swept-back hair. She nodded jerkily several times before saying, "Yes."

She looked, thought Donovan, like a woman struggling to maintain her composure against intense anguish. Aware of her reputation for shrewdness, he wondered if she might deliberately be attempting to convey that impression. He was silent, not wanting to influence what she was about to say.

"Mr. Donovan, this afternoon I got a telephone call from one of my employees in this hotel. I've known him for twenty years and have every reason to trust in his integrity. He said that an incident had occurred that might possibly be connected with the attack on Charles. He asked to see me privately, and I had him come to my room in the hospital. I think that what he had to say should be taken very seriously."

A tremor shook her hand as she inserted a fresh cigarette into the holder. Donovan got up, struck a match, and provided the light. She thanked him as he returned to his chair and watched her taking rapid puffs. He guessed she'd love a slug of booze, refraining only because she'd then have to include him, and so might look as if she were softening him up.

"It happened on the day Charles was shot—one thirty, to be exact. According to my informant, Charles was here at the hotel, in this apartment. He was not alone. With him was"—her mouth worked as though it had run dry—"was a woman."

The hair on Donovan's neck bristled. Had the figment at last become flesh?

Mrs. Dain's voice steadied into a harsh monotone. "This informant—as I said, an employee—was in the lobby when he saw the woman enter the elevator and ride up to the penthouse. He happened to watch the lighted numbers and noticed there were no intervening stops."

"Of course she could have simply been delivering a message."

Mrs. Dain's eyes flashed. "She was there, Mr. Donovan, for more than an hour!"

"I see. You're sure of that?"

"Positive." An ash fell from her cigarette and, unnoticed, dusted her dress. "My informant also saw her when she finally came down in the elevator and hurried to the street."

"Could he describe her?"

"He said she seemed very upset—'mad as the dickens,' were his words."

"I mean her appearance. Did he get a good look at her?"

"He did. She was slim and well-dressed." Mrs. Dain's eyes glittered, and her voice turned bitter. "She appeared to be in her mid-twenties. Small-featured—very pretty. Most noticeably, her hair was quite blond."

Why couldn't her hair have been red or black, thought Donovan. Any color except blond. Then there would have been room for doubt. Now there was none. He became aware that Harriet Dain was regarding him with a sharp, calculating look, as though anticipating enlightenment.

"Are you thinking she might be someone I'd seen?" he said.

"It seemed possible. You've been closely associated with Charles, and you're known to be very observant."

"Sorry, Mrs. Dain, I can't help you."

She flashed a brittle smile and waved her cigarette holder at him. "Oh, I think you can, Mr. Donovan. I think you have the ability and the sources to find out who this woman was. She may have had nothing to do with the shooting, but the fact that she apparently had quarreled with Charles only hours before surely makes her a suspect. You do agree?"

His nod informed him of a numbness in the back of his neck.

"Then you'll do it?"

He felt trapped. "I'll do what I can. But I can't promise—"

"Of course you can't. The only promise I expect is that you'll keep this between the two of us."

"What about Max Wills?"

"He's not to know—not even to suspect. If he did, he'd think it his duty to Charles to make it all appear entirely innocent. Before talking to Max I want to know a lot more about Charles's relationship with this woman."

"I'll look into it. But there's not much to go on."

She raised her eyebrows. "You do have quite an incentive."

"Yes, my friendship for Charles is—"

"I mean something else." She stood up. "A quarter of a million dollars, Mr. Donovan."

Alone in his apartment, sipping a martini, Donovan felt no inclination to concoct a scenario based on what Harriet Dain had told him. The fact was that the blonde in Charles Dain's apartment was Kate Richards. The fact was that Charles had said or done something that had enraged her. The fact was that she had owned the same caliber gun that hours later had shot him down.

Still, there were questions.

Why would Charles ask her to meet him at the town house on the evening of that same day? To effect a reconciliation? To persuade her to remain silent and not create a scandal?

Or had someone else confronted Charles at the town house? Someone who, as Donovan had suggested last night to Kate, might have stolen her gun to set her up as a scapegoat? Was he, Terry Donovan, the *Express's* unimpeachable investigative reporter, being used not to find Kate Richards but to find the gun, which would cleverly be placed in his path? Once matched to the bullets and once it was revealed that Kate had been Charles's outraged mistress, it would take a wizard of a criminal lawyer to keep the sentence down to assault with a deadly weapon.

Now he had implicated Harriet Dain, the only person

he could think of who had reason to seek vengeance against both her husband and Kate.

Incredible, thought Donovan. Even though she could have paid a fortune to set it up. Even though she might have offered the whopping reward in order to immunize herself against suspicion. Still incredible.

He saw no choice but to lay it all out before Kate, tell her everything he knew and suspected, and pray that her response would prove her guiltless. It was the way Charles would deal with it—straight on.

He glanced at his watch. Ten minutes to six. Kate was probably at home, deciding on what bit of finery would be right for tonight's round of revelry. Sorry, he thought, and reached for the phone. His hand snapped back as it rang.

It was Jackie, calling from a pay phone at the hospital.

"Terry, I promised you that if anything happened—"

"He *died?*"

"No, no, there's been no change. But Mrs. Dain just had a meeting with the doctors. That was the second one."

"You know what was said?"

"I know what *she* said. She gave them permission to remove the bullet. It's risky, but not doing it could be worse. The operation's set for day after tomorrow."

"Thank you, Jackie."

"Sure. Sorry it sounds so dismal. Off duty, I'd give you nothing but good news."

"I'll remember that."

Hanging up, he decided not to call Kate. Possibly within forty-eight hours Charles Dain himself would be able to provide the answers everyone was anxious to hear.

Except, perhaps, Kate Richards or Harriet Dain.

Chapter · 13

Harriet Anthony, in late 1923 uncomfortably aware that she was fast approaching thirty, an age at which she was certain she would be doomed to everlasting spinster-hood, was prepared to buy herself a husband. She had but one stipulation—the man must be no other than Charles Dain.

From the moment in the ballroom of the Savoy Hotel when she had spied him standing tall and self-possessed, the strong bones in his face hollowing his cheeks, giving him an exotic look, she had felt a visceral attraction. And when, surprisingly, he had shown wit, roguishly applying it to the jiggling buttocks of an otherwise prim English lady, the mirth evoked in Harriet was tanta-mount to intimacy. For the first time in her life she sensed that laughter of a certain kind could be an ex-pression of sexual desire, a feeling not experienced since an actor had projected it into her inner self, failing, however, in his attempt to make it viable. But the actor had been boring, unimaginative, his interests limited to an insular domain of mimicry, while Charles Dain, she quickly discovered, had a sharp, stimulating mind concerned with the fortunes of continents. How like herself, she had thought, upon hearing he was a foreign correspondent—both for their own purposes investing themselves in the people, places, and politics that were the heartbeat of the world.

But she had not spoken of herself except to convey rather obliquely that she lived alone in London on money provided by her father, whose full name she was not required to mention—an omission that spared her from being recognized as the fabulously wealthy heiress of the late and renowned Calder Anthony. The name Harriet Anthony, though well known in corporate and financial circles, seemed to mean nothing to him, explainable, she thought, by his travels to distant places and his preoccupation with the struggles of foreign political movements. This was exactly as Harriet would have it, for while she now had no compunction about using her fortune to induce a marriage proposal, she insisted on first having evidence that the prospective groom would at least assure her of a companionable bond.

Certainly as they conversed in the Savoy Hotel ballroom there was no question but that she interested Charles Dain intellectually. He seemed surprised and fascinated that she could discuss so informatively the monumental problems then plaguing the countries of Europe and Asia—the rise of the Labor Party in England, the rampant inflation in Germany, the astounding social changes in the Soviet Union, the resistance to white domination in China, the political instability in France and Italy. For more than an hour they talked, sitting on brocade chairs in a carpeted area away from the dance floor, ignoring the lords and ladies, the diplomatic dignitaries, the obsequious sycophants, oblivious of time until he happened to glance at his watch and suddenly sprang to his feet.

"Forgive me, but I'm late. I'm supposed to be on my way to Paris."

She considered driving him to the station, deciding against it when she thought of her Bentley—the one bequeathed by her father and still resplendent—now parked outside in the care of a liveried chauffeur. She had also retained the Rolls-Royce, but that she kept in Paris and seldom used, finding it an embarrassment among all the small, efficient cars.

She had risen and was regarding him with a look of anguish, a look she did not bother to dissemble because she had only this crucial moment either to win him to another meeting or perhaps lose him forever.

"I'm so sorry you must leave, Mr. Dain."

He grinned. "Mr. Dain? Here we've been reshaping the world and you call me—"

"Charles," she said, smiling.

"Much better. When I'm in London again, may I call you?"

She felt a thump in her chest. "Please do." She snatched a note pad from her bag and quickly scrawled her phone number. Handing it to him, she said, "Do you know when that will be?"

"In about eight months."

"Eight months!" It seemed like the rest of her life.

"I'm going to the Far East."

Probably, she thought, he'd return with a Eurasian bride. "Then you won't be staying in Paris?"

"Only for a few days."

"With friends?" She didn't care that it was none of her business, didn't care that he was obviously younger than she, didn't care that her eagerness betrayed a man-less woman. She cared only to delay him, to allow time for him to say that he would phone her from Paris or send a postcard from Peking.

He was turning away but paused to give her a penetrating look. "I'm stopping at the Crillon," he said, then smiled gently, as though he had seen into her heart, and, as abruptly as he had entered her life, was gone, his words of farewell stunning her with their terrible finality.

Returning to her apartment, she thought for a while, then picked up her phone and called a vice-president of one of her companies.

That done, she went to bed and slept soundly.

"Charles? This is Harriet Anthony. Remember, we met—"

"Well, hello! Of course I remember. Yesterday you rescued me from the London bores. How are you?"

"Fine. I was afraid I'd made you miss your train."

"Better if I had. The Channel was rough. Anyway, I made it to Paris a few hours ago. Is there something I can do for you over here?"

"I was hoping you'd ask. This is a frightful imposition, but I have a friend in Paris who is a great admirer of your work. She'd be thrilled if she could meet you. Do you suppose you could possibly spare her a few minutes? She'd gladly come to your hotel."

"Well—"

"I know I'm asking a lot. You're probably on a very tight schedule."

"Actually I'm not. No one knows I'm here. It's just that I'm not very good at playing the great man."

"All you need do is say hello and look wise."

He laughed. "I think I have a pill for that. All right, I'll even buy her a drink."

"Splendid. Suppose, then, she meets you in the Crillon bar. About six o'clock?"

"I'll be there. How will I know her?"

"Oh, she'll recognize you. I'll have her take a table where she can see you coming in."

"And her name?"

"Calder," Harriet said.

In the glow from the backbar and under the pinpricks of light from the ceiling, Harriet knew she looked her very best. Her dark hair, worn more loosely than usual, was a mass of gleaming waves, emphasizing the pale perfection of her skin, particularly her bare white shoulders, which seemed to leap from the coral chiffon of her Schiaperelli gown. Only her breasts caused her concern—too prominent, she thought, despite the tightest brassiere she could endure. Voluptuous, she told herself; that was the word to think of, that was the image she had calculated for herself—the very opposite of a brainy, bloodless woman who could move minds but never hearts. Unchanged, however, was her sense of purpose, as implacable now as it would be had she prepared herself to negotiate a lucrative contract.

She glanced at her watch—five past six—then looked up and saw him standing just inside the entry. He squinted as though to adjust his sight to the semidarkness, then slowly turned his head to survey the room. His gaze swept over her and, undeflected by her mischievous smile, went on past. With a slight shrug, he moved in and took a seat at the bar. The bartender greeted him by name, spoke with him for a few moments, then poured a glass of champagne. Charles sipped it, then picked up a pencil and apparently signed the tab, a signal perhaps that he would linger only for this one drink and then leave.

Disappointed that he had not seen her, she half rose in her chair to go to him, but was stopped by the sudden appearance of a bowing waiter.

"For while you are waiting," he said, smiling and setting down a hollow-stemmed glass bubbling with champagne. "With our compliments."

Disconcerted, she thanked him, adding, "Really, you're much too kind."

He dismissed it with a wave of a crisp, white napkin. Then, staring at it, he said, "Excuse me. This, too, of course is for you." He set it carefully beside her glass, smiled again, and turned away.

Glancing down at the napkin, she saw it was smudged with ink. Peering closer, she read: "Your Miss Calder is ravishing. I can't wait to meet her."

Her head snapped up. From the bar, Charles Dain regarded her solemnly, and with mock ceremony raised his glass.

Her quick intake of breath, suddenly expelled in a burst of laughter, brought him to his feet. He crossed the room with menacing slowness, eyes threatening, hand raised to shake an accusing finger. As he lowered himself beside her she started to speak, but he cut her off with a slashing gesture.

"Duplicity," he said darkly. "Chicanery. Flimflam."

"Please, Charles, let me ex—"

"You are"—his head went back in an effort to contain his emotion—"*marvelous!* Absolutely marvelous!"

She slumped in relief. "Oh, thank goodness! For a moment—" She stopped, seeing that his expression had again become fierce.

"Nevertheless, Miss Calder, I think you should know that I'm deeply resentful."

Confused, she could only gaze at him meekly.

"You're guilty of piracy," he said.

"Piracy?"

"Exactly. This particular brand of deception belongs exclusively to me. I hold the original patent."

She smiled and entered the game, enjoying it. "An inadvertent infringement, sir. I shall cease and desist."

"On second thought, we'll split the rights. Which calls for—ah, there you are."

The waiter, face beaming, had reappeared with a bottle of champagne nested in a silver bucket of ice. Charles thanked him, and as the wine was popped and poured, said to Harriet, "You'll concede that I managed a remarkable counterthrust?"

"Spectacular. I beg for mercy."

"We'll see about that."

They clicked glasses, drank, eyed each other over the rims. "Now," said Charles, "I'll hear your confession."

She had rehearsed it well. By an odd coincidence, she said, she had talked to a friend last night who disclosed that he was flying to Paris today—would she like to come along? Considering that Charles had only just left for Paris, she welcomed the invitation as an act of fate. It took but another short, impulsive step—"aided, I suspect, by ardent spirits"—to invent the worshipful Miss Calder and arrange the meeting.

"You astonish me," he said.

"That was the idea."

He shook his head. "I'd never have thought that you—" He hesitated.

"Could be so bold, so impetuous"—she paused—"so *unladylike?*"

"Well, you did impress me as being more interested in world affairs than—"

"I hope I'm dispelling that impression."

"Overwhelmingly. Now, if you'll forgive my curiosity, where did you decide that I take you to dinner?"

"The plan says we'll decide that later. It's a lovely evening—ideal for a ride in the park."

He threw up his hands. "I'm yours to command. Besides, it's getting crowded in here. Shall we leave?"

"As soon as we finish the champagne."

Outside, on the Place de la Concorde, she took his arm and, ignoring the tooting taxis circling the Obelisque, led him briskly along the Champs-Élysées. To his look of inquiry she responded that it was a fine evening for a stroll and that she needed the air to clear her head of the champagne. Approaching the Arc de Triomphe, she steered him away from the boulevard and then turned into a side street where, under a street lamp, she abruptly halted.

"You look pale," he said with concern. "Are you all right?"

She felt an inner breathlessness and pulled her wrap closer to her throat. "Oh, yes. Still, perhaps we should ride now."

He looked about, somewhat helplessly because they were far from any taxis. "We'll have to walk back," he said.

"Why walk," she said, "when we can travel in splendor."

He turned and saw that her hand was raised, finger pointing.

"In that," she said, smiling.

He looked and saw a large, silver-gray automobile parked beneath the street lamp. Its opulence was proclaimed by the gleaming grille flanked by huge headlights, by the glass panel that separated the tonneau from the chauffeur's seat, by the pristine tire that rode majestically on the runningboard.

"A Rolls-Royce," he said. "Yes, of course. Absurd to hunt for a taxi when we have—"

"A palace on wheels," she said. "Let's get in."

He stared at her. "You *are* joking. I hope so, because the gendarmes are pretty sensitive about—"

But she was already in the chauffeur's seat, jiggling the steering wheel. Exasperated now, he went around and stood on the street side, gripping the top of the door.

"Harriet, let's play someplace else."

She pretended to regard him through a lorgnette. "Please enter, Mr. Dain."

"Now look—" He paused as she beckoned impatiently. "Well, all right," he said, "but just for a second." He opened the door, sat, reached to close the door. "Then we'll . . . my God!"

The engine had roared to life.

"Through the park, Mr. Dain?"

He gawked at her. The Rolls-Royce began slowly to move forward. Just as slowly his consternation was replaced by a look of enlightenment. He sighed heavily and sank back on the cushioned leather.

"I should have known," he said. "This, too, is part of the plan."

"Correct. A dear old friend was kind enough to provide us with suitable transportation."

"How long have you been insane?"

"Since I met you."

"Do you know what you're saying?"

"Yes, I'm saying exactly what you think. Now please relax while I try to fathom how this machine works."

Soon they were zipping along the Boulevard Lannes, Harriet clutching the wheel as though it might fly away, Charles cringing against an inevitable crash. Reaching an intersection, Harriet turned left into the Bois de Boulogne, the enormous park bordering Paris on the west. They sped past lakes shimmering in the moonlight, past the great Longchamps and Auteuil racetracks, sprawling like ghostly astral cities, past a tennis stadium, a polo field, a children's zoo, then entered a thickly wooded area, the trees flashing starkly in the beams of the headlights. There, she slowed and coasted into a clearing at the side of the road.

"I've lost my bearings," she said.

"More likely your mind. Just turn around and go back the way you came."

She cut the engine but not the lights. "Let's sit here a minute. I'm a bit nervous."

"You're fortunate. I'm deranged. I hope they serve brandy at the asylum."

"That's what we need—brandy. Come with me." She switched off the headlights and was out of the car before he could reply. He joined her in the richly upholstered rear seat, his despair reported by a small groan. She flicked on the interior light, revealing a red-carpeted floor, gray shades on the windows, and a tulip-shaped vase mounted at the side that contained a single rose. Reaching forward, she pressed a button below the glass partition and a panel dropped down to become a tray, beyond which were several bottles and an array of crystal. She placed two snifters on the tray, then selected a bottle, uncorked it and poured.

"Brandy, my lord," she said, handing it to him.

Sipping it, he stared at her as he might at a wraith. "You are real, aren't you?" he said. "We're actually sitting here, in a forest in Paris, in the dead of night, drinking brandy in the back seat of a Rolls-Royce?"

"It's all true."

He shook his head. "Would it be gauche of me to ask why?"

She smiled mysteriously, took his empty glass and set it with hers on the tray. She felt his hand touch her bare shoulder, where the wrap had fallen away. It was as though he had squeezed a trigger, releasing a mass of fired-up, molten energy that had been seething inside the crucible of her flesh since she had seen him enter the Crillon bar. She shoved the glasses into the compartment, flipped the lid closed, turned swiftly, shrugged off her wrap, twisted to thrust frontally against his body, threw back her head, parted her lips, and joined them to his in a passion experienced only through the books on her father's forbidden shelf. She reached up behind him and snapped off the light.

He resisted for an instant, but only because of the suddenness of the assault. Then he shifted slightly and drew her across him, arm beneath the nape of her neck so that he could kiss her more thoroughly. Her hand crept beneath the lapels of his Savile Row pin-striped jacket, unbuttoned the top of his crisp, white shirt, stroked the hard slabs of his chest, descended to run fingertips inside the line of his leather belt, continuing down to grasp the burgeoning core of him. Her mouth and all the inner richness it was yielding felt his sharp intake of breath, resounded gently to his murmur of protest, addressed not to her but to this Rolls-Royce bedroom that seemed inadequate to the feverish maneuverings of two tall people. In the darkness he could not know, as she did, that the interior was spacious, the upholstered seat broad and long, the carpeted floor designed for the stretching of legs.

She sat up, kicked off her shoes, unsnapped the back of her dress, let it drift to her waist and, wriggling her hips, dwindled to her pink-lace chemise and long silk stockings. Then she returned to him, helping to unfasten, untie, undress, divesting him of the fabrications that insulated his body from the heat rising from her skin like a scented vapor. Finished, she lay back while he slowly stripped her, pausing to kiss and caress her unleashed breasts, the hollows beneath the quivering cage of her ribs, the taut, creamy smoothness of her thighs. Now, all her latent lubricity rushed forth to engulf her, pound at her temples, panic her heart, rob her of breath until, faint with ecstasy, she felt a sudden commotion in her loins, as suddenly released in a frothing wave.

He sensed her completion and rose up to clasp her in his arms, unaware that her pent-up passion had only been skimmed, enabling her now to participate in pleasure without loss of control. She arched back, swelling her breasts, then slid to the floor to tease him with her tongue, savor him, envelop him, engorge him, her head rising and falling in frantic rhythm, her thin lips ravenously demanding. Spinning vaguely through her mind was a montage of all the women he must have possessed—great ladies, stunning actresses, emancipated writers, celebrated courtesans, exotic dancers—all so much more knowing and artful than she, all symbols of a sensual standard that must now be surpassed. She had fantasized the myriad convolutions of sex, selected and mentally rehearsed those that would incite the greatest response in the smallest space, and here she was, well on her way, eager to transport him through lascivious byways to the summit of joy, when suddenly he grasped her shoulders, jerked her to the seat, rolled her on her back, dropped to his knees, parted and jackknifed her legs, and slowly, so very slowly, hands ravishing her breasts, entered her.

And now she was the enthralled captive, every nerve, muscle, and sinew slavishly obedient to the tumescent instrument that relentlessly impaled her, that went on and on, gaining in force, retaining its stamina amidst her multiple climaxes—until finally, as she soared to still another peak, she was rocked by a violent and prolonged tremor, joining with it as it erupted into a lather of warmth.

Then they lay still.

Charles was the first to move. He slid up beside her, cradled her head against his cheek, traced with his fingers the curve of her hip. He kissed her mouth, her nose, her eyes, tasting the tears born of joy.

"If I'd only known," he said, "I'd have stayed in London."

She smiled. "You didn't guess I could be such a wild *fille de joie?*"

"Only for a moment—yesterday, when we said goodbye. Later I thought: It would be like making love to a statue." He ran his hand down her body. "You make me feel like Pygmalion."

"You are. And I'm your Galatea. Only yours."

She felt him stiffen, clueing her to his thoughts: No woman could be so uninhibitedly erotic unless she had lain with many men.

She turned and faced his dark silhouette. "You think there have been others?"

"It doesn't matter."

"But it does. Let me confess my lurid past."

She told him about the actor.

His white teeth flashed in a smile. "And he was the only one?"

"Yes, and a very poor instructor. But at least he taught me that I wasn't entirely frigid."

"Frigid! You could melt the polar ice cap." His head bent forward and she knew he was regarding her dubiously. "It's a wonder you're so wise," he said.

She told him about her father's books.

He laughed, holding her closer, as though to signal his belief. "Well, now that we've enjoyed chapter one, let's get on with it. But first I'll take you to dinner."

"Come to my place. I'll cook for you."

"At the Crillon? They'll let you use their kitchen?"

"I'm staying in a house. We can have it to ourselves."

"All night?"

"All night and the next day—to eternity."

He seemed to think she was joking.

She could feel the intensity of his gaze as she chauffeured the car across the ancient bridge, the Pont Neuf, that led to the house on the island in the Seine called Ile de la Cité. Now, she thought, he's sorting it all out, evaluating it, wondering what kind of woman this was who, in a matter of hours, had duped him into this second meeting, descended on him from the skies, astonished him with a Rolls-Royce, seduced him in the back seat, and was now abducting him to the home of an absent friend to continue their carnival of love. He had to be more than intrigued, more than flattered. He had to be telling himself that here was someone unique, a woman forthright in her desires and shameless in their execution, a woman of intellect who could also be frivolous, a woman who—ah, the dream of all men— appeared unapproachable in public but was brazenly erotic in private.

On the other hand, he could be thinking that he had been beguiled into the company of the ultimate nymphomaniac.

The latter view seemed more probable when they drew up in front of the house. Getting out, he stepped back and peered up uneasily at the two-story structure of rose-colored brick. His smile seemed directed at himself—an odd, ironic smile.

"One of the elegant old houses," he said. "It must date back two hundred years."

"Closer to three hundred."

"Which floor is Miss Calder's?"

She knew he was baiting her, didn't care, in fact was pleased. "Both floors," she said.

He glanced back at the Rolls-Royce. "She lives well."

"Lucky for us. Come see."

She took his arm and led him to the carved front door with its polished-brass knocker. Opening it with her key, she stepped inside, flicked the light switch, and watched his face as he entered.

He was silent as his glance took in the mirrored foyer and, straight ahead, the broad, burnished staircase. And he remained silent when he trailed her into the living room and observed the plush carpets, the authentic period pieces, the marble fireplace, the crystal chandeliers, the paintings by Picasso, Cézanne, Utrillo. Catching his eye, Harriet smiled tenuously, half in apology, half in embarrassment, as though to say she was unaccustomed to all this opulence. He responded with an ingenuous look and the suggestion that they have a brandy and take it along on a tour of the upper floor.

They were in a large bedroom, brandy half drained, standing and inspecting a canopied bed, when he said, "I seem to have been rather slow this evening."

"Slow?"

He shook his head. "Later," he said, and took her glass, set it with his on a night table, came back, stroked her shoulders and, still standing, eyes fixed somberly on hers, proceeded to undress her.

She reached to do the same for him but he drew back and, with a sort of studied grace—carefully folding his foulard tie, his pin-striped jacket, his pearl-gray trousers —made the transition to nakedness. Coming back, he kissed her, caressed her, gently explored her, then, with a quick, strong motion, swept her from her feet and took her to bed.

It was not until they wakened to see sunlight slanting through the tall windows, streaking the rooftops of Paris and turning red chimney pots to brilliant orange, that he revealed what had been on his mind.

"My lovely Miss Calder," he said against her cheek.

His tone, she thought, sounded ominous. Nervously she fussed with the hem of the satin sheet. "Darling, perhaps we should forget about that."

"Forget? That was my problem." He pushed up on

the pillow. "Miss Calder. Miss Anthony. Put them together—"

"Wait, Charles—"

"—and you have Calder Anthony." He gazed down at her. "The corporate Croesus. The man who, eight years ago, went down with the *Lusitania* and left all his worldly—"

"I planned to tell you, Charles. Believe me, I did. But first I wanted you to, well, care about me for myself."

"Would you say now that I do?"

"Yes. Am I wrong?"

"You're not wrong."

She released a breath. "Then it doesn't bother you that I'm rich?"

"I'm bothered you didn't tell me in the first place." He grinned. "I'm delighted you're rich. All my life I've wanted a woman who was rich!"

September 4, 1923

Dear Max:

Sit down, light a cigarette, pour yourself a stiff one, and listen to a story that will warm your foolish heart. I'll wait. . . .

Now then. In June I wrote you that I'd hired on at the Paris *Herald,* taken an apartment, and was seeing a good deal of a woman named Harriet Anthony. What I didn't say, lest you think me a romantic imbecile, was that all this necessitated canceling a trip I'd assigned myself to the Far East. Steady there.

A week ago I quit the *Herald,* forsook my apartment, and moved to what I have christened the Palais Anthony, a magnificent abode occupied in lonely splendor, before my merciful arrival, by its namesake. After two days of whatever you want to imagine, we decided to take a holiday in Brittany. We traveled of course by Rolls-Royce, equipped with hampers of delicacies and an intimate, well-stocked bar. We stayed at a resort in La Baule that sits on a rocky cliff overlooking a white sand beach and is staffed by courteous people who speak Breton, a Celtic language that only a Welshman or Cornishman would understand. However, that proved no barrier, as we were not concerned with asking directions to such local attractions as—and here I consult my guidebook— the megaliths of Carnac and the dolmens of Locmariaquer, whatever they may be. We wanted nothing more than to find a church, preferably one run by a kindly clergyman with a sentimental wife. We found it.

And so we were married.

Have another drink.

Onward. Harriet is the sole child of the late, fabulous Calder Anthony who, as you may recall, owned all the money in the world except a dollar and sixty-nine cents, and he was working on that when he died. All this plunder, and the businesses that provided it, fell into the lap of his daughter, who had been prepared almost since infancy for just such an event. During the war, when you and I were battling the Hun with typewriters and roistering at Nini's, Harriet was dashing madly about flogging her companies to turn out increasing quantities of the stuff the Germans found so objectionable. She's a superb businesswoman—

smart, informed, tough when she has to be—and she earns every penny of her income, which makes mine look like it belongs in a piggy bank. This is not to say she is lacking in the more enticing attributes of womankind—a fact which, knowing me, I'm sure you assume. But it does emphasize the feasibility of what I'm about to propose.

Since leaving the *Herald,* I've had no gainful employment. I've decided that I'm sick to death of traipsing around the world prying provocative quotes out of megalomaniacs who, if they were in New York, would be running a restaurant or a laundry or, more likely, firing sawed-off shotguns in those gang wars I keep reading about. Aware of my boredom, Harriet plumbed my soul in an effort to release from my subconscious some secret ambition that I've always wanted to fulfill. The torturous process took all of six seconds. "I want to own a newspaper," I said. Her response took but three seconds. "You shall have it," she said. I pushed my luck. "A New York newspaper," I said. She hesitated a moment, then, indulgent wife that she is, said, "Of course a New York newspaper. Why not ask your friend Max Wills to advise you?"

Will you, Max? Not just out of friendship but also because it might please you to see atop the masthead of a great metropolitan newspaper: Max Wills, Editor in Chief. How's that for a bribe?

I'm not interested in picking up and trying to rejuvenate some butcher-paper sheet that's bought mainly to wrap fish. I want to start from scratch and develop a paper that will hit New York fully grown, even though a bit awkwardly at first, a paper that's got blood in its eye and fire in its belly, a paper that's even more alive and exciting than the *Daily News* and the *Journal* but that has the respect given the *Times*.

That's a tall order, but I haven't the slightest doubt we can do it. We'll need a plant, presses, Linotype machines, the works. But that's no problem—all of that can be had with money, and we'll have plenty of it—however many millions it takes. My chief concern is personnel. Granted that we start with two certified geniuses, we'll still need people to fill up the pages. And, Max, I want the best. I'd have no compunction about raiding the competition with offers of big pay and benefits.

Right now what I'd like from you is a list and the credentials of those people you think would make the ideal staff—editors, rewrite men, reporters, photographers, columnists. (Later we can discuss the syndicated stuff.) I'd appreciate your ideas on what kind of paper you'd like to see—its character, its tone of voice, its stance on local, national, and foreign affairs, even its format—anything and everything you've ever thought of to make a paper more stimulating and worthwhile.

Harriet and I will arrive in New York in about two months. She's preparing herself to give full time to this project until it's off the ground, after which she will confine herself to the small matter of running her international enterprises. Her experience will be invaluable in acquiring facilities and arranging contracts for newsprint and distribution, as well as in providing an entree to a number of big advertisers. But first we'll need a cadre of highly skilled professionals to design and produce an actual newspaper, which we'll publish in small quantities several times a week. It will be experimental, to be seen only by ourselves. We'll try to view it objectively—admire it, detest it, yawn at it, kiss it, and keep changing it until we've got what we want. This process, along with the mechanical acquisitions, will take, I estimate, about a year from the time we start. Our gift to the literate public should be ready for presentation in the summer of 1925.

That's it for now. You've probably got a million questions, so send them along. But first say yes.

Max, can you imagine us working together again!

Think about that while you finish the bottle.

> Your solid-gold friend,
> Charles

The next morning, in a haze of glorious fantasy, I sent Charles a cable:

HOORAY AND CONGRATULATIONS AND BEST WISHES ON YOUR MARRIAGE EXCLAMATION POINT I HAD THE STIFF DRINK STOP I FINISHED THE BOTTLE STOP AS YOUR NEW EDITOR IN CHIEF I SHALL PROCEED AS DIRECTED STOP AM PLANNING TO FURNISH OFFICE WITH CAFE TABLES STOP LETTER FOLLOWING STOP LOVE MAX

Chapter · 14

Terry Donovan parked his feet on my desk and said, "Max, you know about Kate and me. As boss, does that bother you?"

I exercised my eyebrows. We'd just been adding up the progress of the police, concluding that the sum was zero, so the sudden switch caught me by surprise. For a moment I wondered if it was a sneaky lead-in to questions about the disappearance of Kate's gun. But he seemed so sincere, so open, as though speaking to a lodge brother, that I decided he was simply obeying an impulse to talk about his ambiguous romance.

"Not at all," I said. "Why should it bother me?"

"Some places they fire guys who fraternize with the help."

"Not here," I said. "We stand with Jefferson—the unalienable rights of life, liberty, and the pursuit of beautiful blond columnists."

He gave me a pleasant smile, said "That's the spirit," got up to leave, then turned back. "By the way, you know Kate's parents. What are they like?"

That should have tipped me that he was up to something, but I was about to call the hospital, and my mind was preoccupied with Charles. Besides, the question seemed innocent enough. Considering his friendship with Kate—even before they became lovers—it would have been only natural for her to confide my close relationship with the family.

"Great people," I said. "You'll like them."

"That I'm sure of. The point is will they like *me*? He's an engineer and probably thinks reporters drink like fish, play the horses, and sleep in their underwear with their hats on."

Well, I thought, if he was worried about meeting her parents, he must have accepted Kate's explanation about the missing gun. I suddenly felt expansive. "Do you?" I asked, smiling.

"Drink and play the horses—moderately. Sleep—hatless and raw." He came back and sat down, but kept his feet off my desk. Opening a fresh pack of Camels, he plucked one out with his lips, started to pocket the pack, then, glinting his eyes in mockery of the Devil, offered it to me. As with the hell-bound Faust, I yielded, lighting up and sitting back to savor the iniquitous weed.

"Maybe I'll put in a good word for you," I said. "I'll tell him you can't wait to serve your country."

"Fine, if that'll impress him. I gather he was in the war—*your* war, I mean."

"No, he didn't make it."

Donovan's eyes got sleepier, a sign he was thinking. "That's right, they'd have skipped him, a married man— in fact, a father."

Despite all the years that had passed since Tom Richards had married Sharon Fletcher, the memory was still vivid, the wound still sensitive. I could recall Mr. Dain's somber voice on the phone announcing that Charles had enlisted, an act precipitated by Sharon's wedding just days before.

"He'd been married less than a week when we declared war," I said. "And he didn't become a father until the following year." My thoughts flashed back to my farewell call to Sharon, right after I'd volunteered— early November of 1917—catching her when she was in the midst of packing. "That was after they'd moved to New York. The reason Tom didn't—"

"I thought they were both born New Yorkers."

"No, just Kate. Her parents were originally from New Jersey—South Orange." I offended my lungs with more smoke. "Anyway, the army turned Tom down because of a heart murmur. Nothing serious, but back then they'd disqualify you for flat feet."

Donovan shook his head. "There goes my conversation starter. I was going to ask him about all the pontoons and airfields he'd built."

I regarded him sympathetically, remembering how I'd once wanted George Fletcher's approval. "Try him on pipelines in Arabia," I said. "Or, better still, ask him about the foul-ups in war production. Stick to things like that, and he'll love you like a son."

Smiling self-consciously, Donovan got up. "Thanks for the tip, Max. If it works, I'll buy you a bottle of Scotch."

"The cork will do. These days just the smell gets me pickled."

As soon as he left, I called Harriet at the hospital. Though it was ten in the morning, she sounded as though she'd been wakened from a deep sleep. Her voice was guttural, the words slightly slurred. If I hadn't known her so well, I'd have thought she'd been hitting the brandy. Apparently the stress had finally got to her and she'd been chain-smoking for hours. The operation, she said, was scheduled for nine A.M. the next day.

"I'll come up," I said. "We'll suffer together."

"Thank you, Max. But we won't know anything until afternoon. They think it may take five or six hours."

"I'll get there about eleven. We'll do crossword puzzles and play backgammon. You can blow smoke in my face."

"Oh, Max—" Her voice broke, then recovered as she said, "God help me if I made the wrong decision."

"You didn't. Look, Charles is going to beat this. That's what you've got to believe, just as I believe it." I felt my chest tighten. The thought that I might lose my dearest friend was too awful even to contemplate.

"I do believe it, Max." She paused, and I heard her light a cigarette. When she spoke again, it was more like her business voice, brisk and unemotional. "There's one thing I'd like you to do."

"Name it."

She cleared her throat. "After it's over and he's in the recovery room, I want any doctors or nurses cleared out. I want to be alone with him."

"But they'll have to check him out, monitor him."

"I know. But they're not to be there when he regains consciousness. If he's able to speak, I want it to be only to me. As his wife, I think I have that right."

"I'll take care of it, Harriet."

I felt no need to ask why.

Terry Donovan was sure that their friendly little chat had not aroused Max Wills's suspicions. Why should it?

What could be more guileless than the wish to make a good first impression on your lover's parents? Shrewd as Max was, there was enough sentimentality under his crusty hide to make him a willing victim of the deceit.

Deceit—that troubled Donovan. It never did when the setup was a crook or a pretender, but when the target was a man with the integrity of a Max Wills, the art of surreptitiously extracting information seemed close to thievery. Still, it was essential that it be done—a decision made shortly after two A.M. that morning, when Donovan's mind, churning to produce something solid out of random scraps of knowledge, had exploded with nightmarish conjecture. Jolted awake, he had snapped on all the lights to verify the real world, then sat at his desk while attempting to reduce the dream-inspired notion to absurdity. Instead it had grown in substance until it competed in importance with the question of whether Charles Dain would live or die.

The conversation with Max had provided circumstantial support for the shocking thought—specifics that when added to the recalled words of Charles's father encouraged conjecture to become conviction.

Now there was no need to suffer in ignorance. The answer would have been indisputably recorded in the archives of the City of New York.

Twenty minutes later he was standing in a huge room occupied by a few clerks and banks of file cabinets. Hunting through the file on Richards, he found that the job would take longer than anticipated—everyone in New York, it began to seem, was named Richards, from Aaron Richards to the simplified Z. Richards. But there was not a single Richards named Kate, the name, she had once told him, she had been christened with.

Abandoning the search, Donovan returned to the office of the man in charge—a squat individual with a sallow complexion and expressionless eyes. The name he was seeking, said Donovan, was not in the file—were there additional files somewhere else?

"No, that's it. If the person was born in New York City, the record would be there. Absolutely."

Donovan distinctly recalled Max saying that Kate had been born in New York, after her parents had moved from New Jersey. Did he know that for a fact, or had he merely assumed it? He may have been in the army at the time, perhaps overseas, thus could easily have been mistaken. In that case the most likely birthplace was the town where the Richardses had previously lived—South Orange, New Jersey. That would be in Essex County, whose vital statistics were probably housed in the nearby city of Newark.

After a verifying phone call, he was on his way to cross the Hudson River.

This time the name was there, seeming to leap from the certificate Donovan had plucked from the file drawer, Kate Edna Richards. Parents: Sharon and Thomas Richards. Place of birth: Essex Community Hospital. The date . . . Donovan squinted, unsure of the numbers that had him catching his breath. He backed off from the cabinet, then moved into the pale sunlight glazing a grimy window. The numbers though handwritten a quarter of a century ago, were clear, unmistakable—and horrifying.

Donovan stepped to a table, slumped into a chair, drew out a pad and pencil, and transcribed everything printed and written on the certificate. His hand twitched as he wrote the date of birth: September 20, 1917.

Finishing, he got up and stalked from the long room, barely nodding to the smiling woman at the desk who had been so cooperative. Outside he was oblivious of the jostling crowds, the clanging trolleys, the indignant horns of jammed-up cars. Crossing Broad Street and elbowing through the throngs milling about Bamberger's department store, he finally saw, on the corner ahead, what he had been seeking—a bar. Entering, he took a stool near the window and ordered a double Scotch. He knocked back half of it before taking out the pad and staring again at what he had transcribed. The only item of significance was the date. The sight of it was as unnerving as the conjecture that, in tortured sleep, had erupted through his brain.

On the day Kate was born—September 20, 1917—her parents had been married less than six months!

There was no doubt of the approximate time of that marriage. Old Mr. Dain had indicated it when he said it occurred shortly before Charles joined the army ("As soon as President Wilson said that we must fight") in early April. And Max Wills had been equally precise, stating that Tom Richards had "married less than a week before we declared war."

Put another way, Sharon Richards was at least three months pregnant when she became the bride of Tom Richards, thus placing the time of conception back to the last days of the previous year—a time when, presumably, she was still deeply involved with Charles.

The conclusion seemed inescapable: Charles Dain was the father of Kate Richards!

Unless Kate had been born prematurely.

Unless Tom Richards had been sexually intimate with Sharon several months prior to their wedding. (But why, then, would they have waited so long to marry?)

The question of Kate's paternity was minor compared to its dreadful implications. Now Donovan had to cope with the suspicion that the woman who had enamored him might have previously been conducting an incestuous affair with her father. Granting that neither would have known of the genetic relationship, the stigma, the revulsion, remained.

Did Max Wills know of it? He had been a close friend to both Sharon and Charles since the height of their romance and later had become virtually a member of the Richards family, judging by his treasured snapshots. But perhaps he had not seen Sharon for some time prior to reporting for military duty and had not been told of the birth (though surely he would have phoned her, if only to say good-bye). Returning from France more than a year later, he would not think to question the legitimacy of a child whose age, particularly to a bachelor, would not have been obviously determinable.

And what about Tom Richards? Had he married Sharon without suspecting she was pregnant? And once he knew, what explanation had she given?

Questions, questions, questions—and Donovan had no hard answers to any of them, least of all to the one that was most crucial: Should he remain silent in the hope that Kate and Charles had forever terminated their liaison, assuming there had been one? The answer must await the outcome of the operation. Should Charles die, the only sensible course would be to let the truth die with him.

He was sure of but one thing—if Charles Dain was

indeed Kate's father and they had been lovers, there would be many more people than she with a motive for murder. He did not exclude himself.

Arriving home, he picked up the mail, opened an official-looking envelope, and was confronted with the word "Greetings." According to the undersigned—President Franklin D. Roosevelt—Terence Donovan's good neighbors had selected him for induction into the armed forces of the United States. He was to report in two weeks.

Strangely, he felt only relief. No longer would he have to make a single important decision. He would simply be a body, a number, his destiny controlled by an invisible, disinterested hierarchy whose profession was killing. But until they actually had him, he would continue as the investigative reporter for the *Express*, assigned to cover the shooting of Charles Dain.

Unless, of course, Max Wills learned he'd been drafted and—ostensibly out of kindness, patriotism, and the need to indoctrinate another reporter—ordered him on vacation.

But why should Max find out? Or anybody—including Kate?

"Stay awhile, Max," Harriet said. "Have a drink."

"Well, now," I said, smacking my lips, "this is certainly the place for it. But you'd better alert an orderly. Have him stand by with one of those snappy canvas jackets that tie in the back."

"Oh, I forgot." She smiled. "But that's all right. I have some really delicious soda water. It's imported." She took my fedora. "From Brooklyn."

I had left work early to stop by and talk to the key members of the medical team that would operate on Charles the next morning. None of the three—surgeon, anesthesiologist, head nurse—objected to Harriet's request that she be the first to speak to her husband when he regained consciousness. (The word "if" was not mentioned.) I had then drawn aside the surgeon—Dr. Wayne Haskell—and asked if he would mind giving me a general idea of what the operation involved. Dr. Haskell, a thin, white-faced man, with hair as straight and black as a movie Indian's, was happy to oblige, in fact, would have qualified as an evangelist for his profession. Speaking with great zest, he told me far more than my stomach could comfortably tolerate. I would have liked nothing better than to have responded to Harriet's unthinking invitation by imbibing a quart of hundred-proof whiskey.

"I appreciate your getting that settled," she said, pouring me a glass of aqueous bubbles. "I suppose they thought it a strange thing to ask."

"No, why should they?" I folded myself into one of the angular Swedish chairs, reached in my shirt pocket for the cigarettes that weren't there, then fiddled with my hands.

"Naturally they'd wonder if I thought Charles would name the person who shot him." She raised her eyes from her bartending to give me a searching look.

"Assuming he knows," I said.

"Yes, of course." She splashed Scotch into her glass, her face suddenly grim. "I can't help wishing he doesn't," she said.

It was as close as she could come to praying that he didn't name a woman.

She sat, drank, smoked, and talked of Charles. Not the comatose creature who lay in twilight down the corridor, but the strong, vital Charles Dain who had stormed into her heart, stripped her of all propriety, made her laugh and lust and love, redeemed her lost youth, become her friend, partner, confessor, convinced her that her worth as a person far surpassed all her millions. It sounded almost like a eulogy to the dear departed, as though she were fashioning an image that must be rendered flawless before it was stored away in memory. Knowing Charles so well, I had moments of cynicism, which, like a mourner in church, I masked with looks of pious Amen.

Then, my mind wandering, I was brought back by her saying, "I think he was happiest when he first started the paper."

And suddenly I was in my element. My thoughts wheeled back eighteen years, to 1924, when I was a lad of forty-two and Charles was a man of twenty-six.

We were in the drafty offices of the loft building on Park Row, overlooking the green dome of City Hall— "Red Mike" Hylan still installed—and the block-square park where I could see the statue of Horace Greeley and imagine him offering a benediction to our embryonic enterprise. Down the street stood the headquarters of the *Daily News,* whose boss, Joe Patterson, had generously allowed us to rent his mechanical facilities—a privilege perhaps granted in compensation for the time when his meteoric tabloid had used the presses of the *Daily Mail.* (Not until 1930 did the *News* occupy the towering brick structure on East Forty-second Street.) Once again I was managing editor, city editor, telegraph editor of the four-page standard-size *Evening X* (the X soon elongated to *Express*), while Charles stripped stories from the *Times*, the *Tribune*, the *World*, the *Sun*, the *Post*, pasted them on sheets of yellow copy paper, added notes and comments, then passed them on to the small group of recruited newsmen for rewrite. Now in my mind I could hear him exclaim his dissatisfaction: "The headline should shout, not whisper!"; "Pictures, pictures, we need more pictures!"; "This lead is limp. Get more excitement into it!"; "I want more city news on page one. New Yorkers don't give a damn about the King of Italy—they can see him on a sardine can!"; and, more gently, "Harriet, have you talked to the wild man yet?"

The wild man was Frank Munsey, the flamboyant buyer and killer of newspapers who, rumor had it, was interested in disposing of the *Herald*. But even as Charles was considering some sort of deal, Munsey was agreeing to sell it to Mrs. Whitelaw Reid for five million dollars. She merged it with her *Tribune*, moving it uptown, where the *Times* had also gone. Despite these defections, Park Row was still Newspaper Row, and we were in the thick of it, inspired not only by the phenomenal success of the five-year-old *Daily News*, but even more by the fighting tradition of the *World*, housed beneath the golden tower of the Pulitzer Building and employing such luminaries as Harvey Bayard Swope, Heywood Broun, F.P.A., Walter Lippmann, Frank Sullivan, and cartoonist Rollin Kirby. "We can lick the *World*," Charles would say, and then proceed to add muscle to our experimental infant, doubling the number of pages, hiring more staff, building in features and special-interest sections, writing inflammatory editorials, refining his beloved Op-Ed page; all this while Harriet entertained potential advertisers, scouted for building sites, investigated the purchase of mechanical facilities, negotiated contracts with suppliers.

I recalled that hot summer day in 1925 when Charles called a staff meeting to announce that we were ready. Everyone in the room felt, I think, as I did—like a father awaiting word that the newborn child who had kicked and screamed his way into viable life was truly beautiful. Charles presented our introductory promotion advertising, created by Leo McGivena, who had conceived the famous "Tell it to Sweeney" campaign for the *News* ("Tell it to Sweeney. The Stuyvesants will understand.") The ads were arresting, forceful, exciting —projecting what all of us believed to be the character of the *Express:* a crusading newspaper that also appealed to the intellect.

Now, in the hospital room, refilling her glass, waving her cigarette holder, Harriet said, "Then, after all that, he had the nerve to say he was holding off publication until the election. We could have killed him."

"That's right," I said, laughing. "He was determined to wait for Jimmy."

Chapter · 15

I had known Jimmy Walker professionally since his early days in the state legislature, admiring him if only because he was the antithesis of the stuffy, self-righteous Mayor Hylan, whose bumblings I had for so long covered—and covered up—for the *American*. Robert Moses, the crusty human dynamo who built Jones Beach, once likened Walker to Sabatini's *Scaramouche:* "born with the gift of laughter and a sense that the world was mad"—a description I wish could have been applied to me.

In 1925 Jimmy was the eloquent speaker of the New York State Senate, depended upon by Alfred E. Smith, the brown-derbied, cigar-chomping governor, to push through such progressive measures as workmen's compensation, the eight-hour day for working women, safeguards for tenement dwellers. But though he spoke for the common man, Walker himself was as uncommon as anyone ever to rise from the littered streets of the city that newspaper columnists romanticized as Baghdad-on-the-Subway.

He was handsome, with dark, sleek hair, twinkling

blue eyes, a mouth that, even when serious, was hooked at the corners with ironic humor. His slim figure was enhanced by custom-fitted double-breasted suits, white silk shirts, polka-dot ties, and wide-brimmed fedoras turned up on one side and rakishly down on the other. To see him parading up Fifth Avenue in support of his bills for Sunday baseball, Sunday movies, legalized boxing, or 2.75 beer was to witness the personification of all the urbanity, sophistication, and nonchalance that New Yorkers so proudly imputed to themselves.

In fact, with his charm, his style, his joy in living, he was not unlike Charles Dain—a resemblance seemingly recognized by both when I introduced them at about the time the sachems of Tammany Hall were debating who to run for mayor in the fall elections. The mutual attraction was heightened for Walker when he remembered that Charles was about to launch a major metropolitan newspaper backed by Harriet's millions. However, he made no appeal for support, nor was it offered until after he had defeated Hylan in the primaries, at which point the two men met privately at the Walker headquarters in the Commodore Hotel. It was then that Charles announced to his staff that publication would be postponed until election day. He was convinced that the *Evening Express* would make a far greater impact on the city if it marched in side by side with the man who was a hero to the average working citizen.

The polls had been open only a few hours when the first issue of the *Express* hit the streets. The banner headline read: LANDSLIDE FOR JIMMY! Beneath it was a posed photo of Walker, mouth agape as he stared at a copy of the same paper with the same headline.

The reaction was exactly as Charles had hoped.

Throughout the five boroughs, people passing newsstands stopped to gawk, perhaps wondering if this upstart newspaper had consulted the famed mentalist Joseph Dunninger, who only recently had visited Walker at the Commodore and, after reading his mind, predicted victory.

Under the by-line of Charles Dain, the reader was quickly set straight.

> The headline above [wrote Charles] is a prediction. It is not yet the fact that we believe it will become when the polls close tonight. We print it now to demonstrate a basic policy of this newspaper—a willingness to stick our necks out.
>
> Fine, you may say, but must you be quite so loud about it?
>
> We think so. The *Evening Express* is a newcomer in a city with nine daily newspapers, all shouting to be heard. Like the newest member of a family, we may at first have to shout a bit louder, be a bit more brash, in order to be noticed. (Our first headline was simply, "Hello, New York," but we feared you'd reply, "Hello yourself" and keep right on walking.)
>
> A more important reason for the headline is to indicate our support for the principles of James J. Walker, a man who epitomizes everything the *Evening Express* stands for. Like Jimmy, we intend to be fearless in our opposition to those who seek unfair advantage, those who foment racial and religious strife, those who hypocritically profess sanctity while lining their pockets, those who extort tribute from lawabiding businessmen, those who raise their blue noses at anything that might be interpreted as "having fun."
>
> We are—again, like Jimmy—for the five-cent subway fare, for the legal consumption of beer, for the ex-

pansion of transit and highway facilities—and also for
Clara Bow, the Charleston, Mah-Jongg, and the right to
read James Branch Cabell's *Jurgen* as well as Bruce
Barton's *The Man Nobody Knows.*

None of this should imply that we will stand with
Mr. Walker if we think him wrong. We will say so—
vigorously and without equivocation. The same goes for
Tammany Hall, which, though it has contributed much
to the progress of New York, has had the misfortune
to provide us with an occasional crook.

The editorial went on in this vein, placing the *Express*
indubitably on the side of the angels. As though this
weren't enough, a front-page box featured accolades to
the *Express* from such notables as Bernard Baruch, Will
Rogers, Jack Dempsey, Bishop Manning, George Jessel,
George M. Cohan—the last two having been pals of
Walker since his Tin Pan Alley days, when he wrote the
popular "Will You Love Me in December as You Did in
May?"

"What if he loses?" I said to Charles as we stood on a
street corner observing a newsboy hawk the *Express.*

"He can't lose. I talked to Olvany. He says they'll get
every last Democrat to the polls even if it takes stretchers accompanied by priests giving the last rites. Before
the Democrats would take a beating, I think they'd vote
all the tombstones in Queens."

George W. Olvany was the head of Tammany. He
had only recently replaced the revered Charles Francis
Murphy who, though serving without pay, had died
leaving an estate of more than two million dollars.

Olvany's prescience was sustained by the huge headline in the next day's *Express.* Playing back to the election day screamer, it chortled: SPEAKING OF LANDSLIDES,
WALKER GOT IT!

Apparently New Yorkers liked such jubilant journalism. We sold some three hundred thousand papers, up almost fifty thousand from our maiden issue.

We were on our way to lick the *World*.

Never in history had there been such a favorable time to start a big-city newspaper. The nation was riding an ascending wave of prosperity, powered by the demand for automobiles, refrigerators, radios, telephones, washing machines, vacuum cleaners, cigarettes, rayon, cosmetics—all of which must be advertised, and with newspapers as the major medium. America was playing the stock market, investing in the Florida real estate boom, going to the movies, motoring down six-lane highways, cruising to Europe, joining country clubs, acquiring unaffordable luxuries on the installment plan. Shrewd advertisers were winning customers with appeals to "reach for a Lucky instead of a sweet," banish BO with Lifebuoy soap, astonish your skeptical friends who had laughed when you sat down at the piano, use Listerine mouthwash or risk becoming "Often a bridesmaid but never a bride," heed the nightgowned, yawning boy and buy Fisk balloon tires when it was "Time to Re-Tire."

"The chief business of the American people is business," said President Calvin Coolidge, a creed that glorified the salesman, the go-getter, the man with the muscular smile who played golf, attended church, joined Rotary, all for the sake of making "contacts." And this reverence for false gods, this ravenous acquisitiveness was not restricted to the men. After all, if a fellow was to get ahead, his wife must bedeck herself in the latest fashions, entertain with the finest china and cutlery, and of course have a home and a car (now offered in a rainbow of colors) that would properly publicize her husband's rise to success.

Deplorable as this materialism might be to the intellectuals and the truly pious—not to mention the forsaken farmers, who shared none of it—it was the source of life for the *Express*. Wary at first of an untested vehicle, advertisers soon flocked to its pages, attracted by constantly rising circulation and an editorial vigor that appealed to people who went places, did things, spent money. Anticipating red ink for the first year, Charles was happily surprised to find we were soon substantially in the black—a position reversed only when we invested in our own building overlooking the East River. At that point Harriet withdrew from the scene, bought the mansion in Mount Kisco, outfitted a section of it to resemble a military control center, and from there—like Hearst at San Simeon—directed her corporate empire. Aside from her financial commitment, her interest in the workings of the *Express* was confined to what Charles wished to tell her, which was considerable inasmuch as he relied heavily on her judgment. Otherwise, in the evening and on weekends, she delighted in the role of adoring wife, pampering, flirting, and—intimated to me one night when we were awash with brandy—ravishing him on their elegant assortment of beds, sofas, and Oriental rugs. I often wondered if Charles was not so much in love with her as he was fascinated by her contradictions—cold yet warm, calm yet turbulent, serious yet frivolous. In one respect, however, she was totally consistent—if she was your friend, she was as steadfast as Gibralter. I felt fortunate to be her friend.

* * *

Coolidge prosperity was not the only reason for the spectacular growth of the *Express*. Just as influential was the social revolution which provided the press with material that would have stunned the Victorians. Few newspapers would have sold in such numbers without enticements like "heart balm" for jilted mistresses, annulments based on sexual impotence, murders triggered by adulterous passions, not to mention the crimes of pederasty, miscegenation, and whoring in high places. Nor was it probable that Walter Winchell would have achieved great success with the first Broadway column —credited with attracting more than half the readership of Bernard MacFadden's sensational tabloid, the *Evening Graphic*—if scandal had not been so ubiquitous.

An even bigger news bonanza was struck in the pervasive defiance of Prohibition. The attitude of Charles Dain typified the great paradox of the time. As a member of the so-called carriage trade, he considered the speakeasy an acceptable way of life, its charming hosts and hostesses no more censurable than the lobbyists for soulless corporations or the women who entertained men in exchange for mink coats. The real villains, and the targets of the *Express*'s wrath, were the coldblooded criminals who controlled the traffic in booze, dope, and prostitution; who employed goons and assassins to terrorize shopkeepers into paying for "protection"; who corrupted politicians and further impoverished the poor with their betting parlors, slot machines, numbers rackets; who made a profitable business of mayhem, murder, arson, bombing. For men like these, the *Express* became a scourge, a relentless pursuer, emblazoning their iniquities in boxcar headlines, scathing editorials, penetrating articles, incriminating photos. When beer baron

Dutch Schultz broke with Vincent "Mad Dog" Coll, who then declared war on his former boss, the *Express* scored a beat on the final showdown: Coll, lured to a phone booth in a Twenty-third Street drugstore was calmly and efficiently machine-gunned to death. When racket king Jack "Legs" Diamond, survivor of enough bullet wounds to destroy a platoon, eventually had his brains blown out while sleeping off a hangover in Albany, an *Express* reporter had it on the wire before his pulse quit. When killer Owney Madden, after serving seven years in Sing Sing, moved into the laundry and coal protection rackets, it was the *Express* that exposed him, harried him until he decided to take early retirement in the salubrious quiet of Hot Springs, Arkansas.

The *Express*'s vendetta against the underworld bosses soon won the admiration and gratitude of every honest cop in New York, officers who too often had been thwarted in court by such silver-tongued mouthpieces as Bill Fallon, Sam Liebowitz, Max Steuer. Police Commissioner Grover Whalen was often publicly outspoken in his praise while privately encouraging his minions to provide *Express* reporters with inside information. In return the paper lauded New York's finest, likening them to the centurions of Rome and the soldiers of the Crusades. Charles, as publisher, was looked upon by the men in blue as god, brother, confidant, a man who must be protected against reprisal from the gangsters he pilloried. He was advised to employ bodyguards, carry a gun, notify police of his comings and goings—precautions he refused, saying that if the crime lords were determined to get him, nothing could stop them. Written and telephoned threats on his life were frequent but presumably were deterred by the fear that injury or death to Charles Dain would trigger a massive manhunt and crackdown, which would drastically disturb the flourishing status quo.

So Charles remained a highly visible target—addressing a conclave of editors at the Waldorf, attending, with Harriet, the openings of Broadway shows, appearing at Park Avenue parties, testimonial dinners, charity benefits, riding up Broadway in a ticker-tape parade for the latest overnight celebrity—Channel-swimmer Gertrude Ederle, transatlantic flyer Amelia Earhart, polar explorer Richard E. Byrd. Ironically Charles was most vulnerable to attack when he relaxed among the friends he most enjoyed—show business personalities I'd known through my activities in the Lambs and Friars and introduced to Charles—for these gatherings generally took place in mid-Manhattan speakeasies frequented not only by the smart set but also by racketeers, musclemen, and professional killers. My ever-present anxiety for Charles's safety did much to increase my intake of alcohol, even though the only signs of danger were occasional glares from men in tight dark suits that bulged ominously at the lapels.

A more insidious threat—to Harriet as well as to Charles—came from women. Though traditionally barred by custom from the saloons, women were warmly welcomed into the underground resorts by the dapper men who first eyed you through the sliding panel in the front door. To me it was somewhat distasteful to see spike heels gripped to the brass bar-rail, to hear soprano laughter and endless chatter, to inhale exotic perfumes in a place dedicated to serious drinking. But not so with Charles. It amused him to be greeted by a hatcheck girl skinned into a strip of gold lamé or to buy cigarettes from a temptress wearing little more than black fishnet stockings or, once seated, to observe the seductions proceeding at surrounding tables, the outright gropings in cushioned booths, the casual pickups at the crowded bar. There was nothing covetous in his interest. He was simply reacting as a healthy, under-thirty male should, stimulated by the sight of pulchritude, enjoying vicariously the premating ceremonies of attractive couples. He behaved no differently when Harriet was present—a situation that became increasingly rare due to the odd hours he worked and the commitments forced on her by her many business interests. No, I thought, there was no danger that Charles Dain—respected publisher, happily married man— would succumb to the fleshly attractions that adorned the world of the speakeasy.

Until the evening when we were seated near the piano at the Club New Yorker on East Fifty-first Street, and Bonnie Prince walked in.

Charles, facing the entrance, saw her first. Whatever I was saying trailed off as I observed his eyebrows raise, his eyes grow luminous, his jaw descend—an expression I'd expect to see on a person confronting a benign ghost. I turned my head and, with a pump of the heart, shared Charles's experience. The girl stood poised atop the three carpeted steps, her head slowly rotating as she scanned the smoky scene. The impression was not of an actress making a grand entrance—though to us it was all of that—but of a curious child peeking down from a staircase at an adult party. But if child she was, she was indeed precocious, her body snugly capsuled in flowered chiffon, curved and rounded to maturity, her silken legs long and tapering. Still, her form was secondary to what had so transfixed us. It was her face—smooth skin naturally pink, lips full and ripe, nose delicately wrought, eyes—ah, those eyes—radiating, even from a distance, an amethyst blue. And her hair. . . . It seemed an impossible stretch of coincidence that it should be blond, that it should sweep across and back from her cheeks into what could be imagined—erroneously, it turned out—as a soft bun. If she had been crowned with a feathered hat, I would have felt certain that I was back in George Fletcher's dining room glancing up from the cards to stare in awe at his ravishing daughter.

The spell was broken by the arrival around her of several men and women who had come from the cloakroom. Charles's gaze remained fixed on the girl as the party was escorted down the length of the room in our direction. Suddenly he pushed his chair back, stood up, and strode toward the man in the lead. He said something and held out his hand, which the man at first shook limply, then with vigor, his face lighting up as he realized who Charles was. "Why, yes," I heard him say, turning to the others for approval, "that would be very nice." And in a moment there was a fetching of chairs and I found myself surrounded by five cast members of *Whoopee,* the hit show of the season. Charles had recognized the young man he had spoken to as one of the juvenile leads, but I'm sure he would have approached him if he'd been no more than an usher.

It was an education to watch Charles in action. First, without seeming to arrange anything, he manipulated the chairs so that Bonnie Prince sat beside him. Then, through artful questioning and casual remarks, he established that there were no intimate alliances between the three women and two men—they were simply meeting for a drink before they were due at the theater for the evening performance. Next he jokingly accused Bonnie of being an impostor—"I saw the show. You weren't in it. If you were I'd have packed your dressing room with roses"—which elicited the information that she was a recent replacement for an ingenue who had been stricken with pregnancy.

She was charming, soft-spoken and self-effacing, reminding me of a well-mannered child carefully exhibiting her good training. Close up, of course, she was not a replica of Sharon—her face was fuller, her mouth smaller, her eyes more closely set—but for Charles, I think, the original image persisted, and he mentally revised those deviations to accommodate his nostalgia. She was obviously attracted to him, often flashing him appraising glances, gently grasping his wrist when he lit her cigarette, adjusting her chair, ostensibly for comfort but actually to move it closer to his. Charles had the pianist play the title song from *Whoopee*, then followed it with requests for the more romantic show tunes of Berlin and Gershwin. As I sought to contribute to the general conversation—affecting, I'm afraid, the role of omniscient journalist—I was continually aware that across from me was a lovely girl dazzled by a man determined to bewitch himself into falling in love. It struck me then that no matter how much he might care for Harriet, no matter how strong their union of minds and hearts, he had never stopped yearning for the rapture that had been his with the girl he had cruelly and forever lost.

"You would?" I heard Bonnie say. "Oh, I'd like that."

"Not the stage door, though," Charles said. "I refuse to be one of your Johnnies."

"I have no Johnnies. Could we meet at Sardi's?"

"And lose you to some matinee idol?" He sipped his drink, thinking. Then he shot me a look, his face cleared, and a smile tugged at his lips. "Why not the lobby of the Algonquin Hotel?" he said. "It's not far from the theater. From there we can decide where to go."

She gazed at him ingenuously. "Is that where you're staying?"

"No, but I drop by fairly often. I have a friend who lives there."

So I became Charles's "beard"—the man who, in public places, appears to be the one with the girl. My credentials were impeccable—a well-to-do bachelor in his mid-forties who lived alone in a hotel and often indulged in Manhattan's night life. When, shortly after eleven, Bonnie entered the Algonquin lobby and saw me with Charles, I'm sure she knew immediately the reason for my presence. Without being told that I was to join them, she said how flattering it was to have two such handsome escorts. In the taxi she took both our arms, paid us equal attention, laughed at my lame jokes, and all but convinced me that I was either Charles's rival or that she was agreeable to a dual romance. The masquerade continued at Lindy's where, between bites of cheese blintzes, she inquired into my life's history, while Charles, appearing to be on some higher plane, waved to friends, greeted table-hoppers, and all in all acted as though Bonnie was at most a distant cousin.

Apparently satisfied that the pretense was impenetrable, we went on, at his suggestion, to the Central Park Casino where we joined a party presided over by Jimmy Walker and Betty Compton. The mayor, himself an old hand at such deceptions, was so taken in that he congratulated me on my excellent taste in women and, in a rush of boozy Irish sentiment, offered his sincere wishes for our future happiness.

My night of glory ended the moment we settled back in a limousine for our homeward trip. Immediately Bonnie's blond head tipped to rest on Charles's shoulder and her hand crept up to sneak beneath his jacket. I, the raconteur, the fascinating journalist, the debonair man-about-town, was totally ignored as we proceeded in sensual silence to the Algonquin. Getting out, I paused beneath the canopy as the limousine glided away. Framed in the rear window, like a full-screen close-up of movie lovers, were two gorgeous heads joined in a passionate kiss. It seemed inevitable that Bonnie Prince —physically drawn to Charles at first sight, impressed by his godlike eminence, overwhelmed by his friendship with the popular mayor—would spend the remaining night in Charles's bed at the Waterford Hotel penthouse. (I suspected he had provided for that eventuality when he had telephoned Harriet earlier.)

Which, of course, was the case—a fact verified late the next morning when Charles called me at the office to say that he would not be in until midafternoon. That had never happened before; no matter how late the roistering he had always managed to appear at his desk promptly at ten A.M. I could only conclude that what he had enjoyed in darkness he anticipated would be at least equally enjoyable in daylight.

The suddenness of the liaison—his willingness to compromise, on impulse, his loyalty to Harriet—I found not particularly offensive. He had, I thought, been swept away by a fantasy in which he was once again the youthful Charles Dain experiencing the enchantment of first love. It was different only in degree from listening to a bygone song and mentally committing adultery with the girl you had first lain with, perhaps only regretting that you had not then dared to explore all the extremes of lust. As with any illusion, it could not last—of that I was sure.

Imagine, then, my astonishment when I learned that he had provided Bonnie with the funds to rent a suite at the Waterford Hotel! I would not have believed it if he himself had not told me—a necessity, he felt, inasmuch as he expected me to continue as his "beard."

"Charles," I said, "this is absolutely crazy. You're not in love with her. You can't be!"

We were in his office, the door closed. He smiled across the desk at me, an odd, somewhat sardonic smile, seeming to imply that I had a lot to learn about the vagaries of human nature.

"But I am," he said. "Why should that shock you?"

"Because, well, my God, there's Harriet!"

He didn't flinch. "This has nothing to do with Harriet. It won't affect our marriage in any way."

"You told that to Bonnie?"

"Of course. She understands perfectly. In fact, she's relieved that she won't have to be a homewrecker."

"But to put her up in Harriet's hotel—isn't that asking for trouble?"

"Bonnie arranged it on her own. Outwardly I'm not involved."

I felt a rising indignation. "That's not what I mean."

"I know. You think she's too close for comfort."

"Don't you?"

"Well, these days Harriet rarely comes into town

and—" Suddenly he grinned. "Max, you haven't studied these things. If Bonnie lived someplace else, I'd either have to stay over, which would mean moving in a lot of my clothes and junk, or—"

"Or you could simply go back to the hotel. What's wrong with that?"

"What's wrong is that I'd be dragging in at ungodly hours and I'd be seen by the help. The word would get around. This way—with her just two floors below and at the opposite end of the building—I simply use the fire stairs and no one's the wiser. If we happen to pass in the lobby, we're nodding acquaintances. It's convenient for her and convenient for me."

I could not help thinking that the arrangement appealed to him mostly because it excited him to play close to the fire. He was still the same Charles Dain who, as a war correspondent, had delighted in braving the front lines.

He gripped his lapels and assumed the pose of a pompous lecturer, "Now, are there any more questions?"

"Yes. What happens when you take her out?"

He laughed. "Max, my friend, you're going to have a wonderful time. And it won't cost you a cent."

For a while everything worked out exactly as Charles had planned. Often he would leave the office around five o'clock to rendezvous at the hotel with Bonnie, leaving her before showtime to go on to Mount Kisco. Occasionally he would join her in her suite for lunch—breakfast for her—afterward plunging into a frenzy of work, as though in compensation for his prolonged matinee.

Only once or twice a week did he stay overnight, and

these were the times when I became the apex of the loving triangle. In the better speakeasies and restaurants, I was looked upon with envy by suave men notorious for their conquests of beautiful women as Bonnie fussed over me and Charles blessed us with avuncular smiles. I confess that all this attention—which I fancied at the moment as sincere—was balm to my ego, allowing me to act with the savoir faire I so admired in Charles. But later, alone in my rooms, I was made miserable by the thought that I was a pawn in a conspiracy against Harriet, just as I had once been a pawn in the deception of Sharon's father. My sense of guilt was not eased by rationalizing that Harriet was in no way being harmed, secure as she was in the knowledge that a publisher's work was usually long and erratic and often subject to the social demands of important advertisers. The fact remained that the role I had been chosen for was not much more respectable than that of a panderer. Finally I decided to end it, even if it meant a cooling of Charles's friendship, which I was sure would be temporary.

The opportunity arose one day when we were having lunch in the Oak Room of the Plaza Hotel. After an hour of newspaper talk, we were lingering silently over coffee when I said;

"Charles, about Bonnie and you—" I was stopped by his look of surprise.

"You mean you heard?" he said. "She told you?"

"Told me what?"

"That we're"—he peered at me closely—"no, she didn't tell you. Well, I will." He sipped his coffee, his face grim. "It's all over. We're finished."

I didn't bother to hide my relief.

"She's moving out tomorrow," he said, adding with a wry smile, "complete with diamond pendant, wardrobe from Saks, and a prepaid lease on a new apartment. Believe me, Max, it was a bargain."

He told me about it. Bonnie, it seems, was not quite the unselfish, guileless girl Charles had thought. After a few weeks of feverish devotion, she had begun hinting that it might be profitable for her lover to invest in motion pictures, the obvious implication being that she would sacrifice her privacy for stardom.

"She figured," said Charles, "that I was Hearst and she was Marion Davies. I set her straight. If she was interested in the movies, I said, I'd gladly give her a letter of introduction to Adolph Zukor or the Schencks. That didn't get a laugh but she didn't mention it again, and everything returned to normal."

"Well, then—"

"Well, then she took a different tack. The reason her career wasn't a smashing success, she said, was lack of publicity. This time she was very direct about it. She wanted me to order stories about her in the *Express*. Photos. Interviews. Items in the columns."

I couldn't help smiling. "Editorials?"

He recovered his good humor. "Only on Valentine's Day. Max, can you believe it? She actually thought I'd turn the *Express* into a house organ for Bonnie Prince!"

"I suppose it wouldn't hurt to give her a plug in the drama column."

"Not a line, I told her, not a word—unless she died, and then I might okay an obit. I was mad as hell. I stormed out, saying I'd send her a rate card so she'd know what it would cost to run an ad."

"And that was the end?"

"Not quite. She called me, said she was sorry, and she'd never mention it again. I went back, but it wasn't the same. She wasn't really that girl I'd seen that first night. She didn't even look the same. I suddenly realized I'd been playing some sort of damn fool game with myself and I'd better quit before the losses got any heavier. The other day we had a quiet little talk, she cried, and I dried her tears with my checkbook. So now you can turn in your beard."

"Good. It was beginning to itch." I looked at him seriously. "You're lucky, Charles. At least Harriet didn't find out."

He cocked his head. "I'm not too sure about that. Harriet's a damned perceptive woman. Sometimes I had the feeling she knew that all those nights in town weren't spent to coax more linage out of Macy's and Gimbels."

"But she didn't say anything?"

"No, but she wouldn't. She knows that what we've got is too substantial to be wrecked by some stupid affair."

So now it was a stupid affair, not paradise regained. I just looked at him, wondering if his disillusionment would convince him that you can't recapture the past.

"Anyway, I've had my fling," he said. "From now on, I'm sticking close to the hearth."

Looking back on those years in the late twenties and early thirties, it's clear to me that Charles was emotionally impaired. He was like an alcoholic who maintains long periods of productive sobriety, then takes that first drink, goes on a bender, recovers, and in time repeats the performance. I can't remember all the young women Charles loved and left, only that each of them met the same criteria: blond, blue-eyed, fair-skinned, girlish yet dignified, discreet yet reckless, and, above all, utterly yielding—essential if she was to satisfy his compulsion to mold her to his inner vision. Confronted by what he thought was such a woman, he became euphoric, separated from reality, neglectful of his wife, his friends, his business.

A neurotic, someone has said, merely *builds* castles in the air, while a psychotic *lives* in them. Charles, it seemed, leaned toward the latter, except that his castles —complete with plastic princesses from the stages of Broadway—were comfortably furnished little apartments near Times Square. For a manic month or so he would regress to romantic adolescence, lavishing gifts on his latest beloved, taking her on picnics to New Jersey, to theaters featuring old movies, to intimate speakeasies where men with their mistresses were commonplace. (He no longer, thank God, felt a need for my presence.) Then the fanciful bubble would burst and the charade end, generally for some obscure reason his lover could not possibly fathom—a sudden realization that her voice was affected, her blondness fabricated, her character superficial. Magically he would revert to the Charles Dain I knew—the hard-driving publisher, crusader against crime, devoted husband of the woman who would forgive him anything.

Oh, yes, Harriet knew—intuitively at first, and then with pragmatic certainty as his behavior became more eccentric with each illusory interlude. One night in early September of 1929—I remember the time well because on that day the stock market had soared to its highest point—I got a glimpse of her attitude. We were standing in a theater lobby between the acts of a play called

Candlelight, and Charles was out on the sidewalk talking to a politician who was accompanied by one of those brassy Broadway blondes. I was commenting on the performances of Gertrude Lawrence and Leslie Howard when Harriet suddenly interrupted:

"Max, I know about Charles."

Startled, I stared at her and saw she was looking out the open doors at the blonde, who was then speaking to Charles.

"Know what?" I said stupidly, feeling my flesh start to crawl.

"About his women." She smiled sympathetically at my discomfort.

I tried to look incredulous. "His *women?* Really, Harriet—" I didn't go on. Her smile, now fixed and knowing, told me that she was not blindly fishing for information.

She waved her long cigarette holder—the equivalent of a shrug. "I've been aware of it for a long time," she said. "Max, you needn't say anything. It's just that I don't want you thinking I'm being fooled."

I could only look anguished.

"For my self-respect," she added.

"You'll always have mine," I said. "I'm glad that whatever it is you know you're taking in stride."

"I have my bad moments. Anyway, Charles will eventually outgrow it. I think he's trying to make up for what he missed when he was young and poor."

"Whatever he missed," I said, "he's found with you."

"My thought exactly. Now all I have to do is be patient until he realizes it."

"Have you ever spoken to him about—"

"No, and I won't. If he found out I knew, he'd start resenting me. I'd become the domineering wife—Maggie to his Jiggs. Then I'd lose him. If that happened, I might"—she gave her head a shake—"I'm afraid even to think about that."

The buzzer sounded for the next act. Suddenly her lips stretched into an adoring smile. Turning my head, I saw Charles approaching.

Less than two months after that conversation—when John J. Raskob was insisting that "everybody ought to be rich," when waiters and elevator operators were driving Pierce-Arrows, when the new President, Herbert Hoover, was predicting nothing but golden years ahead —the stock market crashed. Charles suffered only minor personal losses, but the *Express,* indeed all newspapers, was suddenly faced with dwindling advertising revenue. Whereas most other publishers cut staff, pages, editions, Charles was determined to go on as before, in fact, in some areas—crime, in particular—he intensified our coverage. His aggressive policy paid off in 1931, when the revered *World*—the paper Charles had set out to lick—went to its tragic death. (But the *Express* had not licked it; its demise was due to indifference on the part of the great Joseph Pulitzer's three sons.) From its ashes Charles was able to pluck talented writers, popular features, and much of its circulation, which in turn attracted more advertising. Circulation was further increased the following year when the despised *Graphic,* which had built a huge audience on scurrilous sensationalism—and in so doing, repelled respectable advertisers—declared bankruptcy.

Throughout this period Charles failed to meet Harriet's expectation that he would grow up. He remained the strangely dual personality who could publish a newspaper for mature intellects and at the same time lose his heart in juvenile passions.

And then, in the spring of 1933, shortly after Franklin D. Roosevelt had been inaugurated as President, Charles was astonishingly transfigured into the stable, responsible citizen that he remained till the day he was shot.

Nine years, I thought, as I left Harriet's hospital suite. Nine years of apparent rectitude while the bullet forged so long ago was slowly winging toward his brain.

Tomorrow, when it was removed, would he recognize the nature of the force that had driven it?

Chapter · 16

A thunderstorm, driven by howling winds, was flooding the streets when I arrived at the hospital the next morning. Entering Harriet's suite, I found her at the window gazing out at the pelting rain, recoiling slightly as a zigzag of lightning flashed in the distance. She wore a bright-yellow dress, the bodice artfully fashioned to flatter her breasts. Her dark hair was meticulously combed in smooth, even waves, and her makeup would have done credit to Hollywood's Perc Westmore. Obviously she intended Charles's reentry into the corporeal world to be a thing of beauty. I suppressed the thought that she might have to change into something more becoming to a widow.

She greeted me with a warm smile and a cool cheek, hung my damp fedora and raincoat in the closet, and said with false cheeriness, "I can't think of a nicer day for a vigil."

I put my arm around her waist and said, "You don't have to be Harriet Happiness for me, you know."

She touched my jaw. "No, I don't, do I? All right then—I'm scared to death. I can't rid my mind of that look in his eyes."

"You mean they were open?"

"Yes, when he was being wheeled into the operating room. Like a fool, I went with him as far as the doors. His eyes were wide open—which has happened off and on, a doctor said. But they didn't see anything, just stared blankly at the ceiling and then rolled a bit. It was as though a light had gone out inside his head."

"No wonder you're scared."

"I thought, my God, suppose he has to live like that—not able to see or speak or even move."

I held up my hand like a traffic cop. "Enough of that. Once the pressure is off, he'll come around."

She nodded, pretending it was as simple as that. In fact, pressure was not the major concern. The crucial question was how much damage had been done to the brain tissue and arteries, both by the penetration itself and the scattering of bullet fragments and bone splinters. That could not be determined until the surgeon got inside and took a magnified look—a procedure that involved the risk of fatal hemorrhage.

"What time did he go in?" I asked.

"Nine thirty—just after you called from the office." She glanced at her watch. "He's been in there for an hour and a half." She stuffed her cigarette holder with a king-size Pall Mall.

I lit it, saying, "Shall I see if I can find out something?"

"Yes, but not yet." She took a Vesuvian drag. "Let's wait until we think they've had a good look at it."

I went to a table by the window, where she'd set up the backgammon. "In that case, suppose I reduce your bank account."

"You're on."

We played a couple of games—enriching her by just over six dollars—then gave it up. There were too many distractions—the rain beating against the window pane, the grumble and roar of thunder, and of course, worst of all, the rising, almost tangible suspense. Lunch came and went, scarcely touched. We talked in brief spurts, lapsing into heavy silences, during which I shamelessly smoked cigarettes, extinguishing them when half burned and then relighting the stubs. I had the strange sensation that I had been spun back two years in time, to the summer of 1940, when I was the patient and Charles was the one anxiously awaiting the decision of life or death.

The attack had struck as I was lifting a Scotch at the Algonquin bar—a sudden shortness of breath, dizziness, a stabbing pain in the chest that seemed to streak down my arm. (The doctors later said it might not have occurred if I'd had time to drink the Scotch.) I had been rushed to the hospital, where it had taken hours to get me stabilized. Then, recuperating nicely, buoyed by optimism, I was informed that I had a cirrhotic liver, which, if further abused by alcohol, would make excellent material for my headstone. Ironically, that diagnosis came at a time when I had my liquor consumption under reasonable control.

Now that episode was revived by the routine sounds of the hospital—the squeak of crepe-soled shoes, the rattle of dishes, the soft whir of carts and stretchers, the startling slam of an elevator door, the hushed voices of visitors, the incongruous laughter of passing interns. For an instant I experienced the delusion that it was my body stretched out on the operating table, my skull that had been split open like a melon, my brain that was being scrutinized through barrel-shaped glasses by a green-masked man who then turned to his colleagues and sadly shook his head.

I got up and looked at Harriet who, for the third time, was giving herself a manicure. "It's been more than three hours," I said, my voice sounding like someone else's. "I think I should nose around."

She stared at me as though I were about to consult a mortician. "Try not to be long," she said.

I went to the floor below and stopped at the nurses' station outside the operating room. In answer to my question the middle-aged woman in starched white said that "everything is going as expected." Asked if it wasn't taking unusually long, she replied, "Not necessarily." Considering such definitive answers, I was about to suggest she run for public office when I felt a tap on the shoulder. Turning, I looked into the grim face of Terry Donovan. I was surprised to see him, knowing that the story here was being covered by Dave Hewlett; but then I realized that Terry's reason for stopping by was the same as mine—we were both Charles's friends. He was probably as fearful as I that we would never again see him alive.

"They got the bullet," he said. "Now they're working on the damage. It's a tricky business and takes time."

"You were in there?"

"No, I heard it from a friend who works here—a nurse. There's a spectator room if you want to take a look. I was just going in."

I hesitated, wondering if I could tolerate the sight of someone I cared for so deeply being dissected as though he were a dead rat. But the need to know, instilled in me as a newsman, broke my resistance, and I followed Terry through a door next to the operating room.

Mounting a short flight of stairs, we stood in an aisle fronting a tier of seats and gazed through a half-wall of glass at the medical team working below. It looked like a tense scene from a Dr. Kildare movie, except that we could hear no sound, and the operating field was eclipsed by the huddled medics in green gowns, caps, and masks.

To make some sense of what was going on I had to recall items from the interminable briefing so zestfully given me the day before by the neurosurgeon, Dr. Wayne Haskell: "First we make a bicoronal incision—a cut across the top of the head from one ear to the other. Then we drill a number of holes in the skull and connect them with a fluted blade. We remove this section of bone and thus have a window into the brain. . . . Chances are an artery or two will be severed, so we can expect brisk bleeding. No problem really; we can control that. Also, there appears from the X rays to be a large blood clot, but again no problem—we simply suction it out. Then we *do* face a problem—locating and removing the fragments of metal and bone, an extremely delicate procedure, tedious and time-consuming. . . ."

Perhaps, I thought, that was what Haskell was doing now. He was jackknifed over the upper portion of the sheeted figure on the table and, from the movement of his arms and shoulders, I guessed he was probing the labyrinths of Charles's brain. One slip, just a slight twitch of his long fingers and . . .

"I've had enough," I said to Donovan.

"Yeah. I can get more than this from my spy."

Outside in the corridor, he said, "I talked to Kate just before I saw you. So she knows as much as we do."

"Good. I planned to phone her when it was finished."

"No need to. I'm meeting her then." He said it gloomily, as though he dreaded the prospect. "Besides," he added, "you may have your hands full with Harriet."

"Well, she may need a little—"

He interrupted, as though unaware that I'd spoken. "Max, does she know Kate?"

I thought a moment. "No, I don't think they've ever met."

"But she does know who Kate is?" There was an urgency in his tone.

"That she writes a column? Oh, I would think so."

His jaw set. "I mean does Harriet know how much Charles has helped Kate's career?"

I paused to look at him. His usually sleepy eyes were alert and inquisitive. "I doubt that Charles would think to mention it," I said. "Does it matter?"

He flushed. "Only that there might be some jealousy."

"Harriet jealous? Nonsense. Oh, I see. You're concerned that if Charles . . . let's say that if Harriet had to take over the paper, she might want to clip Kate's wings. Is that it?"

He blinked as though in surprise, then caught himself and smiled ruefully. "Just a thought," he said.

I sensed that my answer wasn't what he expected, but I let it go; there were more important things on my mind. "Forget it," I said. "There's not a jealous gene in Harriet's body. And forget about her taking over. Charles is going to make it."

We took the elevator to the floor above. Approaching Harriet's door, I asked if he'd like to look in, but he declined, for a moment appearing disconcerted. He was on his way, he said, to a press room set up next to the Administrator's office; if he heard anything significant, he'd call me. I said I'd do the same, then watched him as he strode down the corridor and stopped at a nurses' station. The nurse on duty—a pretty redhead—gave him a smile that was provocatively unprofessional. She turned, saw me, and raised her hand in a beckoning gesture. When I got to her, Donovan had left. "Message for you, Mr. Wills," she said, and handed me a slip of paper. I started when I read, "Please call Mrs. Thomas Richards." Sharon. I had talked to her only once since the shooting, when she had phoned me at the Algonquin to ask about Charles's condition.

I walked to an alcove down the hall and used the pay phone to call her back.

"I read that Charles was being operated on today," she said. "Did they do it? Is it over?"

"They're doing it. They started almost four hours ago. It seems to be going well. He should be out of there pretty soon."

"Will you let me know what happens?"

"I'll let you know."

"What about you, Max? Are you all right?"

"I'm fine. Anxious, that's all."

Her voice lowered. "I just talked to Kate. She's—"

"Can we discuss that later, Sharon? Right now I've got to see Charles's wife."

"Yes, of course. Good luck, Max"—her voice caught— "to both of you."

"Thank you, Sharon. Give my best to Tom."

Harriet was again standing at the window when I knocked, and she called for me to come in. Her usually erect figure appeared to droop, and her cigarette holder was no longer at a jaunty angle. She didn't react when I told her what little I'd learned, but when I mentioned Donovan, her eyes sharpened.

"Did he ask to see me?"

"No. But if you want to talk to him, he's in a press room upstairs. I can call him."

"Thanks, but don't bother. I just thought he might have something new on the case."

"If he did, I'm sure he'd have told me."

Her eyes flickered—as though in doubt, I thought, then decided I was mistaken. It was simply another symptom of the unremitting stress she had endured and must continue to endure. My heart went out to her and, on impulse, I crossed the room and took her in my arms. For an instant, she stiffened—a reflexive reaction to the embrace of anyone but Charles—but then she sagged against me and an almost inaudible mewing sound escaped from her throat. For a minute or more I held her—this hard-surfaced woman with the molten core who could influence the destinies of unknown millions but was helpless when confronted by the ordeal of the one she held most dear. I murmured words of comfort, as I once had to Kate when her cat had been crushed by a car, and I thought how terrible love can be and wished I could have suffered it, not from afar, but in union with a woman I adored. When I released Harriet, I saw that her face was stamped with pain, but her eyes were dry. I turned away because mine were not.

"Thank you, Max," she said.

"Don't tell Charles. He always was suspicious of you and me."

"With good reason. I've loved you since the day I stepped off the boat." She straightened my bow tie. "To prove it, I'll let you get even at backgammon."

"Now you're talking."

We had just sat down at the table when the phone rang. She picked it up, said a few words, and hung up. Her pale skin had gone dead white.

"Dr. Haskell wants to see me," she said. "He's coming up."

Dr. Haskell, still in his green, pajamalike surgical clothing, mask slung around his neck, pushed his fingers through his straight black hair, sat back in the angular chair, and crossed his arms. From where I was standing against the wall, I looked down at his canvas shoes and noticed they were spattered with blood.

"It's over, Mrs. Dain," he said.

Alarm rounded her eyes. "Over?"

Haskell's narrow face split in a thin smile. "I mean the operation is finished."

Harriet stirred as if to rise from her chair. "He's in the recovery room?"

"Not yet. A few routine things are now being done— inserting drains, suturing the flap of skin—nothing to worry you."

"How is he?"

"He's alive, Mrs. Dain. And his vital signs give us reason to be cautiously optimistic."

"Optimistic? You mean—"

I cut in: "Forgive me, Doctor, but are you saying you can't be sure the operation is a success?"

"Not at this moment." He turned back to Harriet. "That's why I'm here. It's important that you know what we found and what we did."

So she wouldn't sue him for malpractice in the event of death or paralysis, I thought.

"As you know," Haskell said, "the bullet entered the head just above the left eye, close to the temple. It penetrated a section of the left frontal lobe, causing little damage, and came to rest in the parietal lobe, which is at the rear of the brain. Between those two points we found fragments of metal and specks of bone, which of course caused severe bleeding. We—"

"Really, Doctor," I said, "can't we save the gruesome details until later? Right now we're concerned only about the prognosis."

He gave me a condescending look. "Yes, but first—"

"You'll please be brief, Doctor," Harriet said, her eyes glittering. It was an order.

His face froze, and he gazed down at the moving fingers of his priceless right hand. "All right, then, but it's best you know these things if you are to understand what might be in store. Suffice to say that the bullet was removed, as were all fragments and the damaged brain tissue. His blood pressure is now within normal range. Fortunately the shock to his system was minimized by the small caliber of the bullet and the fact that its velocity was impeded by first glancing off his upper arm and cheekbone. Now, as to what you might expect . . ." He paused and glanced up at the ceiling.

I stepped over and lit Harriet's cigarette.

Haskell sniffed slightly at the smoke and went on. "I can only say that at this time I don't consider his life to be in jeopardy. As for the future, it is beyond the power of anyone to predict. Your husband, Mrs. Dain, is a physically strong man and, I understand, possesses an equally strong will. These factors will count heavily in his recovery and form much of the basis for my optimism."

"When will you know?" Harriet asked.

"I can't be definite. There have been numerous cases where the patient becomes virtually normal within hours. With others, it can take weeks, sometimes months, before it can be determined whether he will achieve a complete recovery."

Harriet leaned forward. "Then I'm to understand that some of his faculties may be impaired at first?"

"Quite possibly. His bodily movements may be limited. He may experience difficulty in speech, hearing, comprehension. All temporary, in my opinion. You should not be unduly alarmed by such aberrations."

I moved closer to Harriet, saying, "When can she see him?"

He kept his eyes on Harriet. "I understand you wish to be alone with him as soon as possible."

"That's correct."

"It will be a while before he comes out of the anesthesia. Also there are a number of postoperative procedures that must—"

"When, Doctor?"

"Late this afternoon, I'd say. I will see that you are notified."

Shortly after five o'clock I sat with Terry Donovan outside the recovery room waiting for Harriet to come out. She had been in there for ten minutes, leading us to believe that she and Charles were somehow communicating. Two resident doctors and a nurse idled about, ready to rush in should there be a sudden emergency. Down the corridor at the nurses' station stood two bulky men who were, Donovan had informed me, homicide detectives. Dave Hewlett had phoned the story to the paper (the operation, he reported, was a success and Charles Dain's condition was listed as serious but stable) and he had returned to the press room to await developments.

The storm had blown through, and now the wall opposite us was daubed with sunshine. I prayed it was a good omen.

The nurse said to the two doctors, "I think it's been long enough."

All three started for the door. As they were about to enter, it sprung open and Harriet stepped out. She looked around uncertainly, as though she had lost something but couldn't recall what it was. Getting up, I saw from the corner of my eye the two detectives striding toward her. Donovan rose and went to head them off.

I moved close to Harriet and asked quietly, "Was he conscious?"

She had to squint to get me in focus. "Yes. At least he knew I was there."

"Did he speak to you?"

She shuddered. "Max, he can't talk. He can't make a sound."

My innards felt as though they'd been knotted and the knot yanked tight. "Can he hear?"

"Yes. I spoke to him, and I could tell from his eyes that he understood. Then I played a sort of insane game. I pointed to myself and said, 'Charles, do you know me?' and his head gave a tiny nod. I said, 'Is my name Harriet?' and he nodded again. Then, to make sure the nod wasn't just a reflex, I asked, 'Am I your sister?' and he shook his head, no. 'Am I your wife?' He nodded yes."

"Did you ask if he knew why he was there?"

"Yes. But there was no response. He just closed his eyes and kept them closed."

"Then you didn't ask who shot him?"

"Yes, I did. But his eyes stayed closed and his head didn't move. Finally I said I'd be back later, after he'd rested."

I asked her to wait a moment and went to the detectives and Donovan, who had halted out of earshot. Quickly I explained what had happened.

One of the detectives said; "Okay, then, he can see and he can hear and he can signal. So maybe he can identify who did it from mug shots."

"Mug shots?" My mind was disconnected from police procedures.

"Yeah." He tapped a large manila envelope under his arm. "We've got pictures of every known triggerman in the country."

"You can't go in now," I said. "He's in no condition to—"

"We'll wait," the other detective said.

I looked at Donovan. He was regarding the detectives with patent disdain, as though to say they were wasting their time.

I went back to Harriet. She no longer looked bemused. Her jaw was set and her eyes glowed with a sense of purpose.

"Max," she said, "the important thing is he can think. Anything else won't matter so much if his mind can function."

As I escorted her back to her suite, I wondered what thoughts might be spinning about in Charles's mutilated brain.

Chapter · 17

When a creeping awareness signified that he had undergone some strange transformation, Charles Dain concluded he was dead. So this was how it was, the answer to the eternal mystery—no great flash of light, no pearly gates, no angelical choir; just a feeling of unearthly suspension, a mind empty of care, a sense of benign inertia.

His eyes fluttered open and saw, somewhere beyond his feet, a woman dressed in white. She was smiling and saying something, the words unclear. He tried to move his lips, perhaps to return the smile, perhaps to speak; he was unsure. But it didn't matter—nothing at all mattered. The woman spoke again, this time to some other presence, and he heard a male voice quietly reply. Then he felt a warmth on his eyelids, prompting them to open and blink rapidly as they were struck by a fierce incandescence.

"He's reacting well to light," the male voice said.

Charles heard the words but could not comprehend their meaning.

Another male voice said, "Can you raise your arm?"

Stupid thing to ask. He raised his right arm about six inches.

"Very good. Now the other arm."

That was more difficult. A fraction of an inch was all he could manage.

"Fine, fine. Get Mrs. Dain."

They had left and, in a minute or so, another woman came in. She looked only vaguely familiar, like someone met at a party that he couldn't quite place. So he'd had to pretend, nodding and shaking his head in answer to absurd questions that established her identity. Something inside his head knew she was his wife and that her name was Harriet, but the words conveyed no significance, evoked no images aside from the one that confronted him. And when she persisted with questions even more nonsensical—Why was he here? Did he know who shot him?—it was as though the circuits of his brain, already overloaded, suddenly shut down and the interior of his skull became a dark void.

He swam back to sensibility on a wave of multicolored lights, then plunged into a vortex of spinning faces—his father and mother, sisters and brothers, Harriet, Max, Kate. . . .

Kate. Her image dissolved into the one so like her own—Sharon's.

And now, filling the entire screen of his mind, there was only Sharon. She was a luminous face coming toward him along a crowded corridor, pausing as they passed to press into his palm a tightly folded square of paper. In history class he spread it out, fingers fidgeting, heart pumping, and read: "I'll be studying at Janet Newmiller's house this afternoon. Would you like to stop by and help?" This from Sharon Fletcher! Why, they'd only just met—in the school newspaper office when she'd brought him items about her classmates. But they'd talked for an hour, and she'd gone away saying what a fine mind he had. So that was it, exactly what the note said: she wanted a free tutor, nothing more. Ridiculous to think she could have any other interest in a boy who looked sort of foreign, wore patched clothes, and whose father supported a pack of kids and dogs by working with his hands. Well, Sharon Fletcher, if you needed brains to pick, try finding them among those rich kids who were always chasing after you. He'd tell her so, politely, right after morning assembly.

Now there was a myriad of faces, glowing in the golden sunlight that flooded the vast auditorium. On stage the school band struck up a familiar melody, signaling monitors to rush down the far aisles and with long poles fling open the huge windows to the born-again spring—the scent of damp earth and flowering plants, the chatter of birds, the splash of the rocky brook. And then, in rhythm to the swinging arms of the small man up front, the voices rose and mingled in ardent greeting:

> Welcome sweet Springtime,
> We greet thee in song,
> Murmurs of gladness
> Fall on the ear. . . .

And Charles saw, across the aisle and two rows down, the face of Sharon Fletcher turned to gaze at him, to smile as no one could ever have smiled at a mere tutor, to entice him with the sparkle of amethyst eyes and the inquiring tilt of her silky-blond head. And he gave her a vigorous nod—yes, he would be there—and for a fleeting moment his whole being surged with the joy of life.

She stood in Janet Newmiller's parlor looking ethereal in her white ruffled blouse and long pale-green skirt and solemnly recited:

> She walks in beauty, like the night
>   Of cloudless climes and starry skies;
> And all that's best of dark and bright
>   Meet in her aspect and her eyes:
> Thus mellowed to that tender light . . . .

"Exactly," Charles said.

"But I haven't finished."

"It's enough to describe you exactly."

Her eyes rounded to full moons. Her lips parted like a budding rose. "Such talk," she said. "Such"—smiling archly now—"lovely talk."

"Byron must have dreamed you," he said, and closed the book.

She made a mock curtsy. "Thank you, sir."

He stood up and gazed at her boldly, knowing now why she had asked him over, knowing why Janet Newmiller had excused herself to help her mother, knowing why Sharon had chosen to memorize romantic poetry—knowing that he was merely the object of a playful flirtation that must be conducted surreptitiously lest she suffer the contempt of her elite peers. It didn't matter, of course, that Janet Newmiller knew, because she was Sharon's slave and would keep her mouth shut while vicariously sharing this teasing interlude. All right, then, if that's how it was, he could afford to be reckless; he had nothing to lose but the false identity existing only in

Sharon's fanciful mind, and in losing that he would regain his pride.

She was regarding him curiously, as though seeking to anticipate his next move. From the kitchen down the hall he heard the muffled voices of Janet and her mother and the rattle of pots on the iron stove.

"I guess I'm making love to you," he said.

Her gaze remained steady. "Are you? Is that what you're doing?"

"Isn't that why you asked me here?"

"Oh, no. My goodness, what must you think of me?"

He shrugged and turned away. "Sorry I was so wrong. For a minute I thought . . . Well, it doesn't matter now. Anyway, I've got to leave."

"But it's still early."

He stepped close to her. "Good-bye, Sharon."

"Charles, I wish you wouldn't—"

She was silenced by the sudden encirclement of his arms, by his mouth crushing against hers, and when he quickly released her, she was too breathless, too stunned, to utter a word. He left her there, strode to the front door and, without looking back, was gone.

He was halfway down the street when he heard her call, "Charles! Charles!"—but he did not turn around, even though her voice was edged with panic.

Standing on his porch he saw the spoked wheels spinning dust from the dirt road. He waited, staring in disbelief as Sharon sped past the squatters' shacks, then coasted her bike along the hard-packed earth of the front yard.

Getting off, resting the bike on its side, she stalked up and confronted him with a look of defiance.

"Your face is dirty," he said.

"What's wrong with a little dirt?"

"Nothing, if it's used right." He descended the steps and grasped her elbow. "Come on, I'll show you."

They worked side by side in the garden, along with his brothers and sisters, who looked with awe at this genteel girl who didn't seem to mind if her fine long dress became soiled or if her beautiful blond hair fell limply over her eyes.

"So you came to study farming," Charles said.

"I came because you've been ignoring me at school."

"I had to."

"Why?"

"Look around you," he said. "I don't have the background for a girl like you."

"If you mean you're poor, you're not."

"I'm not?"

For the first time, she smiled. "You have me."

He was startled, disconcerted, skeptical of the notion that anyone so refined, so universally desired, could think of him as more than an offering to her vanity, a small trophy soon to go unnoticed in her splendid collection. Still, he was aware that he was good-looking (though not in the preferred way of the men in the collar ads), and even she, who should have not cared, had admired his intelligence. So it was just possible . . .

He smiled, shrugged, said, "Sure I have you; you're a great hired hand"—then turned away and began to gather up the tools.

She helped, fetching a hoe and a rake, then followed him to a rusted metal shed at the rear of the garden. Inside he hung up each item carefully, taking his time, conscious of her presence behind him, her gaze on his back, her musky scent in the sun-baked air. And when he slowly swung around, grazing her breasts, it seemed inescapable that their bodies should join, dusty-damp cheeks meet, lips touch, cling, breathlessly immerse.

When finally they parted—interrupted by approaching footsteps—he knew, looking into her caressing eyes, that never again would he be the Charles Dain who deferred to the rich and the mighty. Why should he when with certitude he knew that someday he would be one of them?

Walking back to the house, she said, smiling, "Am I still your hired hand?"

"You just got a promotion."

"Thank you. But please don't change the working conditions."

As he reached the front of her house he heard her voice from an upstairs window telling him to come in, the door was unlocked. Inside, he found himself alone, explained when Sharon called down that her mother was at the grocer's. He reflected a moment, then asked if he might use the bathroom. Yes, of course; it was upstairs at the end of the hall.

Passing the open door of her room, he glanced in and saw her standing before a chiffonier putting up her long hair. He paused, caught by the reflection of her smile in the wood-framed mirror. She turned to him, releasing her hair to flow in untamed waves down the shoulders of her pink, floor-length robe. Their meeting in the center of the room was spontaneous, a reflex of the heart, as were the kisses, the stroking, and the sudden loosening of her sash, presenting the flashing whiteness of her curtained body. His hands, unbidden by thought, parted the curtains to reveal her taut ripeness, then slipped around her waist and drew her into him, feeling the responsive pressure, the warmth of her quickening breath, then hearing . . .

. . . hearing the creak of a board, the wrench of a doorknob. They froze, split, and before he realized it he had bounded down the stairs, grasped the edge of the door as it opened, and was unburdening Mrs. Fletcher of her bagged groceries.

His only thought was a thanks to God that it hadn't been Sharon's father, that hulking, red-faced creature who, at first meeting, had eyed him as he would a burglar.

Later he sat with Sharon on the porch swing. They spoke very little, and then only of trivial things, just enough to distract them from the terrifying knowledge that youth and empathy were conspiring in their seduction.

They tried to pull back from the precipice. Walking in the woods, lingering at the soda fountain, sitting on her porch, they discussed the economic theories of Adam Smith, the philosophy of Emerson, the works of Shakespeare, the books she was reading in class— George Eliot's *The Mill on the Floss*, Charles Dickens's *A Tale of Two Cities*, William Dean Howells' *The Rise of Silas Lapham*. But there were also her borrowed copy of Theodore Dreiser's shocking *Jenny Gerhardt* and the marked passages found by Janet Newmiller in her mother's copy of D. H. Lawrence's *Sons and Lovers*. The feelings that inflamed them were only partially those of the adolescents in Booth Tarkington's best-selling and parent-approved *Seventeen*, theirs being much more turbulent and all the more frightening for being recognized. They were in love, insanely, recklessly in love, oblivious of all but themselves, their thoughts when apart ruled by wild fantasies that expanded the intimate scene in her bedroom into an overwhelming climax. And then came reality, instigated by a catalyst named Janet Newmiller. . . .

"Mom's at a club meeting," she said. "She'll be there all afternoon. So I've got to go and buy things for supper."

Charles felt an inner stirring. He looked at Sharon, beside him on the sofa. "Shall we give her a hand?"

Sharon dropped her eyes. "Well—"

"Don't bother," Janet said. "I can do it faster by myself." She went quickly to the door, pausing to give them a metallic smile—how she hated the braces, the glasses, the unmanageable hair—and add, "I'll be back in about an hour."

Then they were alone, quiveringly alone.

He tried to be debonair. "All right, then, as I was saying about the Pythagorean theorem—"

He was stopped by the look in her eyes. "Damn Pythagoras," she said.

His voice lowered. "Maybe you'd prefer the Dain Hypothesis?"

Her face moved closer. "I think so, if I knew what it was."

"Let's see, it goes something like this. The juxtaposition of two young people in love invariably produces . . ." He paused, shaking his head. "Forgot the answer."

"This?" She kissed him lightly on the cheek.

"Eureka!"

Their laughter was subdued by the pressure of lips, converted to sighs by the panic of hearts, lost in a flurry of frantic hands that somehow unfastened her skirt, unbuttoned her blouse, loosened his belt, opened and lowered his trousers, blazed a silken passage through her summer undergarments. And then he was there, as they both had imagined it, she yielding, cooperating, hands on his hips, guiding him to the virginal thrust— which suddenly was not at all as they had imagined it, but was desiccated and wounding and dissociated from love or passion.

They lay frozen against each other while she murmured words of reassurance—it was too sudden, they were too tense, and, after all, this was the first time for both of them. It *was* the first time for him, wasn't it? He nodded miserably, feeling childish and impotent, chilled by the certainty that he had lost her. He shifted to sit beside her, embarrassed by what now seemed his indecent exposure—like some beggar lying drunk in an alley—and he started slyly to rearrange his clothing. But she stopped him, wiser now than he, her hand gliding to his loins to fondle him as she might a treasured object, shameless of her own disarray, in fact seeming to flaunt it by gazing wantonly into his eyes.

And so it resumed, this time in fading light, this time with the removal of encumbering clothes, this time with the remembrance of how it had been in fantasy, this time slowly and tenderly and, in its prolonged, breathtaking climax, with an all-consuming rapture.

She had made him a man—strong, courageous, indomitable—one of that breed who had scaled the Matterhorn, defended the Alamo, plunged over Niagara Falls in a barrel.

Whatever the future might hold, she would glow in his heart for the rest of his life.

Now all the pretense that had stood between them was abandoned. They talked not only of their love—

unselfish, romantic, idyllic—but also of their sexual needs, verbally sharing each discovery, planning how and where and when they could be alone, uncaring of where it might be—in the bed, happily provided, of Janet Newmiller; in the recessed doorway of the dark, deserted school; in a bower deep in the woods; in the cramped space of the Dain toolshed; in the depths of a picnic grove when Max Wills hiked off to explore.

There were notes passed in school—"I can't wait for Friday night. I love you, love you, love you!"—the pressing of knees beneath a library table; the adoring sight of her, ethereal in black robe and broad white collar, as she sang in the choir; the furtive kisses in the last row of the movie theater; the Saturdays of boating on a lake, rowing lazily to a hidden cove; the serious talks over banana splits as they sat in wire-backed chairs at their special table, their commitment made secure by unabashed revelations of self. Nothing could ever separate them, he thought, not even a college man like that Tom Richards who was so crazy about her, not even her ferocious father who distrusted anyone born of immigrant parents—unless they were Irish.

Oh, God, that man, that Neanderthal son of a bitch who had come storming out of the moonswept night into the school doorway, where the blackness was relieved only by Sharon's pale hair and the flashing whiteness of her bare thighs. . . .

"Mr. Dain?"

It was the woman in white again, smiling toothily, as she might at someone else's baby.

"Can you hear me, Mr. Dain?"

Yes, he could hear her, but to admit it would be to

enter a strange world that he sensed, without knowing why, would be hostile and unforgiving.

"I'm your nurse, Mr. Dain. Miss Ferber, Anna Ferber. You do *see* me, don't you? Your eyes are open."

He closed them. Keep them closed, he thought. His eyelids were now the only barrier to whatever it was out there that threatened to destroy him. Satan? No, but someone with a satanic look of vengeance.

"I think he's in a coma again, Doctor."

"Odd. He shouldn't be. Vital signs are okay. Better get Dr. Haskell."

So tired, so damnably tired. Boneless, inert, like a sackful of jelly. But there was a friendly light glowing inside his head. An oval light, like a luminous face. Ah, yes, that's what it was, the features slowly emerging, like a photographic print in a developing solution—the sensual mouth, the delicate nose, the sparkling amethyst eyes, the sweep of flaxen hair. His mind was an album, and on every page was that beloved face. . . .

He had seen that face floating above his canvas bunk at Camp McClellan, seen it hovering over the battlefield at Cantigny, seen it lurking along the corridors of the hospital near London, seen it perched on his café table at *Stars and Stripes* and at Nini's and the Napolitain and on the ceiling of his room at the Y.M.C.A., seen it pinned to the spire of Notre Dame, seen it in Rome, Constantinople, Athens, Budapest, Prague. . . .

It had never left him, not for a single day of all the years. It came to him most poignantly in the night, a smiling apparition that beckoned and tantalized and tortured, becoming more than a face, becoming a body as well, a body remembered in every lovely detail, every sinuous movement, as much a part of him as his beating heart, and, like his heart, forever untouchable. When he heard she had married Tom Richards, it was as though he had been smothered, drained of vitality, sentenced to everlasting agony. He truly wished for death, thankful only that it need not be accomplished by his own hand, that there were millions of uniformed Germans who would be glad to oblige him. He would end his life in glory, a martyr to the cause of civilization, and then perhaps she would weep, not as he had wept—inwardly, beneath a jesting facade—but visibly, extravagantly, interminably, so that she and Tom Richards and all the world would know that for her there had been only this one love.

But death had passed him by, leaving but a single alternative to impress upon her the magnitude of her loss—fame. And what could be more suitable to his talents, what could be more glamorous than to become a foreign correspondent, a man respected and sought after by the high and the mighty, a man who might one day lecture to an enthralled audience, knowing that somewhere among those awed faces was hers, attentive, admiring, but also punished by the thought of what might have been?

Harriet had restored his sanity. Harriet was real, of this world, and intriguing in her paradoxes—haughty in business, a hellion in bed; prim in public, profane in private. She was a woman, all woman, but pretending otherwise until he had happened along and unlocked the vault that had for so long imprisoned her yearnings. She was friend, confidante, lover—*wife*. What more could he ask except that she be rich? Oh, what a fine thing it was to discover she was rich—rich enough to think nothing of making him a gift of a New York newspaper. But money aside, she was so many things to him, so understanding, so dear. . . .

But she was not Sharon. She was not the girl who had astonished his heart with the joys of discovery, who had produced a universe in which every minute of every hour was charged with excitement, who had elevated him to equality with all those moneyed young men he had once considered his betters. But that girl, he kept reminding himself, was gone, married, a mother; and it was senseless to think she could ever be duplicated. It was just too bad that acceptance of the loss failed to destroy the emotion; but eventually it would fade, absorbed by his deep affection for Harriet and the fulfillment of his grandiose dreams as a journalist.

But it did not fade, in fact, became more vivid as he mingled with the Broadway crowd and observed actresses and showgirls still dewy with youth, uninhibited in speech, sexually precocious, all aspiring to the indefinable something that author Elinor Glyn publicized as "It"—a something that Sharon had not had to contrive because it was innate. Thus it was easy to dismiss these pretty young things who, while often provoking nostalgia, were mere parodies of the girl who had utterly possessed him.

And then along had come Bonnie Prince—standing like Sharon herself atop stairs that appeared as a pedestal in the Club New Yorker—and it was as though she had come there determined to escort him to a reunion with the glorious past.

What a fiasco that had been—not only because of her avarice, her affectations, her absurd ambitions, but also because she had been born with a mind incapable of

comprehending anything more subtle than the philoso-
phies reflected in *True Confessions* or in the writings of
Faith Baldwin.

He had tried desperately to keep the illusion alive—
having her dress in old-fashioned clothes in private,
insisting she augment her blond hair with a fall, guiding
her to reminiscent techniques in bed—but soon he had
despaired of creating even a reasonably accurate
facsimile of the prototype fixed indelibly in his mind.

But once having tasted the forbidden fruit, having
enjoyed, however briefly, a delirious flashback to romantic youth, he was powerless to resist further pursuits. He became like a compulsive gambler whose
losses are forgotten in the recalled excitement of the
game and returns to the tables confident that this time
he will walk away rich. That shapely blonde at the bar
who turned from her escort to smile at him—was she
not Lady Luck? That tawny-haired singer who directed
her torch songs to him—was she not inviting him to
pool their beautiful memories? That fair, long-legged
dancer who said she liked dominant men—wasn't she
really saying that she'd be anything he wanted?

Invariably he was right, invariably he left the gaming
establishment—a speakeasy, a supper club, a theater—
as a big winner—only to discover too late that what he
had won was counterfeit. Disillusioned, wounded in
spirit and bank account, he would then revert to full-
time husband, enchanting Harriet as he had in the beginning—until one day he would again be beguiled by
eyes projecting a certain look, a smile that was faintly
familiar, a body that moved in a remembered rhythm.

Inevitably there were interludes of danger—the girl
in the fur coat, a gift from him, who had stripped to her

skin in his limousine; the girl who had responded to rejection by slitting her wrists; the girl who had yanked a small pistol from her purse and ...

Now, in the recovery room, his inert body was suddenly electrified.

... and shot him! With a small pistol!

My God, that's why he was here! He had been shot! Not, as before, while standing in his office, but while standing in the living room of the town house trying to reason with a visitor who had abandoned all reason.

His brain erupted in a hemorrhage of images—traumatic, intolerable.

He lapsed into a coma.

The voices, subdued and melancholy, drifted in through the open door.

Harriet's voice: "Dr. Haskell, I'm frightened. He's been unconscious for more than an hour."

"No cause for alarm, Mrs. Dain. I have examined him thoroughly and found nothing extraordinary."

Max's voice: "Can you say how long he'll be under?"

"It's unpredictable. It might be as long as several hours. The reason is not attributable entirely to the wounds. The fact is, his mind needs time to adjust."

"To reality?" Max said.

"You might put it that way. The recovery may well occur in stages. The next stage is often amnesia."

"What!" From Harriet.

"Temporary, Mrs. Dain, only temporary. It is not unlike senility. Events of the present are perceived dimly, if at all, while those of the past are recalled quite clearly. But, as I say, this is merely a transitional state."

Silence.

"Mrs. Dain, you look fatigued. Understandable, of

course. I suggest you try to rest. You'll be called the moment he shows signs of consciousness."

The voices trailed away.

The past, the doctor had said. Was this a scene from the past that was now slowly unwinding inside his head? If so, it seemed irrelevant, trivial compared to all his other mental churnings. He was on a platform nodding and waving to an applauding audience. The Waldorf-Astoria, that's where he was. He had just made a speech to retail advertisers—a stem-winder of a speech, exulting in the promise of great days ahead for newspapers and the merchants who used them. Does Macy's tell Gimbels? Now why had he thought of that old line?

Because he'd been stopped in the corridor by Bernie Gimbel, head of the department store and longtime friend. Bernie, smiling as usual and clapping him on the back, had declared that he was absolutely right, this New Deal plan to put more money in the pockets of the less fortunate was just what the country—and the retail business—needed. Let the Old Guard Republicans rail against the alphabet soup of agencies in Washington, and the Brain Trust, and the so-called social radicals—those diehards embalmed in their plush clubs would soon have to admit that Roosevelt had done more in his first hundred days than Hoover had done in four years. "Let's have a drink on it, Charles." "Sorry, Bernie, Harriet's in town. We're meeting for lunch."

So it must have been the spring of 1933—June perhaps, because F.D.R. had been inaugurated in March. Wait a minute. It had been the twenty-first of June, the first day of summer. How could he be so precise? Well, for one thing, as he stepped out on Park Avenue, summer was all around him—women in flimsy dresses and colorful millinery from Lily Daché and Mr. John, vestless men carrying their snap-brim hats, open convertibles with radios tuned to Martin Block's "Make Believe Ballroom," shirt-sleeved passengers crowded on the top decks of buses, taxi drivers actually smiling—yes, summer had come to New York. But none of these things accounted for the date being so firmly fixed in his mind. There was something else. . . .

He remembered walking crosstown to Madison Avenue, taking his time because he was early for his appointment with Harriet. He was on the west side of the street, strolling south, passing Tripler's and then Abercrombie & Fitch, where he paused to admire a window display of safari gear. Turning, he saw a woman emerge from the Eastman Kodak store on the opposite corner and cross the street, coming toward him. He stood there, breathing shallowly, studying her carefully so that this time there would be no mistake.

Her blond hair, beneath a mere token of a hat, fell almost to her shoulders. Her skin was like pink whipped cream, her mouth a rich confection, her eyes a startling amethyst-blue. And she was slim, poised, her long silken legs seeming to glide rather than walk. Incredible that after almost sixteen years, at the age of thirty-three, she should look scarcely a day older than the girl he had first kissed in the parlor of a house in New Jersey.

He found himself standing in the middle of the sidewalk, confronting her as he might a long-lost child. She reached the periphery of his shadow, slowed, looked up—and her lovely face fell apart.

"Charles!"

That's why he remembered it was the first day of summer.

Chapter · 18

He had felt somewhat as he did now—an airiness inside his head, a dryness descending from throat to chest, a weakness in his limbs. For a moment he could do no more than say her name, stare at the miracle of her face with its rounded blue eyes, open-mouthed smile, deepening pinkness. Then he took her arm, grasping it just below the short sleeve of her lime-colored dress, his palm thrilling to the smooth resilience of the remembered flesh, and drew her back to the safari window of Abercrombie & Fitch, where, for all their awareness of the passing throng, they might as well have been in darkest Africa.

"Charles, isn't this—"

"—haven't changed—"

"I always thought this—"

"—at all. Look, Sharon—"

"—might happen. But—"

"—why don't we—"

"Charles, we don't seem to be making sense."

And they burst into laughter—laughter that seemed to bridge all the years and, here in Manhattan, return them to tree-lined streets and the promised excitements of a suburban summer.

"The meeting will please come to order," he said. "The first item on the agenda is to find a nice cozy place and—"

"Oh, Charles, I can't. I'm meeting Tom, my husband, for lunch."

For the moment he had forgotten about Harriet. Now there was no reason to mention her or their lunch date.

"Later then," he said. "Whatever time you say."

"Well—" She looked dubious but at the same time tempted.

"We'll talk about whatever happened to what's-her-name."

She smiled. "Oh, *her*. Charles you just wouldn't believe."

"Not now. Only when we can sit down and really tear her to shreds."

She half shook her head, glanced nervously out at the traffic, said she was on her way to Grand Central, where her husband worked in the Graybar Building, and after lunch she must shop for a gift for her daughter, and— her eyes swung back and gazed full into his—"Would two thirty be all right?"

"Two thirty would be fine. I'll buy you an after-lunch drink."

"Don't tell me it's legal."

"Not yet, but soon." He took a card from his wallet and handed it to her. "Meanwhile—"

"A speakeasy?"

"Think of it as a social club."

She grinned. "I prefer speakeasy. I've never been to a speakeasy. The closest I've come is a bottle of near-beer in my kitchen. And, oh, yes, at Christmas, some home brew with the neighbors."

"You're beyond redemption. I'll be waiting for you."

The speakeasy was known simply by its address on East Forty-sixth Street, chosen because it was close to Grand Central, making it easier for her to be on time. He refused to believe he'd been influenced by the ambience of the place—deep-piled gray carpeting, softly-lit, red-velvet booths, college-boy waiters in white mess jackets, instrumental music from a remote record player. It was frequented mostly by the younger men-about-town, accompanied by a spectrum of sex-mates ranging from strippers at Minsky's and taxi dancers at Roseland to free-thinkers from Hunter College and budding secretaries from Katharine Gibbs. The few times he had dropped in he had left feeling middle-aged and isolated, intolerable for a man who was now only thirty-four, had a flat stomach, a tight-skinned face, and whose thick black hair betrayed filaments of gray only in bright sunlight.

Thirty-four. Hell, on this first day of summer in 1933, he was a mere eighteen, his virility only beginning to peak, his emotions tuned to the piped-in song which inspired his mind to supply the lyrics:

> Just one more chance
> To prove it's you alone I care for
> Each night I say a little prayer for
> Just one more chance.

God, how banal. God, how absolutely wonderful. Keep it going, Mr. Guy Lombardo, because it's just right for this rendezvous with a seventeen-year-old girl of thirty-three who's about to arrive in a Model T flivver to join him for a two-scoop soda—two straws, please—and then . . .

"I'm sorry I'm late."

He looked up, the semidarkness confirming she was only seventeen, the music affirming his own youth, the few young couples scattered about signifying that a party was about to begin. He rose, wanting to say, "You're not late, you've never left me," but instead murmured something unintelligible while helping her into the red-velvet booth and sitting beside her, but not so close as to prevent a direct view of the enchanting face that had haunted him all of his adult life.

"So this is a speakeasy," she said, looking around. "It's so nice, I may write Senator Wagner to vote against Repeal." The waiter approached and she said to Charles, "What shall I drink?"

"I don't recommend the near-beer."

"Whatever you think. But I warn you, I didn't have much lunch. I left half of Schrafft's blue-plate special."

He ordered white crème de menthes, but as the waiter turned away changed it to stingers, explaining to Sharon that the liqueur became more festive when wedded to brandy. She rolled her eyes, said, "Good-bye, it was nice seeing you," and they laughed a bit nervously, then lapsed into silence and just looked at each other. For a moment he thought of his lunch with Harriet at the Colony, where they'd been surrounded by austere women with monolithic bosoms, flowered hats, and ropes of pearls, and its contrast with this intimate, illicit hideaway quickened his excitement.

Finally she said, "I always thought that someday I'd meet you when you were with Max."

He had to remind himself that Max had remained friendly with Sharon, a fact he'd mentioned on a few occasions when in his cups. But he didn't want to talk about Max or about Sharon's family or about anything except—"

"We see Max quite often," she said.

"Fine," he said, "that's fine," and was grateful that the waiter had arrived with the stingers.

"He adores Kate," she said, and took a quick drink. "Delicious. Really delicious."

He nodded, smiled, and raised his glass to offer a toast to this tense, fumbling reunion—then drank instead.

"I guess you know that Kate's my daughter," she said.

Her voice seemed strained now, and he thought, Oh, God, let's get it over with; let's hear about her fabulous child and her sweet, kind, wonderful husband—Tom Richards, the college man—and about her friends and her clubs and all the marvelous years she's enjoyed since her wise, good, son-of-a-bitch father had murdered her love for the no-good hunkie who'd stolen her virginity. Let's hear it all, but please, let's hear it fast and then go on to why it was they were sitting here in this underground establishment designed for lovers.

"Yes, I know," he said. "Do you have a picture of her?"

And it just so happened she did, in fact a lot of them, in a special leather case that she drew from her bag. Even before he took it from her, he was ready with the words: "Say, she really is a beauty"—steeling himself against the awkward stance, the braces on the teeth, the pony-tail hair tied with a ribbon. So he was astonished when, looking at the first one, he felt his breath suck in and heard himself exclaim, "Well, I'll be damned!"

He went slowly through them all, fascinated by the images of this girl—fifteen, her mother said—so blond, so sleek, so poised, so much like . . .

"She's you," he said, "you exactly. Put her in a long, ruffled dress, add a chignon to her hair, and she'd be Sharon Fletcher, circa nineteen sixteen."

She smiled, relaxing slightly as she shared his emotion. "Everyone says we look alike. I don't deny it. I just enjoy the flattery."

"It's not flattery, it's the truth. You could be twin sisters. You're still as beautiful—"

Quickly she interrupted. "Guess what she wants to be? An ace reporter. Max's influence, I guess."

"She's made a tough choice. Newspapers hire very few women. But maybe I can help. When she thinks she's ready, have her tell Max to get on me about it. I may come up with something."

"That's very generous, Charles."

"Why not?" He paused to look at her. "She'd come recommended by an exceptional person."

"Yes, Max is—"

"I mean her mother. I used to know her very well."

The dim light did not conceal the flush rising to her cheeks. She dropped her eyes and, as though unaware of it, picked up her glass and drained it. "That seems so long ago," she said.

"Does it? To me it was yesterday."

She was silent, staring into her empty glass. He swung around and raised two fingers to the waiter. Turning back, he caught her gazing into his face—wistfully, he thought.

"Wasn't it yesterday?" he said.

She hesitated, looked away, then quietly said, "Yes." But before he could pursue it, she added with false brightness, "Now tell me about yourself—Charles Dain, the famous publisher."

He refused to be put off. Dammit, did she think he'd come here to be interviewed? Well, she'd just have to be disappointed because Charles Dain, the famous publisher, had vanished somewhere back on Madison Avenue. However, if she'd like to talk to the eager young man who'd replaced him . . .

He didn't say anything, just looked at her, his mouth hooked in a satirical smile, but his eyes glimmering with the look that had once preceded fantastic intimacies. He saw her take a breath, saw her eyelids fluttter, saw the pink tip of her tongue dart out to circle her lips—saw the waiter sidle up with the second round of stingers. She smiled then, partly in relief, partly in humorous appreciation of this intrusion into a poignant moment, and she gazed out at the room, head cocked, as though seeking the source of the music that floated insidiously into the red-velvet booth.

She shook her head. Perhaps, he thought, to rid it of notions that didn't belong in the mind of a contented housewife and devoted mother who should be home planning what to buy at the butcher's.

"So you want to hear about me," he said as the waiter left.

"Yes, I certainly do." She spoke with calculated enthusiasm, as though he had suggested showing his home movies.

What the hell, he thought, why not come right out with it? Sixteen years ago he'd lost her and now he was losing her again, and by default at that. What was he supposed to tell her—what a fine, rich wife he had and how she'd bought him a great newspaper and that he had a chauffeured limousine and a showplace house in

Mount Kisco and wasn't that pretty wonderful for a penniless outsider whose father spoke with a foreign accent and was proud of his homemade dandelion wine? Is that what she was expecting to hear as she peered over her glass with a look of polite anticipation?

He said matter-of-factly, "Sharon, there's only one thing about me that should interest you, and that's that I've never stopped loving you. I remember every minute we spent together and everything we did. I remember you in Janet Newmiller's bed and in the toolshed and in our secret place in the woods and—"

"Charles!"

"—and every other place where two people in love could sneak away and take off their clothes, or at least some of them, and celebrate their feelings. I remember—"

"Charles, *please!*"

He went on relentlessly, exulting in her look of shocked confusion, which could so easily be translated as a sudden arousal of desire. "—the way you looked and spoke and moved. I remember every part of you, which right now is very easy to do because it's still all there, just as it was, and crossing your arms like that isn't going to make me forget it."

"Charles, you've got to stop!"

He did stop, but just for a moment, just for the time it took to look into her distraught face, then lean forward and say, almost belligerently, "Why must I stop?"

"Because . . ." She fluttered a hand.

"Because you've got a husband and I've got a wife?"

"Yes. Yes! It isn't fair to them."

"Is that why you haven't even mentioned your husband? And why I haven't mentioned my wife?"

"It just didn't seem—"

"Proper? You're right, it wouldn't seem proper to talk about two people who have nothing to do with what happened between us. And you know why, don't you? You're afraid it would spoil what we're both feeling right now."

She stared at her hands, now clenched on the table. "What I'm feeling, Charles, are the drinks and the music."

"Are you saying that, alone, cold sober, with the radio turned off, you've never thought of me?"

"Of course I've thought of you."

"In what way? As an old-time friend or as your lover?"

She squeezed her eyes shut.

"Which?"

"Both," she said.

"Often? Every day? The way it's been with me?"

Her eyes opened and gave him an imploring look. "Charles, I'm afraid."

His voice softened. "Say it, Sharon."

She whispered, "Yes, it was like that with me."

"Was? Or still is?"

"Charles, we can't do this. I'm a mature woman, with a grown daughter and a fine husband, and I'm happy, very happy, truly I am, and I like my life the way it is, without any complications, and"—her eyes suddenly moistened—"and I don't know why I'm going on like this because the answer is yes, I still feel that way. I can't help it; for all these years I haven't been able to help it. And sometimes I thought I'd go out of my mind thinking about you and remembering and wondering and—"

"Sharon, my dearest, my darl—"

"—and finally I told myself, convinced myself, that I was just being sentimental, that I wasn't that girl and never would be again—"

"But you are."

"—and that it had just been part of growing up and here I am washing away my makeup and—heavens, Charles, what did they put in these drinks?"

"Truth serum. Drink up."

She finished her stinger.

"I have a place near here," he said, "where I stay when—"

"Oh, no, we can't, we simply can't. I've got to think of Tom and you've got to think of your wife, Harriet—yes, I know her name—and it's all very well to say what we said, but that's where it has to end, *has* to—oh darling, what am I saying? Tell me what I'm saying."

"That you want us to be together. Isn't that it?"

"Yes, that's it, that's what I'm saying. Can we go now? Can we go right away?"

Her snug, lime-colored dress was fastened in back with square white buttons, which she all but ripped from their moorings the moment the door to the penthouse closed behind them. Her eagerness did not startle him. How could it when, in the taxi, oblivious of the unshaved face in the rearview mirror, they had flung themselves together as though in panic? How could there be the slightest inhibition when, alone in the elevator, they had clung to each other, hips undulating, she whispering, "Charles, Charles, I'd have done it in the taxi," and they had laughed huskily, laughter that was like a sexual joining?

Now she had escaped from her dress and was wriggling from her slip, saying, "Isn't progress wonderful? There's so much less to take off than there used to be." Then she danced away, clad only in creamy bra and panties, and stood with her high-heeled, open-toed shoes anchored in the pale-yellow carpet and, gazing at him from under thick lashes, said, "You always did the rest. Remember?"

"Sure, I remember. I did it over the drinks, and yesterday, and the day before—all the days."

He went to her, jacket and tie discarded, and slowly slipped the straps from her shoulders, exposing breasts still vibrant with youth, jubilant to the touch of hands and lips. Drawing down her panties, he kneeled to breathe islands of warmth on pulsing flesh, then rose as she kicked off her shoes and smiled up at this man suddenly grown taller. She arched her back, curving her hips into his while she unbuttoned his shirt, a service interrupted by the encirclement of his arms, drawn there by the erotic paradox of her nakedness against his clothed body.

Then, both dressed in glowing skins, he offered a suggestion, which she ratified by skipping to the gold-cloth drapes and opening them wide to reveal the terrace, drenched in late-afternoon sun. Stepping outside, he removed thick blue mats from the divans and placed them side by side on the pink tile. They met there, falling to their knees to embrace and explore and entangle, directed by memory to all the ways and all the words that had smoldered and echoed in their hearts for sixteen years. And when the tempestuous reunion was finished, when finally they rose to contemplate quietly the huge theatrical set of midtown Manhattan, it seemed only to have begun.

"You'll stay," he said, "at least for a while?"

"Oh, dearest, I really can't. I—" She paused to rebuke her mouth with her fingertips. "Enough of saying *can't.* No more. I'll make a phone call."

They went inside, and he led her to a guest room where she could talk in privacy. Returning, he sat on the sofa, lit a cigarette, and tried not to think that the man she was speaking to had enjoyed all the pleasures that had just been his.

No, no, not *all* the pleasures. There were things they had done that she would not duplicate with another man, not even her husband, Tom Richards, who, he recalled, had been a proper, conservative youth, traditionally respectful of the lie that women were much less sensual than men. Besides, throughout all those years of her marriage, she had remained in love with him, Charles Dain, and it was therefore absurd to think that Tom Richards or anyone else could have aroused the same uncontrolled passion. Was he being naïve? Perhaps, but at this moment it seemed vital to believe that her conjugal relations were little more than obligatory acts conducted with affection but never with abandon. But why think about it at all? What he and Sharon had was something completely separate from any other person or experience, a love sealed off from the lives they otherwise led, existing in an enchanted compartment that kept them forever young, forever foolish.

She came back smiling and stretched out on the sofa, resting her head in his lap, her silken hair flowing over his thighs. "It seems that right after lunch I bumped into an old friend from school," she said. "We're meeting for coffee at five. Naturally, that should last at least until six." She raised her head and kissed him. "So, my old friend, we have two whole hours. A little longer if for some delightful reason that seems necessary."

He stroked the gleaming curve of her hip. "Did you also tell that to your daughter?"

"Kate's at camp. She'll be there all summer."

"Good for Kate."

"Good for us." She sat up and looked at him seriously. "Am I presuming too much, Charles? Am I wrong to think we'll go on seeing each other?"

He felt a need to hear her commit herself. "Is that what you want?"

"Not just want. I have to see you. Oh, darling, I couldn't stand losing you again."

"You won't. It will be just the way it was."

"Yes, yes. It's like that now, isn't it?" She returned her head to his lap and stared at the ceiling. "But we both know what that means, and I guess we'd better face it. It means doing what I just did—telling lies, pretending you're in one place when you're in another, acting at home like you're the same person you always were."

"I know. Just as it used to be." He felt a twinge of conscience and lit another cigarette. "Of course," he said slowly, "there's another answer."

Her body twitched. "Divorce? Charles, I couldn't. I love you, but I couldn't. Tom has been so fine . . . but, well, I won't go into that. And Kate—it would tear her to pieces, I know it would."

"I understand," he said. "I'd have a similar problem."

"Yes, with Harriet. I know she must love you terribly, and I guess you—"

"She's a fine person. We have a good relationship." He ground out his cigarette, aware of a sudden sense of betrayal.

"Do you want to talk about her?"

"No, just about us."

"I'm glad. That's how I want it too. We just won't talk about them unless we have to. There'll just be us, the way it always was."

"Yes." He smiled down at her. "You used to be very good at arranging things."

"I know, and I will be again. It's not pleasant to talk about, but I realize we've got to be practical. He usually doesn't get home until about seven, so some days we could meet in the afternoon, like today, and have a few hours together. And anytime you can take a long lunch, well, you call me and I'll go wherever you say."

"You're a lovely girl."

"You'll see, it will get even better. I've got so much stored up inside me—dreams of the way it could have been for us. And now I can make some of it come true. He often has to go away on business for days, sometimes weeks, and all that time I'd be free for anything you want." She laughed and reached up to touch his cheek. "Just imagine, I could be here waiting for you to come home."

He felt himself recoil. "No, not here. She owns this hotel and stays here when she's in town."

"Oh. Well, there are other hotels." She laughed again, forcing it. "Or you could find us a nice furnished toolshed."

"They're all taken. Don't you know there's a Depression? And forget the hotels. I won't have us sneaking around like some lecherous boss and his file clerk. I'll think of something." But he already had. "What you deserve is an elegant town house, a place where we can relax, maybe keep a change of clothes."

"Oh, how marvelous! I could even dress up for you— you know, in things I used to wear."

"You've still got them—those long silk dresses?"

"A few, packed away in a steamer trunk. Not all that stuff I used to wear underneath though. But who wants that? Oh dearest, dearest, we're going to be so happy!"

She turned her face to where the back of her head had rested and kissed him.

This time he took her to the guest room.

Now, in the recovery room, he was aware that something had been placed over his nose and mouth—a respirator, he thought, and was surprised that his mind was so quick to recognize it. That had to mean that his brain was functioning normally, connecting him with the present as well as the past. But why should he think his brain had been affected? The bandages, that's why. He could feel them swathed about his head like a turban.

So it was his head that had taken the bullet. An accident? Or had someone deliberately tried to kill him? Why? Who would want to . . . gangsters? Perhaps— there were any number who'd like to see him dead. But the thought brought no response. He closed his eyes and let his mind drift, hoping it would pick up a clue. Nothing except the low hum of machines, and then, above it, a voice:

"I said you'll have to wait. No one can see him now, not even his wife."

From beneath his eyelids he saw that the door was ajar. A man in a loose pale-green top stood there. A doctor—the one who had just spoken so sharply.

Now, from outside, a deeper voice: "Doc, I want five

seconds, that's all. Just time enough so he can say who gunned him."

A cop.

"Forget it. He can't talk."

"Can't or won't?"

"Can't."

The door clicked shut. He heard the doctor moving about, saying something to a nurse. Then he heard nothing as his mind again whirled into darkness. But in the distance there was a light. No, not a light. A face—*her* face.

He was in a bedroom of the Twentieth Century Limited, on his way to make a speech in Chicago, when he heard the tapping on his door. He opened it, and she slipped inside and into his arms. They sat facing each other on the wide, cushioned seats, drinking tall Scotches, smiling like conspirators who had just made off with Fort Knox. She said that she'd have to mess up her bed next door so that the porter wouldn't be embarrassed. Meanwhile it was only five in the afternoon, and it seemed silly to wait until the beds were made up. He admired the way she thought, he said, and pulled down the shades, and she was ready for him—beneath the modest dress there was nothing but her—and they made love on the seats to the traveling music of steel spinning on steel and the compressed-air gasps of doors opening between the cars and the far-off, eerie shriek of the train whistle. And in Chicago's Drake Hotel they sat in the dark little bar off to the right as you walk up the broad entrance stairs and talked of long ago, but it was not long ago, it was never long ago, it was that time reclaimed for this moment. . . .

❋   ❋   ❋

It was mid-December, the snow falling and gathering soot in the streets, and when he walked into the bar he had the feeling that something was wrong. Probably, he thought, it was because Prohibition had been repealed and this bar was not really a bar but a "cocktail lounge," an atrocity composed of bright-orange modern furniture, chromium fittings, huge mirrors, Venetian blinds, and, God save the drinking man, cellophane palms! His uneasiness mounted when he saw her at a table in the rear. Her eyes were troubled, her manner subdued, which was explained when, over a legal drink, she said that Kate would be home for the holidays and Tom— big-hearted Tom Richards, he thought bitterly—was taking them to Miami Beach for ten days. Ten days! Two or three days without her had had him growling at his secretary and snapping at editors. But she'd phone him, she said, somehow she'd phone him every day. And she did—furtive, fast-talking calls that were litanies of love, sometimes aborted when she abruptly had to hang up. And when she'd returned, he had skipped going to the office for two days and, on the third, had to drag himself in, a casualty of a sexual riot. . . .

She was with him at the Statler Hotel in Washington, confined to her adjoining room reading *Anthony Adverse* while he went out to discuss the RFC with Jesse Jones, the WPA with Harry Hopkins, the FBI with J. Edgar Hoover. From G-man Hoover he brought her the inside stories of the capture of "Baby Face" Nelson, "Pretty Boy" Floyd, John Dillinger, and Bruno Hauptmann. She was fascinated but also worried, because the *Express* was then thundering its support of New York's special prosecutor Thomas Dewey in his relentless war against racketeers, and she feared reprisal. But she seemed reassured after he joined Franklin Roosevelt at the White House for cocktails, questioning him on the workings of the New Deal, the battle over the Supreme Court, the rising threat of the German Nazis; after all, who would dare assault a man who shared the personally-concocted martinis of the President of the United States? ...

They were at the Republican Convention in Cleveland, he in the press section, she in the gallery, on the night Alf Landon, "the Kansas Coolidge," was nominated, and they were at Franklin Field in Philadelphia when Charles's idol, Franklin Delano Roosevelt, accepted renomination with a speech blistering the "economic royalists." They were in a Vermont ski lodge when King Edward VIII quit the throne in favor of "the woman I love" ... on the beach in Bermuda when the German airship *Hindenburg* exploded in flames over Lakehurst, New Jersey ... on the Albany night-boat for his morning appointment with Governor Lehman when Hitler marched into Austria ... in his Packard driving to the Adirondacks when news commentator H. V. Kaltenborn announced over the radio that the man with the black umbrella, Neville Chamberlain, had returned from Munich boasting of "peace for our time". . . at a boardwalk hotel in Atlantic City when Orson Welles panicked the nation with his broadcast of *The War of the Worlds* ... at a restaurant on Lake Champlain when word swept the room that Germany and Russia had signed a ten-year nonaggression pact, triggering the Nazi invasion of Poland a week later. ...

All those years of planning, lying, maneuvering to be together . . . justified, they felt, because theirs was a union formed and consecrated in early youth. Their love was the first love, the original patent, invulnerable to infringement by assaults of conscience. Her excited phone calls to say that "he" would be going to Detroit or Anchorage or the Persian Gulf; his inventions of business trips out of town, sometimes unnecessary because Harriet, too, would be gone, consulting with her managers in other cities, here and abroad. Their meetings at the town house for lunch, or for late-afternoon drinks, or occasionally for dinner—and always for making love. Her girlish pleasure when, in their enchanted enclave, she changed to a long, silk, ruffled dress, topped with a feathered hat, and his delight as she modeled it, daringly permitting a glimpse of well-turned ankles, escalating to flashing thighs, culminating, with his eager help, in the tantalizing removal of all but the hat, which she waited to discard until they were in bed. She was better, he said, infinitely better than ecdysiasts like Ann Corio and Gypsy Rose Lee, an opinion, he added, that might possibly be influenced by the fact that he loved her with all his heart. . . .

It made no difference that he also loved Harriet. There was no conflict, because that love existed in a different world, a world in which he was the distinguished, responsible publisher and she the aggressive custodian of vast enterprises. Their talk was not of an idyllic past, of the racing excitement of forbidden meetings and the exchange of eternal vows, but was more apt to concern the grim present of bank failures, sit-down strikes, government regulations—subjects which he was inclined to discuss with optimism due to his constant euphoria. He was, in fact, a more cheery person around the house, and more attentive, which Harriet seemed content to accept as compensation for their diminished sexual activity. It was, said Sharon, so like her own situation. Nothing, they thought, could come between them. . . .

Except Kate.

Sharon spoke of her daughter constantly, reporting, it seemed, every movement she made, every thought she expressed; her progress at school, her skiing trips to Lake Placid, her latest crush; the movies she'd seen (oh, to be like Carole Lombard!), the books she'd read (oh, to write like Virginia Woolf!); and on and on it went.

Until one day at lunch in the town house, when, eager to take her to bed and due back in the office in an hour, he interrupted, unable to conceal his exasperation.

"Look, Sharon, must we always spend so much time talking about Kate?"

She drew back as though he had raised a fist. "Sorry," she said stiffly. "You always seemed interested."

"Up to a point, sure. But my eyes get a little glazed when I hear about things like slumber parties and how she's wearing her hair these days."

"Charles, that's not fair. I've never mentioned anything so trivial."

"All right, it's not fair. But look at it my way. Assuming I had a daughter by Harriet, would it thrill you if I made her the center of conversation?"

Her mouth contracted. "This is different."

"Why? Because I don't have a daughter, or a son, and never expect to?"

"No, because—" She gave her head a shake, pushed to the edge of the sofa, and picked up her coffee cup. It was empty, and she rattled it back in the saucer. "Let's please forget it, Charles. I'll try not to—"

"Now you're angry. Hell, I don't want to hurt you, not ever. But let me say one more thing, then I'll quit." He sat up straight, grasped her shoulders, and turned her to look at him. "Sharon, we keep pretending that there is no Tom Richards, just as there is no Harriet. And that's fine, that's how it has to be. But when I'm away from you, when you and he are together, doesn't it occur to you that I think about him and wonder what he and you are doing?"

"But we agreed—"

"We agreed not to talk about it. But I can't control what pops into my head. Anyway, that's not too important—I can handle it. What's tougher to handle is hearing about Kate whenever we see each other." His voice softened. "Sharon—look at me—I envy Tom Richards for the daughter you gave him. I can't help wishing she could have been ours. Every time you tell me about her, I feel like an outsider and—"

"Oh, no, Charles. You mustn't!"

"—I keep thinking of how satisfying it would be if I had the right to be a part of her growing-up. That's selfish, I know, and I'm a damn fool for making a big thing of it, but I want you to understand why—"

She shook from his grasp, jumped to her feet, and burst into tears. Her eyes flashed him an agonized look, then squeezed shut as she pivoted away and dashed to the kitchen.

He caught her at the sink. The water was running and she was reaching toward it with cupped hands. He turned off the tap and took her in his arms.

Between sobs she said, "That's what I've been . . . been trying to do . . . trying to make you part of . . . of Kate growing up."

"Yes, I know. I know."

"You don't know . . . and I just can't stand . . . can't stand . . . your not knowing . . ."

He didn't try to comprehend, just rocked her as he would a child.

"I wanted to tell you . . . that first day I saw you . . . when we were in that speakeasy . . ."

He pressed her closer, feeling dampness seep through his shirtfront. "Tell me what, dearest?"

She took a shuddering breath. "That *you're* Kate's father."

The memory jolted his brain like an electric shock. He felt his body convulse, heard the nurse exclaim, sensed a sudden rush of movement, felt his eyes bulge and stare as they were struck by jets of light.

"Mr. Dain," the doctor said, "are you conscious?"

His muscles slowly relaxed. His head jiggled in a crazy sort of nod.

"Good," the doctor said, and moved away.

Now there was only the incessant whir and hum of machines. His mind, adjusting to the astonishment of parenthood, was still with Sharon in the town house kitchen. He heard his voice babbling, then Sharon speaking quietly. Her arm was around him, leading him back to the living room.

The doctor returned, arching over his face. "You're all right, Mr. Dain. Do you hear me? You're all right."

Again the jiggling nod.

"Can you speak, Mr. Dain?"

He didn't know, didn't want to know, didn't want to try, so fearful was he of the words that might burst from his lips.

"No hurry," the doctor said. "No hurry at all. We'll be right here when you're ready."

His eyes closed and once again he appeared to be in a coma.

But he was not in a coma. He was fully conscious, his brain illuminated by the image of Sharon, controlled now but speaking in a tone that implored compassion.

She had not discovered her pregnancy until after their affair had violently ended, shortly before his army enlistment in early April of 1917. Frantic but refusing to involve him lest he feel trapped, she had been forced to turn to her parents for help. Her father—stunned, outraged, and terrified of scandal—hit upon a solution: marry Tom Richards, the respectable college man who for so long had adored her; the birth of the child could then be declared premature. She was appalled; it was unthinkable. Her father insisted, and finally she agreed to accept a proposal, but only on one condition: she must first tell Tom the complete truth. Defying her father's strenuous objections, that was what she did.

"Are you saying your husband knew I was Kate's father?"

"Yes."

"But, knowing that, how could he possibly have—"

"Married me? Because he loved me, and he chose to think of what I felt for you as an infatuation. Temporary insanity, he called it. I knew better, but I thought I'd never see you again."

"Has he ever thrown it up to you?"

"Not once. He's been a good husband, Charles, and a good father. I'm terribly grateful to him and always will be. I love him—I've got to say that—but not the way I love you."

It was easy for him to understand, because he felt the same way about Harriet. He listened in silence as she told him that while she was still pregnant her mother died, leaving her father to endure alone the anticipated humiliations of whispering neighbors; but he was spared when a job offer enabled him to escape to Philadelphia. She, too, feared there would be talk, which could be harmful to the child, so she and Tom had moved to New York right after Kate was born.

"I remember Max phoning me just before he went into the army. I hadn't seen him in a long time, and he didn't know I'd been pregnant. Kate was then only about a week old, and I was afraid that if he knew about her he'd figure out that you might be the father. So I didn't mention her, and I put off seeing him. When he did meet her it was after he got back from France, and there was no way of telling exactly how old she was."

"Max still doesn't know?"

She shook her head. "There were times I thought of confiding in him, probably because, unconsciously, I hoped he'd tell you. But that wouldn't have been fair to Tom, so I managed to keep quiet. I had a feeling, though, that some day I'd have to tell you. I couldn't stand the thought that you might come to resent her."

"If I did, I certainly don't now." He took her in his arms. "Dearest, I'm going to do everything I can to help her. And only the two of us will know why."

Now the memories flooded in: his elation when Max had brought her to the office; his pride and satisfaction in her skill in running down a story; his vicarious sense of achievement, shared with her mother, when he elevated her to writing a column; his pleasure when he heard from Max that she was seeing Terry Donovan; his . . .

Suddenly another memory detonated a small explosion in his mind. My God! That day when Kate had asked to see him alone, away from the office! That day in the penthouse when they had argued so fiercely, when she had stomped out in such a fury . . .

That was the same day he had been shot!

Oh Kate, Kate, why couldn't you have stayed out of it?

Worst of all, knowing what he did, why hadn't he used his phone call from the Stork Club to cancel rather than confirm the meeting in the town house?

He was thinking clearly now, recalling every detail.

Chapter · 19

"Max," Kate said, "will you call me as soon as he says anything—anything at all?"

"*If* he says anything," I said, almost whispering into the mouthpiece. "It's possible his vocal cords are paralyzed. How long will you be at your place?"

"I'm not going out. Tomorrow's column has been put to bed—mostly canned stuff—so I've nothing to do but wait here by the phone."

It was late afternoon of the next day, more than twenty-four hours since Charles had been wheeled from the operating room. After Harriet's visit no one but the assigned medical team had been allowed to see him. He was making a remarkable recovery, Dr. Haskell reported, though he was still unable to speak, a fact, I sensed, that the doctor found puzzling.

"Have you talked to Terry?" I asked.

"A few minutes ago. He's supposed to come here later, but I'm not so sure of that. He's taking over from Dave Hewlett, hoping to get more out of Charles than Dave could. When I talked to him he was practically going steady with a couple of detectives." Her voice thinned, as though about to snap. "He says he'll get in there before they do even if he has to break their legs."

I said, very calmly, "He just wants a beat, Kate, that's all. If the detectives get there first, they'll leak it to every reporter in the press room. Anyway, I've arranged it so that I'll see Charles before any of them."

"Before Harriet?"

"I hope so. Look, I'd better get off. I'll call you as soon as I've got something."

I eased the phone into its cradle, hoping that its one quick ring had not roused Harriet. I went to her bedroom, opened the door a crack, and saw that she was still asleep, breathing long, throaty sighs of exhaustion. Earlier, agreeing to lie down, she had said that sleep would be impossible, then proved herself wrong within minutes. It was a bad trade-off, I thought, an exchange of wakeful anxiety for terrifying nightmares.

I went back and stood at the window, the phone within reach, and gazed out at Park Avenue, still slick with rain and shimmering in the headlights of crawling cars. My mind was on Kate, whom I'd known and loved since her infancy—the closest I would ever come to having a child—and again I had the recurring thought that all this horror might have been avoided if only I had kept her with me on the night of the shooting.

She had phoned me that evening at the Algonquin just as I was about to go downstairs for dinner, saying she must see me immediately about a matter of urgent importance. Twenty minutes later—shortly after seven —she stalked into my living room, flung her purse on a chair, muttered a few creative obscenities, and proceeded to explode.

Her mother, she shouted, was the mistress of Charles Dain!

I was stunned, petrified, mute.

What's more, the affair had been going on since 1933. Nine years! Her father had been a cuckold for nine years! I uttered a strangled protest, staggered to a chair, and collapsed. For a moment I thought I'd hallucinated —that she'd said one thing and my mind had registered something else. I just sat there, staring at her, shaking my head in disbelief.

"Goddammit, Max, it's true! Absolutely true!"

My voice tore loose. "No, goddammit, it isn't! You don't know what you're saying!"

"The hell I don't." She stood over me, eyes glaring, lips drawn back. "I got it from the best possible source."

"You mean those gossip-hounds you run around with? Oh, Kate, for God's sake—"

"That's where I heard it first. In the powder room at El Morocco when I was in the john. Two old bags repairing their makeup while they bloodied a few reputations. One of them had sat next to Charles and my mother in some cocktail lounge. She'd recognized Charles, of course, but not my mother. She'd heard Charles say her name, though—Sharon—and she said she was blond and beautiful. Well, that made me suspicious and—"

"Get off it, Kate. There are probably hundreds of beautiful blondes named Sharon."

"Maybe. But how many are there who knew Charles when he was a teenager? I'll tell you. Only one."

"That still doesn't prove—"

"No, it doesn't. So I decided to get the proof. Yesterday around six o'clock I followed Charles in a taxi. He went into a brownstone town house on East Sixty-third Street. I waited in a doorway across the street, and pretty soon another taxi drove up and out stepped my mother. I saw Charles meet her at his front door."

"Oh, no!"

"Oh, yes! I knew my father was on a business trip for a few days, so it seemed likely that my mother planned to spend the night. Apparently she did, because I phoned her at home at about eleven and there was no answer. I tried her again at nine this morning. Still no answer. *Now* tell me I don't know what I'm saying!"

I groped desperately for another explanation. "She might have met him to discuss your career—after all, they were once friends, as you said. She might have spent the night somewhere else—with a woman friend."

"And she might have been Snow White visiting the seven dwarfs. But forget the guesswork. I've got the facts. And I got them from none other than our great friend Charles Dain!"

"You *what!*"

"I phoned him just before lunch today and said I wanted to meet him someplace—someplace private. He suggested the Waterford Hotel, in his penthouse. The minute I saw him I let him have it. I told him everything I just told you and a lot more besides. I said that if he wanted to wreck his own marriage, to go right ahead, but I was damned if I'd stand by while he wrecked the marriage of my mother and father."

"He admitted everything?"

"And then some. He didn't want me thinking he was just having a fling, using my mother like she was some chorus cutie. He said that she loved my father and he loved his wife but this was something entirely different that had started way back when and . . . oh, Christ, it was sickening. Anyway, that's when I found out they'd been sneaking around together for the past nine years."

Just as they'd sneaked to avoid the wrath of George Fletcher, I thought. I, too, felt sickened, but not for the same reason as Kate's. She saw the affair as a despicable insult to her beloved father. I saw it as a demonstration of undying love.

"Did he agree to stop seeing her?" I said.

"He did not. He said it would be up to my mother to make that decision. My mother! Didn't he realize, I said, that she's now forty-two and it wouldn't be too long before he'd think of her as old and want someone younger? Why not end it now, I said, while she still had the pride and the stamina to bounce back? Lousy arguments maybe, but I was throwing everything at him I could think of. None of it did a damn bit of good. I even threatened to tell my father, but the way he looked at me, I could tell he knew I was bluffing." She paused, breathing rapidly, looking wildly about the room. "I need a cigarette. Where did I put my purse?"

I found I was sitting on it. As I fetched it she went to the liquor cabinet in the corner, opened it, swore when she saw it was empty, and turned back. I was standing, holding out a pack of Camels taken from the purse. She grabbed one, I lit it, and she inhaled until the tip resembled a torch.

"And that was it?" I said.

"Yes. Except that I quit my job."

"Kate!"

"I had a choice? You think I should go on working for the man who's banging my mother?"

I couldn't answer. "Look, maybe if I had a talk with your mother—"

"Sure. Great idea. You can talk to her tonight. You can, that is, if you don't mind going to that town house and pulling her out from under Charles Dain!"

"Nonsense. After the way you blasted him today, I don't think he'll be seeing her tonight."

She stoked her cigarette. "Think again, Max. After I left his penthouse—his wife's really—I phoned my mother and asked to see her for dinner. She put me off, saying she had to be at some sort of meeting. I knew by the way she sounded that she was lying. Then I asked when my father would be home and she said sometime late tomorrow. So then I was positive she was going to a meeting—of the Charles Dain Sex Society!"

I said quietly, "I think it goes a lot deeper than sex, Kate."

"All right, so do I. And that makes it worse. If it was only sex, it would have burned out long before this, and they'd be back where they belong. The way it is they could go on until my father or Harriet—" She stopped, cigarette poised, her eyes suddenly opening wide. "That's *it!*" she said.

"What," I said, "is *it?*"

"Harriet! Why didn't I think of her? Probably because, from what I've heard, she used to tolerate his playing around. But I can't see her standing still for what practically amounts to bigamy."

"Now, just a minute, Kate—"

"Perfect! My God, it's perfect! She'd crack down, and the famous publisher would either rush back to momma and stay there, or he'd find himself without a paper, without a job, and without a wife. Hell, he doesn't own the *Express*—*she* does. She's got the millions, not him. If she shucked him, he'd probably have just enough capital to buy into a four-page weekly in Crossroads, Montana."

"Stop it, Kate! Stop it right there!" I was furious.

And so was she. "That's what I can do—stop it! So Harriet's your friend, and you don't want her hurt. Well, that's tough, but my mother's your friend, too, and so is my father, and unless my mother and Harriet get hurt now, he'll end up getting the worst of it."

"And what about Charles? He—"

"He had his chance. He turned it down. I could have killed him." Her eyes glittered. "That's what I should have done—killed him! That would have solved everything!"

At that moment, she looked capable of it. Startled, I backed off and sat on the arm of the chair.

She turned away and began pacing in circles, saying bitterly, "I came here thinking you might have some sensible answers. But no, all you give a damn about is your precious Charles!"

"Let me talk to him," I said. "He's always listened to me."

"Listened, sure. Then did what he damned well pleased."

"This is different. I'll talk to him in the morning."

"Great, great. Meanwhile he's over there in his love nest . . . Oh, that bastard, that rotten bastard!"

"Be reasonable, Kate."

"You be reasonable. It's easy for you—You're not involved!"

"At least promise you won't say anything to Harriet."

"I won't promise anything! I've got to think about this." She veered to the table next to me and snatched up her purse. "But I can't do it here." She reached the door as I got up. "Thanks for seeing me."

"Kate, stay for a minute."

"Sorry, Max, it wouldn't do any good."

"Kate!"

But she had gone. By the time I got to the door and opened it, she had disappeared from the corridor. Nor did I find her at the bank of elevators. It took me a while to realize that she had used the fire stairs a few steps from my apartment.

It was then about seven thirty. Ninety minutes later a bullet from a .25 caliber semiautomatic pistol crashed into Charles's brain.

Now, standing in Harriet's hospital suite, I was thinking of shrewd Terry Donovan coming into my office the next day to say that he suspected the assailant was a woman—when the phone gave its sharp little ring.

"Mr. Wills?"

"Yes, speaking."

"This is Nurse Ferber. It seems—"

"He's all right?"

"Coming along as expected, Mr. Wills. He's asked to see you."

"Fine! I'm delighted he can talk."

"Oh, no, he still can't talk. But he can move his hands, and he signaled that he wanted to write something. I have his note here. It says, 'Get Max Wills.' Then he heard that Mr. Donovan had been waiting to see him, and he nodded that he should be included."

"Not Mrs. Dain?"

"I asked him that. He shook his head. I hope that won't be embarrassing."

"No, she'll understand."

"Good. You can come right down. You're allowed ten minutes."

Gently replacing the receiver, I was aware of the moisture on my palm and the quaking sensation in my stomach. I had hoped to see Charles alone, so that we might collaborate on a statement for the press. But the fact that he had included Donovan suggested a willingness to reveal all, regardless of consequences.

I wrote a quick note for Harriet, saying I'd be back shortly, and left it on a table, anchoring it with her cigarette holder. Dread rising in me like an illness, I went downstairs.

Donovan and the nurse were waiting outside the recovery room. He looked as grim as I felt, his somnolent eyes seeming to glimmer with apprehension, his face drawn and drained of color. From the nurses' station, the two detectives glowered at us as though we were escaping convicts.

Donovan grimaced a smile, pulled a notepad and pencil from his wrinkled jacket, then put them back, patting the pocket as though to remind himself where they were.

"I'll talk to him first," I said.

He raised an eyebrow, but agreed.

The nurse, smiling sweetly, opened the door, and we went in.

We paused inside the threshold, adjusting our eyes to the gray dimness, broken at intervals by the greenish glow of the monitoring machines. Moving forward, I saw that the bed had been raised so that the upper half of Charles's body rested at an angle. His face below the bandages appeared serene, the eyes closed, the mouth immobile, an image that, together with his slow, regular breathing, made me think of a swami in deep meditation.

Standing at the foot of the bed, Donovan beside me, I said, "Charles, it's Max. Terry's with me."

His eyes remained closed, and he did not stir. I

looked at Donovan. He shrugged slightly and shook his head, confirming my own thought that Charles had again slipped into a coma.

"Charles," I said, "you wrote a note that you wanted to see me." I paused. "Do you hear me, Charles?"

His eyes slowly opened. I had the eerie sensation that I had raised him from the dead.

I said, "I know you can't speak but—"

"But I can," he said, and I thought my legs would give way.

"You mean," Donovan said, "that just this minute—"

"No, Terry, I could have talked earlier. But I wasn't ready then to have it known."

He spoke very quietly, but his voice was firm. I had the impression that he had carefully rehearsed this scene.

It seemed stupid to question him about his health. "Charles," I said, "do you recall anything of what happened?"

For a long moment he didn't answer, just looked at me from under heavy lids, his eyes suddenly intense, as though trying to deliver a message. Then he said, "Max, I remember *everything*."

Before I could speak, Donovan said, "Charles, this may be a hell of a thing to ask, but what the hell, we're all newspapermen—are you ready to talk for publication? Or would you rather—"

"—rather wait," I cut in, "until you're feeling better? Until you've had more time to think?"

He gave me the same intense look. "No, Max, it's as clear in my mind now as it will ever be." His eyes shifted to Donovan. "Terry, take this down. Maybe you can make the next edition."

"Don't rush. We can always replate." Donovan drew

out his pad and pencil and moved around to the head of the bed.

"It's been a long time since I wrote a news story, so I'll just report the facts. You can do the rewrite."

"Go ahead."

Speaking slowly and with obvious effort, Charles said, "First, about the town house—why I used it and why I was there on the night I was shot. As you may know, it was set aside back in the twenties as a place to accommodate out-of-town business associates of Harriet's. Some years ago—I can't recall exactly when—I stopped by to see a visitor and caught him just as he was about to leave and return to Europe. As a courtesy, I took his key, meaning to drop it off at the management company. But I didn't, because that key gave me an idea." He paused to take a heavy breath. "Why not, I thought, use the town house to meet with people I couldn't afford to be seen with in public?"

Donovan, scribbling notes, glanced at Charles in surprise. I could read his mind: give me the headline, give me the lead, give me the stop-press news of who shot you and why; save this boring stuff for a follow-up.

"You know the sort I mean, Terry—certain politicians . . . informants . . . sometimes influential men who want to remain anonymous."

"Yeah. Some of 'em I've had to meet in sewers."

Charles gave a quick nod. "So that's why I occasionally went there. And that's why I thought I was going there when I got a phone call from a man on the morning of the shooting. The caller identified himself as a top reporter for another paper. I knew the man casually and had admired his work. I can't mention his name or the paper because it might ruin him with his boss if it was known that he wanted to discuss moving over to the *Express*. We both knew, of course, that it could be embarrassing for him if he was so much as seen with me."

"Uh-huh."

"My first suggestion was that he come to my apartment at the Waterford. But even that seemed too conspicuous for him, so I then suggested the town house. He agreed to meet me there at nine that night." Charles paused. "Got that?"

"Got it," Donovan said, his tone impatient.

I gazed at Charles in wonder, but he kept his eyes on Donovan's face, as though studying it for evidence of belief. He was silent for a few moments, his jaw flexing as he sought to gather strength.

"I got there a few minutes after eight," Charles said, "and—"

"Was it this reporter that you phoned earlier from the Stork Club?" Donovan said.

Charles's head twitched. "Phoned? Let's see—"

I said, "You've probably forgotten, Charles. Someone at the Stork reported you'd gone to a table and placed a call."

"Hmm. I remember going there." His eyes brightened. "In fact, I think I talked to Billingsley and Max Gordon. But the phone call—"

"It doesn't matter," Donovan said. "Okay, you're at the town house. It's just after eight o'clock."

"Yes. It had been a hot day and I had plenty of time, so I took a shower."

"Yeah. When the cops found you, you were wearing only a robe."

I said, "We assumed it was a robe that a former occupant had forgotten."

Charles rolled his head to look at me, his eyes faintly sardonic. "Correct," he said, then went on as Donovan started to speak. "I was about to get dressed when the doorbell rang. The man was early. I remember looking at my watch and seeing that it was ten to nine. I went to the door, and before I had it half opened it was slammed back in my face, knocking me against the wall. I was pinned there, between the door and the wall, unable to move. Then the door was pulled shut, and this huge figure grabbed me and shoved me back into the living room."

"Huge figure?" Donovan said. He had stopped writing and was regarding Charles with relief.

"Well over six feet," Charles said, "and built like a wrestler. I was stunned, and my first thought was that he'd set me up simply to work me over, maybe break a few bones, and leave. Then, by God, he pulled a gun! He wasn't just a muscleman—he was an assassin."

Donovan said, "You'd never seen him before?"

"Never."

"Would you recognize him from a mug shot?"

"I'm not sure. It all went so fast."

I said, "Probably a hit-man imported from another city, or even another country. The gangsters in this town wouldn't risk sending one of their own."

Donovan blew an exasperated breath. "Go on," he said to Charles.

"That's about it. Before I could move, he shot me."

"You must have moved plenty," I said. "He fired three shots. Two of them missed badly. That wouldn't have happened if you hadn't—"

"You're right, Max. Now I remember going for him. We grappled and—" His voice faded.

"That's probably when he got off the wild shots," I said. "Then you must have knocked him down, and he fired the one that got you. It came from a kneeling position."

Charles closed his eyes. "I vaguely recall hearing shots, but not being hit."

"In a way," I said, "it's fortunate he fired those two wild ones. All that shooting—the noise—must have scared him off. He ran out before making sure he'd finished the job. By the look of you, though, he must have thought he had."

"The door," said Donovan, "was unlocked. Any reason for that?"

Charles's eyes opened, and he looked at me.

I said, "We surmised that he did it accidentally when he yanked open the door."

"Probably," Charles said. "I know it was locked when I answered the bell."

As Donovan finished his notes, I told Charles that a woman passing by had heard the shots and phoned the police. "She hung up without giving her name," I said.

"Lucky for me," he said. "Too bad I can never repay her." A ghost of a sad smile seemed to cross his lips.

Donovan moved beside me at the end of the bed. He peered closely at Charles's haggard face, as though searching for a flaw. "You're sure you want me to—"

"Print it," Charles said.

As soon as the door closed behind Donovan, Charles gave me a long look. "Well?" he said.

"I think he believed it," I said.

He eased back on the pillow, looking exhausted.

"I also think the police will believe it," I said. "And so will the public."

"Good. I think it sounded convincing—with your help."

"I only wish Harriet could believe it," I said.

He flinched. "So do I. But she'll stand behind it. For now, that will have to do." He placed a hand over his eyes and there was a prolonged silence. Then he said, "You know, lying here, I've just begun to realize the importance of living in the world as it is, not as it was."

I was reminded of the final line of Scott Fitzgerald's *The Great Gatsby:* "So we beat on, boats against the current, borne back ceaselessly into the past." The current had proved too hazardous for Charles, as it so often had for me, but now, having recognized its power, he might, as I had, seek a safer passage along a familiar shore. There would be fewer excitements, perhaps, but also fewer defeats.

"It was all a dream," he said, "a dream of never growing old." His mouth twisted in a wry smile. "And the dream got shot down."

"Do you want to talk about it?"

"Not now, Max. Someday, but not now." He sighed heavily. "I'm so damned tired."

"Would it help if I told your story to Harriet?"

"No, no, I'll tell her. And somehow I'll convince her that her middle-aged husband has resigned as the romantic rover."

"She'll be happy to hear that, Charles."

"So will Kate," he said.

There was a knock on the door and the nurse entered.

I left him to look in on Harriet. After that, I would call Sharon and Kate. There now seemed no reason at all for Kate to confront her mother about a relationship that could not possibly be resumed.

Chapter · 20

"I think this calls for my ten-year-old Napoleon brandy,"
Kate said. She gave Donovan the same radiant smile
she had greeted him with at the door. "Or should it be
champagne?"

"Brandy's fine. I'd settle for day-old shellac."

She unfolded her legs from the sofa, got up, and
paused for a moment, as though modeling her garment
of shocking-pink silk; elegant, thought Donovan, in all
but name—hostess pajamas. Very seductive, as were her
sweptback hair, artful makeup, and Chanel No. 5.
Physically, she had already seduced him. Mentally, not
quite.

Despite his acceptance of Charles's story—devoutly
believed by the authorities because it vindicated their
implacable theory of an assault by gangsters—it did not
entirely erase his suspicion of an affair between Kate
and the publisher. In fact, it had deepened when she
told him Max had called to report Charles's press statement and inform her that he was improving dramatically and the doctors now predicted complete recovery.
Her joy seemed to imply emotions that far transcended

feelings of friendship. Also, there was that meeting at the Waterford Hotel. . . .

"Want yours in a snifter?" she said.

He glanced back to where she stood before an ancient rococo cabinet holding up a pear-shaped brandy glass. "Certainly a snifter," he said. "Only proper for a gentleman-journalist."

She laughed and poured the brandy.

"That's an interesting cabinet," he said. "Looks like it belongs in a Venetian palazzo."

"It belonged to my great-grandmother," she said, bringing the drinks. "And it's Irish, not Italian. She probably kept elderberry wine in it." Dropping to the sofa, she tossed the key on the glass top of the cocktail table. "Which she kept locked away—maybe because my great-grandfather was a lush. Who knows?"

He glanced at the key and gave a start. It was the old-fashioned iron key he had once lifted from her purse, suspecting it might open the door to Charles Dain's town house. Another hypothesis shattered, but trivial compared to his monstrous conjecture that the bullet fired into Charles's brain had come from her gun, a conjecture demolished by the victim himself. The key, he thought, was a symbol of his rampant imagination, which might better be used for shoot-'em-up fiction. Nevertheless . . .

"Kate, when Max phoned you, had he talked to Harriet?"

"Yes. He waited until after she went in to see Charles. When she came out, Max said, she looked happier than he'd ever seen her." Kate smiled, as though mentally observing the scene.

"Glad to hear it. Apparently he convinced her she didn't have a rival."

Kate's smile vanished. "Why would she have thought that?"

"Because on the afternoon of the shooting Charles met with a young woman at his Waterford penthouse. An employee saw her leave the hotel looking mad enough to sock a cop. He told that to Harriet, probably hoping for a cut of the reward."

Kate eyed him warily. "Did he know who she was?"

"No, but he described her. In her mid-twenties, well dressed, slim, pretty"—he paused—"and very blond. Harriet thought that, knowing her husband so well, I might be able to identify her."

Kate sniffed her brandy, eyes contemplating it. "And could you?"

"Yes."

Her glass clicked against her teeth.

"But I didn't tell that to Harriet," he said.

She sat back and gazed at him steadily. "All right, let's clear it up. Charles asked me there for lunch. That was a ploy to make it easier for him to tell me that he wanted to move my column—back near the comics, for God sake! Mad? I could have thrown him off his terrace. Needless to say, we didn't have the lunch, even though I think I changed his mind. Leaving there, I must have looked like I'd just had an audience with Hitler."

Donovan felt the last of his doubts fade away. All that remained was the question of her paternity, and now that she had been absolved of an affair with Dain, what did it matter? Perhaps someday, pretending amusement, he would confess his suspicion to Max Wills, if only to enjoy being told he was out of his mind.

He shrugged. "I figured it was business and said so.

But I can't blame Harriet for what she was thinking. There was a time when she had plenty of reasons to be jealous."

"So I've heard. But I'm sure that's all over with."

"I'll drink to that." He started to raise his glass.

"Here?" she said, then nodded toward the bedroom. "Or there?"

"There sounds better."

Soon, he thought, the clothes he'd divest would be government issue. But he'd tell her about that later.

"Evening, Mr. Wills. What'll it be?"

"Good evening, Mike." I hiked up on a stool and scanned the enticing labels on the backbar. After the ordeal at the hospital I had an impulse to line them all up in front of me and imbibe until I had to be carried to bed.

"Scotch?" Mike said. He had noticed my covetous stare and was regarding me dubiously.

I placed my folded copy of the *Express* on the bar and gave him an innocent look. "Mike, you know I never touch hard liquor. I'm a reformed man."

He laughed, nodding approvingly. He'd worked behind the stick at the Algonquin for about ten years and considered himself the guardian of my sobriety. My last defeat by Johnny Walker had, I sensed, left Mike with a feeling of personal failure.

"Soda water it is," he said, and moved his bulging frame down the bar.

I flipped open the *Express* and glanced again at the banner headlines: DAIN TALKS! SHOT BY UNKNOWN KILLER! WILL RECOVER! Terry Donovan's by-line story made it convincingly clear that the would-be assassin could have been none other than a hit-man sent by gangsters in reprisal for what they considered the publisher's persecution—a view supported by quotes from the mayor, the district attorney, and the chief of police. The man Charles had been tricked into thinking he was to meet was described only as "a trusted journalist who Dain said would prefer to remain anonymous." In reporting the struggle in the town house, Donovan had Charles sounding like a composite of Joe Louis, Errol Flynn, and General George Patton.

Mike brought the soda water and said, grinning, "Go easy on that stuff," then left to serve the two other customers in the bar. Coming back, he noticed my paper and said, "Hey! Heard it on the radio. Boy, am I glad he's gonna make it." He eyed me solemnly. "Guess that makes you feel pretty good."

I said that it did.

"The fight he put up"—Mike shook his head in admiration—"the guy's a hero." He went off to polish glasses.

Charles a hero, I thought—what a magnificent irony. He almost destroyed the Richards family, he wantonly flouted his obligations to Harriet, he heedlessly risked his good reputation—and he had emerged a hero.

All because of a trumped-up story made credible by the power and authority of the newspaper he had once boasted would never knowingly print a lie.

Not that I blamed him for his plausible scenario; in fact, he had said what I hoped he would, and I was more than glad to collaborate in the deception. Had he told the truth, the lives of all the people dearest to me—Harriet, Kate, Sharon, Tom Richards, not to mention Charles himself—would have been devastated, and I would have been faced with an isolation I doubted I could endure.

I sipped my soda water and again thought back to the evening just before the shooting when Kate had stormed into my suite shouting that Charles was her mother's lover. Kate, usually so cool, so easygoing, spouting words as lethal as the look in her eyes. I had been stunned, outraged, then suddenly terrified when she declared, "That's what I should have done—killed him! That would have solved everything!" In that instant my only thought was to somehow prevent this distraught woman from seeking justice through bloodshed. Moments later, when she slammed out of the room and vanished, I could only hope that she was not on her way to Charles's town house.

At that point I had lost my appetite for dinner, so I stopped off at the bar, sitting about where I was now. Mike delivered the usual soda water and then, at my request, added a jigger of Scotch. That, when mixed and stirred with Kate's accusations, was enough to release a flood of memories about the man who had so deeply affected my life. Like blackouts in a stage revue, Charles Dain appeared, disappeared, reappeared, acting out all his roles—the respectful teenager absorbed in my tales of flamboyant newspapermen; the brash young lover slyly engaging Sharon Fletcher in the back of the Model T; the desperate outsider crushed by her father; the suicidal doughboy wounded at Cantigny; the devil-may-care combat correspondent of *Stars and Stripes;* the roisterer of Paris who had won and then spurned the heart of Ann Tyson; the replica of Richard Harding Davis who fraternized with the mighty; the glamorous playboy seduced by Harriet Anthony into marriage and millions; the acclaimed publisher who warred against crime; the debonair man-about-town who sacrificed nubile women to the goddess of his dreams; the reckless adulterer who for nine years had possessed that goddess and materialized those dreams. . . .

All this swirled through my mind on that terrible night, borne on wave after wave of Scotch, which, in my anxiety, I was helpless to resist and which Mike allowed because I was, in effect, at home and could be transported safely up to my room. And as the whisky seized and distorted my thoughts, I began to fantasize acts and scenes which edged me toward panic. I saw Kate fulfilling her threat to inform Harriet, and Harriet reacting by speeding down from Mount Kisco to the town house. I saw Kate intercepting her mother and brawling with her in the street. I saw Kate telephoning her father, wherever he was, and insisting he rush back to confront his wife's lover. I saw all of them together in the town house, shouting, brandishing improvised weapons, inciting hostilities that could never be healed.

And then I saw myself as the peacemaker, devoted friend of all but partial to none, a man above the battle, who, in his dispassionate wisdom, could produce calm out of chaos. I felt duty-bound to intercede, to preserve the love and unity of these two families—the Richardses and the Dains—who, for most of my lifetime, had been *my families*.

Oh, God, I was drunk!

Not until the next day did I recall going to the town house. And even then the scenes penetrated my brain in flashes and bursts, as though projected by some bizarre piece of artillery.

"Max! What brings *you* here?"

I asked—demanded—where Sharon was.

"What makes you think . . . Oh, you've been talking

to Kate." Charles's face was grim, eyes flashing in anger. "Max, you stay out of this!"

The hell with that. We had to talk. The three of us had to talk and put some sense in their heads. Where was Sharon?

"She's not here. Max, you're drunk, crazy drunk. Go sleep it off. We'll talk in the morning."

I searched the kitchen, the bedrooms, the bathroom. I came back and stood facing him in the living room. He wore a bathrobe. Nothing else. He was waiting for Sharon. Waiting to slip off the bathrobe and . . .

". . . so I'm telling you, Max, this is none of your goddamn business. I'm calling a taxi, and you're getting into it!"

I refused. I called him every gutter word I could think of. I said he was fucking, literally fucking, his way to oblivion. I said that Kate knew and I knew and soon Harriet would know and so would Tom Richards, if they didn't know already, and if he didn't quit it right now he'd end up divorced, disgraced, and maybe dead.

He was silent, gazing straight at me. That look in his eyes—never had I seen it turned on me. Contempt. He stepped to the phone, picked it up. I grabbed his wrist and slammed down the receiver.

I shouted at him. I shouted that he'd spent most of his life manipulating women, destroying them, turning them into his personal whores, and I'd be damned if I'd let him go on making a whore of Sharon.

"Whore! That's what you think she is to me? Whore? Max, for Christ's sake, you don't understand!"

I hardly heard him. I was busy yanking the gun from my jacket pocket—the .25 caliber pistol I'd discovered in Kate's purse when I got her the Camels and later removed while she paced the floor ranting about killing

Charles. Ah, I couldn't take the chance that in her murderous mood she might steal into the town house and blow out Charles's brains. It had not occurred to me that I—gentle, tolerant Max Wills—could be the executioner.

"Max, listen to me! I'm the father of Sharon's daughter!"

The words meant nothing to me.

"Of Kate!"

Then he saw the gun.

"Max, what the hell—"

I fired as he lurched away. The bullet tore into a leather armchair.

He jumped at me, knocking me back.

I fired again. The bullet splintered the ceiling.

He butted me with his shoulder, sending me sprawling. I scrambled to my knees.

I fired again.

He stopped, stared, blood streaming down his face. He thudded to the floor.

There was a deathly silence.

Then, as I stood there, paralyzed, gun frozen in my hand, the front door opened, and Sharon walked in, her face bright with anticipation. . . .

I remembered nothing else. Not until Sharon phoned me the next morning did I learn of the frantic aftermath; her throwing clothes into a suitcase, unlocking the door to permit quick access, rushing us from the house, stopping at a pay phone to call the police, helping me into a taxi, then getting another for herself, which she left on Third Avenue to walk to the East River and fling away the gun.

She was of course protecting herself as well as me.

But it's comforting to think that, even if she had not been involved with Charles, she would have done all in her power to spare the man who, unknown to her, had loved her so deeply and with such constancy through all the years.

It would be easy to say that I shot Charles because of a noble desire to avenge Harriet and to preserve the integrity of the Richards family.

But it would not be true.

Hatred, not love, was the force that squeezed the trigger. Hatred so long repressed and suddenly released by the look of contempt in Charles's eyes. Hatred for the war hero, the foreign correspondent, the admired press lord, the idol of beautiful women—hatred of my dearest friend for possessing all that I had so deeply yearned for but had never obtained.

The bullet that ended its career in Charles's brain, I thought, had begun its flight twenty-six years ago—on the day in 1916 when Sharon had unwittingly crushed my romantic hopes by demonstrating her passionate love for Charles Dain.

Now, finishing my soda water, I said to myself: Charles, thank God, is truly a great man. Great enough to understand and forgive and go on as before.

I went in to dinner, glad, for once, to be alone.